TACITURN IN THE TON

Misfits of the Ton
Book Nine

by

Emily Royal

Dearest Reader;

Thank you for your support of a small press. At Dragonblade Publishing, we strive to bring you the highest quality Historical Romance from some of the best authors in the business. Without your support, there is no 'us', so we sincerely hope you adore these stories and find some new favorite authors along the way.

Happy Reading!

CEO, Dragonblade Publishing

Additional Dragonblade books by Author Emily Royal

Misfits of the Ton
Tomboy of the Ton (Book 1)
Ruined by the Ton (Book 2)
Thief of the Ton (Book 3)
Oddity of the Ton (Book 4)
Harpy of the Ton (Book 5)
Heartbreaker of the Ton (Book 6)
Doxy for the Ton (Book 7)
Duelist for the Ton (Book 8)
Taciturn in the Ton (Book 9)
The Taming of the Duke (Novella)

Headstrong Harts
What the Hart Wants (Book 1)
Queen of my Hart (Book 2)
Hidden Hart (Book 3)
The Prizefighter's Hart (Book 4)
All I Want for Christmas is My Hart (Novella)
Haunted Hart (Novella)

London Libertines
Henry's Bride (Book 1)
Hawthorne's Wife (Book 2)
Roderick's Widow (Book 3)
A Libertine's Christmas Miracle (Novella)

The Lyon's Den Series
A Lyon's Pride
Lyon of the Highlands
Lyon of the Ton
The Lyon and the Unicorn

CHAPTER ONE

Rosecombe Chapel

"ARE YOU READY?

Olivia winced at the sharpness in her brother's tone and tightened her grip on his sleeve. Though she focused her attention on the stitching in gold thread around the cuff and the perfectly formed buttons that had been polished until they shone, she could still feel his gaze upon her.

He was not a man to be denied.

In fact, he'd *never* been a man to be denied. He commanded the admiration and respect of hundreds of souls whose lives depended on him, who spoke his name in hushed tones.

His Grace, the Duke of Whitcombe.

Aristocrat, landlord, master. Husband, father…

And brother.

Or *half*-brother, though he threatened to destroy anyone who dared make the slightest reference to Olivia's birth.

"Sister?"

She winced and lifted her gaze.

Though he was silhouetted against the morning light, she could see the intelligence gleaming in his deep-set eyes. Their expression spoke of a strength of will that could never be matched, let alone conquered.

In short, he was the most imposing, terrifying man she had ever encountered. Save one.

The man waiting at the end of the aisle who, with his bare hands, could crush whole armies.

The man she was soon to call husband.

Olivia's brother lifted his hand to her face and frowned as she flinched. He cupped her cheek and his lips curled into a smile as he spoke, his tone softening.

"Olivia, are you ready?"

She nodded.

"He's an honorable man. He'll treat you as you deserve to be treated."

"As a bas—" she began, but he took her wrist.

"As the sister of the Duke of Whitcombe," he said, the hardness returning to his voice. "How can you expect the world to respect your position if you cannot respect it yourself?"

Moisture stung her eyes, and she blinked. A tear spilled onto her cheek, and he brushed it away with his thumb.

"He's a fortunate man to have you," he said. "He'll come to realize that. If not, I'll—"

"Yes, brother," she said, wincing at the bitterness in her tone. "I know what you'll do. I've seen the marriage contract."

He sighed. "The stipulations in the contract are there to protect you."

"Do I need protection?"

He glanced toward the altar. "No more than any woman."

She turned and followed his gaze. On one side of the chapel sat her sister-in-law, Eleanor. Her bonnet was trimmed with the pale-green ribbon to match the sash around Olivia's waistline. The two of them had chosen it the day the modiste fitted Olivia with her hurriedly made wedding gown, and Olivia's cheeks warmed at the memory of the pointed glances Madame Dupont had made toward her belly.

Did the rest of the meager congregation—the dowager duchess sitting next to Eleanor, smothered in black-lace-trimmed silk, a handful of friends in the pew behind, the housekeeper and butler, the steward, and a smattering of tenants—share the modiste's suspicions?

The vicar stood at the end of the aisle, a Bible open in his hands, his expression impassive. As a child living on the estate, Olivia, like the rest of the village children, had been a little afraid of Reverend Ouston. But from the moment her brother had recognized her as a member of the Whitcombe family, the vicar showed her nothing but kindness and deference as the duke's sister. But did he now suspect her to be a fallen woman? Would he look upon her with the kind of disdain that the majority of the world turned upon her merely due to her birth?

Her gaze slipped sideways to the groom's side of the chapel—empty, save a solitary guest at the front. The sunlight formed a halo around his hair, bathing him in light. And standing within a few feet of him at the front of the aisle…

Oh, heavens!

Her stomach fluttered as her gaze settled on the one thing she dared not look at…

The bridegroom.

His tall, powerful frame dwarfed that of every other soul in the chapel. Dressed in a dark-blue jacket, with a thick head of dark hair curling about his shoulders, he seemed to absorb the light. He stood, his back to her, body tense, as if ready to engage in a fight to the death. His jacket seemed to stretch in protest across his shoulders. His hands hung at his sides, curled into fists. Then he moved his left hand, and Olivia caught a flash of light reflecting off the signet ring on his fourth finger—a dark-red ruby to match that on the ring on the third finger of her left hand, the large red stone that seemed to wink malevolently at her like a silent, watchful eye.

Stop being such a fool!

Silently, she cursed her imagination.

He was not the devil, nor even a demon. He was a living, breathing man. One who deserved compassion, for he did not fit into the mold of the Society gentleman.

He was, perhaps, as much of a misfit as Olivia herself. And he wanted this marriage as much—or rather, as little—as she.

Eleanor said that two hearts could unite when they were

compelled to face adversity together. What better way to describe the situation Olivia found herself in now, standing at one end of the aisle, on the brink of cleaving herself to the man awaiting her at the other?

"Come, Livvie," her brother whispered. "Show the world, and the groom, that today he is to become the most fortunate of men."

She nodded and forced a smile. Her brother returned it, then he raised his hand and gave a sharp nod.

Almost at once, the music stopped. Then the organist filled the chapel with a fanfare to the tempo of a march, as if announcing the arrival of royalty—the princesses that Olivia used to read about in storybooks.

Only she wasn't a princess. She was the bastard child of the late duke who, having compromised herself, was being hastily married to save her reputation and that of the present duke.

No. That was unfair. Her brother loved her and believed he was doing what was best to make her happy. She was like any other Society bride, embarking on a journey with a stranger. The bridegroom was an honorable man—his coming here today was evidence of that. And honor was as good a reason as any to marry. From honor came respect. And from respect, perhaps love might blossom.

"I'm ready," she said, curling her fingers around her brother's arm. "I'll make you proud of me."

"I already am," he replied, smiling. "Shall we?"

She nodded and, head held high, let him guide her along the aisle. Buoyed by the music, Olivia felt her hope soar as they passed Eleanor, who smiled encouragement, her eyes shining with tears of happiness.

Then the groom turned.

Olivia's stomach clenched in fear as he fixed his gaze on her. Eyes so dark they were almost black, mouth set in a hard line, he showed no sign of honor, hope, or joy. Instead, his very soul seemed to vibrate with anger—directed at her, the bride he never wanted.

And, in a matter of moments, she would become his, in the eyes of the law and the church, to do with as he pleased.

CHAPTER TWO

London, six months earlier

"WELCOME BACK TO England, Lord Devereaux."

Charles winced.

Curse that name! To most, it signaled breeding—a family line dating back to the Plantagenets with which it would be an honor to associate oneself. Or, most likely, a name that the ambitious wished to ingratiate themselves with to further their advancement in Society…

…whatever the fuck *that* meant.

How dare you curse in my home! Insolent, dim-witted boy!

Devil's breeches, did that old bastard seek to plague him from beyond the grave?

"Lord Devereaux?"

The voice spoke again, tinged with a thin veneer of irritation. Charles blinked and focused his attention on the man before him.

Clad in black, the clerk had all the appearance of obsequiousness, but it could not disguise the impatient contempt that many in business had for the clients they served, seeing them as merely a means to an income rather than a client in whose best interests they were supposed to act. But then, he couldn't expect any man to act in accordance with anything other than what was best for himself. Men of the world—whether those in trade, or the idle gentlemen who languished in their country estates—only sought to serve their own gratification. As for women of the world…

Women were a good deal worse. Men acted out of self-interest, but women preyed upon men to take advantage of that self-interest.

"Lord Devereaux!"

Charles gestured toward his valet. John was one of the few men, perhaps the *only* man, whose loyalty surpassed self-interest.

"My master is here to see Mr. Stockton," John said.

"I know *that*," the clerk replied, "but servants must enter through the back door, not the front."

Charles gestured with his hands. *Arrogant arse.*

The valet suppressed a smile.

"My master insists on my accompanying him wherever he goes."

"I don't think that's entirely…" the clerk began, but his voice trailed off as Charles stepped across the threshold. Fear shimmered in the man's eyes as he craned his head to look up. A little shorter than average, he'd have to look up to most of the clientele, but Charles topped him by a head and a half. He itched to grasp the clerk by his lapels and toss him down the steps, and, as if he'd read his mind, the clerk lowered his gaze to Charles's gloves. Were Charles to remove them, the little man would see the callouses on his knuckles—trophies of his childhood that uttered a silent warning to anyone who had the wit to recognize danger.

At length, the clerk stepped back and bowed.

"O-of course, your lordship. I'll tell Mr. Stockton you're here. And Mr.…?"

"Richards," John said.

The clerk nodded, then ushered them into a large room on the upper floor overlooking the street. Its occupant, a gray-haired man with soft eyes, rose to his feet from behind a large mahogany desk.

"Mr. Stockton, Lord Devereaux for you," the clerk said. "I'm afraid he's insisted on being accompanied by—"

"Yes, yes, Billings, I can see that," the solicitor replied. "That'll be all, thank you. Gentlemen, sit, please."

After the clerk retreated, closing the door behind him, Charles slid into a seat, motioning to John to occupy the adjacent chair.

The solicitor reached for a sheaf of papers, bound with a pink ribbon, which he untied. Then he met Charles's gaze.

"Please accept my condolences on the loss of your father, Lord Devereaux. I…"

He paused as Charles raised his hand.

"Very good, your lordship. I understand. You're not here to discuss pleasantries." He flicked through the papers. "The estate accounts are, I'm afraid, in need of your attention. The death duties were substantial."

Of course they bloody were. Charles gritted his teeth to stem the anger vibrating through his bones. Did the arrogant fool not realize he already knew that?

Stockton raised his eyebrows, as if awaiting a reply. Then he nodded and continued. "Your father passed over four months ago." He tilted his head, looking at Charles over his spectacles, in the manner of a judgmental schoolmaster.

Charles leaned forward, his frame casting a shadow over the desk, and the solicitor's eyes widened in apprehension. He glanced at his valet, then gestured with his hands. The solicitor watched the motion, confusion in his expression as Charles continued to move his hands in a fluid motion. Then the valet nodded.

"My master says that he's fully aware of the circumstances surrounding the estate," he said. "He sold his property in Italy to pay the death duties. Surely there can be no requirement for further payment?"

"There's already a substantial loan secured on the estate," the solicitor said, "but the trustees aren't amenable to selling any heirlooms to service the loan."

Charles raised his hands again, making a series of gestures. Then his valet spoke.

"Are the trustees amenable to the bank seizing the property if the loan cannot be serviced?"

"The loan is being serviced, Lord Devereaux," the solicitor said, "but the estate's income is barely sufficient to meet the interest, which is twenty per cent."

Twenty per cent?

Devil's breeches, what the fuck had his wastrel of a father been thinking?

"I share your concern, Lord Devereaux," the solicitor continued. "Coutts Bank did not consider your father to be an acceptable risk and therefore levied a premium on the interest rate. I warned him at the time, but you know what the late earl was like…" He shrugged.

Yes. I know damned well what that old bastard was like.

Charles closed his eyes, suppressing the memory that had threatened to resurface. The skin of his back itched and he shifted position in his chair and leaned back, crossing his legs. He reached for the signet ring on his left hand and rotated it with his thumb, focusing on the repetitive motion to divert his mind from the image of his father's face, twisted in anger and disgust…

"Lord Devereaux?"

Charles opened his eyes to see the solicitor staring at him, his head tilted to one side. Stockton gestured toward a decanter half filled with a dark amber liquid. "Perhaps a brandy?"

Charles made a series of gestures to his valet.

Doubtless he'll add it to his bill to increase the profit he's making out of me.

John frowned, and the solicitor raised his eyebrows.

"My master says he'd greatly appreciate a brandy," John said, "but only if you pour one for his valet also."

Charles frowned at John, whose eyes twinkled with faint amusement. The solicitor poured two glasses and pushed them across the table.

"While the estate income can service the interest on the loan, the problem is the repayment of the capital. There's nothing to spare to reduce the capital outstanding. I'm sure you'd rather the profit from the estate be used to benefit the estate rather than its creditors."

Charles gestured with his hands.

"What is to be done?" John said.

"If you can raise the funds to reduce the loan," Stockton said, "even if not eliminate it entirely, then the interest will similarly reduce, leaving sufficient income to reduce the capital further. I trust you understand?"

Yes, you condescending fool, I'm aware how loans operate. Insult me again and I'll throw you out of the window.

John raised his eyebrows as Charles signed his response.

"Ahem, my master says that he understands you, and he'll make arrangements to sell any assets that are not under trust."

Stockton poured himself a brandy, then leaned back and sipped it. "Are you married, Lord Devereaux?"

I don't think that's any of your...

"Lord Devereaux is not married, Mr. Stockton," John said, ignoring Charles's gestures.

"Then forgive me for being frank, but the solution seems perfectly clear," the solicitor said. "A substantial enough dowry should clear the loan, and there are plenty to be had this Season, or so I'm told. Once Society's matriarchs know that Earl Devereaux is in Town, I imagine your hallway will be littered with calling cards. You'll have your pick of the—"

Charles leaped to his feet and his chair tipped onto its side with a clatter.

Was there no end to the torture? Not only was he forced to surrender his home and return to that godforsaken mausoleum in the middle of bloody nowhere, must he now be plagued, within hours of setting foot on English soil, by the prospect of being pecked at by desperate debutantes and their overbearing mamas?

"Yes, yes, very good." Stockton rose and offered his hand. Charles stared at it for a moment, then took it, his larger hand engulfing the older man's. One squeeze and he'd be able to crush Stockton's fingers...

"I apologize if I gave offense, Lord Devereaux," Stockton said. "I understand how difficult it must have been to leave Italy after having lived there for so long, and under such trying personal circumstances. But I trust you'll be happy at Penham Park. There's sometimes comfort to be found in knowing that one is doing one's duty to one's heritage."

Charles released Stockton's hand. Then the older man escorted them out of the building to the waiting chaise. Charles climbed on without a backward glance and, as soon as John joined him, the chaise set off.

He focused his attention on the surroundings—row upon row of identical houses with imposing, colorless façades. Then he reached for his signet ring to rotate it, focusing on the feel of the hard metal against the base of his finger, until the swell of anger receded.

"If I may be so bold, sir..." the valet began, and Charles moved his hands.

When are you not *bold?*

John smiled. "Mr. Stockton was right on one matter, at least."

Are you about to lecture me on the merits of duty?

"Not duty, sir. The merits of ready cash."

Would you have me sell the shirt on my back? I've nothing else to sell.

"There's one thing, sir, if I may be so bold."

Bold? Why would John confess boldness as if he expected fury from his master? What could he possibly suggest that Charles could sell which would elicit such a response?

Unless...

Charles turned to stare at his valet. Fear flickered in the younger man's eyes before he blinked, and the veneer of stoicism returned.

Do you mean...

"Begging your pardon, sir, I wouldn't make such a suggestion unless out of absolute necessity. But it—"

Charles gestured, then punched his palm with his fist.

He's a he, *not an* it.

The valet flinched. Doubtless, most servants were used to their masters roaring at them in fury. But John had long since understood the potency of dark stare and angry gesture. Over the years, he'd learned to recognize Charles's tempers such that he regulated his conduct, knowing when to be silent and attentive and when to steer clear. That was the curse of being in service— to be beholden to the whims of another.

It was a curse that he paid John for handsomely. Until now, when ready cash had been almost exhausted.

"Forgive me, sir. I wouldn't mention it—*him*—if there were any other option. But Destriero is a valuable horse. I could arrange a sale at Tattersall's, or privately if you prefer."

Charles closed his eyes.

Curse you, Father. Not only have you cost me my home, but my horse, whom I loved a great deal more than you.

Perhaps he should have attended the old bastard's funeral. Then he could have spat on the coffin.

"Sir?"

Charles opened his eyes and a needle scratched at his heart at the compassion in his valet's eyes. But compassion was the last thing he needed. Compassion made a man weak. And Charles had no intention of growing weak.

Not again.

I'd prefer a private sale. But only with a man I trust.

John nodded. "That narrows down the list of potential purchasers. But I'll start making inquiries before we leave London."

I'll accept nothing less than five hundred guineas.

"Very good, sir."

And an assurance that the horse will be treated well.

"Naturally."

Charles let out a sharp sigh and resumed his attention on the world outside—the soulless London townhouses that the creatures of Society valued so much. As unappealing as it may be, his exile to Penham Park would at least remove him from London.

He curled his hands into fists to temper the rising anger. Was this how a caged beast felt, trapped in a life he never wanted?

"Sir, perhaps…" John hesitated.

Charles lifted his eyebrows in inquiry.

"Perhaps, before we leave for the country, I could make arrangements for a woman? You're in need of a little recreation before you leave."

I no longer have money to waste on a doxy.

"If you sell Destriero you'll have enough to reduce the loan, with plenty to spare for a whole coven of doxies."

Charles let out a snort. *So, I'm selling a horse and buying a woman?*

The valet grinned. "At least the woman will be cheaper."

But far less pleasurable to ride.

"I'll find an Italian doxy if you like," John said. "To remind you of home."

Charles sighed, then motioned again. *England is my home now.*

"An English doxy it is, then."

The chaise drew up alongside Charles's lodgings.

Yet another colorless building. Like every other house in England, it was filled with damp and mold, the stench of which not even the strongest of colognes could mask. The furnishings were torturous—hard chairs that caused the bones to ache, as if Society measured elegance in direct proportion to discomfort—with dull, muted colors, soulless compared to the vibrant hues of Italy. As for the servants within—stiff with disdain, engaging in bland conversation and serving even blander food. The item they'd placed before him last night, which they tried to pass off as steak, had almost dislodged a tooth.

Devil's breeches, was this what life would be like from now on? Perhaps he ought to take pleasure where he could.

Charles glanced at the valet, then nodded.

Better make it two.

CHAPTER THREE

Penham Park, Hampshire

D EVIL'S BREECHES, IT was worse than he'd imagined.

The vast building of Penham Park stretched before him, a monolith of gray stone, dotted with windows that stared out across the landscape like dark, lidless eyes. Two staircases climbed toward each other at an angle at the front, meeting on a large balcony that wrapped around the whole building, edged by a balustrade.

The gardens, that had once been so finely manicured as to have wiped out all evidence of the beauty of nature, were overgrown as if, now given freedom from the chokehold of the previous earl, Nature had taken vengeance.

Charles stepped out of the carriage and onto the gravel drive where weeds poked through the tiny stones. He thrust his hands into his pockets and cast his gaze over the building he'd be forced to call home.

Buildings from a man's childhood ought to harbor the fondest of memories—secret hideaways, a treasured nursery, a favored bedchamber, and a multitude of dens in the surrounding estate. And they were always expected to be smaller than recalled, distorted by a child's memory.

But the main building of Pelham Park elicited no such emotions. It was larger, more imposing than Charles recalled from the last time he'd seen it, before he'd effected his escape into manhood and out of England.

It was a mausoleum, a memorial to years of torment and

bitter unhappiness.

Charles climbed the steps, John in his wake, then approached the main doors, the lawyer's words playing in his mind.

There's sometimes comfort to be found in knowing that one is doing one's duty to one's heritage.

What comfort could ever be found in this godforsaken place? The only inhabitants were most likely spiders and bats.

The only *living* inhabitants. Doubtless, the building housed the spirits of the dead, the souls of the condemned. Who else would find comfort here—a dark and forbidding place to suit his dark soul. Wasn't that what Father accused him of being?

You're a dark soul, boy—cursed spawn of your mother...

"Bloody hell, you weren't wrong about the place," John said. "Beg pardon, sir, I meant no offense."

The doors creaked and cold fingers circled Charles's heart as a deep groan echoed through the air.

He stepped back as the doors swung inward, forming a gaping, toothless mouth.

Then a figure appeared in the doorway—a human form, blurred by the darkness.

Charles took an involuntary step back, but the figure followed, moving into the light. Then it solidified into the shape of a woman, of diminutive stature with iron-gray hair scraped into a neat bun. Her dress was an unremarkable shade of dark blue, and she wore a set of keys on a chain about her waist.

Her face bore the wrinkles of age, but though her skin was pale, a flush of rose adorned her cheeks, and her eyes, a pale shade of blue, twinkled beneath her brows.

"Viscount Penham..." She hesitated. "F-forgive me, I suppose I should call you Lord Devereaux now. I did not hear the carriage. We weren't expecting you until tomorrow."

Charles glanced at John and signed.

What does she mean, we?

"Who are you, ma'am?" John asked.

The woman glanced at Charles's hands, then her face cracked

into a smile.

"Bless me, Master Charles! Have I aged so much that you don't recognize me?"

Charles stared at her then tilted his head to one side.

Mrs. Brougham? Surely this wizened creature couldn't be the housekeeper?

Her eyes filled with understanding, mixed with a little judgment, and she nodded.

"I see your memory serves you well, Lord Devereaux, even if your gallantry doesn't. The years have been kinder to you than me. But fifteen years is a long time to be absent from one's home."

Was it really fifteen years since he'd last set foot in the place, leaving for Oxford and vowing never to return until his father was cold in his grave?

It was a vow he'd kept. But, unlike most vows, it had been driven by hatred, not honor.

"We thought you might return when your father..." the housekeeper began, then she sighed and shook her head. "It matters not. What matters is that you're home, to take up your rightful place as the earl."

My rightful place...

He reached for his signet ring and ran his thumb over the stone, taking comfort from the feel of the sharp edges of the facets. The housekeeper lowered her gaze to his hands and smiled, her eyes filled with understanding.

"Please, come inside," she said. "You must be tired from your journey, and your man...?" She raised her eyebrows and directed her gaze at John.

"Lord Devereaux's valet, ma'am," he said. "John Richards, at your service."

"I'm pleased to meet you, Mr. Richards," she said, stepping aside. "Please, come inside, both of you, and I can arrange for some tea."

Both of us?

Charles glanced at the valet who, by right, the housekeeper should have insisted use the back entrance. Or at least she would have, were his father still alive. Father was always a stickler for propriety—ordering and delivering punishments for the slightest transgression.

As if his body recalled his last transgression, the skin of Charles's back itched. He crossed the floor of the hallway, illuminated by a beam of light from an upper-floor window, in which dust motes swirled in protest at their disturbance. His footsteps clicked on the marble floor as he approached the main staircase—an enormous flight of stairs that swept upward to a wall bearing a huge painting of the third earl, staring darkly at all comers, before dividing in two to ascend either side to the upper floor. A cold hand clawed at his stomach as he approached the stairs and his gaze landed on the lowest step, then moved along the floor to the third stone from the bottom. His chest constricted at the memory, the image that formed in his mind…

A pool of dark red, spreading across the floor, arms frozen like marble trapping his body, and…

…and two dark, lifeless eyes, staring into his soul, drawing him toward the mouth of hell…

"Lord Devereaux!" the housekeeper exclaimed as she swam into view before him. He blinked and her features came into focus, concern in her soft blue eyes.

Concern and pity. The last thing he wanted was pity, especially from a *woman*.

She reached for his arm, and he snatched it free. Her eyes narrowed, but the compassion in their expression did not waver. If anything, it deepened.

"How about that tea?" she said brightly. "Then you can tell me all about what you've been up to since I saw you last."

Charles nodded.

"I've always wanted to visit Italy. I hear Rome is particularly beautiful. But, as they say, there's nowhere on God's earth like home, is there? And it gladdens my heart to see you finally come home."

What foolish nonsense was she speaking?

"Are you well, sir?" John asked.

Charles gestured. *I will be once I'm spared the girlish nonsense that women always feel the need to speak when a man returns to his childhood home.*

Mrs. Brougham raised her eyebrows, then nodded. "I'll see to that tea," she said. "Then perhaps we ought to discuss hiring staff, if you intend to stay."

A flicker of hope shone in her eyes.

"Have you a wife? A family?"

Charles shook his head.

"A pity," she said. "You ought to take a wife. You don't want Jacob inheriting, seeing as he cares not one jot about the place. No sense of duty. But then, that's to be expected, seeing as—" She broke off, and her smile returned. "Never mind. Now you've returned you can find yourself a good English girl. There's plenty to be found who'd be delighted to be mistress of this place."

Charles glanced about the hall, taking in the stench of neglect. No girl in possession of her wits would want to be mistress of such a place.

"It would be good to have the house filled with children," the housekeeper continued. "It's high time love and laughter returned to the place."

Since when had love or laughter ever taken residence *here*?

Charles signed to John. *Now she's talking rot. Dim-witted, like all women.*

John's cheeks colored. "My master agrees with you, Mrs. Brougham."

She tilted her head and eyed Charles through her lashes. "Oh, he *does*, does he? Even though he thinks me dim-witted for considering that light and laughter could return to this house?"

Devil's breeches! Surely she didn't…

"Did you think I'd forget?" the housekeeper said, moving her hands to convey the exact same phrase. "I should be flattered that you consider my nonsense to be girlish, given my advanced years.

As to my lack of wits, well—the purpose of my sex, at least among my class, is not to shine a light on our own wits, but to convinced members of your class and sex of your superiority. Of course, *my* role is to ensure that you have a comfortable and well-functioning home. To this end, I trust you'll grant me enough of your time to listen to my recommendations for hiring a full complement of staff."

She smiled then curtseyed to convey her subservience, but why did Charles feel as if he were an errant boy being chastised by his nursemaid?

Forgive me, he signed to the housekeeper, and she patted his arm.

"When you were a boy, I forgave you anything, including when you stole a basket of eggs from the kitchen and threw them out of the upper-floor window to see if they'd bounce. Mr. Phelps wanted to thrash you, if you recall, but I convinced him that an inquiring mind was to be nurtured rather than beaten into submission."

She lifted her hand as if to caress his cheek, then withdrew.

"You always were a good-hearted boy, Master Charles," she said. "Do you recall, afterward, how you stole a dozen roses from the garden and presented them to me to say thank you?"

Charles frowned, and she let out a soft laugh.

"Perhaps you don't care to recall an act of kindness that, while praised in a boy, is thought to be a weakness in a man. But I've never forgotten how sweet-tempered a lad you were, until—"

She broke off, her color deepening, and glanced toward the foot of the stairs. Charles pushed her away and motioned with his hands.

We'll take tea in the morning room.

"Of course," she said. "You remember where the morning room is?"

Charles nodded.

She curtseyed again, then disappeared toward the kitchens, and he made his way through an oak-paneled door into a room decorated in dark purple. The color of wealth, Father had always said—to show all comers that the Devereaux family was to be revered.

Revered, indeed! The family name had been blighted by scandal since *that* night. From that moment, Charles had been nothing but a disappointment to his parent.

Fuck you, Father.

He lowered himself into a threadbare chair, and motioned John to sit. *What do you think of our new home?*

"Do you require honesty or diplomacy, sir?"

Charles let out a snort. *I am not in the mood for either.*

"Very good, sir," the valet said. "I should see to your trunk. It appears that Mrs. Brougham can understand you enough to take your instructions. Shall I speak to her about your requirements for supper, or will you?"

You do it. And tell her not to bother with the tea.

John bowed, then exited the room.

Charles leaned back and closed his eyes, breathing in the scent of damp, dust, and doom.

Was he really supposed to find some perfect English girl and bring her back to this godforsaken place? Nobody deserved to be a prisoner here like he now found himself to be.

Then he allowed himself a smirk.

Perhaps it would be a fitting punishment for whatever grasping debutante he was forced to shackle himself to merely to keep this bloody estate solvent. At least the place was large enough that he wouldn't be forced to spend any more time with her than necessity demanded.

As soon as he'd settled his belongings here, he'd return to London, find the largest dowry he could, then return to a life of solitude. Whether the bride followed him mattered not. All he craved now was a peaceful existence, away from the rest of the world—free from debt and, most importantly, from other people.

CHAPTER FOUR

London

"A SOMEWHAT UNSUCCESSFUL Season so far, Olivia. We must discuss what to do about it."

Olivia paused, her teacup at her lips, and eyed her brother. Then she set the cup back on the saucer with a clatter.

His eyes narrowed and she withstood the instinct to cringe.

"I'm only stating the facts as I see them," he said.

"Perhaps now's not the time to state *facts as you see them*, my love," a soft voice spoke.

Olivia glanced at her sister-in-law. Eleanor seemed such a timid creature, at least in public, with mild features and hair an unremarkable shade of brown. But the unusually intense expression in her dark-green eyes spoke of a sharp intelligence beneath the awkward exterior—intelligence and a passionate concern for the few people she loved.

And Olivia was fortunate enough to be one of those few.

"Nevertheless, Eleanor, you cannot fail to agree with me," Olivia's brother said.

"Perhaps, Montague, but there's no harm in showing a little compassion."

Montague? Eleanor rarely addressed him by his full name, save in admonishment.

He arched an eyebrow.

"You speak as if Olivia's lack of success—however one might define *success* in Society—is entirely her own fault," Eleanor continued. "But there's nothing in Olivia to fault."

Except one thing.

Evidently unwilling to point out her one fatal flaw, Olivia's brother did not respond. The silence stretched, punctuated by the ticking of the drawing room clock while the specter of Olivia's birth remained suspended, like a ball having been tossed into the air waiting for someone to catch it.

Like it or not, Society valued birth above all. The sister of a duke might command respect and adoration of the sycophants who paraded about the ballrooms of London and exchanged gossip at Almack's, but only if she were a legitimate sister. Lady Olivia Whitcombe would have been the toast of Society. Plain Miss Whitcombe, however, carried the indelible stain of her birth, which pretty gowns, diamond necklaces, and a large dowry did nothing to diminish.

"We ought to consider our options," Montague said, "such as—"

"My love, did I overhear your speaking to Jenkins about buying a horse?" Eleanor interrupted, and Olivia shot her a look of gratitude.

"Yes, but..."

"Surely it's not the season for it," Eleanor continued, "and it would be unfair on the horse to keep him here in livery in London, isolated from your other horses."

"A horse doesn't require the company of friends, Eleanor," Montague said. "But I won't keep him in London. He's too fine a hunter for that."

"Did you purchase him through Tattersall's?"

"No, a private sale. Cost me five hundred guineas."

Olivia stared at her brother. "Five *hundred*? That's a lot for a horse."

"It's a bargain, given his pedigree. Italian, you know. An entire horse, so I might use him for stud. Beautiful animal. Devereaux clearly didn't want to part with him."

"Who?" Olivia asked.

"Earl Devereaux," Montague said. "He's recently returned

from Italy and brought his horse with him."

"From Italy?" Olivia said. "How did he transport a horse from Italy?"

"With difficulty, I presume," Eleanor said, smiling. "But why not sell the animal in Italy and save himself the cost of passage?"

"I get the feeling he wasn't expecting to have to sell the animal at all," Montague said. "His estate's deep in debt, so Stockton tells me."

"I thought lawyers weren't supposed to engage in gossip," Eleanor said. "I'm surprised at Mr. Stockton. He's usually a man of integrity."

"I believe it's due to that integrity that he encouraged Devereaux's man to contact me to broker the sale," Montague said. "Devereaux was only willing to sell his horse to the right sort of man."

"You mean one with a title and pedigree as pure as the horse?" Olivia said, wincing at the bitterness in her voice.

"Surely you're not comparing your birth to the bloodline of a horse."

"Montague!" Eleanor cried. "Must you distress your poor sister further?"

He raised his hands in supplication. "I meant no injury to you, Olivia," he said. "In answer to your question, no—Devereaux seemed to care only for one thing, that his horse be treated well. When he visited Rosecombe, I managed to convince him that I would."

"He visited us?" Olivia asked. "When?"

"During our house party."

"I don't recall a Lord Devereaux being at the party," Olivia said.

"He refused to stay," Montague replied. "He arrived just after dinner and left the moment we shook hands on the sale. But I doubt either of you would value an acquaintance with him."

"Why not?" Eleanor asked. "Is he a dishonorable man?"

"On the contrary—he seemed overly honorable, but he's

somewhat ill-tempered."

"No wonder, poor man," Olivia said. "He'd just lost his horse. Wouldn't you be bad-tempered if you had to part with something you loved?"

He snorted. "One horse is like any other."

"To *you*, perhaps, my love," Eleanor said. "When do you take possession?"

"He arrives at Rosecombe next week."

"Then when we return to the country, perhaps I'll ride him."

"I'd advise against that, Eleanor. By all accounts, Destriero is not suitable for a woman."

"Destriero?" Olivia said. "What a beautiful name."

"Even if his former master's temperament sounds decidedly less beautiful." Eleanor laughed. "Perhaps it's as well that you didn't introduce him to us, Monty. Though if he has nothing else to recommend him, his favorable opinion of you is to be commended"—her eyes sparkled with mischief—"even if I find you infuriating at times. Have you met him before?"

"We were at Eton at the same time," Montague said, "but I only knew him by sight. He was several years above me and went up to Oxford while I was still in the lower school. He was in the same year as Dunton."

Eleanor wrinkled her nose. "*That* unsavory creature! Were they friends?"

"Not at all. Devereaux was always getting into fights—mostly with Dunton."

"Then that's one more thing to recommend him," Eleanor said before sipping her tea.

"He was an excellent boxer," Montague continued.

"What, *Dunton*?" Olivia asked, recalling the red-faced, portly duke she'd had the misfortune of being introduced to at the beginning of the Season.

"Heavens no!" He laughed. "Devereaux. He was awarded a boxing blue. Rumor at White's has it that he flattened his opponent from Cambridge with a single blow."

"Surely you exaggerate," Olivia said, shuddering at the notion of such violence.

"Unlikely, given the size of him," her brother said. "He looks more like a pugilist than an earl."

"Perhaps it's as well you didn't introduce him to us at our house party," Olivia said. "He sounds like a man to fear, though doubtless like every other man you've introduced me to, he'd not consider me worthy of his attention."

Montague sighed. "Don't lose heart just yet, Olivia. How about we hold a ball in your honor?"

"What," Olivia said, unable to disguise the sharpness in her voice, "so I can be paraded around like a prize heifer? You're aware of my pedigree, brother. The bull that sired me may have had a known bloodline, but not the cow."

"Sister, I—"

"What was it?" Olivia said, no longer able to temper her despair. "A quick rutting in a paddock? What suitor wishes to be stained with *that?*"

"That's enough!" he roared. "I'll not have you utter the language of the guttersnipe in my home, and certainly not before my wife."

"Montague," Eleanor said, "your sister was only—"

"No, Eleanor," he interrupted. "Olivia has to learn that she, more than anyone, must act with decorum." He turned to Olivia. "You're upsetting your sister-in-law. Don't you know she dislikes loud voices?"

"The only loud voice in the room is yours, Montague," Eleanor said. "Olivia cannot help her birth, and I won't have her forced to wed any man who thinks less of her because of it. I would advise against holding a ball."

"But…"

Eleanor raised her hand. "I know you have good intentions, my love, but we wouldn't want Olivia's marriage to come about through an act of coercion—not on her part, nor on the young man's. Let the suitors come to her of their own free will."

"And if they don't?"

Olivia winced at her brother's tone.

"Then they don't deserve her," Eleanor said. "What would you prefer, Montague, a man who would not love her? Love can be found in the most unlikely of circumstances, when you're not looking for it. After all, is that not how you and I met? Did *you* intend to marry me at first?"

He colored and shame flickered across his expression. "Our initial engagement was not a usual one, I'll admit…"

"Quite so. If I recall, you confessed, the day after proposing to me in public, that you never intended to marry me and you'd only offered marriage to put paid to your mother's plans to match you with Lady Arabella Ponsford."

"Sweet heaven!" Olivia cried. "Mr. Baxter's wife? Were you going to marry *her*?"

His color deepened, then Eleanor let out a laugh.

"Come, come, Monty, my love. I'm only teasing you. It's long since forgiven and forgotten. I'm merely attempting to point out that forcing Olivia into a conventional courtship may not be in her best interests."

His shoulders relaxed and he sighed. Then he approached Olivia and offered his hand.

"Forgive me, sister," he said. "I only want you to be happy. I wish I knew how to achieve that."

His voice wavered as it always did when he revealed his heart—the living organ that he concealed behind a layer of cold steel.

Eleanor rose. "I must see to the cook about supper. Please excuse me."

Without waiting for a response, she exited the drawing room, closing the door behind her.

Montague drew Olivia into his arms.

"Please forgive your overbearing older brother," he whispered, placing a kiss on her forehead. "There's no urgency to find you a husband. I'll sponsor as many Seasons as it takes. None but the best of men for my little Livvie."

She suppressed a cry at his pet name for her, only uttered at the tenderest of moments. His anger, dominance, and belligerence she could withstand, but when the moments of kindness broke through, like a ray of summer sun from behind a thick thundercloud, her resolve crumbled.

She buried her head in his chest. "What if I don't..."

"Hush," he said, stroking her hair. "You'll always have a home with Eleanor and me. You know the children adore you. Horatio told me the other day that you're his 'favoritest person in the whole world,' and you know how difficult *he* is to please."

"But I want a home of my own," she whispered, "children of my own. I want what you have with Eleanor—someone to love me without condition, without expectation, whom I can love in return."

"Such a thing is rare in our world."

"You mean *your* world."

"No. *Ours.* You belong to this world, and I'll beat into a pulp anyone who says otherwise."

"Except perhaps this Lord Devereaux," Olivia said with a grin, "seeing as he can flatten a man with a single blow."

He let out a soft laugh. "Aye, except him. But it's unlikely you'll ever meet."

His chest rose and fell in a sigh, and Olivia grew still, taking comfort from her brother's solid embrace and the faint echo of his heartbeat.

"Did you speak the truth back then?" she asked. "About how you and Eleanor met?"

He nodded. "I'm ashamed of it. I behaved abominably, with no thought for Eleanor and her feelings. But it turned out for the best. For me, that is. I'd never have noticed her ordinarily, until we were thrust into each other's company on a silly whim of mine. But that whim was the one action that redeemed me and found my soul mate. And more than anything, I want you to find yours." He patted her arm. "And he'll be the most fortunate man in the whole world. Perhaps you'll find him at Lady Fairchild's ball next week."

"I thought you disliked the Fairchilds."

"They're more amenable now their daughter's safely married," he said. "Lord Fairchild made a point of saying at White's yesterday that he very much looked forward to seeing you dance."

"I don't think I can face another ball, brother."

He placed his fingers under her chin and gently tilted it upward until their eyes met.

"You don't have to go, Livvie, but it's the last ball of the Season. How about you come to one more—for me? Then we can return to Rosecombe, where I'll even let you ride Destriero—defy his previous master's insistence that he's not fit for a woman. In fact, I'll let you do anything if it makes you happy."

Her heart softened at the love in his voice. Perhaps, if she could not find a husband to love her as she wished, she at least had a brother who would strive to make her happy, a loving sister-in-law, and four nephews and nieces whom she loved as if they were her own children.

My own children...

"Very well." She nodded. "One last ball."

CHAPTER FIVE

"OH, MY LORD! Yes! Ride me hard, you wondrous beast!"

The whore's throaty cries filled the bedchamber as Charles pounded into her.

She let out a scream, jerking her body from side to side, throwing her legs open wider in an overly exaggerated gesture.

Curse the woman! Didn't she know that such obviously feigned pleasure was almost as effective in dousing a man's lust as a bucket of cold water poured down his breeches?

He closed his eyes, ignoring her lusty cries and focusing on his breathing, which came out on short, hoarse bursts as his body tightened in its elevation toward his climax.

Then it came. With a surge of base instinct, he plunged into her one final time and exhaled sharply as he shuddered with release.

Her writhing continued for a heartbeat, then she jerked her body upward.

"Magnifico!"

Charles opened his eyes to see her face at close quarters, covered in a layer of powder so thick that little cracks appeared at the corners of her eyes. Her cheeks were smeared in grease that glistened an unnatural shade of red—a shade to match her lips.

Ugh.

The bed would have to be stripped as soon as she left the building, and the room aired, before he'd consider sleeping in it again.

Nausea gripped his stomach, and he climbed off the whore and reached for a cloth to wipe himself.

A hand caught his wrist with the speed of a striking snake.

"Let *me*, my love," she said, "I'm here to serve you, my *bella* lord."

Devil's breeches! Was she still trying to keep up the pretense of being Italian? Her poorly executed accent was enough to give her away, let alone the smattering of ill-timed Italian words. Doubtless she'd told Charles's valet that she hailed from the finest brothels in Rome, and most men would have been fooled by her act.

But Charles knew enough Italian to see through her façade. And he'd fucked her before, when he was a raw youth before he left England.

He allowed himself a wry smile. To think—doxies always argued that, to a man, one whore was the same as any other. But the reverse was also true. Anne Brown—or, as she'd called herself today, Angelina Bellissima—hadn't shown a flicker of recognition when John escorted her to Charles's bedchamber. In her eyes, one man ready to part with cash as she parted her thighs was like any other.

To her credit, she'd learned a trick or two in the fifteen years since he last rutted her, wrapping her bony fingers around his cock the moment he lowered his breeches, parting her lips to receive him. But now, he slapped her hand away.

She pouted, her lips glistening in the candlelight. "Did I please you, my lord?"

He shrugged, then caught a flash of irritation in her eyes.

"There's time enough," she said, pitching her voice low in an attempt at seduction. "I know all manner of ways to pleasure the discerning gentleman. And you strike me as a *very* discerning gentleman."

Discerning—*ha!* Doubtless others fell for her pretty speeches, but, to Charles, the act of rutting was merely a means of gaining release. Men, and women, rutted for two purposes only—to achieve a base, physical release, and to further their bloodline. Anyone who believed otherwise was a fool.

And anyone who believed in love was an even bigger fool.

He pointed toward the door. Her smile broadened and she reached for his cock once more.

"Let me show you the pleasures that only I can give, my *magnifico* stallion," she said. "I'm yours for the night."

Devil's breeches, a whole night of her false moans and screeches, not to mention the stench of sweat and cheap cologne?

Charles slid off the bed and, turning his back to her, approached the bellpull. She let out a low cry, and when he turned, he caught a flicker of disgust in her eyes before the veneer of false seduction once more gleamed in them.

"That mark on your back," she said. "What happened? Are you perhaps a hero from Waterloo?"

He wrinkled his nose in a sneer.

Yes, because in battle, an army always prefers to use whips instead of guns or swords.

She stared at his hands as he signed, confusion in her gaze.

"What are you doing?"

He gestured to the door once more, then pulled the cord over the fireplace. Within a suspiciously short space of time, a knock came on the door, then John opened it.

Get rid of the woman.

John knew better than to argue. He nodded to the doxy.

"My master's done, miss," he said.

"But you paid for the whole night," she whined petulantly. "You're not expecting me to return my fee, even if your master couldn't—"

She broke off as Charles drove his fist into his palm with a sharp slap. Then he motioned to John.

Get the slut out before I throw her out myself. Give her an extra sovereign for her trouble—and her silence.

"Very good, sir."

The doxy moved her gaze from Charles to his valet and back, her brow furrowed in concentration.

Tell her that if she breathes a word of what she saw, I'll hunt her down and toss her into the river.

John had no need to translate. The doxy's eyes widened in fear as Charles plucked her discarded gown from the floor and held it out. She reached for it and slipped it on, securing a sash about her waist. Then the fear was replaced by greed as the valet fished a coin out of his pocket.

"For your discretion," John said. "We may require your services again…"

No, we fucking well won't.

Ignoring Charles's signing, John continued, "Therefore, it's in your interests to maintain the discretion that your profession is noted for."

She sidled up to John, her eyes gleaming with seduction, then palmed the coin. "You're a right proper gentleman, Mr. Richards," she said, all trace of faux-Italian accent now gone. "I'll be happy to accommodate *you* anytime. What do you say?"

"I say that it's time for you to go."

"Very well," she said, pouting. "But you know where to find me."

She eyed Charles, dipped into a curtsey, then let John escort her out.

By the time John returned, Charles had stripped the sheets from the bed and dropped them in a bundle beside the door. The valet arched his eyebrows.

"Fancy yourself as a chambermaid, sir?"

Charles frowned, and John raised his hands in appeasement.

"Very well," he said. "I take it the woman was not to your satisfaction?"

She satisfied me well enough, but I've no wish to have a woman in my bed longer than necessary.

"A pity," John said. "She's known to be very accomplished, both in giving pleasure and in teaching men of limited experience how to pleasure women."

Why would a man want to learn how to pleasure a woman?

John rolled his eyes.

Charles tempered the flare of irritation. What the bloody hell did he pay the man for if not to show respect?

"The art of pleasuring a woman is considered an accomplishment among men, sir."

Only insofar as the man wishes to boast about it in the clubroom at White's.

John shrugged. "Perhaps, but I hear that a well-satisfied woman can be a boon. And you'll want to be ready for your bride, will you not? A well-pleasured bride is supposed to be more fruitful."

This time John had gone too far.

Charles slapped his fist into his palm, then gesticulated in sharp, angry motions.

A bride has one use. To give me a dowry.

"And an heir."

Do you wish to be dismissed?

"There's nothing wrong with wanting an heir," John said. "Mrs. Brougham said Penham Park needs light and laughter, and to be treasured as a family home. I agree with her."

Are you also turning into a weak-bellied woman?

John eyed Charles's hands, then sighed. "If you fear that you'll turn out to be like your father just because…"

He stopped, flinching as Charles rammed his fist into the door then pointed to the discarded bedsheets.

Get rid of those. They reek of her stench. This whole chamber reeks of her stench. Have another chamber made ready.

"There's no other bedchambers in the apartment, sir, unless you want my room. I didn't see the need for unnecessary expenditure on rent, seeing as you're only in London for a few—"

Charles cut him short with a dismissive gesture. *Then I'll sleep on the sofa in the drawing room.*

John stooped to gather the bedsheets. "I'll see to these, sir. If you'd care to wait in the drawing room, I'll bring you a brandy while I see to your bedchamber."

I said I was content to sleep in the drawing room.

"It's not the done thing, sir. Besides, you'll need a proper night's sleep to ensure that your usual good sprits have returned in time for the ball tomorrow night."

Charles raised his hands to respond while the valet eyed him with not a trace of irony in his gaze, then he lowered them and nodded.

That bloody ball.

Already it had cost him enough—precious funds in lieu of parting with his beloved horse—to purchase that bloody jacket. The tailor had simpered all over him while making the measurements, complimenting his good taste in fashion and praising the Devereaux name.

But, apparently, the right sort of bride could not be acquired by placing an advertisement in the newspaper or brokering a deal via Mr. Stockton. She was to be gained by Charles's parading himself about a ballroom in a jacket that cost more than the footman's wages.

Of course, in this context, the *right sort of bride* was one with a dowry large enough to fund his father's debts.

Very well, Charles signed. *Bring me the brandy when you're done here.* He paused. *Don't bother with a glass. Just bring the bottle.*

The valet frowned. "I'd advise against too much brandy, sir. It's not the best quality, and you wouldn't want to attend Lady Fairchild's ball with a sore head, would you, sir?"

And you wouldn't want to spend the rest of our stay in London with a sore head, would you?

John's mouth twisted in a smile, then he nodded. "Of course not, sir. I'll bring the bottle as soon as I've finished here."

Charles pulled on his breeches, then exited the chamber, almost colliding with a chambermaid in the hallway. She glanced at his half-naked form and tipped her head up to meet his gaze. Her eyes widened in terror, and she let out a whimper.

John appeared at the doorway. "It's all right, Millie; you've done nothing wrong. Come and see to his lordship's bedchamber."

If anything, her eyes widened further. Trembling, she approached the door. Charles stepped aside to make room, and she darted past him faster than a rabbit that had scented a fox.

Devil's breeches, could he not wander about his own lodgings without instilling fear into every creature he encountered?

But at least, if she feared him, she'd keep out of his way from now on.

If only the rest of the world would keep out of his way.

Shortly after Charles entered the drawing room, John appeared brandishing a decanter half filled with a deep amber liquid and a glass on a silver salver.

Charles motioned toward a table and John placed the tray on it.

"I wouldn't drink it if I were you," John said. "The landlady charges extra, and it's of inferior quality."

How do you know? Have you been drinking it?

"I saw Milly polishing the silver with it."

Who?

"That maid you startled just now."

Charles let out a sigh.

He'd done more than that. The poor creature had looked terrified.

Give her a sovereign for her trouble when we leave London.

John's eyes widened and he glanced over his shoulder, in the direction of the bedchamber.

"Good God almighty! You're not thinking…"

Devil's breeches, did John think him so much of a beast that, not content with frightening a girl barely out of the schoolroom, he sought to defile her?

Charles fisted his palm, then shook his head, gesturing to his valet.

I pay you extra for enduring my poor temper. It only seems fair to pay the girl for the same thing.

John's mouth twitched into a smile. "Perhaps her life won't be entirely miserable."

Who? The maid?

John backed toward the door. "Your bride—whomever the unfortunate woman may be."

Before Charles could issue an admonishment, John darted out of the drawing room and closed the door.

Perhaps he paid the valet too much after all—though he wasn't paying him extra for his impertinence.

But then, few, if any, would endure John's role—and Charles's temper—with grace, let alone aplomb.

Though Charles would never tell the impertinent fool that he valued John's company almost as much as he'd valued his beloved horse.

Destriero…

Charles poured himself a brandy and sighed. It was insult enough to be forced to sell Destriero, but tomorrow night, he'd have to face the bastard who now owned him. Whitcombe might be an honorable fellow who'd paid a pretty price and made even prettier promises about caring for the horse, but nevertheless, he deserved to rot in hell for owning Destriero when Charles did not.

No, that was unfair. It wasn't Whitcombe's fault that Charles had lost his beloved horse and was being forced to shackle himself to some Society harpy.

It was Father's.

Charles raised his glass and uttered a silent toast before draining the contents.

Curse you, Father. Curse you to hell.

CHAPTER SIX

IT WAS EASY to understand why Olivia's sister-in-law did not like balls. For one thing, the noise. Inane chatter filled the ballroom, stifling the air as the ladies exclaimed over the cut of each other's gowns. As to the gowns themselves, the cacophony of colors was enough to induce a megrim.

From her position, seated on the periphery of the company, Olivia leaned toward her sister-in-law and took her hand.

"Are you well, Eleanor? I can accompany you to the terrace if you need a little quiet. Or I could ask Montague to attend you." She gestured toward her brother, who stood at the opposite end of the ballroom, deep in conversation with a group of young men.

"No, no, Olivia," Eleanor replied, her voice betraying her discomfort. "I've no wish to leave you on your own. But I might take a turn about the terrace once you've secured a dance partner."

In which case, Eleanor will be stuck here with me for the duration of the evening.

Olivia glanced about the company, unable to ignore the voice whispering in her mind—a voice to echo the whispers that had drifted across the ballroom as some of the less congenial members of the party had passed her by.

Natural child…

Bastard…

Each time she heard those words, she snapped her head round to see a group of young women who nodded and smiled before opening their fans to giggle and whisper behind them.

Olivia's gaze fell upon Miss Aurora Young—or, as she'd been sharply reminded by the young woman herself, the *Honorable* Miss Aurora Young. Arm in arm with Sir Heath Moss, she radiated the brittle beauty that spoke of years of breeding. The awkward encounter earlier that evening when Lady Fairchild introduced them had resulted in Miss Young giving Olivia the cut direct before sauntering off with Miss Peacock, another young woman who wasn't above pointing out Olivia's many faults, with a sweet smile that belied the spite glittering in her eyes.

Bitches.

"That may be so, Olivia dear, but it's best not to voice it."

Olivia turned to her sister-in-law. "Forgive me, Eleanor. I didn't mean to speak aloud."

Eleanor patted her hand. "You're worth a hundred of them, Olivia."

"Not if you compare their dance cards to mine."

"Then it's the young men's loss," Eleanor said. "Imagine what a sufferance it must be to stand up with women such as Miss Young or Miss Peacock!"

Olivia eyed the couples lining up for the next dance. "None of them look like they're suffering."

"I assure you they are," Eleanor said, with a grin. "Society ladies are supposed to suffer—to endure the company of men such as Sir Heath Moss and restrict their conversation to conceal any unladylike displays of intelligence or emotion." She lowered her voice to a whisper. "That is, of course, assuming they're in possession of intelligence or emotion. Miss Young seems to have a little more wit than her friends, but I daresay the influence of Miss Peacock will obliterate all trace of human decency. Why must titled ladies be so unpleasant?"

Olivia managed a smile. "You have a title. Don't they see you as one of them?"

Eleanor laughed. "My dear Olivia, I'll never be one of them, for all that I'm a duchess. My title is courtesy of marriage, not birth. As the daughter of a man who had the vulgarity to acquire his fortune through trade, I'm not generally deemed acceptable in Society. Besides, I lack the qualities expected of a Society lady. For one thing, I dislike company."

"Which is perhaps why I prefer you to every other living soul," Olivia said.

The murmur of conversation intensified, filling the air with harsh voices and soulless laughter. Eleanor began to pick at her bracelet before twirling it about in her hands.

"Would you do me the honor of partnering me for the next dance, Miss...?"

Olivia glanced up to see a young man bowing before her, hand extended—one of the men Montague had been speaking to earlier.

She stared at the newcomer. Handsome enough, though his reddened cheeks spoke of a little too much liking for Lord Fairchild's champagne.

"F-forgive me, sir," Olivia stammered. "We've not been properly introduced."

He bowed and clicked his feet together. "Mr. Arnott, at your service. I've had the pleasure of being introduced to your brother the duke." He bowed to Eleanor. "Your Grace, I'd be honored to make your acquaintance. The duke speaks very highly of you, and I now see that his praise of you is vastly underrated."

"Do you seek to flatter me, Mr. Arnott?" Eleanor said.

He colored, his artlessness not obliterated by age and experience, and Eleanor laughed.

"No matter," she said. "You're not the first young man to flatter a duchess, and I doubt you'll be the last."

"I-I'm not come here to flatter, Duchess," he said. "I'm come to beg His Grace's sister's hand for this dance."

Eleanor tilted her head to one side. "So, you're here to flatter a duke's sister?"

"Unashamedly so, Duchess." He turned his gaze to Olivia. "Dear lady, with your chaperone's permission and your consent, I'd be honored to partner you."

His eyes sparkled with a hope that mirrored the hope rising in Olivia's heart.

"Eleanor, may I?" she asked.

"Of course, Olivia. You've no need for my permission."

Olivia rose and took the proffered hand. "Then it would be my pleasure, sir."

His smile broadened and her heart fluttered at the expression in his eyes. With perfectly proportioned features, a strong jaw, and a physique that, though slighter than her brother's, possessed a degree of athleticism that filled out his jacket perfectly, he was one of the handsomest men in the room.

And he'd asked *her* to dance!

He led her to the dance floor, and Olivia smiled at the young women she passed who eyed him with curiosity and her, envy.

By the time the music began, Olivia had conquered most of her apprehension. Though she'd practiced the steps many times at home under the guidance of a dance teacher Montague had employed, tonight was the first time she'd had the opportunity to perform this particular dance at a real ball, with a real man as opposed to Miss Revell.

She smiled to herself as she recalled her teacher's words.

One, two, three, one, two, three, forward and back. One, two, three, one, two, three, look straight ahead. One, two, three, one, two, three—and turn!

"I beg your pardon?"

She glanced up from the floor. Curse it! She'd not been looking up—unable as she was to share Miss Revell's confidence that she wouldn't trip over her feet if she didn't stare at the floor for the duration of the dance.

"Forgive me, Mr...."

Heavens! What was his name again?

"Mr. Arnott," he said, frowning in an expression of mock

hurt. "Lady Olivia, am I so far below you in station that you've forgotten my name already?"

"Of course not," Olivia said, "b-but my name is not…"

But at that moment, they were separated by the steps, and she found herself face to face with Sir Heath Moss. With a sneer, he held out his hand, and she took it, suppressing a shudder as he steered her about in time to the music.

"I say, Miss… What was it?" He shook his head. "Forgive me, I cannot recall your name. You seem extraordinarily accomplished on the dance floor, considering."

"Considering what?" she said. "The skills of my partner?"

"Tut-tut, would you impugn Mr. Arnott's talents?"

"I wasn't referring to Mr. Arnott."

"Of course," he said, "when a woman has few offers at a ball, she must accept whichever young men are disposed to dance with her."

"I'm not so desperate as to accept the most objectionable offers, Sir Heath," she said. "But, of course, some dances require an exchange of partners—which can be most unfortunate, can it not?"

His eyes narrowed, and they continued in silence until she was reunited with Mr. Arnott.

"Are you enjoying the dance, Lady Olivia?" he asked.

Olivia caught Miss Young's spiteful smile and felt her cheeks warming.

"Y-yes, very much," she said. "A-at least, I am *now*."

"I daresay you've had many dance partners this Season," Mr. Arnott said.

"Not that many, sir."

"Surely the sister of the Duke of Whitcombe will have had many offers. He's a remarkable man."

Olivia glanced about the ballroom in search of her brother, who was now sitting beside Eleanor, holding her hand.

"He's the best of brothers," she said. "He's very kind to me, and he dotes on Eleanor—I adore her."

"The duchess is a little…eccentric, is she not?"

Olivia tempered the flare of anger.

"Eleanor is the best of women," she said. "She merely dislikes crowds and is discerning when it comes to the company she keeps—a sentiment I agree with."

To his credit, he colored. "Forgive me. I meant no disrespect. I value eccentricity over conformity."

"As does my brother," Olivia said.

At that moment, as if he'd heard, Montague glanced up, and they exchanged a smile.

More than anything, she wanted him—her beloved brother who recognized her as his sister when many men of his station would not—to be proud of her.

Then she caught sight of a lone man standing in the corner of the room and her skin tightened in apprehension. He was more beast than man, and his large, muscular frame strained against his closely fitted dark-blue jacket. He seemed to be cast in a permanent shadow—not only the color of his hair, which was black as night, but the expression in his eyes, glittering darkly beneath a furrowed brow. A footman approached him with a tray, and he waved the fellow away with scowl.

He was the antithesis of Olivia's mild-mannered, good-tempered—not to mention good-looking—dance partner. It was a wonder he bothered to attend a ball if he was going to remain in the corner ready to snarl at anyone who dared approach.

In fact, men who were disinclined to dance ought to stay away from balls, for they only furthered the shame of the unfortunate women unable to secure dance partners.

But tonight, for once, I am not one of the unfortunates.

She turned a grateful smile toward Mr. Arnott. "Had you met my brother before tonight, sir?"

"No, Lady Olivia, but Lord Fairchild introduced us."

Olivia cringed at his address. But how could she correct him in the middle of a dance?

"I knew I'd like him the moment we were introduced," he

added.

"Because he's a duke?"

"Because he's an Oxford man, like myself. Different college, though. I was at New College."

"Oh?"

Olivia cursed herself. Doubtless she was expected to make some witty response to his declaration of having attended Oxford, but all she could muster was...*oh*.

"I always thought it amusing that New College was so named, given that it's one of the oldest colleges. Of course, we weren't at Oxford at the same time. I've only recently come down."

"And what did you study?"

"History...or was it English? Perhaps both."

"Don't you know?"

"Of course," he replied. "I'm only jesting."

"An education at Oxford is to be envied," Olivia said. "My brother is always saying how much he appreciated the experience. He's sponsoring the education of a tenant's son."

"A tenant? Such as...a *farmer*?"

"You disapprove?"

"O-of course not," he said, his forehead creasing into a frown.

"The boy's currently at Eton," Olivia said, "and my brother means for him to go to Oxford afterward. I used to teach him at the school in the village. Exceptionally clever, he is. I'm sure he'll do very well."

"*You* taught in a village school?"

"You disapprove of women having an occupation, Mr. Arnott?"

"I know ladies often bestow charity on the less fortunate," he said, "but few children can boast of being taught by a titled lady."

"Oh, I'm not..." Olivia began, but the dance came to a close and applause rippled through the company.

Mr. Arnott bowed over her hand then lifted it to his lips.

"I must thank you for your excellent company, Lady Olivia.

Such unmatched pleasure that I am in pain now it has come to an end. I trust, in the interests of not furthering my pain, you'll permit me to claim another dance."

Ordinarily Olivia would have laughed at his affected gallantry, but after weeks of receiving snubs at every ball she attended, she allowed herself to enjoy a little flattery.

"I'd be delighted, sir."

"Then I'll come and claim you for the set after next."

He brushed his lips against her hand again, then escorted her back to her seat beside Eleanor. He bowed to Montague and took Eleanor's hand. Eleanor gave a slight frown and tilted her head to one side, unsmiling as he kissed her hand. Then he clicked his heels together and returned to the dance floor.

"A gallant young pup," Montague said. "Decent enough, but a little too quick to ingratiate himself. But I daresay that's due to the inexperience of youth, which can make a man lose all sense when engaging in conversation with a beautiful young woman." He glanced at Olivia. "I take it you found his conversation pleasing?"

"Pleasing enough, brother," she said. "When there are so few willing to engage in conversation with me, I must accept what there is."

"You shouldn't feel compelled to enjoy his company," Eleanor said.

"You didn't like Mr. Arnott?" Olivia asked.

"I'll grant, there are worse men to spend an evening with. Besides, whether I like him is immaterial. It's *your* opinion that matters. I rarely like anyone, but I'll give Mr. Arnott credit for one thing."

"Which is?"

"His eagerness for your company, dearest. That shows good judgment."

Olivia smiled, a nugget of hope swelling in her heart. A young man, fresh from Oxford and eager to dance with her, was something to treasure. And, as Montague had said, she wasn't in need of scores of young men eager for her hand.

She only needed one.

She glanced across the ballroom, and her eyes once more fell on the scowling giant in the corner. A shiver rippled through her as he shifted his gaze toward her.

Eleanor was right. There were worse men to spend an evening with.

CHAPTER SEVEN

*D*EVIL'S BREECHES, IN all his life, Charles hadn't encountered a more unremarkable set of people as the company here tonight. The men—ranging from puppyish young bucks eager to demonstrate their prowess to foppish old fools even more eager to convince the rivals that their virility was as potent as their younger rivals'—were nothing more than foxes, prowling the dance floor as if it were a field, looking for the tastiest hens to devour.

The women were no better, parading about like bitches in heat, flicking their fans in an attempt to entice and seduce.

And the conversation! Did they have nothing better to discuss than the number of doxies they'd seduced during the Season, or the number of names on their dance cards?

Beasts and whores, the lot of them, no different to the lowest creatures residing in the slums of London, save for their titles and their wealth.

Which meant that Charles was no different to them. Or worse—he was already in possession of a title, and he had come to London with the express objective of obtaining wealth.

And not just obtaining it—*marrying* it.

But coming to Lady Fairchild's ball to parade himself among the braying members of Society was a waste of an evening when he could have been...

Been what? Rutting that painted doxy with the faux-Italian

accent who'd screamed his name with false ecstasy then pouted in a fit of temper when he failed to scream hers in return?

A footman approached bearing a tray of champagne glasses. Fighting the temptation to steep himself in liquor, Charles thrust his hands into his pockets and glared at the man. If he were to seek a bride among these people, he needed a clear enough head to protect himself against the wiles of women seeking a titled partner. One false step while under the influence of too much champagne and a man could find himself in the clutches of an ambitious young harpy desperate for a husband claiming that he'd compromised her, followed by an overly aggressive male relative calling him out.

The footman smiled and raised his eyebrows, offering the tray. Charles gritted his teeth and took a step toward him. The footman stepped backward, his eyes glistening with fear, and almost collided with one of the dancers—a painted harpy with the name of Miss Peacock, a name that suited her strutting, conceited demeanor. She admonished him, and the footman mumbled his apology and scuttled off, his jacket now covered in a dark stain where one of the champagne glasses had toppled over on the tray.

Doubtless Lord Fairchild would insist the cost of cleaning the jacket come out of the poor boy's wages, but his fate would have been worse had he spilled champagne on Miss Peacock's gown. A woman with such spite in her eyes would have insisted the boy be whipped...

Charles caught his breath as the memory pushed itself to the fore—the searing pain on the skin of his back, his father's insults filling the air. He fisted his hands and focused his attention on the dancing, the brightly colored silks moving together. Or almost together. A poor young lady was partnered with Viscount De Blanchard, a man who moved his body as if he were in the middle of relieving himself. He'd bumped into several of the other dancers already but, his being a viscount rather than a footman, any transgression was instantly forgiven.

Charles cast his gaze over the unpartnered, unwanted women sitting around the perimeter. One of them might make a suitable bride. The less beautiful the woman, the less attention and devotion she'd expect from a husband. Provided the dowry was large enough, he cared not how pretty his future bride was, given that he had no intention of actually spending any time with her. A stallion didn't take a mare because of what her face looked like.

His gaze settled on a lone woman—another unremarkable creature with insipid pale-brown hair and a dark-green gown, which, though accentuating her curves, lacked the brightness of color of the dancers, as if she wished to be overlooked. A diamond necklace, elegant in its simplicity, lay about her throat, the gemstones twinkling in the light as she turned her head.

She seemed to dislike being here almost as much as Charles. Her whole body vibrated with discomfort, and she was moving her hand about her left wrist in a repetitive gesture. Charles observed her for a moment, then caught the flash of gold about her wrist. It was a bracelet, and she was rotating it, her body moving slightly as she did so. Charles lowered his gaze to his own left hand and the signet ring on the little finger, which he was rotating in a similar gesture. Did she, too, strive to drive away an unknown fear, to restore the balance of temper when in a hostile environment, such as a Society party filled with noise and people?

Then she glanced up, and he caught the intense expression in her dark eyes. What color were they? Green? Brown? They were narrowed so much that he couldn't tell.

She lowered her gaze once more, focusing her attention on her bracelet. But, as Charles watched, she glanced in his direction once more, before frowning and resuming her attention on her hand.

A misfit as much as Charles, she'd be lucky to find a dance partner.

Then a gentleman approached her and Charles recognized Whitcombe, the fortunate blackguard who now owned his horse. He tempered the little spike of resentment. Where was Destriero?

All alone in some stable in the middle of the country? Was he being well looked after?

Whitcombe took her hand and her lips curved upward. Her eyes widened to reveal a rich emerald color, shining with joy and love. Whitcombe, wearing a similarly besotted expression, kissed her hand then sat beside her.

So *that* was Whitcombe's duchess!

Charles tempered the little twinge of regret. Perhaps he should have taken up Whitcombe's offer to be introduced to her when he'd had the chance. Her expression spoke of a depth of character not to be found among most ladies of Society. Perhaps that explained why Whitcombe, who possessed more discernment than most, had chosen her, despite her outwardly plain appearance.

You're getting more ungallant with the passing of each day, sir.

Charles succumbed to the voice of his conscience, which sounded uncomfortably like his valet. Were John with him tonight, he'd have admonished Charles for not placing himself in front of the prospective brides, offering his title for a dowry. But, given the unpalatable array of choices before him, his objective was not to seek the most favorable woman he could find, but the least objectionable.

The dance came to an end and the couples dispersed. Charles cringed as the noise increased, the ladies exclaiming over the prowess of their partners' dancing and the gentlemen bestowing shallow compliments in reciprocation. One couple approached the Whitcombes—a puppyish youth with hunger in his eyes and yet another unremarkable female specimen. Dressed in a plain pale-blue gown, she lacked the elegance of the other ladies, in that she waddled across the room rather than glided and fidgeted where she stood.

In short, she looked like a chambermaid attempting, and failing, to masquerade as a lady.

Now, sir, you're being unkind.

Curse his bloody valet! John wasn't even in the room, yet he lived in Charles's mind, ready to point out his every fault.

The young man bowed before the duke, who gave him a curt nod. Then the duchess patted the seat beside her. The young woman sat and glanced across the room, stiffening as she met Charles's gaze before looking away.

Yes—unremarkable in every way, save for her eyes, which were the exact same shape as Whitcombe's. But rather than an expression of confident superiority, they carried a note of misery and inadequacy, as if she believed that she did not belong.

Perhaps, given the likeness to Whitcombe, she was a relation, maybe an impoverished cousin whom he'd chosen, as an act of charity, to sponsor for the Season.

Which meant that she'd be desperate to bag herself a husband. Whitcombe would be equally desperate, given that charity only lasted so long, particularly if it incurred the expense of a young woman's Season.

"Oh, I say! Is your dance card not yet full, Aurora?"

Charles cringed as the sharp, nasal tones cut through his senses, and he glanced to one side to see two ladies approach—Miss Young and Miss Peacock.

"I've partners enough, Louise."

"Nonsense! You want to dance every dance tonight, do you not? I cannot imagine anything worse than being overshadowed by that Whitcombe brat."

"That's unlikely, given that she's spent most of the evening seated."

"She managed to persuade Mr. Arnott to dance with her. Some men are clearly not so fastidious as to—"

Miss Peacock broke off as she met Charles's gaze, and the slyness in her eyes morphed into hunger.

"Is it not a fine evening, sir?" she said. "I don't believe we've been properly…"

He turned his back and walked away. No dowry was large enough to tempt Charles to saddle himself with one of those two for the next dance, let alone the rest of his life.

"Well, *really!*"

He headed for the terrace doors to escape their indignation, then another pair of young ladies blocked his path. Their eyes widened in unison, and they giggled, fanning themselves vigorously, presumably in an attempt to look alluring.

Devil's breeches, they hunt in pairs!

A true hunter ought to blend in with his surroundings, all the better to approach his prey undetected. But these two creatures were bedecked in eye-watering shades of pink and orange.

He strode toward them, his boots clicking against the polished marble floor. Wide-eyed, they continued to stare, the frank desire in their gazes turning to astonishment, then Miss Pink Gown tugged at the sleeve of Miss Orange. Charles made no move to swerve, and they darted to one side as he strode past, Miss Pink letting out a low cry as he clipped her with his shoulder.

Good. Perhaps she might think again before throwing herself into the path of a man she set her cap at. Without a backward glance, he reached the terrace doors and slipped outside.

He crossed the terrace toward the balustrade, breathing in a lungful of cool air. Then he surveyed the vista before him. Though in London, where the residents lived cheek by jowl compared to the country, the Fairchilds' house had a garden large enough such that no other buildings were visible, save a handful of chimney pots above the tree line. But he could still tell they were in London. Even if one were blindfolded, the stench of dust, dirt, and people sat heavy in the atmosphere.

The moonlight bathed the terrace, picking out the outlines of the plants lining the perimeter. Charles approached one and ran his fingertips over the leaves, relishing the feel on his skin—the smooth upper side, and the rougher underside covered in veins. He closed his eyes and ran his fingertips over the bush until they reached something softer, more delicate, with the texture of silk—the petals of a flower.

The music struck up once more, and he caught the sound of

laughter as the fools inside resumed their hunt.

So many people crammed together, reeking of cologne and sweat as they pranced about for no other purpose than to outdo each other in terms of prowess, availability, and desirability. What shallow creatures they were, stifling the world! Why could they not be more like plants—the flowers, shrubs, and trees that gave air to the world rather than sucking the life out of it for their own gratification? Too many were wont to bully a tree or a bush into a shape they deemed suitable to meet their notion of aesthetics—or to cut down a tree altogether merely for the purposes of convenience, not caring for the tree itself or for the need to live in harmony with nature. Most of the trees lining this very garden had been alive years before the people inside the house were born, and doubtless would live for years after those people were buried.

Perhaps you should marry a tree, sir.

Charles smiled to himself at the notion of what John might say. But trees were considerably less trouble than brides. And at Penham Park he could live in harmony with nature, living alongside it rather than attempting to conquer it.

It was a pity, then, that to achieve such an objective, he must stoop to the practices of Society and pander to some conceited little miss who—

A rattle at the terrace door interrupted his thoughts, then it opened, and Charles caught sight of a blue skirt in the moonlight.

Damn. He retreated into the shadows. The last thing he needed was company, particularly female company.

Perhaps if he told her to go to hell, she'd leave him in peace. Or he could shock her into silence by telling her to fuck off.

If only I could.

He glanced over the edge of the balustrade. The drop wasn't too far—six or seven feet at most. He'd spent most of his childhood falling out of trees, scaling walls, and running from his tormentors until he was large enough to stand his ground and fight back, so a mere six or seven feet was a trifle, the only likely damage a tear or two to this damned expensive jacket.

But that was what John was for—to launder and mend his clothes. It was John, after all, who'd persuaded him to stand and be tortured by that pin-pricking tailor in Saville Row in the name of "bringing my master up to the latest fashions so that he might live in the manner that befits the Devereaux name"—or whatever nonsense he'd spouted at the man.

His mind made up, Charles lifted his leg over the balustrade. Then he paused as the newcomer stepped onto the balcony, shut the door, and promptly burst into tears.

Bugger.

There was nothing more guaranteed to draw a crowd than a sniveling woman. And the last thing any man wanted was to be caught climbing over the balustrade in an attempt to get away from one.

That sort of encounter never ended well for the man.

CHAPTER EIGHT

THE NEXT TIME Olivia glanced about the ballroom, the mysterious, brooding stranger had disappeared. She drew her shawl about her to temper the shivers rippling across her skin at the anticipation of his dark gaze meeting hers once more. But he was nowhere to be seen.

Perhaps he'd been a figment of her imagination—a demon materialized from the darkest depths of her soul to taunt her inadequacy and inferiority. And, in truth, she'd have preferred a demon from Hades to the flesh-and-blood tormentors in the ballroom tonight.

Excepting Mr. Arnott, who'd been gallant enough to ask her for a *second* dance! It was almost too good to be true. Nearly every ball Olivia had attended, she'd been without a partner all evening. For a handful, she'd been partnered once—though an offer from one of Montague's married friends, given with sympathy and doubtless at her brother's insistence, didn't altogether count as a genuine offer. But tonight, she was to dance a second time. It was almost enough to make all those dance lessons worth the effort.

She caught sight of him, leading Miss Peacock about in time to the music. Miss Peacock glanced across the room, her eyes glittering with spite, then resumed her attention on Mr. Arnott. Olivia allowed herself a smile. Miss Peacock's spite would be tempered when her partner exchanged her for Olivia at the end of the dance.

As the dance continued, Olivia rose and circled the perimeter of the ballroom, compelled by the need to observe the party. At least, that was what she told herself. A little voice in the back of her mind whispered that she wished to set eyes upon the dark demon again—or, at least, confirm whether he existed—much as a deer wished to court danger by approaching the lair of the wolf.

She caught sight of the familiar figure of Mrs. Stowe sitting alone. Dressed in a plain gown of dark blue muslin, her graying hair fashioned into a simple chignon, Mrs. Stowe exuded an air of crumbling elegance and exhaustion.

"Miss Whitcombe, is it not?" she said, rising. "What a pleasure. Have you danced tonight?"

"I have, ma'am. And you?"

The older woman gave a smile of amusement. "My dancing days are done, I'm afraid."

"Is there no one here with whom you'd wish to be partnered?"

Mrs. Stowe glanced at the company, and Olivia caught a flicker of apprehension in her eyes. She followed her gaze and caught sight of two men deep in conversation—Earl Staines and the Duke of Foxton. The duke glanced toward them, his lip curled in a sneer, before resuming his attention on the earl.

Mrs. Stowe sighed. "Balls are for the young, Miss Whitcombe," she said. "But my charge is dancing, as you see."

She gestured toward a young woman in the center of the dance floor, dressed in a gown of pale yellow that complemented her rich auburn hair.

"Miss Turton's mother was taken ill, and I offered to chaperone her. I couldn't see the young woman deprived of the last ball of the Season when she'd been looking forward to it so much."

"You're too kind, Mrs. Stowe," Olivia said.

Mrs. Stowe let out a soft laugh and resumed her seat. "I am more enterprising than kind, Miss Whitcombe," she said. "Lady Turton expressed her gratitude with twenty guineas. Which came at an opportune time, as my son is in need of a new suit before he returns to Oxford." She gave a smile of affection and indulgence. "Suits are so expensive, and my darling boy will insist on growing. He'll be taller than your brother if he grows any more— or even that rather imposing man I spotted earlier."

Olivia's heart gave a little flutter. "Which man?"

"I cannot see him now. Perhaps he left. He looked decidedly out of place and not at all happy. A distant cousin of our host, perhaps. I've not seen him about Town before."

"I-is your son enjoying his studies?" Olivia asked, maintaining her composure despite the frisson of disappointment.

"I believe so. Of course, I possess a mother's indulgence and am therefore all too likely to exaggerate his academic prowess if asked. But he'll not want for friends or acquaintances when he finishes his studies next year. I fancy everyone here tonight has an Oxford education."

"Every *man*," Olivia said, unable to disguise the bitterness in her voice. "Don't you think it unfair that men are given the opportunities for intellectual advancement that are denied our sex?"

"Ha!" a male voice barked, and Olivia glanced up to see Sir Heath Moss standing before them.

"May we be of assistance, Sir Heath?" Mrs. Stowe said, her voice hardening. "Or is there anything in particular you wished to say?"

"No, madam," he said, his handsome mouth curled into a sneer, "I was merely expressing my surprise at the notion of providing a woman with an education."

"Do you fear intelligent women?" Mrs. Stowe said.

"How can I fear something that doesn't exist?"

"Just because you fail to see it, does not necessarily mean that it doesn't exist," Mrs. Stowe said. "Men can be extraordinarily unobservant. They only see what they wish to see."

"I beg to disagree, madam," came the reply, "for I find myself compelled to see you and your"—he turned his attention to

Olivia, his eyes glittering with disdain—*"friend."* He folded his arms and smiled. "Would you permit me to bestow some friendly advice upon you, madam?"

"I find it unlikely that any advice offered would be given with the intent of friendship, but I will hear anything you wish to say, Sir Heath," Mrs. Stowe said.

He narrowed his eyes, but his smile broadened. showing white, even teeth. "Just so," he said, the undertone of a snarl in his voice. "If not friendship, then a concern for your reputation. A widow may benefit from her late husband's status in Society, but only if she's in possession of a title and a fortune. A penniless widow compelled to reduce herself to trade, however, must take the greatest of care not to risk her reputation by associating herself with those who may cast a stain on it."

Mrs. Stowe raised her eyebrows—the only sign that Sir Heath's insult had hit home.

"I fail to see how attending Lady Fairchild's ball is likely to place my reputation at risk, sir," she said, "unless you fear I'm at risk of being compromised by predatory males, of whom there are plenty here tonight." She met his gaze, unblinking. "Well, *one*, at least."

He let out a cold laugh. "You can be assured, madam, that any predatory males in the room tonight would not stoop to sniffing round widows past their prime"—he glanced toward Olivia, wrinkling his nose—"or bastards."

Olivia stepped back, wincing at the contempt in his voice. Mrs. Stowe rose to her feet.

"If I were a man, I'd call you out for that, Sir Heath. However, it would not be of any benefit to the world, given that you're too poor a shot and too much of a coward to face me by yourself at dawn. I believe you pay others to undertake the task for you."

She stepped toward him, and his eyes flared with fear.

"But," she continued, "I do not tolerate incivility, and neither does Lord Fairchild. If you wish not to be thrown out onto the street tonight, I demand you retract your insult toward Miss

Whitcombe."

"Yes," he sneered, "Miss Whitcombe, not *Lady Olivia*, as some poor, deluded fools have been deceived into believing. Though I've heard that at one time you were known as Miss FitzRoy. How tiresome it must be to have such uncertainty over one's name."

He dipped his head in a bow, his lips curled into a mocking smile.

"Do forgive any transgression, Miss Whitcombe," he said. "I ought to have referred to…*natural children*. I believe that's the term we must use in Polite Society. But I must express my concern on behalf of those of us in possession of a name and good breeding. Those of low birth, or no birth at all, can never truly belong in Society."

"How dare—" Mrs. Stowe began, but Olivia caught her arm.

"It matters not," she said. "I-I've no wish to discuss my birth with this…*gentleman*."

"I see no gentleman," Mrs. Stowe said. "I see a—"

Sir Heath raised his hand. "I'm sure your description of me would be most intriguing to any man who considered your opinion worth hearing. Unfortunately, I fail to see any such man in the company tonight." He glanced over his shoulder. "Ah, I see the dance is coming to an end. I must find Miss Peacock, who is promised to me for the next. You'd both do well to resume your seats. Unpartnered women in a ball exude such an air of desperation when standing, do they not?"

"I am not unpartnered, Sir Heath," Olivia said. "Mr. Arnott asked me to dance a second time."

"Oh, *did* he?" Sir Heath gave a sly smile, then retreated.

Olivia curled her hands into fists to temper the trembling in her body. Hot tears stung her eyes, and she bit her lip to stem the flow as her cheeks warmed.

A thin, lace-gloved hand took hers.

"Pay no attention to him, my dear," Mrs. Stowe said. "Men such as him, and women such as Miss Peacock, take their pleasure from seeing the distress of those whom they wish to torment."

"But what he said…"

"Is of no consequence to anyone who really matters. Those who cannot see your worth are, in turn, of no value themselves."

"Eleanor says the same."

"A sensible woman," Mrs. Stowe said. "Not all men are like Sir Heath, and for that we can thank the Almighty. There are many men of value."

"Was the late Mr. Stowe such a man?" Olivia asked.

Mrs. Stowe's brow furrowed in pain, but before she could respond, her charge appeared, her cheeks rosy with exercise.

"Did you enjoy the dance, Miss Turton?" Olivia asked.

"Oh yes!" Miss Turton flopped onto her seat and heaved a sigh.

"Posture, Margaret, dear," Mrs. Stowe said, a smile of indulgence in her eyes. Miss Turton straightened herself and let out a huff.

"I don't see why I must sit up straight when I'm so tired," she said. "Dancing is *exhausting!*"

"It is when you've danced very dance tonight with such vigor," Olivia said, smiling at the younger girl. "You enjoy dancing, I take it?"

"I love dancing!" came the reply. "Mr. Potterton said I was a true proficient. That's my dance partner, you know," she added, gesturing to a fresh-faced young man approaching the punch bowl. "I danced with him twice."

"He must be an agreeable partner, then," Olivia said.

"Very agreeable. I'd have liked to dance with him a third time, but Mrs. Stowe said it was inappropriate."

"Quite right," Olivia said. "My brother says that to dance with the same man twice in an evening displays a marked preference, but a third time invites scandal."

"Have *you* danced with a man three times tonight?" Miss Turton asked.

"No, but I'm partnered a second time for this next dance."

"To whom?"

Olivia glanced about the room as the musicians began tuning their instruments. "Mr. Arnott, though I cannot see him."

"I danced with him at the start of the evening," Miss Turton said. "*There* he is!"

She pointed toward the dance floor, where Mr. Arnott was leading a young woman toward the center. Olivia rose and approached him.

"Mr. Arnott, are we…"

He turned, and she froze at the cold expression in his eyes.

"M-Mr. Arnott?"

The young lady on his arm tilted her head to one side and fixed her pale-gray gaze on Olivia.

"A-are we not…" Olivia began.

"Acquainted?" he said. "I believe not—at least we've not been properly introduced. Now, if you'd excuse me, Miss…?" He raised his eyebrows and fixed his gaze on her.

"M-Miss Whitcombe," she said, a knot of apprehension in her stomach.

"Yes, that's it," he said, nodding. "I fear I mistook you for another: a woman of noble birth—or, perhaps, it was a Miss FitzRoy?"

Olivia swallowed the rising nausea and glanced about the ballroom. Her gaze fell upon Miss Peacock, a cold smile on her thin lips, pale eyes glittering with spiteful satisfaction.

"I-I…" Olivia stammered, stepping back.

"Do forgive me if I gave you the impression that I was not otherwise engaged for this dance," Mr. Arnott said. "I'm promised to Lady Mary Chadbury, and I trust you'll understand the nature of her superior claim."

"Oh yes," Olivia said, curling her hands into fists, "I understand it perfectly."

"Perhaps you ought to take a seat, Miss Whitcombe," Lady Mary said. "You look a little distressed, which is to be expected, given that you are in somewhat unusual surroundings—or, at least, unusual given your station."

"Oh, you're *too* kind," Olivia said, forcing a smile. She dipped into a curtsey, then, the spiteful smiles of the ladies filling her vision, she turned and strode away, almost colliding with a footman holding a tray of filled champagne glasses.

Oh heavens! As if the evening couldn't get any worse.

"I beg your pardon, sir," she said, her voice wavering. Through the mist of tears, she saw him raise his eyebrows, then hold the tray toward her.

"Take a glass, miss."

She took one, mumbling her thanks. The tears that she'd kept at bay spilled onto her cheeks, and she glanced about the ballroom for a means of escape. Then she caught sight of a door and rushed toward it, exhaling with relief when it swung outward at her touch, and slipped through the doorway.

A rush of cold rippled across her skin and she drew in a sharp breath, then let out a sob.

Would she never escape the stain of her birth? She'd have been better off living in obscurity, enjoying the simple life of a village schoolteacher. Montague had done what he believed to be an act of kindness by recognizing her as his sister. But, in reality, he'd taken her from the life she belonged to and thrust her into a world in which she did not fit—a world where her validity would always be questioned.

Don't let them win, Olivia. Don't let them see you upset, or angry.

Eleanor's words whispered in her mind, and Olivia drew in another breath. Her sister-in-law was right, of course. Any bully relished the prospect of seeing their victim in distress. The best way to fight Sir Heath, Miss Peacock, and everyone who sought to torment her was to show them that she cared nothing for them and their taunts.

But first, she needed to give vent to her anger.

"Bastards," she whispered. Then she took another sip, letting the bubbles burst on her tongue. "And...bitches!"

She drained her glass, coughing as the bubbles ticked her throat, and paced across the terrace toward the balustrade and back.

"Bastards!" Gripping the empty champagne glass, she paced to and fro, drawing in lungfuls of cool night air. But the anger failed to dissipate. Instead, a tide of despair rose blackly in her heart. She bit her lip to stem the tears. The last thing she wanted was for Eleanor, or Montague, to suspect she'd been crying.

She cast her gaze about the terrace, her eyes growing accustomed to the darkness. The thin sliver of moon in the sky cast a faint blue light, picking out blurred shapes—the tree line in the distance, broken by the occasional chimney pot, the stonework of the balustrade, and the more solid shapes of the shrubs and bushes at the far end of the terrace. She blinked, letting her gaze wander over the shrub in the shadows that moved slightly in the breeze. Then she froze.

There was no breeze.

"Wh-who's there?"

She paused, and the silence seemed to stretch across the air.

You fool!

Montague had admonished her over her overactive imagination during soirées and parties when she could have sworn she heard whispered taunts from the company. She'd dismissed his admonishments as the words of a loving brother seeking to protect her from the derision of Society. But perhaps he'd been right. For what purpose would a ruffian, or otherworldly creature, be prowling Lord Fairchild's terrace in the center of London?

Then she heard it—an intake of breath.

"C-come out! I can see you!" she said, forcing a note of boldness in her voice that belied the terror rising in her throat.

The shape moved—a dark form among the shadows, swelling in size, towering over her, and she stepped back as the blurred lines solidified into the shape of a man.

No, not a man, a *giant*, with broad shoulders and thick arms that showed the faint bulge of tensed muscles. With slow, steady breaths, he moved closer, seeming to glide across the ground, and a whimper escaped her lips as two luminous eyes materialized as if by witchcraft.

Then the form stepped out of the shadows and his face came into view—features sharp as if cut from marble, strong cheekbones, a straight nose, and full lips set in a firm, angry line. He stared at her, his eyes glittering with fury beneath a furrowed brow, topped with a head of thick, dark hair—the mane of a lion approaching his prey ready to tear out its victim's throat.

Then he curled his lips into a snarl.

Olivia caught sight of a set of teeth, gleaming and white in the moonlight, and opened her mouth to scream. She lifted her hands to fend him off, and the glass slipped from her grasp and shattered on the ground.

CHAPTER NINE

*C*RASH!

Charles winced at the sound of splintering glass. The interloper raised her hands and let out a cry.

Bloody woman! It served her right for disturbing his peace. Why wasn't she inside, simpering over the young men she sought to entrap? Or perhaps she'd ventured out for a tryst with some unsuspecting young fool.

He raised his hands in a gesture of appeasement and stepped toward her. She let out a whimper and her eyes widened, two dark pools in a face made pale by the moonlight.

The girl looked terrified. Why were women always so weak-bellied? Did she expect him to toss her over his shoulder and carry her off, when there must be at least fifty people inside who'd stop him?

Or perhaps she was playacting, like most women, feigning emotions to fool him into doing their bidding.

"Who are you," she said, "and what are you doing here, hiding in the shadows?"

He lowered his hands.

After a pause, she spoke again, her voice a low whisper. "A-are you *real?*"

Of course I bloody am.

She dropped her gaze to his hands as he gestured his response.

"What are you doing?" she said. "Do you dismiss me as if I am nothing?"

He cocked his head to one side. The fear in her voice had been replaced by another emotion. Sorrow. And despair.

Perhaps she believed that she did not belong here.

Neither do I.

She tilted her chin. The action emphasized their difference in height, and, given the fear that had transfixed her at first, like a rabbit caught in a fox's stare, he had to applaud—albeit grudgingly—the courage with which she looked up met his gaze straight on. Few men dared stare at him so openly.

He exhaled, and she set her mouth into a firm line, a flicker of defiance in her eyes.

"Will you not introduce yourself, at least?"

He arched an eyebrow. Most women he could read as if they wore placards declaring their intentions. But the little creature before him now—he couldn't make her out. Pretty enough, though as unremarkable as most women. But he had to admit that the expression in her eyes spoke of a little more intelligence than the typical female.

Perhaps that was why she believed she did not deserve to be here tonight. According to Society, intellect was a flaw for which the woman could not be forgiven. When entering the marriage state, a woman relinquished her fortune and her person. But intellect could not be surrendered. And no man wanted a woman who could outdo him in a battle of wits.

As he continued to stare at her, she folded her arms.

"I see," she said. "Like all the others, you think me unworthy."

All the others?

He glanced toward the terrace doors. Had she been mistreated?

He curled his fists, tempering the anger rising in his gut as the memory pushed into his mind—a group of boys, bare-teethed and grinning, issuing taunts, pushing him, pinching his flesh while the schoolmasters were occupied elsewhere, then feigning innocence when adult eyes turned to them once more, before he returned home to an unforgiving father.

I showed them. I showed them all.

His skin itched at the memory of fighting back—the feeling of triumph when, after learning to defend himself, his fists had at last connected with his tormentors. The fear that plagued his nightmares had dissipated and been reborn in their minds—until, at last, the tormentors feared the boy they had tormented.

Was this little thing standing before him also prey to tormentors? If she believed she didn't deserve her place in Society, then the worst of the predators would sniff her fear out and exploit it.

Until she learned to fight back—or was crushed beneath their spite.

Don't be a fool.

He gritted his teeth to dispel the brief flare of compassion. He couldn't afford such weakness in a world where compassion and tenderness had no value.

At length he became aware of a soft voice, and he resumed his focus on the young woman before him.

"...don't you think?"

Bugger. She'd been speaking.

She raised her eyebrows then blinked, and Charles caught a sheen of moisture in her eyes.

"I see," she said. "You consider me not only beneath your notice, but also unworthy of a response."

He gestured toward her.

Of course not.

"So, you dismiss me, is that it?" she said, her voice hardening as she glared at his hands. Then she gave a cold smile. "A great shame, given that we've been indulging in *such* an interesting conversation." She gestured about the terrace. "Consider yourself fortunate that I deign to converse with you, given the greater intellect of our companions."

He glanced about the terrace then raised his eyebrows.

"The plants, sir," she said, an edge to her voice. "I fancy I could elicit a more quick-witted and interesting response from a shrub, do you not think?" She placed her hands on her hips, nodding in an exaggerated manner. "Oh yes, Miss Whitcombe," she said, deepening her voice. "I'm a simpleton, come to speak to the plants because they're my intellectual equal."

She raised her voice to its usual feminine pitch. "Oh, *thank* you, kind sir, I'm *so* glad we're of one mind." Then she lowered the pitch and gestured to the terrace doors. "Quite so, Miss Whitcombe. Not even the numbskulls inside with their heads filled with wool such as that coxcomb Sir Heath Moss, who'll rut any creature with a pulse—and most likely many without—are able to match my lack of mental acuity."

Her voice wavered, then she blinked, and a fat droplet splashed onto her cheek, glistening in the moonlight.

"But a lack of intellect is a sin that can be forgiven, for it is indeed no sin," she said. "You are to be envied, sir. Your defining characteristic is lauded in Society, whereas mine…" She hesitated, her breath catching, and her lips trembled. "I-I'm committing the gravest of all sins, merely by existing. I—"

She broke off and a sob escaped her lips.

Devil's breeches, that was all he needed.

He approached her, hands outstretched, willing his conscience to believe that the action was purely to stop her wailing, ignoring the little voice that whispered in his mind of the need to ease her pain.

"No!"

She stepped back, then let out a scream as she lost her balance and tripped. She lurched sideways, and Charles caught sight of the shards of glass, their sharp edges gleaming malevolently in the moonlight like a thousand sinister smiles.

He lunged forward and caught her in his arms. She screamed again and struggled, but he tightened his grip to prevent her from falling. After a moment, her struggles ceased and she surrendered, with the prey's instinct that she was in the clutches of a stronger beast. Her body heaved as her breath came out in sharp gasps, and he held her close.

Beneath that plain little gown lay a body with deliciously soft curves and perfect, round breasts that were pressed against his chest. He caught his breath as his breeches tightened at the feel of two little peaks poking at his shirt. Then he inhaled, relishing the soft scent, the faint undertones of rose, that stiffened his cock.

What the devil was she doing to him, this unremarkable little thing? Eyes squeezed shut like she were readying herself to have her throat torn out by the wolf, she stilled in his grasp as if welcoming her fate. She opened her eyes, and for a moment they stared at each other, two souls meeting across a chasm.

Then she spoke and broke the spell.

"Let me go."

Another tear spilled onto her cheek as she whispered a plea. The despair in her tone threatened to breach the armor he'd fashioned around his heart.

"*Please…*"

Slowly he set her upright, but rather than release her, he paused. She made no attempt to move. Instead, she curled her fingers around his arms as she glanced toward the ground and the smashed glass. Understanding glimmered in her eyes and she parted her lips.

Then the doors crashed open, and a deep male voice bellowed with fury, "You *blackguard!*"

The woman in Charles's arms stiffened, and he released her and stepped back. But it was too late. The newcomer strode onto the terrace, his eyes blazing with fury.

Shit. It was Whitcombe.

The woman turned to Whitcombe and let out a cry. "Montague!" she said. "It's not—"

"Be quiet," he said. "You've lost the right to speak. As for *you…*" He strode toward Charles and jabbed a finger at his chest. "You will marry her, or so help me God, I'll shoot you where you stand."

Charles shook his head, then Whitcombe twisted his face into a cold, cruel smile as he delivered the one threat capable of destroying Charles—the threat to the one thing in the world that he cared for.

"Or," Whitcombe said, "I'll shoot that horse of yours and feed him to my dogs."

Shit.

He was trapped.

CHAPTER TEN

OLIVIA CRINGED AS her brother advanced on her.

"Montague, I—"

"Silence!" he roared. "Haven't you done enough?"

"I've done nothing!"

Seemingly oblivious to the other man's obviously superior strength, Montague again jabbed a finger at his chest. "You think you can debauch my sister? Is that what you both came out here for?"

The man tensed his shoulders but said nothing. Wasn't he going to defend himself, even if he didn't consider Olivia worth defending?

"Brother, we weren't doing anything wrong."

"You were out here a long time," he replied. "For what purpose other than to offer yourself to—"

"I didn't *offer myself*!" she cried. "We—we"—she glanced at the tall, silent figure about whom the air seemed to shimmer with menace—"were engaging in conversation, that's all."

"Oh, *really*? What, pray, were you discussing in your...conversation?"

Olivia glanced about the terrace. "W-we were discussing the plants."

"I didn't know you took such a keen interest in horticulture," her brother said. "What were you discussing? Did he tell you the names of all the plants?"

Olivia glanced at the silent man, who continued to stare at her.

Help me, sir.

"Y-yes," she whispered.

Her brother strode toward a plant set in a pot on a pedestal. "And what, pray, is this?"

She stared at the plant—its dark green leaves in the shape of sharp, pointed tongues, clustered thickly together.

"A fern."

Montague let out a sharp sigh. "I think you'll find it's an aspidistra. How about this?" He gestured to another plant dotted with flowers.

"A rose. He told me so." Olivia met the silent man's gaze, begging with her eyes. But he remained impassive, a slight sneer on his lips.

"Then I take it you know the gentleman's name, given that you've been deep in conversation."

"Do *you* know it, brother?" she said.

"Of course. But I'm not the one under scrutiny."

"What do you imagine I've been getting up to, brother," Olivia cried, "when no man will have anything to do with me?"

"What is all this?"

Olivia's heart almost cried out in shame as her sister-in-law stepped onto the terrace.

"Eleanor, this is none of your—"

"Be quiet, Montague!" Eleanor said. She approached Olivia and linked their arms. "Can't you see your sister's distressed?" She turned her attention to Olivia. "What's happened, dearest?"

"That's what I'm trying to ascertain," Montague said. "My sister is not in a position to compromise herself, given her background, and—"

"Please!" Olivia cried, shame threatening to overcome her. "Must you humiliate me in front of others? I merely came out to the terrace for some air, yet you accuse me of...of..."

"I see," Eleanor said, glaring at Montague. Then she turned

her attention to the silent, brooding man. "What is *your* purpose here, sir? If some mischief has occurred, I doubt that my sister is wholly to blame."

"You'll get no reply from him," Montague said.

"Why not?"

"For the same reason that I know my sister is playing me false when she claims to have engaged in a discussion with him. He does not speak."

Eleanor let out a snort. "*I* do not speak. I loathe conversation and meaningless social niceties and do my utmost to avoid it at all costs."

"I know that, my love," Montague said, exasperation in his voice. "But this fellow here does not speak *at all*."

The giant set his mouth into a hard line, and Olivia shivered at the quiet anger in his expression.

"Not *at all*?" she whispered.

"He's not spoken a word since I've known him," Montague said. "Renowned for it, he was, at Eton."

"You were at school with this man?" Eleanor asked. "So, you know him well?"

"We were in different houses. But I knew him by sight. Some of the other boys used to taunt him and…"

He paused as a low growl emanated from the dark figure.

"That's right, is it not?" Montague said. "They used to call you—"

"Stop it!" Olivia said, stepping forward. "Must you torment him as you torment me, brother?"

"Why defend him, sister, unless you have compromised yourself?"

"Of course I haven't!" Olivia said.

"Then why utter falsehoods, spin tales about your reasons for being out here tonight? It doesn't paint you in a particularly good light."

"Montague…" Eleanor began, but he raised his hand.

"No, I must have satisfaction. *We* must have satisfaction for the sake of the family." He turned to Olivia and spoke in a low voice. "I want what's best for you, sister, believe me. At this moment I care not whether you've tossed up your skirts to trap a man into matrimony. It's not what I'd have wanted for you, though I understand your desperation. But the very least you can do is pay me the courtesy of speaking the truth."

A knife sliced through Olivia's heart at her brother's words. Though his tone conveyed the love he bore her, did he really think she'd stoop so low as to act the slattern to ensnare a man—and not just any man, but the huge, towering beast before her?

The urge to strike her brother swelled within her, but before she could surrender to it, Eleanor drew back her hand and struck him across the face with a resounding slap that echoed across the terrace.

"Eleanor!" Montague said, rubbing his cheek. "I—"

"How dare you blame your sister in this!" she said. "This man is culpable."

"He's done nothing!" Olivia said. "Neither of us have."

"Then why did I find the two of you embracing?" Montague asked.

Olivia opened her mouth to respond, then her heart sank as a familiar, nasal voice spoke.

"I say! Is this a private party, or can anyone join?"

Sir Heath Moss stood in the terrace doors, the light from inside forming a soft halo around his deceptively angelic face.

"Begone, Moss," Montague said. "You've no business intruding on a family discussion."

"A family discussion?" Sir Heath said, gesturing toward the silent man. "Am I to wish you joy?"

Olivia stifled a sob, and Eleanor drew her into her arms.

"Excellent!" Sir Heath said. "The *London Daily* will sell faster than hot muffins at Michaelmas when the editor hears about this. I can imagine the headline now—*Ducal Debauchery*. But, given your...ahem...*sister's* origins, it should come as no surprise to our acquaintances."

"Don't be a fool, Moss," Montague said.

Sir Heath's smile broadened and he stepped toward Olivia, the stench of his cologne thickening the air.

"*I'm* the fool, am I, Whitcombe?" he said. "Why, then, did I hear you speak of your sister tossing up her skirts to entrap a man? She'd have fared better had she set out to find herself a protector rather than a husband. Her lack of success in securing a dance partner tonight is evidence of her poor prospects."

"I *did* secure a partner!" Olivia said. "Mr. Arnott asked me to dance twice."

"Under false pretenses," Sir Heath sneered.

The silent man let out a huff, then moved toward the doors. Montague blocked his path, placing his hand on the man's chest. A shiver rippled through Olivia's body at the expression in the larger man's eyes as he lowered his gaze to her brother's hand—a hand that he could easily crush with the slightest effort.

"Montague, there's no need..." she began.

"There's *every* need," he said. "Sir Heath has cast aspersions on your honor and slighted our good name." He fixed his gaze on the silent man. "*All* of our good names."

"With good cause," Sir Heath said. "The gossips are going to *love* this!"

"Perhaps they will," Montague said, his gaze still locked on the tall, dark figure. "But I doubt my sister, or...her *betrothed* would take kindly to false accusations, just as much as I doubt you'd take kindly to a lawsuit or a bullet through the heart."

My betrothed?

Olivia met the man's gaze, and a shiver rippled through her at the mixture of cold anger and disgust in his eyes.

"Brother..."

"It's the only way, Livvie," Montague said, and Olivia's heart cried out at the endearment. The anger in his voice had gone, replaced by resignation and disappointment.

Sir Heath let out a snort. "Not even this fellow would be foolish enough to shackle himself to a bas—"

"Be quiet!" Montague snarled, his hand still pressed against the giant's chest. "Speak one more word, Sir Heath, and, so help me God, I'll see that you never speak again." Then he turned to the tall man. "You *are* betrothed to my sister, are you not?" he said, a warning in his voice. "Speak now, or forever hold your peace."

The man raised his eyebrows and fixed his cold stare on Olivia. Then he raised his hands, as if in surrender, and stepped back.

Montague let out a low growl. "Now, for the sake of Sir Heath Moss, tell me, sir…are you engaged to my sister?"

Deny it, sir, please!

Olivia clasped her hands together, sending up a silent plea. He stared at her, his expression softening a fraction, and a flame of hope flickered in her heart.

Then it died. Slowly, the huge beast of a man—the silent stranger who had emerged from the darkness like a menacing phantom—nodded, and sealed her fate.

"FOR THE SAKE of Sir Heath Moss, tell me, sir, are you engaged to my sister?"

Whitcombe jabbed his finger at Charles, gritting his teeth as he uttered the question.

Fuck. I'm trapped.

Charles glanced about the terrace at his companions—his very *unwelcome* companions: the angry couple, the sneering rake, and the young woman whom he'd thought unremarkable at first but, perhaps, if the events of tonight were orchestrated, deserved some praise for her efforts, even if they were driven by greed.

But the expression in her eyes showed neither greed nor triumph—only horror.

Sir Heath let out a bark of laughter that grated on Charles's senses, so reminiscent it was of the braying taunts of the boys who'd tormented him at Eton. Sir Heath would have been just such a boy at school—attaching himself to the vilest creatures to inflate his sense of self-worth by preying on those he deemed weaker than he. Doubtless he'd been the kind of boy who took pleasure in tormenting kittens and pulling the wings off flies.

The urge to remove the smile from the man's face threatened to overcome Charles, swelling higher than the need to extract himself from the clutches of a grasping harpy.

If she were a harpy.

The young woman he'd been holding in his arms earlier stared at him, a plea in her that even the most dim-witted soul could understand.

Please, no…

Her distress was so potent he could almost taste it. But it would be nothing to the distress she suffered were the scandal reported in the papers.

Charles closed his eyes for a moment, and the image of his beautiful horse filled his mind—before being slaughtered at Whitcombe's hands. There was no doubt that the duke would carry out his threat. The man had a reputation for implacability. Perhaps, in another lifetime, the two of them might have been friends. In *this* lifetime, it was better to have such as man as a brother-in-law rather than an enemy.

Cursing his fate, Charles met Whitcombe's gaze and nodded, slowly.

The anger in Whitcombe's eyes morphed into relief. Charles glanced about the terrace, taking some consolation in Sir Heath's evident disappointment. That vile reprobate would have to find others to torment.

But the disappointment in Sir Heath's eyes was nothing in comparison to the cold fury in the duchess's vivid green gaze. She stared at Charles, her mouth set in a firm line. Then she blinked and turned her attention to the young woman—Charles's betrothed.

Shit. My betrothed.

But perhaps it was not all bad. He needed a wife, and tonight's events had, at least, saved him the bother of having to play the gallant suitor. Whitcombe was wealthy enough to give the girl a substantial dowry, and the threat of scandal might persuade him to increase it.

For the first time Charles permitted himself to indulge in a little optimism, which faded as he set eyes upon his fiancée.

The duchess pulled the girl close. "Hush, dearest, all will be well."

"B-but I don't like him."

The young woman glanced at Charles and flinched.

"You've no need to *like* him," the duke said. "Just marry him." Then he offered his hand to Charles. "Well?"

Charles held his hand out, and Whitcombe took it in a firm grip—a sign of domination, though Charles could have easily crushed the duke's hand if he wished.

"I shall await you in my study at nine o'clock tomorrow morning," Whitcombe said. "I trust you'll be on time."

Charles withdrew his hand and nodded.

"Very well. Now, take my sister's hand in honor of your pledge."

"Brother!" the young woman said. "*Must* I?"

Whitcombe stared at Sir Heath before fixing his gaze on the girl. "Yes, you must. And you know why."

Before he could stop himself, Charles found himself reaching for her, as if his body sought to have her in his arms once more.

"Olivia, take his hand," Whitcombe said, an edge to his voice.

Olivia…

So that was her name.

Lady Olivia Whitcombe. A respectable enough name for his intended. At least John would approve, and doubtless the valet would fall for her doe-eyed act of innocence.

But were her innocence only an act, would she be looking at him now with such fear in her eyes?

"Olivia…" Whitcombe repeated.

She flinched, and a spark of anger ignited in Charles's heart.

There was no need to be cruel toward the girl.

Fuck, I'm getting soft.

Her chest rose and fell in a deep breath, as if she summoned courage at the mouth of hell. Then she strode toward him, hand extended.

Charles darted toward her and grasped her arm, and she stumbled against him.

"I say!" Whitcombe cried. "I'll not have you manhandle my sister as if she has no worth."

Still holding her—*Olivia*—in his arms, Charles gestured toward the ground, and the broken glass that, had he not caught her, she would have stepped on.

Whitcombe glanced at the shards, the corner of his mouth curling into a smile.

"Perhaps you're not such a total blackguard after all."

Olivia glanced at the ground then met Charles's gaze. The fear in her eyes lessened, and he caught a flicker of gratitude.

"Come here now, Olivia," Whitcombe said. "I think you've had enough excitement for one evening. It's time we returned home."

She approached her brother, veering around the shards of glass.

"Sir, I'll expect you tomorrow morning on time," Whitcombe said. "Do not disappoint me. I trust you understand the consequences if you do."

Charles nodded and bowed, remaining on the terrace as the duke exited, arm in arm with his sister and the duchess. As they crossed the threshold, the young woman glanced over her shoulder at him, a flicker of gratitude in her eyes, before the trio slipped back inside the ballroom, leaving Charles alone with Sir Heath.

"Well, well," Sir Heath said. "I don't know whether to congratulate you or commiserate with you. I'd say you've been well and truly hooked. It remains to be seen whether you're also gutted. Stand me a brandy at White's and I'll appraise you of the young woman's history. Best to be forewarned if you're to marry the *natural daughter* of the late duke."

Devil's breeches! So *that* explained the girl's timidity, and Whitcombe's anger.

Sir Heath let out a chuckle. "Caught you properly, didn't she?"

Perhaps she had, but Charles didn't know who was worse—Whitcombe for foisting his bastard sister onto him, or Sir Heath, who took such pleasure in witnessing the misery of others.

Suppressing the urge to smash the grin from the fool's face, Charles strode past him in the wake of the Whitcombes, taking care to bump the other man's shoulder, knocking him off balance. Before he closed the door, he heard the very pleasurable sound of Sir Heath toppling to the ground, together with a volley of curses.

Good. Let Sir Heath fall on the broken glass. Charles had no desire to protect him, not like…

He froze.

Not like the young woman—Olivia. Natural child or not, she still elicited in him the urge to protect. When she'd been in danger of stepping on the broken glass, his instinct had compelled him to pull her to safety. And how good it had felt to have her in his arms!

He really *was* getting soft.

And that would not do. A man who was soft was no man at all. Women, especially wives, took advantage of softness in a man. And if he were to be forced into the marriage state, he had no intention of being taken advantage of—not even by a diminutive woman with a quiet voice and soulful eyes.

CHAPTER ELEVEN

THE CARRIAGE SET off with a jolt and Olivia jerked forward, almost losing her seat. Her brother caught her hand and pulled her back. She snatched it free and folded her arms.

"Olivia…" he began, but Eleanor raised her hand.

"You've said enough for one night, Montague," she said, an edge to her voice that Olivia hadn't heard before.

Eleanor was angry.

Rarely did Olivia's sister-in-law display emotion—at least not with her voice. When distressed, Eleanor grew quiet and withdrawn, toying with her bracelet in a repetitive circular motion until she was ready to speak. But tonight, the quiet demeanor had gone, replaced by angry determination.

Eleanor reached for a blanket and drew it around Olivia's shoulders.

"It's not cold," Montague said.

"Your sister's shivering," Eleanor said crisply. "You might be incapable of seeing her distress, but you must at least have noticed *that*."

"A blanket's no remedy for distress."

"But a loving brother *is*," Eleanor said. "For heaven's sake, Montague, can't you see what you've done?"

He leaned back, his eyes widening. In her entire life at Rosecombe, Olivia had never seen Eleanor speak with such anger toward her husband.

"What I've done?" he said, the tremor in his voice betraying his bewilderment at his wife's assertiveness. "*I've* done nothing wrong."

Eleanor drew her arm around Olivia's shoulders. "Neither has your sister," she retorted, "unless you wish to criticize her for the circumstances of her birth. In which case, I'd thought better of you."

"Of course I'm not," he replied, "but tonight's incident, though not Olivia's fault, will ruin her reputation. She has been humiliated by circumstances—"

"How *gracious* of you to admit it's not Olivia's fault," Eleanor huffed.

"As I said, she's been humiliated by circumstances," Montague continued. "But we've salvaged some respectability."

"Oh, we *have*, have we?"

"For heaven's sake, Eleanor, even you must admit that—"

"Will you stop!" Olivia cried, tearing the blanket from her shoulders. "I don't need a blanket, and I don't need your disapproval! Why can't you leave me alone?"

"Dearest, I'm only trying to defend you," Eleanor said.

"I know," Olivia said, "and I love you for it. But I'd rather forget it happened."

"I'm afraid it's too late for that," Montague said. "You heard Sir Heath. If no betrothal announcement is forthcoming, then what happened here tonight will be the subject of every tawdry gossip rag in London. We—*you*—will be the laughingstock of London. We might have weathered the scandal had you not been..." He hesitated and glanced toward the window.

"Had I not been a bastard?"

Her brother flinched.

"He's an honorable man," he said, after a pause. "He'll make you as happy as any other man—and, I suspect, happier than most."

"How can you say that?" Eleanor said, taking Olivia's hand. "He seemed most unpleasant."

"Why? Because he doesn't speak? He at least agreed to do the honorable thing by my sister. Had he cared nothing, he'd have walked off that terrace leaving Olivia's reputation ruined, and most likely flattened me on the way. You saw the size of him. Do you think a man like that wouldn't hesitate to beat anyone into a pulp to get what he wants?"

"And you expect me to marry him," Olivia said, "to be *owned* by him."

She shuddered, but despite the fear, a secret thrill coursed through her veins at the notion of surrendering herself to such a powerful beast of a man—the man who'd drawn her to him and held her tight as if she weighed no more than a feather. A man who, despite the enormity of his strength, held her with a tenderness that almost broke her heart.

What might it be like to feel those strong hands on her, bringing her to the pleasure that drove so many to ruination? Olivia had seen the spark of love between Montague and his wife. The gleam of female satisfaction in Eleanor's eyes most mornings at breakfast spoke of their love, and the pleasures they shared.

Montague took her hand. "Believe me, little Livvie, I wish we weren't in this predicament. But the world is what it is."

"I wanted to marry for love," Olivia whispered, tears stinging her eyes, and she bit her lip to keep them at bay lest her brother think her weak. "Wh-what if he won't love me?"

"Love will come," he said, his voice softening. "Love does not spring from our hearts overnight. It takes time, but it will come. Do you know why?"

Olivia shook her head.

"Because *you* have great capacity for love," he said. "You're a good soul—kind and loyal. Anyone who comes to know you won't be able to help falling in love with you. In time, you'll look back to tonight and smile at how Fate dealt you a hand more blessed than anything you might have wished for."

"Do you really believe that?" Olivia asked. He paused, doubt flickering in his eyes, and she wrenched her hand free. "Or are you merely trying to convince me?"

"You must understand that this is the least painful option."

"Least painful for whom?" Olivia said. "*You* don't have to marry a great big beast of a man who does not speak!"

"For heaven's sake, Olivia, I—"

"Montague, is there no other option?" Eleanor asked.

"Such as what?" he said. "To return to Rosecombe the subject of gossip, to be censured and ostracized from Society for the rest of her days?"

"We care nothing for reputation," Eleanor says. "Surely that ought to be enough?"

"I thought we'd already discussed this at length," he said. "It matters not what we think. Society will forever condemn Olivia for her birth. Her chances of securing a respectable match were slim at best. After tonight, they're nonexistent unless she accepts this man. Assuming he bothers to attend me tomorrow."

Olivia suppressed a cry.

"Montague, how dare—" Eleanor began, but he interrupted.

"I dare because one of us must face up to the truth. I like it no more than you, my love, but now's not the time for emotion or regret. Now is the time for rational action to ensure that Olivia has the best possible chance of happiness." He reached for Olivia's hand, a plea in his eyes. "Believe me, sister, I wish it were not so."

She tried to free her hand, but he tightened his grip.

"I will do what I can to ensure you're treated properly."

She shook her head. "Why did you have to do it?"

"Make him offer for you? Surely you understand—"

"No," she said, her voice rising. "Why did you have to recognize me as your sister? I was happy before. My life was simple. I rose early, went to the school, taught the children, then came home, with no fear for my reputation, or the need to make a respectable match. Why didn't you leave me there in obscurity? Isn't that what most lords do with the bastards in their families?"

"With this match you can live as you please," he said. "You'll have a title, wealth, respectability. You'll have your own children to care for—servants, tenants, all to benefit from the love you have to give."

"And what if he doesn't permit me to live as I please?" she said.

"I'll make sure you're given every freedom in your marriage."

She shook her head. "You cannot guarantee that—not when I become the property of another man."

He squeezed her hand. "I can, and I will. I can stipulate it in the marriage contract. Tell me what you want, and I'll ensure that it becomes not just your wish, but a legal obligation."

"You'd do that for me?"

"For my beloved sister, yes." He blinked, and a tear splashed onto his cheek. "Tonight, I failed you. What happened on the terrace was my fault for not protecting you as a brother ought. For that, I am deeply sorry."

His voice wavered, and the tears stinging her eyes threatened to spill over. This man—this stern, strong man who elicited silence and respect the moment he stepped into a room, for whom loyal servants and tenants would do anything and from whom those who transgressed against him cowered in fear—she had never seen such emotion.

"I know I've been firm with you," he said, "but it's because I want to protect you from a world that is cruel. Perhaps I ought to have left you in the village, handed you a coin or two as an act of charity, as all men of my rank are expected to do. But I couldn't. You're my sister, Olivia, my flesh and blood, and I-I wanted to give you everything that would have been your due had you been Lady Olivia Whitcombe. And the title you will gain on marrying this man will ensure that nobody in Society will ever again treat you are being of no worth."

Eleanor placed a hand on his arm. "Montague…"

"Forgive me," he said. "Please say you forgive me. If you really don't wish to marry this man, then I'll think of something. I'll not force you to enter into something unwillingly. I only want to present the options before you so that you can make an informed choice."

"I…" Olivia paused, ready to plead her freedom. The path of her life stretched before her, forking into two. In one direction lay scandal, ruination, and misery—not only for her, but for those dearest to her. In the other lay uncertainty.

Perhaps every gamester found themselves faced with such a choice—certain ruination, or the chance of victory at the turn of a card.

At length, she made her choice. Surely the chance of happiness, however slight, was preferable to certain misery?

"Very well," she said. "I'll do as you ask."

"Are you sure?" Eleanor took her hand, and Olivia's resolve almost cracked at the tenderness in her sister-in-law's voice.

"Yes," she said, "but I have one final question."

"Which is?"

"What is his name?" she said. "I-I don't even know his name."

"His name is Charles Henry Stephen Devereaux," her brother said. "Fifth Earl Devereaux. You're going to be a countess."

At his words, Olivia's resolve did crumble. The tears unlocked and rolled down her cheeks in silence.

Chapter Twelve

THE CARRIAGE DIPPED sideways under Charles's weight as he stepped out onto the pavement. His valet followed, and together they stared at the building before them. It towered overhead, as imposing as the buildings at Penham Park. But where Penham was shrouded in darkness, Whitcombe's townhouse gleamed in the morning light, its façade almost bone-white.

To the side a small staircase led downward, presumably to the servants' entrance. A wider set of steps swept up from the pavement toward the main entrance—twin doors embellished with shining brass handles fashioned into the shape of lions' heads. The doors were flanked by white pillars, either side of which were enormous, bowed windows, fashioned from multiple panes that reflected the sunlight at different angles. Two stories stretched above the first, and though the topmost was likely inferior due to being the servants' quarters, the view from there must be particularly impressive, given the building's proximity to Hyde Park.

In short, the entire structure reeked of wealth and status far above Charles's own.

"Impressive," John said. "Can the same be said for your intended?"

Charles kept his hands still, despite the inquiring look on the valet's face.

"I suppose," John continued, "one wouldn't expect Whitcombe to lodge in a small suite of rooms in Cheapside." Charles frowned, and the valet gave a grin. "Have I said anything that's not the truth?"

I see little point in wasting funds on a house in Mayfair. Not when I've debts to pay. Perhaps, to reduce the capital outstanding, I should consider selling you.

The valet's grin only broadened. "You'd not get ten shillings for me, sir. As you've told me many times, few men of your rank would care to pay an income for a slovenly servant who cannot hold his tongue."

Perhaps some merchant with little knowledge of propriety might take you. Or I could sell your body for parts to the hospital.

"Ha! There's grave robbers enough for that. Far better for the surgeons to procure a corpse than end a man's life. Though, granted, they'd get a good half a crown for my cock."

"Ahem."

Charles glanced up at the sound of someone clearing their throat to see a black-clad butler filling the doorway, his expression resembling that of a judgmental schoolmaster.

"I take it you're Earl Devereaux, here to see His Grace, the Duke of Whitcombe?"

The butler eyed John, then arched a dark brow.

"The entrance for your man is *there*, Lord Devereaux," he said, gesturing toward the steps at the side.

Charles climbed the front steps, his bulkier frame towering over the older man's. The butler's throat bobbed as he swallowed, a flicker of fear not quite completely concealed behind his impassive expression.

"M-my master expects propriety," the butler said.

Ha! If that were the case, the man wouldn't have tried to pass off his father's bastard as a lady or let her run wild and compromise herself.

"My master insists I accompany him everywhere," John said.

"But..." the butler began, and his voice trailed away as

Charles raised his hand. His eyes widened, a shimmer of apprehension in them, as if he expected Charles to circle his fingers around his throat.

"You're at liberty to refuse us entry, of course," John said, "but if we're not both permitted to pass through this door, then neither of us will. You must therefore convey my master's regret that he's unable to see your master this morning—or at all. I trust your master will not be overly disappointed."

The butler cast an inquiring look in Charles's direction, but Charles remained still, displaying no reaction, despite the anger simmering within. In his experience, an adversary responded more favorably to an absence of emotion. Silence often elicited more than words.

Which was just as well.

At length, the butler sighed, then stepped back.

"Very well," he said, "though it's most improper. Come inside. Quickly."

Charles allowed himself a little smile at the notion of the butler wishing to usher his valet inside before anyone noticed such an outrageous act of impropriety in permitting a servant to use the front door. John returned the smile, and the two of them followed the black-clad figure through the hallway to a solid wooden door.

"Come," a deep voice said as the butler knocked. He opened the door and Charles entered as the clock struck nine.

The study was as Charles would have expected—fashioned in deep, masculine colors to portray male dominance, every wall layered with books, forming a neat pattern, the gold embossing lined up as if someone had taken great care to place each book in exactly the right position. At the far end of the room, across a thick Aubusson rug, was a squat mahogany desk, its occupant silhouetted by the window behind him, his face in shadow.

Charles would have recognized Whitcombe even had he been concealed behind a screen. The very atmosphere in the room reeked of ducal dominance and the woody, spicy scent that had clung to the man last night when he'd threatened to put a bullet in Charles's heart.

And my horse...

"Sir," John said softly, and Charles grew aware of a sharp pain in his palm where he'd fisted his hands, digging the fingernails into the flesh.

"I see you've brought your valet," Whitcombe said, rising. But his voice betrayed no surprise. In fact, two chairs had been placed before the desk.

He gestured toward the seats, then reached for a decanter filled with a dark amber liquid, poured two glasses, and pushed them toward the edge of the desk.

"And you're on time," he added, "albeit only just."

John moved his hands. *Is he always this uncivil, sir?*

Charles responded, *Only when his sister has tossed up her skirts.*

Whitcombe leaned forward, and Charles found himself at the mercy of an unforgiving dark gaze from eyes that, save the expression of barely concealed anger, were almost identical to another pair of eyes that had penetrated his dreams last night.

Might he glimpse them again today? She must be somewhere within the walls of this house. Whitcombe was unlikely to let her wander about London until this damned marriage contract had been signed. Perhaps he'd parade her before Charles once their business had concluded.

Charles's gaze shifted to the papers on Whitcombe's desk.

"Would you care to share what you were discussing with your man, Devereaux?" Whitcombe said.

"My master was remarking on the elegance of your study," John replied.

Whitcombe let out a huff, then picked up a piece of paper. "I've drafted the details of the contract."

Already?

Charles leaned forward, and Whitcombe curled his mouth into a grim smile. "I see no need for delay, do you?"

Charles shook his head.

"Good," Whitcombe said. "My lawyer is due in one hour and I'll have him notarize the particulars. Now, perhaps…"

Charles raised his hand and Whitcombe paused, tilting his head to one side in that judgmental manner he'd displayed last night.

"Yes?" he said, his tone sharp.

Charles gestured toward the papers. *May I at least be permitted to read them, given that I'm the one losing my liberty?*

Whitcombe frowned. "I presume your master wishes to discuss the terms?"

"Ahem, yes," John said.

"Very well. I'm not an unreasonable man, but I should warn you that most of the terms stipulated are non-negotiable."

Why invite me here at all if my fate is already sealed?

Whitcombe glanced at Charles's hands, then let out a huff and handed the paper over. Charles read the first paragraph and inhaled sharply.

The dowry was thirty thousand.

Whitcombe's lips curled into a cold smile.

"Yes, I thought you'd lose some of your scruples on discovering how much you're selling yourself for. But you should read to the bottom before you claim total victory."

Charles lowered his gaze to the page once more, then paused. *You sly bastard.*

Whitcombe's smile broadened.

"Drink your brandy, Devereaux."

Charles handed the paper to John, then picked up his glass.

John let out a low curse. "I'll be damned."

"I rather think it's my sister who stands on the brink of damnation," Whitcombe said. "Which is why I've sought to protect her as much as I can."

Charles sipped his brandy, and the liquor burst with flavor on his tongue. The man may drive a hard bargain, but at least he was discerning enough to know a good brandy from one that rotted a man's insides.

Whitcombe leaned back and folded his arms. "You cannot accuse me of being ungenerous," he said. "I'll even throw in a case of that brandy as a wedding gift." He picked up his own glass and took a sip. "Thirty thousand is a substantial fortune. But, as you see, one-third of it will be invested in an annuity in my sister's name. She may draw an income or capitalize it as she sees fit, and in the event of her death, it shall be split equally between you and her children."

Her children?

Devil's breeches, was the girl with child? Surely Whitcombe would have forced the culprit down the aisle at the point of a pistol. No respectable duke would expect Charles to become father to another man's brat. It was a cruel twist of the law that ensured that if a man had a natural child, he could not recognize it as his heir. But if his wife bore another man's child…

He shuddered at the memory—his father bellowing in anger, Mother's pleas, and the sickening crack followed by the sight of her pale-brown eyes staring at him while he watched the spark of life flicker and die…

"Devereaux?" Whitcombe's voice snapped him back to the present. "Are you finding this interview tedious?"

Swallowing a mouthful of brandy to cleanse himself of the memory, Charles shook his head.

"Then I'll continue," Whitcombe said, an edge to his voice. "The remaining twenty thousand will become yours—ten on the date of your marriage and the final ten to be granted to you as and when I deem it appropriate, provided certain conditions are met."

Isn't marrying her enough of a condition to impose on me?

John eyed Charles's hands. "My master wishes to know what conditions must be satisfied in order to release the final ten thousand."

"I have two," Whitcombe said. "The first is that no derogatory comments with respect to my sister's status must pass your lips, or"—he glanced at Charles's hands—"be communicated in any other fashion.

Her status? So, she *had* been ruined by another.

"And the second?" John said.

"That you consummate the marriage as soon as possible. Preferably the wedding night."

The brandy caught in Charles's throat and he shuddered with convulsions. He let out a cough and spluttered droplets over the desk.

Whitcombe shook his head. "Not how I expect my best brandy to be savored."

Charles set his glass smartly on the desk, and Whitcombe's eyebrow twitched.

"I take it that condition is satisfactory," he said. "After all, it's what's expected of a husband. I merely wish to formalize that expectation."

For what purpose?

Whitcombe glanced at Charles's hands.

"I presume you question my motives," he said. "It seems a small condition to make, given that you stand to benefit financially from it."

He sipped his brandy and set the glass aside.

"It's quite simple. I want there to be no possibility of an annulment. I'm no fool, Devereaux, and neither are you. We live in a world ruled by men where a man can behave how he likes because his title and sex protect him from censure. A woman, however, is not given such luxury. Her actions, whether through her fault or the fault of others, are scrutinized, ridiculed, and used to ruin her if Society deems her unworthy." He placed his elbows on the desk and clasped his hands together. "All of which means that my sister has considerably more to lose, if this marriage fails, than you."

Charles met the man's gaze and caught a flicker of desperation behind the hard ducal stare.

Whitcombe was to be commended for wishing to protect the girl, but the vehemence with which he strove to shield her only served to confirm her guilt.

Nevertheless, ten thousand to be deposited in Charles's account, with the prospect of another ten after rutting her, was not to be sniffed at.

Charles glanced at his valet, whose lips were curled into a smirk. John was thinking the same.

You're a beast.

His conscience whispered in his ear, needling him with the image of the girl's eyes, filled with fear. But, unlike other wives, she'd not have to suffer his attentions when they settled at Penham. He'd rut her and do his duty, then leave her alone to enjoy her jewels and gowns—or whatever young women indulged in when they had an annuity of their own.

"I take it the terms are acceptable?" Whitcombe said, lifting a quill pen from the desk and dipping it in an inkpot.

Charles nodded, took the pen, and scratched his name on the bottom.

"Good. I'll have my solicitor make the arrangements. I've already spoken to the bishop."

What bishop? Charles raised his eyebrows.

Whitcombe let out a huff. "You're to be married in the chapel at Rosecombe as soon as possible. I've taken the liberty of securing a special license. While Sir Heath Moss has assured me of his silence, I've no wish to risk scandal breaking before my sister's safely married. Nor do I wish to keep her confined in this house longer than necessary. I trust you understand."

Charles signed, *Your wish to protect her is your only redeeming feature. Perhaps you're not a total bastard after all, in which case I'll refrain from breaking every one of your fingers.*

John's eyes widened as he watched Charles's hands.

Whitcombe's mouth set in a firm line and his expression hardened. "Please tell me what your master said. I suspect it was not at all pleasant."

Go on, John. Word for word.

The valet colored, then spoke. "My master has said he appreciates your wish to keep your sister behind closed doors, given her birth and the events of last night. He does not want her to disgrace herself and him any more than she has already."

Charles glared at the valet. *Fuck you, John.*

"How dare…" Whitcombe began, but Charles raised his hand, then grasped the pen and scratched out a few words at the bottom of the contract.

That is not what I said. My man is protecting my interests.

"As I'm protecting my sister's," Whitcombe said, rising. "Believe me, Devereaux, I like this no more than you. But remember, if you want your full twenty thousand, you must refrain from such insults."

Charles nodded, then offered his hand.

Whitcombe took it, then withdrew as if Charles's skin burned him.

"You may go," he said, "unless you wish for an audience with my sister?"

Charles shook his head.

"I thought not. Very well—I'll send you a message once the date of the wedding is set. Expect to hear from me later today."

With a flick of the wrist, Whitcombe gestured toward the door. Feeling like an errant schoolboy who'd just been administered a particularly odious punishment by his schoolmaster, Charles rose. He bowed, exited the study, and collided with someone on the way out.

"Oh!"

Charles reached out and curled his arms around a soft, warm body. The air filled with the scent of rose and he inhaled, relishing its sweetness, the scent that had seeped into his dreams last night, causing him to wake with a cockstand fit to burst. His breeches grew tight as his manhood twitched at the memory—the cock he'd fisted to completion before rising that morning.

For a moment, he closed his eyes, relishing the memory of the release. Then the cry came again and he opened them, blinking back the fog of animal lust.

He found himself looking into the eyes of his betrothed, but rather than a lust to mirror his own, he saw nothing but despair.

95

CHAPTER THIRTEEN

"**H**E'S HERE!" OLIVIA said, entering her sister-in-law's parlor, her heart fluttering. "They're in Montague's study and have been talking for a quarter of an hour."

Eleanor looked up from her easel. "Olivia dear, you'll never hear anything to your benefit if you eavesdrop."

"But they're discussing me," Olivia said. "Don't I have the right to hear what they're saying?"

"Men speak very differently to each other when not in the presence of women," Eleanor said. She gave a grin. "Just as we talk very differently when there are no men present. Of course, our reason for doing so is that men lack the intellectual capacity to understand what we're saying. And you wouldn't want to hear what they're saying today, dearest."

"Why not?"

"Because they're discussing the marriage contract." Eleanor swept her brush across her painting, then dipped it into a jar. "To us, marriage is a union of souls, a mark of the love that two people share. To have such a union set out on paper, much as the sale of goods is itemized, is not something a woman wishes to hear, particularly when she's the commodity being discussed. I'd rather see you spared the humiliation of such a discussion."

"There's no love in the marriage I'm about to enter into," Olivia said. "He doesn't even like me."

"He likes you enough to come here today," Eleanor said.

"And he liked you well enough last night. My opinion of him improved when he pulled you away from that broken glass."

"Do you think so?" Olivia asked, giving free rein to the hope that had been simmering inside her from the moment she'd woken that morning.

Last night, he'd entered her dreams and taken her into his arms—arms strong enough to crush the life out of a thousand men but which held her tenderly as if she were as fragile as a blackbird's egg. She had drifted into sleep, filled with sensations of pleasure, of soft, whispered words of love while she soared into ecstasy.

Just imagine! She would soon understand what men and women indulged in—the pleasure that made Eleanor so blissfully happy each morning, such that her eyes sparkled with delight over breakfast.

Olivia approached a mirror on the wall and turned her head to one side, patting the ribbons that adorned her hair. Might he like how Eleanor's maid had fashioned it? Or perhaps her gown, which she'd trimmed with a deep-brown sash to match the color of his eyes?

"Come away from the mirror, dearest. You look very pretty, as you always do," Eleanor said. "He cannot fail to admire you, but if you continue to pull at your ribbons, your hair will come loose. Harriet made it up so carefully."

"What if he doesn't stay for tea?" Olivia said. "Montague might forget to invite him, and I don't want the next time I see him to be at the altar. I want to get to know him a little, to…to lessen the…"

To lessen the fear.

Eleanor had always said that fear arose out of ignorance, that the more she knew about a subject, or a person, the less capacity they had to induce fear.

She set her brush aside and rose. Then she took Olivia's hand and kissed it.

"Have no fear, dearest," she said. "*I'll* issue the invitation."

"Montague forbade me at breakfast to disturb him when Lord"—Olivia hesitated, fighting the apprehension at voicing the name of the man to whom she'd soon belong—"when L-lord Devereux was here," she continued, her cheeks warming.

"He didn't forbid *me*," Eleanor said. "It would be improper to not issue an invitation to tea to your betrothed, would it not? And you know how I insist on adhering to propriety." Her eyes sparkled with mischief.

"Did you not once say 'propriety be damned' in front of the dowager duchess?" Olivia said.

"I think what I said was 'propriety can go and wallow in a pile of horseshit.'"

Olivia couldn't help a smile, and Eleanor drew her close.

"*There's* my Olivia!" she said. "It's good to see you smile again. You have such a kind and merry disposition that Devereaux cannot fail to love you. If he doesn't, I'll personally throw him into a pile of horseshit."

Olivia couldn't contain her laughter at the notion of the duchess picking up such a giant of a man and tossing him about. Eleanor kissed her forehead, then the two women exited the parlor.

As they approached the study, they heard muffled voices. Eleanor lowered her voice to a whisper.

"Go to the morning room."

Olivia nodded, optimism rising in her heart, then a voice filtered through the study door.

"My master has said he appreciates your wish to keep your sister behind closed doors, given her birth and the events of last night. He does not want her to disgrace herself and him any more than she has already."

Olivia drew in a sharp breath, her stomach twisting with horror.

"Come away, dearest," Eleanor whispered. "No good can arise from..."

Tears stung Olivia's eyes as the voices continued.

He thought her a disgrace, to be hidden away lest she taint his good name.

Then she heard her brother's voice.

"You may go, unless you wish for an audience with my sister?"

She paused, grasping a weak flicker of hope—which died at her brother's next words.

"I thought not."

The study door burst open, and the huge man strode out, slamming into her. She caught her breath and cried out, but before she could dart free, two muscular arms wrapped around her—the same arms that had embraced her last night…

…and, to her shame, the same arms she'd dreamed of in her bedchamber while she imagined them holding her, cherishing her.

But it had been just that—a dream. He was no suitor, nor a lover. He was merely a beast who wanted nothing to do with her.

She let out a cry, and the beast's nostrils flared, the anger in his eyes intensifying. Then she caught a flicker of desire in them before he released her.

"F-forgive me, sir," she stammered, and approached the stairs, driven by shame and the need to be in her chamber—anywhere but next to the man who so clearly despised her.

"Olivia."

She froze at her brother's voice.

He emerged from the study, together with a smartly dressed young man. While Montague's expression radiated anger, the young man's eyes showed nothing but guilt, which turned into frank admiration as he cast his gaze over her.

"Where are your manners, sister?" Montague said. "We observe propriety in this house, even if others do not. You must invite your betrothed to take tea."

My betrothed…

"B-but I heard you say…" Olivia said. Shame engulfed her and her eyes misted with tears.

"We were on our way to invite Lord Devereaux to tea, my love," Eleanor said, taking Olivia's hand. "We know how forgetful you can be at times in issuing such invitations."

She turned to the beast. "Lord Devereaux, will you take tea?" She nodded toward his companion. "Your man is invited also, of course. We have some excellent shortbread, do we not, Olivia?"

Olivia cringed as the beast's dark eyes turned to her once more.

"Y-yes, I baked them myself, with a little vanilla to make them—"

"Olivia," her brother warned. "Of course, we keep a cook here, Devereaux. The kitchen is no place for my sister."

She cursed herself. How many times had Montague told her that she was no longer to engage in activities best left to the staff? What must the beast think of her?

His exchanged a glance with his companion.

"My master is of the opinion that an understanding of how a household is run is a quality required of a wife," the other man said. "That understanding will naturally include the practical application of household duties."

The beast frowned, then gestured with his hands. Olivia watched as they moved in a fluid motion, as if engaging in a dance.

The young man let out a sharp sigh. "My master wishes to convey his regrets that he's otherwise engaged this morning. However, he has a gift for Miss Whitcombe."

Olivia cringed.

Miss Whitcombe. Not Lady Olivia. So, he knew she was a bastard. They both did.

And yet he'd still agreed to marry her.

The beast thrust his hands into his jacket pocket then pulled out a small box. He hesitated, meeting Olivia's gaze, then offered it to Montague.

"I think, Devereaux, any young woman receiving a gift from her betrothed would rather he gave it to her than to her brother,"

Montague said. "You're marrying my sister, not me."

"N-no, brother," Olivia stammered. "If he doesn't want to…"

"Sir?"

The beast glanced at his companion, then stiffly offered the box to Olivia.

She took it, and as their fingers touched, her skin tightened at the spark of need. He drew in a sharp breath, the first sound he'd made, and she glanced up and met his gaze. Then he withdrew and gestured toward the box.

She opened it and let out a low cry. Inside, nestled on a bed of black velvet, was a ring bearing the largest ruby she'd ever seen.

"I-I couldn't possibly…" she began, then hesitated as Lord Devereaux raised his hand.

"What do you say, sister?" her brother said.

"Montague!" Eleanor said. "Leave her be."

Her cheeks warming, Olivia plucked the ring from the box and flicked her gaze to her betrothed. He nodded, and she slipped it on the third finger of her left hand, where it met resistance at the knuckle before finally settling at the base of her finger as if it belonged there.

But it didn't. It was a ring for a countess, whereas she was only…

She caught sight of Lord Devereaux moving his hands again.

"My master wishes to know if you like it," the young man said.

"Y-yes, though it's too grand for me. I don't know if I should…"

"It was the late countess's ring, and as you're soon to be the countess, it's yours by right."

Olivia lifted her gaze to her betrothed. "It was your mother's?"

He narrowed his eyes, and she caught a flicker of pain in their dark depths.

She turned the ring on her finger and ran her fingertip over the stone. As she moved her hand it seemed to pulse with life, the facets reflecting the light in differing shades of red, from light pink to deep crimson, as if the stone were alive.

"Thank you," she whispered, meeting his gaze, striving to conquer the need to look away and hide from his scrutiny. "I-I'll do my best to deserve it."

His frown deepening, he gestured with his hands.

Olivia swallowed a knot of shame. He had every right to object to her owning such a precious heirloom. Perhaps he considered her so unworthy that there was nothing she could ever do to deserve the ring—or deserve him.

"Lord Devereaux, are you quite certain that you cannot take tea with us?" Eleanor said. "It seems a pity, given that the next time we meet will be your wedding. Don't you wish to spend time with Olivia?"

"I'm afraid my master has an appointment scheduled with his banker," his companion said. "Perhaps another time."

An appointment with his banker. Presumably he was eager to secure the dowry.

More eager to do that than spend time with me, Olivia thought.

The beast moved his hands again—hands that were large and strong enough to tear a wild animal to pieces, and yet the motion had a fluidity and grace that rendered them more elegant than the perfectly manicured hands of any fine lady.

"My master wishes to convey his sincerest regrets," the companion said, "and his assurances that he'll present himself, as required, at the wedding."

So formal an address, delivered as if Lord Devereaux were promising to present himself before a magistrate, or an executioner, to suffer his penance.

"Th-thank you, sir," Olivia said. "I'm sorry for…"

The beast raised his hand and shook his head. He moved toward Olivia, and she caught the earthy, primal scent of him. She tilted her head back to meet his gaze as he towered over her, and a warmth shimmered in the air as their bodies almost touched. He reached toward her, and she caught sight of the signet ring on his right hand, a thick gold band set with a ruby to match the one now adorning her own finger. She held her breath in anticipation of his touch that had sent a pulse of longing through her before.

Then he let out a sigh and withdrew his hand, running a fingertip over the surface of the ruby.

Olivia shivered as if his rejection cast a frost in the air.

He bowed, stiffly, and his companion followed suit. Then they strode toward the main doors, accompanied by Montague. After a brief exchange, they stepped out onto the street and she flinched as the door slammed shut behind them.

Unable to stem the tears, Olivia let them slip down her cheeks while her brother pulled her into an embrace.

"Have no fear, Livvie," he said. "He's not like other men, but that may be to his advantage. And he signed the contract, so you're protected by the law, at least."

"I don't want to have to be protected, Montague," she said, "at least not from him."

"It's just a precaution," he replied. "For all his outward appearance of uncongeniality, he's an honorable man who will treat you better than most."

"Hardly the best recommendation," Eleanor said, a sharp edge to her voice. "Montague, perhaps you should refrain from—"

"H-he didn't even want to spend time with me!" Olivia said.

"Gentlemen are notorious about wanting to keep their appointments."

"But not about spending time with the women they're supposed to—"

Olivia broke off.

Supposed to what? Love? Lord Devereaux didn't even like her, let alone love her.

In fact, he couldn't even tolerate her company.

Her brother let out a sigh, his warm breath fanning her cheek. "You'll have the rest of your lives to spend in each other's company."

The rest of her life…

With a man who didn't want her—who couldn't bear to be in the same room as her.

Olivia clung to her brother. Montague had a reputation for sternness that was well deserved, but he loved her. And now, she was about to remove herself from his protection and place herself into the hands of a man capable of snapping her in two if she displeased him.

Chapter Fourteen

BLAND ORGAN MUSIC threaded through the air as the chapel began to fill with guests.

Or, at least, one side of the chapel.

Apart from Charles's valet, the groom's side remained empty. Embarrassingly so—or it would have been if Charles cared about such things.

On the bride's side were all manner of folk, from the highest to the lowest, weaving among the pews before taking their seats. A handful of genteel creatures took the frontmost pews—Duchess Whitcombe accompanied an elderly matriarch, engulfed in a riot of black lace, whose cane tap-tapped across the flagstones on the aisle, pausing momentarily as she stepped onto a stone carved with a series of letters—a eulogy to one of the late dukes, perhaps? The second pew was occupied by a smattering of gentility that Charles recognized from London—the duchess's sister Lady Staines and her husband, together with a lone young woman with soft chestnut curls and wide hazel eyes in her pale, sickly complexion. The remainder of the guests were of a different class altogether—men, women, and children bedecked in their shabby Sunday best.

Since when did a duke invite servants and tenants to his sister's wedding? Of course, the girl was a natural child who perhaps had been brought up among these people, but any young women in her position, about to become a countess, would surely want to shun such connections.

Charles glanced at John, who grinned and gestured with his hands.

Anyone would think we're attending a funeral.

A volley of whispers broke out, followed by silence. Then a louder whisper came from the back of the church, a soft voice filled with fear accompanied by a deeper one, and the skin on the back of Charles's neck tightened.

The bride had arrived.

The vicar nodded to John, who rose to stand beside Charles. The moment of surrender had come.

Then a fanfare began as the organist gave vent to his joy—the kind of joy that made a rational man want to expel his breakfast—and the congregation stood in unison.

Firm, steady footsteps drew near, accompanied by a lighter, more hesitant tread. Unable to stop himself, Charles stole a glance over his shoulder.

Whitcombe bore his usual dominant, determined attitude, his expression as dark as his suit. The only light on his form was the reflection of the sunlight off his jacket buttons and the decorative stitching around the cuffs.

The young woman on his arm carried a simple posy of wildflowers and grasses, perhaps gleaned from a nearby hedgerow. She wore a plain white gown trimmed with the minimum amount of lace and a pale-green sash. Hardly the attire of a duke's sister, but thrift in a wife was preferable to extravagance. Perhaps she'd manage Charles's household with equal economy.

Assuming she knew how to manage a household. A village girl would know nothing of such things, and, by her own admission, she was more comfortable baking biscuits in the kitchen than directing a body of staff.

But she was not without wits. The spark of intelligence in her eyes when he'd taken her in his arms the night of the ball had told him that. And, of course, she was intelligent enough to fear him.

That fear shimmered in the air around her now, as she took

each faltering step toward the altar. She wore no veil—evidence, if needed, of her lack of chasteness. Her hair was fashioned into a simple style, but wisps were already breaking free, forming a halo around her head, illuminated in the sunlight.

He might have mistaken her for an angel, graceful and divine in her serenity. But, with her mouth downturned, face flushed, eyes bright with moisture, and quivering lips, she looked as miserable a creature as Charles had ever seen.

Imagine what Father would have made of her! With his elevated opinion of himself and the Devereaux name that had driven Charles's mother to despair, Father would have suffered a fit of apoplexy had Charles brought home a by-blow as a bride—but then, according to his father, Charles had always been "the very worst son a man could have."

He lifted his eyes to the ceiling and sent up a prayer.

I hope you're satisfied now, you old bastard.

At that moment, the bride, who had been studying the floor, lifted her gaze to his. She tensed, like a mouse before a predator, and her eyes widened. She glanced at her brother, but he continued along the aisle, and she almost tripped in an effort to keep up. Whitcombe glanced at her, frowning, and she tightened her grip on his sleeve until they reached the altar, where Whitcombe released her and stepped aside.

The vicar cleared his throat, opened the book in his hands, and began to speak.

Charles stole a glimpse at his bride. She stared straight ahead, clinging to the grasses, their fronds moving slightly as she trembled.

Devil's breeches, he might as well have been standing before a gibbet awaiting execution.

Charles exhaled sharply and his bride stiffened and turned her gaze to him, before resuming her attention on the vicar.

Fuck.

He couldn't let the poor girl suffer a lifetime with him. She was the least objectionable woman he'd encountered. By virtue of that, she deserved to be free.

The vicar droned on, his voice carrying an undertone of superciliousness and lacking any variation. It was a wonder the congregation remained awake, though Charles was sure he could discern a snore or two from the front pew.

He gestured to John, who shuffled closer. Ignoring the vicar's raised eyebrow, he motioned with his hands.

For the love of the Almighty, tell the girl she's at liberty to call a stop to the wedding.

John stared at Charles's hands. His mouth formed a firm line, and he shook his head.

Tell her, Charles repeated.

John raised his hands. *You tell her.*

Damn you! You know I cannot. Tell her or I'll have you dismissed.

John met his gaze, resolve in his eyes. *Dismiss me and be damned. I won't see her publicly humiliated.*

You think humiliation today is worse than a lifetime with me?

"Ahem."

Whitcombe cleared his throat. John let out a snort and gestured again. *Your future brother-in-law likes you not.*

Charles frowned at his valet, but John continued.

Will she be delivered of a child within eight months of the wedding, or sooner?

Charles smacked his fist into his palm then made a crude gesture.

Fuck you, John.

"Devereaux!"

Whitcombe's voice, clear and cold, cut through the air.

Charles glanced up to see the vicar staring at him.

"Proceed," Whitcombe said.

"Therefore, I ask all of you here," the vicar said, "that if any of you know of any lawful impediment to the union of this man and this woman, you should declare it now."

Silence fell, punctuated by a baby's crying, which was quickly shushed.

Whitcombe touched the bride's elbow in a gesture of unexpected tenderness and raised his eyebrows. The anger in his eyes morphed into love—the love of an adoring brother who wished his sister to be happy. It was the love that families shared—a love that Charles had never experienced, nor had he believed existed until this very moment.

Whitcombe, despite his insistence on propriety, was offering his sister, at the brink of placing the noose around her neck, release from her obligation. He leaned toward her and whispered in her ear, his voice inaudible, but the movement of his lips conveyed the words.

Speak now and you can be released, Olivia. I love you no matter what. Do you wish to proceed?

The vicar opened his mouth to resume and Whitcombe raised his hand.

"A moment, reverend."

The bride glanced at Charles, moisture gleaming in her eyes. Then she resumed her attention on her brother. Charles caught his breath, his rational mind willing her to release herself, despite the whisperings of his heart, and the yearning in his body that had tightened his breeches the moment he caught her soft scent.

Then, slowly, she nodded.

The vicar continued, and John proclaimed the vows at Charles's direction, followed by the bride, who spoke in her clear voice, flinching as she pledged her vow of obedience. At length, the vicar closed his Bible shut with a snap and declared them man and wife.

Charles took her hand and caught his breath as his cock surged forward like a rampant stallion eager for the mare. She lifted her gaze to his, and his ardor cooled at the intensity of the fear in her eyes. But the need to take her as his, to declare his ownership by claiming her mouth, was too strong, and he lowered his head as she tilted hers back, parting her lips in anticipation.

What the fuck am I doing?

The fear in her eyes was so sharp, so potent, that he could not, in good conscience, make such a brutal declaration of ownership in front of the people she knew and loved. If she had given herself to another already then perhaps she wished it were him, instead of Charles, who claimed her today.

Like any beast, Charles was ready to surrender to the primal need to obliterate all trace of him who had gone before, as savagely as any rutting stag. But he could not be assured that he'd be able to restrain himself. Though she now belonged to him, body and soul, in the eyes of the law and of the church, he doubted that Whitcombe would stand by and do nothing while Charles rutted his bride in the middle of the chapel.

Conquering the yearning in his body, he withdrew his hand. There would be plenty of time to take her as he pleased, to satisfy the beast growling in his soul, as soon as they were alone.

CHAPTER FIFTEEN

"Y OU MAY KISS the bride."

Olivia faced the groom.

My husband.

Montague stood behind her, the warmth from his body providing much-needed comfort. Even at the brink her brother had offered her a means of escape. But a wicked little corner of her soul had whispered of the prospect of pleasure when she saw the dark hunger in the eyes of the man to whom she now belonged.

Swallowing her fear, she tipped her face up, offering her lips for a kiss.

The moment had come. Eleanor said that the bridal kiss was the tenderest gesture a husband could make. It was the first gesture of affection after a bride uttered her vows before the Almighty, and the groom's duty was therefore to show her, by means of a kiss, that she'd made a wise choice.

It would be the moment when all her fears dissolved, when the spark of tenderness she'd seen in Lord Devereaux's eyes would flourish and bloom.

She held her breath while he met her gaze and lowered his head.

Then he pulled away.

The organist started to play a march, a victorious refrain that filled the chapel as the congregation stood. But there was no victory. The groom could hardly bear to look at her, let alone kiss her.

How abhorrent he must think her!

Olivia blinked and her vision blurred for a heartbeat, then it cleared, and she caught sight of Eleanor in the front pew, and beside her, Montague's mother. When Olivia had first been presented before the dowager, the older woman had stared at her as if she were an insect that needed to be stamped out—understandable, perhaps, given that Olivia was living evidence of the late duke's infidelity. But, in the past year, the dowager had softened a little—enough, at least, that she was not averse to kissing Olivia on both cheeks at each greeting. Her dislike of Olivia, however, could never be completely conquered.

How much more must her new husband dislike her if he couldn't even bring himself to kiss her on the cheek?

In the second pew behind Eleanor stood her sister Juliette and her husband Earl Staines, together with Miss Lucas, whose pale, sickly complexion rendered her perhaps the only creature in the chapel more miserable than Olivia herself. The poor girl looked as if she might faint at any moment.

Olivia fingered her necklace—a simple gold chain with a pearl pendant that Eleanor had given her last night as a token of love between sisters. She ran her fingertips over the pearl, seeking comfort from its smoothness. But there was none to be had. Biting her lip to stem the tears, she caught her husband's sleeve. He stiffened and glanced at her, then he stepped along the aisle in long, slow strides, while she hurried to keep up.

They emerged from the chapel. Olivia blinked, letting her eyes adjust to the sunlight, then a coach-and-four came into focus, bearing the Whitcombe crest. The horses stood patiently, their polished harnesses gleaming, while the coachman sat holding the reins. A footman climbed down from the back, which was already laden with trunks, and opened the carriage door.

This was it—the means by which she would be transported from everything she held dear.

The congregation gathered to wish the couple well, their merry chatter filling the air. Olivia turned to see Eleanor approaching, arms outstretched.

"A word, if you please, Devereaux," Montague said as he emerged from the chapel accompanied by the vicar. The groom withdrew his arm and approached Montague as Eleanor ran toward Olivia.

"Oh, sister!" she cried. "I do hope you'll be happy. Write to me often, darling, so that I may be assured of your happiness."

"I will," Olivia said, her throat tightening.

"And don't merely write pleasantries," Eleanor said. "You know I care naught for such vile niceties. I'm not the kind of correspondent who only wishes to be told how grand your new home is or how fine the furnishings are. I want—*need*—to know how *you* are. I can only bear the thought of you leaving us if I know that you are happier with"—she faltered—"with *him*...than you have been with us."

Olivia glanced toward the chapel doors, where her brother stood beside Devereaux. Both men wore grim expressions, as if a declaration of war had been made.

Perhaps it had.

"Oh, Eleanor!" Olivia said. "If only you knew..." She trailed off as Eleanor's sister approached, together with her husband and Miss Lucas.

"Dearest Olivia, I'm so pleased to see you happily married as you deserve."

"And I trust that you will be," Miss Lucas said, her voice a low rasp. "I wish—" She broke off in a fit of coughing.

"My dear, are you quite well?" Eleanor said. Miss Lucas nodded, but she looked far from healthy. In the dim light of the chapel her skin had looked pale, but in the bright sunlight it carried a sheen of moisture, as if merely existing was taking its toll on her constitution.

"I-I know that Olivia will be happy with such a fine-looking husband."

Olivia opened her mouth to voice her fears, then took in Lady Staines's smile of pure happiness—how she had one hand placed over her already-swelling belly, her delicate features flushed with pleasure. Olivia had no wish to dampen her joy, not when the overprotective Earl Staines stood beside his wife.

"Lady Staines, I'm sure that—"

"Did I not tell you to call me Juliette? We're sisters by marriage, after all." Lady Staines glanced toward Montague and Devereaux. "I cannot think why my brother-in-law insisted on your marrying here, and such a quiet affair. It would have been no trouble for my husband to have presided over the ceremony in London. The bishop's a particular friend, and he would have approved. You are equally as deserving to have your wedding take place in St. George's as any other bride, is she not, Andrew?"

Lord Staines patted his wife's hand and smiled at Olivia. "Miss Whitcombe—pardon me, *Lady Devereaux*—was quite right in insisting on a quiet ceremony here at Rosecombe. And I'll wager much of her decision is due to her consideration for her guests, for you wouldn't have wished to travel to London in your condition, my love."

"I'd have made the effort in Olivia's case. Surely she deserves…"

"She deserves to choose the manner of her own wedding," he said, lifting his wife's hand to his lips. "The ceremony is not about the pomp. It's a sacred vow made by two people in love."

He placed his hand on Olivia's sleeve. "I wish with all my heart that you'll be happy." He glanced toward the chapel doors. "Devereaux is an honorable and honest man. With your sweet nature, you cannot fail to make him happy."

"But will he make Olivia happy?" Eleanor said.

The corner of Lord Staines's mouth twitched into a smile. "Duchess, I daresay he'll find a bullet in his heart courtesy of your husband if he does not. What say you, Miss Lucas? You're very silent on the matter. Are you unwell?"

Miss Lucas nodded and gave a watery smile. "It's the heat,"

she said. "Do forgive me."

Footsteps crunched on the gravel, and Olivia's skin tightened as the air seemed to shimmer with the masculine essence of...*him*. She lowered her gaze and his shadow appeared, stretching across the pathway until it engulfed hers. The faint scent of wood and spices filled her nostrils, and though she anticipated his touch, a fizz of apprehension still rippled through her body as he took her elbow, cradling it in his palm in a gentle but determined gesture.

"I fear it's time to take your leave," Montague said, joining them. "You've a long journey ahead."

"B-but your carriage..."

"Is at your disposal until your husband arranges the purchase of a carriage of his own, which I trust he'll do without delay...in addition to certain other pledges he's made."

Olivia glanced at her husband to see him glaring at Montague, his eyes almost black with anger. Then, slowly, he nodded.

"Good," Montague said. "In which case, I see no further reason for delay." He took Olivia's hand and squeezed it. "Write to Eleanor as soon as you're settled."

"I've already made her promise, my love," Eleanor said. Then she turned to Devereaux. "What shall we make *you* promise, sir? To abide by your vows?"

The groom frowned, then nodded.

"Then take my hand as a gesture of good faith," Eleanor said. "For we are now brother and sister."

He paused, then took her hand, as delicately as if plucking a flower, and lifted it to his lips.

"There!" she said. "Montague, did I not tell you he was a decent sort of man?"

Then her eyes darkened. "I trust my faith will not be misplaced, sir. You have gained more today than Olivia can ever have hoped to gain in her lifetime. But of course, in this world, men always have the better bargain."

His mouth twitched into a smile that did not reach his eyes.

"I don't refer to my sister's fortune," Eleanor added, "though I trust you will treat it, and her, with the respect they both deserve."

She turned to Olivia. "One last farewell, dearest, then you must be on your way before I cry. I hate to cry at weddings, for I fear that tears cannot bode well for a happy union."

Olivia blinked, willing the tears in her own eyes not to fall, as she found herself embraced once more. Then she hugged Lady Staines and finally Miss Lucas. On impulse, she handed her posy to the pale young woman.

"Oh no, Miss Whitcombe—I mean, Lady Devereaux. I couldn't possibly…"

"Take it, Miss Lucas," Olivia said, "as a symbol of my friendship, in the hope that you'll find happiness in your marriage, whenever that may be."

"Very well. I hope I shall be as happy as you."

Olivia forced a smile. Then she caught her breath as a large hand touched the small of her back. For a moment, it remained there, Devereaux's body heat seeping into hers—then, gently but determinedly, he propelled her toward the carriage and helped her inside. He followed suit then beckoned for his valet to climb in.

"Oh no, sir!" The valet laughed. "I have no wish to disturb a newly married couple as they travel to their wedding night. I'll be content seated outside."

With that, he closed the door and the carriage tilted sideways as he climbed aboard. Then, with the crack of a whip, they set off. Olivia leaned toward the window to see her brother and sister-in-law arm in arm, waving her off with their love and good wishes. Then the carriage turned a corner, and they disappeared from view, leaving her alone, for the first time, with the beast of a man who'd been forced into marrying her against his will.

CHAPTER SIXTEEN

"**D**ON'T FORGET, DEVEREAUX, if you want the other ten thousand, you must consummate the marriage tonight."

Whitcombe's instruction, delivered through gritted teeth, might as well have been an executioner's threat—as if, in addition to ten thousand, the reward for Charles fucking his new wife tonight was to keep his head.

My new wife.

He glanced at the young woman sitting opposite. She was a diminutive thing at the best of times—as most women were, compared to his bulky frame—but in the cramped space of the carriage she looked like a tiny, shrunken field mouse.

And as terrified.

Devil's breeches, what was a beast such as him going to do with her?

It was fortunate that she'd already been ruined. At least she knew what to expect tonight, and she was hardly a brittle Society lady who'd faint at the sight of his cock.

To be honest, whether or not she carried another man's child mattered not. It might even be preferable. His family bloodline had hardly produced men of honor or good character. Goodness was supposed to skip a generation, but for the Devereaux family it had never existed.

He lowered his gaze to her belly. No evidence of a child. She didn't even cradle it as women were supposed to. Had she loved the father? Perhaps not, given the shimmer of hope in her eyes when she'd anticipated his kiss in the chapel.

Bloody hell, when she'd offered those sweet, soft lips of hers, a powerful lust had gripped his body, tightening his breeches and obliterating his reason. It was all he could do to stop himself from pulling her to him, parting her thighs and rutting her against the chapel wall.

Ha! That stiff matriarch smothered in black lace in the front pew, face like a smacked arse on a frosty morning, would have *loved* that.

He heard a sigh and glanced up to see Olivia looking at him, apprehension in her honey-colored eyes.

Are you well?

She glanced at his hands, then shook her head. "F-forgive me, I don't understand…"

She broke off and cringed as he let out a sharp sigh. Curse bloody John for abandoning him!

Then he cursed himself. He had less to fear from her than she from him.

A spark of something unfamiliar threaded through his blood—the need to drive that look of fear from her eyes and to see it replaced by trust.

But a girl like her would never bring herself to trust a man such as I.

She drew her shawl around her shoulders. "I-I was wondering how far away your home is…how long it will take to get there today."

Charles shook his head.

"W-will you not tell me?"

We'll be staying at an inn tonight.

She stared at his hands, frowning, then shook her head. "I-I'm sorry."

He let out a sigh and made a dismissive gesture, and she leaned forward and took his hand.

He caught his breath as a fizz of need tightened his skin and swelled his cock.

Devil be damned, if she continued to touch him like that, they wouldn't have to wait until tonight to consummate the marriage.

He inhaled then started to withdraw, but she tightened her hold, curling her little fingers around his.

"No, please. I want to understand you," she said. "I want to learn…" She gestured toward his hands. "But before I do, let me ask the right questions. May I?"

He nodded, and the corner of her mouth lifted a little.

Almost a smile.

How might she look if she smiled properly?

And how might she look with her face flushed with pleasure—not the fake pleasure of whores, but the genuine response of a woman well satisfied? It was not something he'd seen, but he'd heard enough talk among gentlemen to know that it was the most glorious sight a man could behold—a woman screaming her climax at his hands, evidence of his skill and virility.

"Are we perhaps staying at an inn tonight?"

He nodded.

"And the journey. How long is it?"

He held up four fingers. Then, compelled by the urge to see her smile, he raised his hands, as if playing an imaginary violin.

She frowned and folded her arms, watching his hands, then a flicker of a smile touched her eyes for a heartbeat.

"Are we staying at the Fiddlers' Arms, where we'll arrive in four hours?"

Slowly, he nodded.

"I knew it!" she said. Then she checked herself, as if the burst of mirth was once more conquered by her melancholy. "A-and tomorrow?"

He held up three fingers.

"Another three hours then we'll be at your home?"

He shook his head, then pointed to her and back at himself. Confusion clouded her gaze, then she parted her lips, and a faint bloom colored her cheeks.

"Three hours, yes," she said, "but you want to tell me that it's *our* home?"

He nodded, and she blinked, a sheen of moisture glistening in her eyes.

"Thank you," she said, almost in a whisper, and turned to look out of the window. Unwilling to intrude on her distress, Charles looked out of the opposite window at the landscape passing by.

After a moment, he heard her soft voice, the tremor piercing his heart.

"My lord?"

My lord? Bloody hell, she wasn't his housekeeper. She was his wife. Had that bastard brother of hers taught her to be subservient?

He turned toward her, and she lowered her gaze, but not before he caught another glimmer of fear. *Devil's breeches*, he'd have to learn to conceal his anger, or at least tell his little bride that his anger was directed at others, not her.

At length she lifted her gaze, and he raised his eyebrows in inquiry.

"I-I was wondering…"

He forced the frown from his expression and leaned toward her—but not so close as to crowd her.

"I was wondering whether you minded very much being married to me." She spoke quickly, as if she feared the outcome of her question and wished to be done with it as quickly as possible. "Please don't say what you think I wish to hear. I'd rather know the truth."

He raised his hands. *No.*

"I-I don't…"

He shook his head.

"Y-you *don't* mind being married to me?" She repeated his hand gesture. "That means no, am I right?"

Yes.

She watched his hands as he made another gesture, then

repeated it. "And that means yes?"

He nodded and was rewarded with the ghost of a smile.

"Thank you," she said.

What for? Teaching her two simple hand gestures, or not minding being married to her?

Do you *mind being married to* me?

She frowned as he signed. Then he gestured toward her, then to himself.

"Are you asking me the same question?" she said.

He nodded, and his conscience stabbed his heart at the gratitude in her eyes. What a cruel world they lived in where a woman had to express gratitude for a husband who cared whether she minded being his wife.

"No," she said, after a pause. "I do not mind being married to you."

He nodded, and she resumed her attention on the view outside, her body moving with the rocking motion of the carriage.

Charles diverted his attention from her, like a predator focusing his gaze away from his prey to enable her to relax out of his glare, snatching only occasional glimpses. At length, the fatigue she'd barely been able to conceal overcame her and she fell asleep, her chest rising and falling more steadily—at which point Charles allowed himself to observe her more fully.

Her gown did nothing to conceal her form, the swell of her breasts, the way her body dipped in at the waist before flaring at her hips—delectable, rounded hips. Her face, flushed with distress, bore the soft roundness of youth, plump cheeks, a delicate nose, and long lashes that quivered as she slept, and finally...

Finally, his gaze settled on her mouth—the sweet, plump lips that she had offered to him.

How had he ever thought her unremarkable?

The duchess was right. Out of the two of them, it was Charles, not his wife, who'd secured the better bargain.

And consummating the marriage tonight would be the easiest and most pleasurable ten thousand he'd ever earned.

CHAPTER SEVENTEEN

THE ROCKING MOTION of the carriage that had lulled Olivia into delicious oblivion stopped. Voices came from outside, set against a backdrop of the merry air of a violin.

She blinked and rubbed her eyes; her skin tightened with cold.

She was alone in the carriage. Lord Devereaux stood beside the open door, gesturing to his valet, who was relaying instructions to a thick-set, whiskered man with ruddy cheeks.

"Right ye are, your lordship," the man said, before raising his voice. "Daniel, Tom! Get yer lazy arses out here and deal with his lordship's trunks. Hurry, now! We don't want to keep him waiting!"

The carriage tilted sideways, and Olivia spotted two men lowering her trunk from the top.

Then the valet caught her eye and nudged his master. "Lady Devereaux, we're here."

The valet offered his hand and, ignoring the ache in her bones, Olivia uncurled herself and climbed out, almost losing her balance. The valet caught her arm and smiled. Then his smile disappeared as Olivia's husband pulled him away, his brow furrowed into a frown, and she could swear she heard a low growl reverberating from the bigger man's throat.

She cast her gaze over the inn—a white-fronted two-story building with diamond-paned windows and a sloping, thatched roof. Over the entrance, through which music and laughter came, swung a sign that creaked in the breeze, depicting a dancing man, legs akimbo, holding a violin.

The whiskered man, evidently the innkeeper, touched his cap. "Welcome to the Fiddlers', ma'am...pardon me, Countess Dever-axe."

"It's Dever*eaux*, Mr. Smith," the valet said, with a grin.

The man nodded, then raised his voice again. "Betsy! Ger yer bones down here now. Earl Dev-row and the countess are waitin' to be shown to their rooms." He glanced toward Olivia's husband. "We've set aside the best rooms for ye, sir—not that ye'll be needin' both rooms for much of the night, I'll warrant."

He let out a chuckle, and coarse laughter came from the servants carrying the trunk.

Olivia stumbled against her husband's arm, shaking with fatigue even though she'd been sitting in the carriage all afternoon. He placed his hand on the small of her back and steadied her—a gesture that, though insignificant, spoke of possessiveness.

"Mr. Smith," the valet said, "be so good as to have supper ready as soon as possible, then Lord and Lady Devereaux will wish to retire."

"Very good, sir. Betsy, see to it, will ye, lass?"

The maid bobbed another curtsey then disappeared.

The innkeeper glanced at Olivia then patted her arm. "We've a nice bit of venison pie for ye, lass...beggin' yer pardon, Lady Dev-row. That'll bring the color back to yer cheeks. The wife bakes the best venison pie in the county."

"Thank you, Mr. Smith," Olivia said, managing a smile. "That's very kind."

"No trouble." He gave a gap-toothed grin, a flare of interest in his eyes. "Ye're a pretty thing, aren't ye? If I were ten years younger! Yer husband's a lucky lad to—"

He broke off, his eyes widening, and mumbled an apology. Olivia glanced up to see her husband's eyes dark with cold fury.

"I'll see to yer carriage, Lord Dev-row, sir," the innkeeper said. "Ah! Here's the missus. She'll see ye right."

A woman almost as plump as the innkeeper appeared, wiping her hands on her apron.

"Mary, love, here's Lord and Lady Dev-row."

She rolled her eyes. "I can see that, Jim, ye great oaf. Do ye think I'm blind? *Men!* Just because they don't notice what's in front of their noses half the time, they think us womenfolk are equally lacking in wits." She smiled at Olivia. "Bless me! To look at ye, a person wouldn't think ye'd just had the happiest day of yer life. But ye must be right tired after yer journey. Come in out of the cold. Ye need a good bit o' pie to get yer strength back."

Olivia tried to return her smile, then, clinging to her husband's arm, followed the woman inside.

THE INNKEEPER'S CLAIM about his wife's pie was not without foundation. Molded into a smooth, round shape, crimped at the edges and decorated with embellishments in the shape of a stag's head surrounded by leaves, it was a work of art. The cook at Rosecombe, who'd taught Olivia the basics of baking—including how to perfect pastry, such that it was strong enough to maintain its shape but not so tough as to loosen the diners' teeth—had always said that one could recognize who'd baked a pie from the decoration, which was like a signature. Olivia herself had discovered a knack for fashioning remnants of pastry into roses and grapevines.

No countess would be expected to have practiced the skills of the kitchen. But Olivia had never expected to become one. And even though he'd recognized her as his sister and brought her to live at Rosecombe, Montague had known that, for Olivia, a Society marriage with a respectable man had always been unlikely. Instead, she was risk of being preyed upon by the less respectable—fortune hunters who, with overly bright smiles, promised love and devotion but mistreated their wives as soon as the money changed hands.

At least I cannot accuse my husband of deceiving me into matrimony with overly bright smiles or promises of love.

Olivia glanced across the dining table. Her husband stabbed a piece of pie with his fork, dipped it in the sauce, then placed it in his mouth and chewed, his jaws moving up and down with vigor. His throat bobbed as he swallowed, and he lifted his wineglass. Then he paused, glass in midair, and met her gaze.

He'd caught her staring.

Her cheeks warming, Olivia lowered her gaze and resumed eating. But the next time she looked up, he was still watching her, with the same attitude, glass in hand.

She pushed her plate aside, and he glanced at her half-eaten portion then lifted his eyebrows in inquiry.

"I-I'm no longer hungry," she said. "It was delicious—thank you for bringing me here, my lord—b-but I've had my fill. W-would you like to finish mine?"

He frowned, and she cursed herself.

What must he think of her? No well-bred couple would consider passing their plates about and eating each others' leftovers.

"I-I would hate to think Mrs. Smith thought me unappreciative of her efforts," Olivia said. "If she's worked hard to cook supper, I wouldn't want to appear ungrateful. Forgive me if I spoke out of turn."

The corner of his mouth quirked up, then he deftly swapped his empty plate for her half-full one and resumed eating. Not long after he finished, the door opened to reveal the young maid who'd greeted them earlier.

"Mercy me!" she cried, taking their plates. "Mrs. Smith will be right pleased to see you've finished the pie. Been boiling the bones all yesterday, she has, to make the jelly. Will ye be wanting anything else or are ye eager to get to yer chambers? Ye'll need to work off that pie!"

She gave a broad grin, her eyes sparkling with mischief.

"My lord, may I retire?" Olivia asked.

She rose, her stomach knotting with apprehension. He stood and, as she reached the door, he motioned toward a large cabinet that dominated the wall beside the window, where a decanter, half filled with a dark-red liquid, stood on the top. The maid poured a glass and handed it to him.

Of course, after a meal, husbands preferred a moment away from their wives. And Olivia had to admit that she craved a moment away from *his* presence. The very air seemed to bend around him, as if the world yielded to his superior masculinity. And though it gave her a wicked little thrill deep inside her center, that thrill came hand in hand with fear.

Once inside her chamber, Olivia undressed then slipped into her nightgown. As she was brushing out her hair, there was a knock, and the maid entered.

"I've been sent to see to you, seein' as ye've brought no maid of yer own."

"I can take care of myself," Olivia said, "but thank you."

"Mrs. Smith insisted I give satisfaction."

She glanced at the thin young woman in the dressing table mirror. Would she be admonished if Olivia sent her away?

"Very well," Olivia said. "You may brush my hair if you wish."

The girl picked up the hairbrush and ran it through Olivia's hair in soft, gentle strokes.

"Thank you," Olivia said. "It's not often someone brushes my hair for me. I like the sensation."

"You do, yer ladyship?"

Your ladyship…

Would she ever become used to a title?

"Doesn't yer own maid brush yer hair?"

"I have no maid."

"But ye're a countess!"

"I wasn't a countess yesterday."

"Well, ye're right lucky if ye don't mind me sayin' so," the maid said. "A fine, big man the earl is, and good lookin' with it. Ye're in for a treat tonight!"

"I-I suppose so."

"There's no *suppose* about it!" the maid said. "The size of a stallion, I reckon, and he knows his way around a woman, I'm sure of it. Ye'll be moaning his name all night, and I'll not be surprised if ye're bow-legged come the morning!" She let out a peal of laughter, and Olivia startled as the door opened to reveal the innkeeper's wife holding a cup from which wisps of steam arose.

"Betsy Green! What have I told you about making bawdy talk? I could hear every word ye said—doubtless ye could be heard in the next village!"

The maid went as red as fire. "Sorry, Mrs. Smith."

"It's not *me* ye should apologize to."

"Beg pardon, yer ladyship."

"Yes, yes—now be off with ye, lass," Mrs. Smith said. "And for yer bawdy talk, ye can help Tom rake out the fireplaces in the parlor. Mind ye don't fool about with him though, lass—at least, not until ye've seen to those fireplaces."

The maid gave a saucy grin, bobbed a curtsey, then slipped out of the chamber. Olivia cringed as she heard footsteps followed by whispering and giggling.

Heavens! Was the whole inn gossiping about her wedding night?

Mrs. Smith placed the cup on the dressing table. "A little hot chocolate, Lady Devereaux," she said. "It'll help ye relax. Will ye be wanting anything else before yer husband comes?"

Olivia's stomach fluttered with anticipation, and she shook her head.

"No, thank you, Mrs. Smith," she whispered.

The older woman placed a gentle hand on her shoulder. "Ye'll be all right, lass," she said, her tone that of a stable hand coaxing a nervous filly. "I'll send ye some sweet tea in the morning. My ma swore by it for new brides. Sweet tea and a hearty breakfast."

Heavy footsteps approached, the floorboards vibrating as they drew nearer, and Olivia's stomach twisted once more as they stopped outside the chamber next door. Mrs. Smith exited the bedchamber, and Olivia caught her words as she closed the door.

"I trust ye enjoyed yer port, yer lordship. Good night, then— best leave ye to it."

Olivia sipped her hot chocolate, wincing as the hot liquid scalded her lips. But all she could taste was the sharp tang of anticipation. Setting the cup aside, she approached the bed and slipped beneath the sheets.

Shortly after, she heard a murmur of voices coming from next door.

No—a single voice. The valet's, punctuated by periods of silence.

Her heart thudding, Olivia extinguished the candle, settled back, and waited.

CHAPTER EIGHTEEN

LAUGHTER ECHOED IN the distance, followed by a squeal of pleasure.

Doubtless the young maid was "fooling around" with Tom—perhaps they were sweethearts, promised to each other.

Olivia sighed. Most likely Betsy envied her for being a countess. Being a servant, Betsy would be at the beck and call of her employers, but she had one privilege that was denied Olivia—the freedom to marry for love. The innkeeper and his wife clearly loved each other. The friendly, sporting exchanges between them were not due to disrespect or dislike, but the free, easy speech between lovers able to tease one another without fear of reprisal.

Much like Eleanor and Montague.

Oh, Eleanor. How I wish you were here to soothe my fears!

Eleanor had said that tonight Olivia had nothing to fear from her husband and everything to enjoy, provided she relaxed and conquered her embarrassment when her husband touched her intimately.

Olivia had to admit that the prospect of the wedding night sent a little thrill through her. And, if Betsy's squeals of delight were anything to go by, the attentions of a man were something to take pleasure in.

But when she heard footsteps outside and caught sight of a shadow beneath her door she stiffened, curled her fingers around the bedsheet, and held her breath.

Was she expected to invite him in? Eleanor had said nothing about that.

Or would that be too forward and he would think her a wanton?

But then, might he be angry if she said nothing and kept him waiting? He didn't seem to be a man who liked to be kept waiting…

…or disappointed.

What if she disappointed him?

She opened her mouth to call out, then checked herself.

What if it wasn't him?

Oh, heavens! What am I supposed to do?

At length, the door creaked open, and she suppressed a cry.

Foolish girl—do you want him to think he's married a weakling?

Her husband stood on the threshold, his huge body silhouetted against the light outside. Then he entered and closed the door, plunging them into near darkness. In the soft orange glow from the dying embers in the fireplace, she saw him approach the bed, moving as silently as a panther approaching its prey.

He pulled back the bedsheet, and the bed dipped and creaked under his weight as he slipped inside. She caught a flash of light reflected in his eyes as he lay back, staring at the ceiling.

Then he shifted closer, and his body heat almost seared into her skin. Olivia let out a whimper as her stomach somersaulted.

He was naked.

He rolled toward her, his eyes gleaming in the dark, then reached for her nightgown and tugged at it. She held her breath as he pulled it up, but rather than her feeling a rush of cold over her exposed legs, her skin seemed to burn with the heat from his body. He lifted a hand, and she let out a soft cry at the unexpected tenderness with which he touched her cheek, caressing her skin with his thumb. He began to withdraw his hand, and she caught his wrist, arching her back to lean into his touch, seeking comfort from the tenderness.

"Please…" she whispered.

Without friends or family—without anyone who had ever loved or cared for her—even the slightest sign of friendship was like an oasis in a desert of loneliness. And if that was all that he could give her, then she would treasure it.

"P-please, my lord…"

He stiffened as she uttered the plea once more. Then he pulled her nightgown further up, exposing her naked body.

Just relax, Olivia, and you'll be well.

With Eleanor's reassurance in her ears, Olivia swallowed her fears and lay still, conquering her instinct to flee.

Her husband rose up, a dark shadow swelling in the air before her. Then, in a swift, sharp movement, he tore her nightgown apart and climbed on top of her. A shock of horror rippled through her as he grasped her thighs.

Surely this couldn't be the tender pleasure that Eleanor spoke of?

"What's happening?" she cried, growing rigid with fear.

He pushed her thighs apart.

"My lord!" she cried, shame and embarrassment swamping her senses. "Wh-what are you *doing*?"

He parted her thighs wider, and she let out a scream.

"No!"

He jerked back as if she'd struck him.

"M-my lord!" she sobbed. "I-I don't know what…" She broke off, shaking as she drew in a ragged breath. "I-I mean…I haven't…" She shook her head. "F-forgive me… I-is it supposed to be like…*that*?"

He drew in a sharp breath, then leaped off the bed. He approached the door, then she cried out as he rammed his fist into the wall.

"Stop!" she cried. "Don't hurt yourself!"

He let out a sharp huff and turned toward her.

"Please!" she said. "Tell me what's wrong. What must I do?"

He raised his arm and raked it through his hair. Then he approached the fireplace and crouched beside it. She caught a flare of light, then he held up a lit candle, and she let out a whimper.

His body glowed in the light of the candle—the sharp, chiseled features of his face, the broad shoulders and sculpted arms, and the planes of muscles on his chest, nestled together in pairs. A thin layer of downy, dark hair covered his chest, growing thicker lower down, toward a thatch of dark curls from which jutted out…

Oh, sweet, sweet Lord! Even in her mind she couldn't bring herself to voice it.

And he was going to put *that* inside her?

B-but it was so…

So *big*.

He narrowed his eyes and lowered his gaze to that part of him which seemed to shift and throb in the candlelight with a primal need, as if it beckoned to her.

Heaven save me…

A low growl reverberated in his chest—a predator readying himself to devour his mate.

Olivia glanced about the chamber, but there was no escape. He was blocking her access to the door. In any case, she belonged to him now. She had vowed, before the Almighty, to honor and obey him.

For several heartbeats he stared at her. Why didn't he just devour her? Or did he savor her fear like he'd savored his port after supper?

Then he set the candle aside, picked up the cup on the dressing table, and smashed it against the wall. He took a shard and dragged it along the heel of his palm until a fat red droplet appeared, then he advanced on her.

"No!" she cried. "Please, no!"

Ignoring her pleas, he tore the bedsheet from her grasp and rubbed his palm across it, leaving a dark smear. Then he released the sheet and withdrew to the door.

"Don't go!" she said as he opened it. "Come back inside—

you're supposed to…"

She faltered as he raised his hand and shook his head. Then he slipped outside, closing the door behind him.

Moments later she heard another door open and slam shut, then the sound of splintering wood—a fist pummeling the paneled walls in the adjacent chamber once, twice…five times in total.

Olivia held her breath, willing him to return—to tell her what she was supposed to have done. She heard footsteps and a creak, presumably as he climbed into the bed next door, followed by another series of thuds—he was giving a pillow the same treatment as the wall. Then, silence.

She drew her tattered nightgown around her and rolled onto her side, curling up. Only when she caught the distant sound of female giggling elsewhere in the inn did she surrender to her despair. Hot tears splashed onto her cheeks, blurring the glow from the fireplace.

CHAPTER NINETEEN

D EVIL'S FUCKING BREECHES, what the bloody hell did
Whitcombe think he was *doing*?

Charles drove his fist into the wall, but the explosion of pain
in his knuckles did nothing to lessen the shame of what he'd
done.

What he'd *almost* done.

The girl was a maiden, and he'd come at her like a rutting
bull at the behest of her brother to claim the remainder of the
dowry.

The sheen of terror in his bride's eyes had cleaved his heart in
two and shattered his soul. It was the same expression that
haunted him almost every night—the expression in his mother's
eyes the moment before her life had been extinguished as her
broken body lay, inches from his face, while she drew her last, her
final exhalation caressing his skin.

He paused, his knuckles throbbing, but heard nothing from
the chamber next door. Perhaps the girl was too terrified to make
a sound, lest he thrust his way into her chamber to force himself
upon her again.

He climbed into bed and satisfied himself with driving his fist
into the pillow. Then he tossed the pillow across the floor.

What the devil was he supposed to do *now*? His bride lay in
the adjacent chamber—shaken, terrified, in need of comfort. But
he was the last person to comfort her, and he'd be damned if he'd

ask John to do it for him. The young slut who'd served them supper was busy—he could hear her screaming her pleasures elsewhere. Which left the innkeeper's wife.

But what could he say to *her*? That he was sorry for being such a brute that his bride screamed with terror on her wedding night?

He ought to demand an annulment. That might, at least, put the girl out of her misery. But it would humiliate her even more than she had been already. Not to mention Charles would find himself on the wrong side of Whitcombe's pistol.

Perhaps he ought to consider a novel idea—ask his wife what she wanted.

But the poor creature would drop dead with fright if she saw him again tonight. Better to deal with the matter, and with her, in the morning.

Coward. Sniveling little wretch. You're your mother's son, all right.

Charles flinched as his father's sneering voice sliced into his mind. But perhaps Father was right, and he was a coward, a pathetic creature unworthy of the Devereaux name.

But he *was* a Devereaux. The name formed the walls of a prison that ensnared him. He was stuck with it.

And so was his wife.

⁂

THE NEXT MORNING Charles entered the dining room, his valet in tow, to find it empty. He blinked in the sunlight and his stomach growled at a warm, savory aroma.

"The Fiddlers' reputation for good food is well deserved, sir," John said. "Mmm…it smells good enough to wake the dead."

But was it good enough to coax his terrified wife from her chamber?

The table was laden with platters of food—scrambled eggs, bacon, and a dish of dark-brown objects resembling mushrooms that glistened in a brown sauce topped with green flecks.

The decanter of port was still on the nearby cabinet. If there was ever an occasion for liquor, this morning was it.

The young maid from last night scuttled in, carrying a teapot. "Bless me, yer lordship, ye're already down. I just need to fetch the milk, then I'll leave ye in peace."

She cocked her head to one side and gave him a saucy grin. "Shall I make up a tray for Lady Dev-row? I suspect she'll be wanting to keep to her bed for a bit this morning."

John raised his eyebrows, and Charles signed, *I'm damned if I know whether she's joining us.*

"Just bring the milk, miss," John said, "and…"

He trailed off and dipped his head in a bow.

"Good morning, Lady Devereaux."

Charles turned to see his wife—Olivia—standing in the doorway. Other than a slight color to her cheeks, she gave no sign of distress from her ordeal of last night. He reached for his signet ring and ran his thumb over the facets of the gemstone.

"Good morning, Mr…." She nodded to John. "Forgive me, I don't know…"

"It's John."

"John." She fixed her clear gaze on Charles, and he felt his stomach curl with shame. "Good morning, husband."

She dipped into a curtsey then sat at the opposite end of the table.

"I'll wager it's a *very* good morning," the maid said with a chuckle. She bobbed a curtsey then exited the dining room, humming to herself.

Olivia cast her gaze over the table, her eyes bright with distress.

"I think you're supposed to help yourself, ma'am," John said. "If you wish, I could serve you. There's bacon, eggs, and…" He glanced at the final dish and raised his eyebrows.

"Devilled kidneys," she said, a slight smile on her lips. "They're Eleanor's favorite. I'd never had them until I went to live with my brother."

She spooned some onto her plate, then paused and glanced at Charles.

"W-would you like some?"

Charles shook his head, and her smile disappeared. She picked up her knife and fork, hunching her shoulders like a hunted animal striving to make itself appear smaller in the vicinity of a predator.

Bloody hell, what the devil was he supposed to do with her?

The door opened and the maid returned with a milk jug which she placed on the table. She eyed Charles's empty plate. "Not eating, your lordship?"

She glanced at Olivia, then grinned.

"Ah—ladies first," she said. "Might as well continue what ye started last night!"

Olivia looked up, and the maid chuckled.

"Ye've a fine husband there, yer ladyship!" she said. "I heard ye! Screaming yer pleasures, beggin' him to come back inside."

Trembling, Olivia lifted a forkful of food to her mouth, and Charles's heart ached to see the distress in her eyes.

"Ha!" the maid cried. "I see ye blush. It's no wonder ye're eating first. Needin' yer strength, I'll wager. It's a wonder ye can walk, given the size of him!"

Charles slammed his fist on the table. The fork slipped from his wife's grasp and clattered onto the plate. He gestured to the maid, then to John, his hands shaking with anger.

"Please refrain from making such remarks," John said. "They're not suitable for the ears of a lady."

"*I'll* say so," a new voice said.

The innkeeper's wife stood in the doorway, hands on hips.

Devil's breeches, was poor Olivia's discomfort to be witnessed by every soul in this cursed inn?

"Betsy, what have I told ye about making bawdy remarks? Heavens, girl, ye'd think we've not had newlyweds here before! We all know what the wedding night entails, so there's no need to giggle about it like a child fresh out of the nursery. Be off with ye, unless ye want a lick of the strap."

The maid's face reddened. "Beg pardon, Mrs. Smith," she mumbled, then fled.

"I also beg pardon, yer ladyship," the innkeeper's wife said, and Olivia flinched as the woman patted her arm. "It's always the same when we've newlyweds here. Betsy means no harm. She's just not used to serving such fine folk. But we're all right pleased for ye and wish ye a happy marriage."

Olivia gave the woman a bright smile that almost, but not quite, reached her eyes.

"Thank you, Mrs. Smith," she said, the ghost of a tremor in her voice. "I understand. Please don't treat Betsy too harshly. I'm sure her remarks were delivered with kindness in mind."

"That's very good of ye, ma'am. Now, would ye like a cup of tea? I'll make it nice and sweet."

The woman fussed around Olivia, pouring tea and spooning eggs onto her plate, then she patted her shoulder once more and exited the parlor, promising to leave the newlyweds in peace.

As soon as the door closed, Charles gestured to John.

Tell my wife I'm sorry for last night. I didn't realize she was…

Fuck—how could he express that?

John tilted his head to one side and responded, *Had you thought her a whore?*

Charles drove his fist into his palm. *No!*

Olivia flinched and glanced up.

Tell her yourself, John signed. *You cannot expect me to say such a thing, unless you wish me to humiliate her more than you have already.*

Charles let out a huff. *Just do it. It's what I pay you for.*

"You don't pay me to do *that*."

"To do wh-what?"

Bugger. John had spoken aloud. Olivia stared at him, a determined set to her jaw. Despite the moisture in her eyes, she straightened her back and met his gaze unflinchingly.

Brave little soul.

"Please…John," she said. "Tell me what you're speaking of—

at least until I can understand your hand gestures. After all, I am in the room."

Tell her I'm sorry. I didn't intend to frighten her last night. Had I known she was a...

Charles paused, hands in midair.

Bloody hell! How could he say it?

...that she had not lain with a man before, I would have been gentler.

John colored, then nodded.

"Lord Devereaux wishes to apologize, ma'am, for"—he hesitated—"for the events of last night."

Charles raised his eyebrows. *Continue.*

John shook his head.

"My husband wishes to say something else, doesn't he?"

Find me something to write with.

John rose and approached the cabinet, where he opened the drawers and rifled through the contents. At length, he pulled out a crumpled piece of paper and the stub of a pencil. Charles snatched it from his grasp, smoothed out the paper, and scrawled a few words:

Forgive me. I thought you a ruined woman. Had I known you were a maiden, I would not have touched you.

Hardly the flowery words of a poet making love to his sweetheart, but they'd have to do.

John reached toward the paper. Frowning, Charles shook his head, then he folded the note, rose, and handed it to his wife.

She waited for him to resume his seat before she unfolded it. Her gaze darted over the page, then, her color deepening, she crumpled the note in her hands and reached for her teacup. It slipped from her grasp and toppled onto the saucer, splashing tea on the tablecloth.

"I-I'm sorry," she said, in a small voice.

Tell her she has nothing to be sorry for.

John stared at Charles.

For fuck's sake, man, can you not see how distressed she is? Charles signed.

Then comfort her, sir.

I don't know how.

Understanding and sympathy flickered in John's eyes and Charles averted his gaze, unwilling to reveal himself any further. He'd learned over the years that it was easier to discern the thoughts and wishes of another, not by what they said, but by what they *didn't* say—the way they tilted their head, the furrow in their brow, and the expression in their eyes.

And his eyes would have conveyed the revelation that, for the first time in his life, he wanted nothing more than to ease the pain of another—but he lacked the ability, the knowledge, and the experience.

Perhaps Father was right.

I really am nothing but a beast. And a coward.

"What did you say just then, my lord?"

Her voice was soft, laced with concern—a concern that he did not deserve.

"My master said that it's not you who ought to apologize. You are entirely blameless, and he was gravely mistaken in believing that you were anything other than a true innocent. He only wishes to atone, and is anxious to know that you are well enough to travel today."

A fine speech indeed. A little too flowery, but believable, nonetheless. The smile on Olivia's lips was evidence of its success.

"He wishes to reassure you that matters will improve," John continued, "and he appreciates his supreme good fortune in securing your hand."

Her smile disappeared.

Either she still believed herself unworthy or—and this was more likely—was astute enough to know that such gallant words were John's, and not his.

Perhaps John would have fared better as the master and Charles the servant. John, with his classic good looks and open, warm disposition, would have had ladies flocking to him in their dozens. He'd have had no trouble securing a bride—and, no doubt, in giving her pleasure on her wedding night.

Olivia fixed her gaze on Charles. "I thank you for your consideration, my lord," she said. "I hadn't realized you were such an accomplished wordsmith."

A spark of defiance! It was enough to send a surge of heat into his cock.

He leaned forward and she flinched, almost imperceptibly, and the spark died.

Bugger.

But at least the spark was there, even if she kept it hidden. Perhaps, in time, she might emerge from the shell she'd fashioned around herself and come out into the light.

At least, she would if she weren't married to a man that she feared.

A pity, then, that she's married to me.

CHAPTER TWENTY

*H*E APPRECIATES HIS *supreme good fortune in securing your hand.*

Olivia turned her attention from the view outside the carriage window and glanced at her husband, his body hunched and contorted to fit himself onto the seat.

Gallant though the words were, they were evidently not his. Surely if he thought himself fortunate, he wouldn't look so angry all the time.

But she clung to the flash of tenderness in his eyes as he'd passed her the note—a tenderness that belied the awkward words he'd written. Eleanor had always told her that men knew little of fine speeches and pretty words. It was only by their actions that they could express any feeling.

The terror that beset Olivia last night had long since faded, but humiliation had replaced it. Shame had burned deep inside her body as she read his confession that he'd thought her some sort of harlot. And, to further her humiliation, he'd confessed that he wouldn't have touched her had he known she was a maiden. Doubtless he preferred the company of doxies.

He sat before her, rocking softly in unison with the motion of the carriage—hands folded on his lap, fingertips touching the gem on his signet ring. His eyes were closed and had been for most of the journey.

But if he were awake, what would she say to him? And what could he convey to her that would not further her shame? The valet, with his kind eyes and gallant words, might have furthered a conversation between them, but the man had, once again, insisted on sitting outside. His merry conversation with the coachman filtered through the window, and not for the first time, Olivia wished she had remained in obscurity—on the periphery of a Society to which she didn't belong. Then she might have sat outside in the sunshine, enjoying easy laughter with those of the class into which she'd been born, rather than imprisoned in the confines of the carriage with a man who despised her.

Her husband's eyes snapped open, and Olivia's stomach flipped with shame at her being caught watching him. She averted her gaze, then drew in a sharp breath as a large hand took hers. He uncurled his body, frowning as his head bumped on the ceiling, then he glanced out of the window and made a gesture.

"I-I'm sorry, I don't understand."

He pointed to the window and nodded. Through the trees she glimpsed a building.

"Is that your home?"

He frowned, pointed to his chest, then to hers.

"*Our* home?"

He nodded and made a gesture that she recognized from yesterday.

"That means yes, doesn't it?"

The corner of his mouth lifted.

"Will you teach me to understand what you're saying with your hands?"

He frowned and made another gesture.

"Are you saying you think it would be too difficult for me to learn?"

He tilted his head to one side, the expression in his eyes conveying surprise, and she allowed herself to smile.

"It's not just by a person's voice, or their hands, that they tell us what they're saying," she said. "It may take time for me to understand you, but I have the rest of my life."

He frowned, and she caught an expression of guilt in his eyes.

Then he released her hand and leaned back, staring out of the window, his gaze fixed on the building outside, which seemed to have grown in height the closer they drew to it, dominating the skyline.

But rather than express the delight of a man returning home, his expression seemed to darken with each turn of the wheel.

By the time the carriage drew to a halt, the brooding anger had returned, shimmering about his form. The carriage shifted as someone climbed down, then the valet's cheerful face appeared at the window. He opened the door and, without a glance at his master, took Olivia's hand and helped her out.

A row of servants formed a line, at the head of which stood a black-clad butler and a woman, presumably the housekeeper, in a dark-blue gown with iron-gray hair scraped back into a severe style. Next to them were a young man with a mop of black hair, dressed in a rough-spun jacket and breeches, and a young woman with light-blonde hair, pale-blue eyes, and delicate features. The man stared at Olivia with frank appraisal, but his companion narrowed her eyes, hostility in her expression.

Olivia heard her husband's footsteps crunching on the gravel as he climbed out of the carriage, then he placed his hand on the small of her back and glared at the valet, and Olivia could swear she heard a low growl. Then he propelled her toward the waiting servants, who, at a word from the butler, bowed and curtseyed in unison.

Olivia hesitated. How was she expected to respond? Should she greet each one individually?

Was there nobody to tell her what to do?

The gray-haired woman approached, warmth glowing in her eyes. She cast a frown at Lord Devereaux, then took Olivia's hands.

"Welcome, my dear," she said. "What a pretty little thing you are! We've all been looking forward to your arrival. It's about time Master Charles brought a wife home." She glanced at Olivia's husband. "You've chosen well, sir. Hasn't he, Jacob?"

The young man at the end of the line nodded, his eyes sparkling. "I'll say so."

He cast his gaze over Olivia's form. The young woman standing beside him scowled and took his hand, but he withdrew it and approached Olivia.

"How did you manage to reel in such a fine catch, brother?"

Brother?

Olivia glanced at her husband. The young man let out a chuckle.

"I doubt he'd have told you about his reprobate of a brother. Ashamed of me, he is."

"Jacob, that's enough," the housekeeper said. "Haven't you got chores to be getting on with? Those logs won't chop themselves."

"He chopped them yesterday," the young woman said, her gaze still fixed on Olivia, "and he's every right to—"

"That's enough of your lip, miss." The housekeeper nudged the young man. "Well, Jacob, aren't you going to say how-do-you-do to your brother?"

He let out a snort. "*Half*-brother," he said, "as I'm sure Charles would say. That is, if he bothered to speak."

Devereaux stepped forward, his lips curled into a snarl and his eyes darkened until they were almost black.

"Be off with you now, Jacob," the housekeeper said. She gestured to the line of servants. "And the rest of you. The master and mistress will be wanting tea before their supper. See to it, will you, Susan?"

One of the maids bobbed a curtsey. "Yes, Mrs. Brougham." Then the rest of the servants dispersed.

The young woman with Jacob tugged at his sleeve. "Aren't you going to introduce me?"

Jacob rolled his eyes. "Nicola, this is my brother and his new wife." He winked at Olivia. "Lady Devereaux, this is Nicola, my…" He hesitated, and the young girl scowled.

"I'm his sweetheart," she said.

"That's enough of that, young miss," the housekeeper said. "Don't be getting ideas above your station." She gestured to Olivia. "Come along, my dear, let's get you inside. You'll need some tea, and supper's at eight—if that's acceptable, Master Charles?"

Devereaux nodded.

"Have you brought your maid, Lady Devereaux?" the house-keeper asked.

"I have no maid, Mrs. Brougham," Olivia said, her cheeks warming.

The older woman raised her eyebrows. "Oh… Well, I suppose some lady's maids are unwilling to uproot their lives when their mistresses marry. I can make inquiries tomorrow if you like, and Ethel can see to you in the meantime. I suspect you'll be wanting to retire straight after supper."

"Please, don't trouble yourself, Mrs. Brougham. I—"

"It's no trouble, dear. We can't have the lady of Penham Park with no maid, can we? I can't think what Master Charles is about, letting you come here without one!"

Olivia glanced at her husband, whose scowl had deepened. The housekeeper shook her head, then, with a huff, took Olivia's arm and ushered her inside.

The hallway, though smaller than at Montague's estate, seemed more cavernous, perhaps because it was devoid of any of the features that turned a mere building into a home. The floor was covered in polished marble stones, which seemed out of place in a room that was otherwise fashioned almost entirely of wood.

Dominating the hallway was a wide staircase, flanked by thick wooden banisters that swept up to form a gallery. Olivia glanced upward to where a chandelier hung from the ceiling. A black oval studded with thick candles, suspended by a thick chain, it looked more like an instrument of torture than one of light.

She shivered and drew her shawl about her, then glanced toward her husband, who stared at the foot of the staircase, hands curled into fists, jaw bulging as if he gritted his teeth.

The housekeeper tutted and took Olivia's elbow. "If Master Charles won't tend to you, child, *I'll* take you to the morning room, where there's a fire all ready. Master Charles, are you coming?"

He glanced up, his eyes unfocused. Then he shook his head and gestured with his hands. The housekeeper let out a huff.

"Surely the estate affairs can wait when your wife's needing attention?"

With another huff, she led Olivia past the staircase and into a room that carried a smell of lavender and wood polish that could not completely conceal the odor of damp and dust. Then she excused herself and left.

Olivia glanced about the room. Dark-purple curtains—a color that matched the furnishings—seemed to absorb the light. The wood-paneled walls were adorned with candle sconces fashioned in a similar style to the chandelier, with the same hint of rust at the edges. A stone fireplace in which a fire blazed dominated the far wall, and a longcase clock fashioned from dark wood ticked in the corner. Unlike the hallway, the floor was fashioned from polished wood, forming a crisscross pattern. A round table covered in a lace cloth stood in the center of the room on a blood-red rug dotted with a pattern in purples and greens.

A maid entered carrying a tray. With soft blonde curls peeking from her servants' cap, clear blue eyes, and rounded cheeks, she could not have been more than fifteen years of age. She gave a shy smile and bobbed a curtsey, then placed the tray on the table.

"Your tea, your ladyship."

"Thank you...?" Olivia raised her eyebrows.

"Susie, your ladyship," the maid said, curtseying again. "Shall I pour the tea, or will you be wantin' to pour it yourself? Beggin' yer pardon for being so forward."

"I can manage on my own, thank you," Olivia said. "After all..."

After all, I'm hardly a fine lady incapable of serving tea.

"Very good, your ladyship," the girl said. "May I be so bold as to wish you well? We're all right glad that the master's returned and brought a lady to Penham."

"I'm no…" Olivia hesitated, then nodded and smiled. "I'm glad to be here also, Susie," she said.

"I've made your chamber ever so pretty, your ladyship. You just ring the bell when you've finished your tea, and I can show you. I've put some of the roses in a vase to make it bright for you. The rose garden's in a right state, but I managed to find enough, and I'm sure when the master hires a gardener, he'll—"

"Susie!" came a voice from outside. "The mistress won't want your chatter at the best of times, and certainly not when she's tired from her journey."

"Comin', Mrs. Brougham!"

The maid curtseyed again, then exited the morning room, leaving Olivia alone.

And I am alone.

Her husband couldn't wait to get away from her.

Then she admonished herself. What right had she to expect him to be at her beck and call? He must have business to see to. Montague always retreated to his study the moment he returned to Rosecombe to deal with whatever little troubles his steward presented him with. Men were not great drinkers of tea. Neither, as so many ladies of Society deigned to tell her, did they relish the company of ladies.

And Olivia's husband was all man.

She poured herself a cup, then approached the window.

There was no denying the beauty of the landscape that stretched before her, undulating toward a horizon that was dotted with treetops and a hill in the distance, tinged pink in the evening light. Thick forests covered the land to the left, above which a cloud of birds circled and cawed.

Settling in the window seat, Olivia sipped her tea and watched the world outside while the sun slipped behind the hill then disappeared.

BY THE TIME the supper gong rang, darkness had fallen. Olivia emerged from her chamber, which was, thankfully, free from the odor of damp, and descended the main stairs to the dining room that Susie had pointed out earlier. There was still no sign of her husband, and after waiting for him to appear, she ate alone, in silence, under the watchful eye of a footman who stared at her with a glimmer of contempt in his eyes. The slice of pie he'd placed before her had been oversalted and the pastry had the consistency of shoe leather. After nibbling on it and struggling to swallow the first bite, she set it aside and resolved to spend the rest of the evening exploring the building that was now her home.

Our *home*.

That was what her husband had indicated. Why, then, had he abandoned her the moment they entered it? Did he not wish to show her around, puffing out his chest with pride? Montague had taken such delight in giving her a tour of Rosecombe when she first entered it.

But her brother loved her, unlike…

With a sigh, she ambled along the hallway, peering into room after room, each one decorated in dark, forbidding colors, the faded furnishings frayed at the edges and reeking of damp and dust.

Except, it seemed, the kitchen, which glowed with warmth. Its welcoming air beckoned to Olivia as she descended the stairs to the servants' domain. Then she heard voices.

"Poor lamb—to eat alone her first night!" a roughened female voice said. "I can't think what the master's about. And the appetite of a bird. She hardly touched the pie."

Olivia froze and caught the handrail, trembling with shame. Her husband's indifference to her had not gone unnoticed.

"She's pretty enough, though," a male voice said. "I can see why he married her. There'll be a tidy fortune if her brother's a duke. Don't look at me like that, Nicola. Can't a man appreciate a pretty face?"

"Well, *I* like her," a lighter feminine voice said. "She was ever so civil to me."

"That doesn't mean you should prattle away at her," another voice said. "I hope you're not going to plague her with your gossip."

"No, Mrs. Brougham."

"And as for the rest of you—you oughtn't gossip about the lass. She's your mistress, and—"

The voice stopped as Olivia entered the kitchen. Its occupants were gathered around a large wooden table, the housekeeper and butler at either end, eating the remains of the pie. Several pairs of eyes regarded Olivia in silence. Then, at a sharp word from the butler they stood, chairs scraping against the stone floor.

"Lady Devereaux, is there anything the matter?" the housekeeper asked.

"N-no, Mrs. Brougham, I was exploring the house and wanted to see the kitchen."

"Whatever for, lass?" a plump woman sitting next to the housekeeper asked.

"I like to cook."

The butler arched a dark brow.

"The cook at my brother's house let me help her," Olivia said, her frustration giving her voice a note of petulance. "My brother didn't mind."

"Well, I hardly think—" the housekeeper began, but the plump woman interrupted.

"Let the lass cook if she wants, Mrs. Brougham. I've no objection to having her in my kitchen. Is there anything you need tonight, your ladyship? Some warm milk for when you retire? We've no chocolate, but I can send for some from the village in the morning."

"*I'll* bring some tomorrow," the young woman sitting next to

Jacob said, fixing her blue gaze on Olivia. The hostility Olivia had first spotted in her expression seemed to have gone. "Jacob and I can show you round the gardens tomorrow if you'd like that. Have you explored the house yet?"

"That's enough, Nicola," the housekeeper said. "You're almost as forward as your sister." She cast a stern glance toward the young maid who'd served tea.

"I'd like that," Olivia said. "And I'd like to meet all the tenants."

"Lord Devereaux should be the one to give you a tour of the estate," Mrs. Brougham said.

"But my husband is not…" Olivia hesitated, then nodded. "Of course, but perhaps you could show me around the gardens, Miss…?"

"Call me Nicola, Lady Devereaux," the young woman said with a smile. "Jacob can accompany us, won't you, Jake?"

A bell tinkled on the wall.

"That'll be his lordship wanting his brandy," the butler said. "See to it, Albert, would you?"

The cook let out a snort. "Not hungry enough to eat my pie, yet he's time for a brandy."

The butler cast a glance at Olivia, and her heart withered at the sympathy in his eyes. Mumbling, she excused herself and returned to the gloom of the main house. The servants resumed their chatter—doubtless gossiping about their mistress's lack of propriety.

What might they say if they knew she ranked below them on account of her birth? That would give them plenty to gossip about—the bastard Lady Devereaux.

She flinched as she voiced the words in her mind, then surveyed her surroundings. Now that night had fallen, the whole place was filled with shadows that flickered as she passed each candle on her way to the main staircase. The stairs were fashioned from the same color wood that lined the floors and the walls in every room. Why, then, was the floor of the hallway fashioned from marble—so out of keeping with the rest of the house?

Almost as out of keeping as I.

How was she ever to step into the role of mistress of this place? She couldn't even earn the servants' respect, let alone her husband's.

Weariness pressed upon her, and she reached for the stair rail. Her limbs had grown heavy—almost as heavy as her heart. Perhaps she ought to have asked for a brandy to soften the pain of inadequacy. But Eleanor had always said that while liquor might tempt one the most when spirits were low, it was a false cure. The temporary numbing of pain brought about the briefest of respites, shortly followed by a greater pain that endured far longer. With no friends, or even companions, to ease her pain, Olivia had only the memory of her sister-in-law to give her comfort.

She ascended the staircase to the gallery. The chandelier was almost at eye level with her now, and looked less sinister now that it had been lit. The flames of the candles flickered and danced as the structure swayed gently to and fro.

Which servant had risked their neck to light it?

She peered over the balustrade. From above, the marble floor looked even more out of place—cold gray against the warm tones of the wood. The candles cast patterns of light across the floor, and she leaned on the rail to get a better look.

A large hand caught her arm and yanked her back. She let out a soft whimper of pain as the hand tightened its grip, and she glanced up into the dark eyes of her husband. Her stomach clenched in fear at the raw intensity she saw there, which seemed to flash with fury—almost as if he were in a trance or suffering some kind of fit.

"Sir!" The valet approached in quick, purposeful strides.

Devereaux blinked, and the dark sheen in his eyes faded. Then he released her, and she stepped back, rubbing her arm. "What have I done, my lord?"

He stared at her.

"John?" She turned to the valet.

"Lord Devereaux was concerned that—" He broke off as Olivia's husband raised his hand.

"Husband?" She stepped toward him, but he shook his head, then turned and strode along the passageway toward the back of the house.

"What did I do wrong?" she asked John.

"Nothing, my lady," the valet said. "But I would suggest you take care at the top of the stairs. It's a long way down."

"Did he think I was foolish enough to fall over the rail?"

John hesitated, then glanced along the gallery. Devereaux had stopped and stood in the center of the passageway, a silent shadow.

"Good night, my lady."

Before she could reply, the valet followed his master and the two of them disappeared into a room near the end of the passage.

With a sigh, Olivia returned to her chamber. Shortly after, there was a knock, and she tempered the flare of hope. But it was the young maid with a cup of warm milk.

"Thank you, Susie," Olivia said.

"No trouble, your ladyship." The maid colored and stood in the doorway, shifting from one foot to the other.

"Is there something you wish to say?" Olivia asked.

"I don't know as if I ought, but Nicola, my sister, that is, said you'd be kind enough to consider it, so there's no harm in askin'."

"Asking what?"

"Whether you'd consider me as your lady's maid."

"Oh, I've no need for—"

"I'm a fast learner, honest I am, your ladyship. And I'll work ever so hard. Nicola says you're going to be wanting a friend here, seein' as you know no one, beggin' your pardon. I know all about how to look after gowns. Ma Lucy said I was as good as any seamstress you might find in London..." Her smile slipped. "God rest her soul. Passed last year, so she did."

"Your mother died? I'm sorry to hear that."

"Oh, Ma Lucy wasn't my mother. My real ma died when I was a baby. I never knew her, though Nicola remembers her. Da married Ma Lucy two years ago. But I have Nicola. She looks after me right and proper and keeps house for Da, though not for long if Jake offers for her. I think…"

She rattled on, and Olivia sipped her milk, smiling at the easy chatter—so unlike any conversation she'd endured at Society parties.

"So would you consider it, your ladyship?"

Olivia set her cup aside, and her heart softened at the eager expression in the girl's eyes. "How old are you, Susie?"

"I'll be fourteen come Michaelmas."

"You're only *thirteen?*"

Susie colored. "I've been in service since I was eleven, and I'm as good as any other. I know how to plait and curl hair too—did you see Nicola's hair tonight? Did that all myself—and she's promised to let me do her hair for the wedding. Jake's sure to offer for Nicola now Lord Devereaux's back. Nicola says he'll be wanting Jake at his side to manage the estate, seein' as they're brothers. And I do love weddings. I love seein' people so *happy*. Da was happy when he married Ma Lucy, though Nicola disliked her at first."

Susie paused and her eyes grew bright with moisture.

"You're goin' to ask that Ethel, aren't you?" she said, her voice wavering. "She's head housemaid, so I reckon Mrs. Brougham means for her to be your maid."

Olivia took another sip of her milk. Doubtless propriety demanded that she take the housekeeper's advice. But it was her, not Mrs. Brougham, that the maid would serve. And a lady's maid was not merely a servant who dressed her hair and tended to her clothes. Eleanor treated her maid like a trusted friend, and in return, Harriet was a great comfort, providing her mistress with company when Montague was in Town, tending to her when she was sick. Harriet had even helped deliver little Horatio when Eleanor was brought to bed four weeks before her time.

What might Olivia give for such a companion! And her heart had already warmed toward the eager girl standing before her.

She set her cup aside. "Very well, Susie, what do you say to tending to me for the next week or so, to see if we get along? Then, if we're both happy with the arrangement, you can have the position."

"Can I *really*?" The girl's eyes widened with eagerness. "*Thank you, your ladyship!*"

She rushed toward Olivia and wrapped her arms around her. Then she stiffened and withdrew.

"Oh, beg pardon!" she said. "I oughtn't have done that. But you seemed so kind, and…"

Olivia placed a hand on Susie's arm. "No harm done," she said, smiling at the girl's enthusiasm. "I prefer natural joy to cold propriety. Though I suppose if we're to convince Mrs. Brougham that you're suitable for the role, we must observe a little propriety."

"Will you teach me how to behave properly?"

"As much as I can," Olivia said, glancing about the chamber, "though I fear I'm also in need of instruction." She reached behind her neck to remove her necklace, fumbling at the clasp. "Susie, would you help?"

"Of course." The young girl removed the necklace and held it up to the light. "How pretty!"

"It's a gift from my sister," Olivia said. "Eleanor's my sister by marriage, but I love her as if she were of my own blood. I'd do anything for her."

"And I for Nicola," Susie said, placing the necklace on the dressing table. "Shall I brush your hair? I can plait it."

Olivia smiled and turned to face the dressing table mirror. Susie picked up a hairbrush and ran it through her hair in soft, gentle strokes.

"I hope Mrs. Brougham won't be too angry with me," Olivia said, almost to herself.

"Oh no!" Susie said, smiling, as she separated Olivia's hair and began plaiting it. "She's that delighted there's a mistress at Penham after so many years, especially since the previous mistress came to such a tragic end."

Olivia's stomach gave a flutter.

"What tragic end?"

"It was before my time here, but…" Susie shook her head. "Forgive me—Mrs. Brougham said I wasn't to gossip."

"I'll not tell anyone," Olivia said. "My sister-in-law says that what happens between a lady and her maid is sacred, and each must keep the confidence of the other."

"Very well." Susie paused plaiting and leaned closer, lowering her voice to a whisper. "The late mistress, Lord Devereaux's mother, that was, fell to her death on the stairs."

Sweet heaven! Charles's *mother?*

"Wh-when…?"

"Ten or twenty years ago, so Albert says. But he heard it from old Mr. Prosser, him who was gardener before he passed last winter and his brother took over. But he said that Mr. Prosser said that there was foul play."

"Foul play?"

"Lord Devereaux was with her at the time."

"My *husband?*"

"So Albert says."

"Albert should know better," a sharp voice said.

Olivia turned to see the housekeeper in the doorway. Susie let out a cry, her cheeks turning scarlet.

"I've told you before about gossiping, girl!" Mrs. Brougham said. "And what do I catch you doing? Telling tales you've no business telling."

"I didn't say anythin' that wasn't true."

"That's enough! Back to the kitchen with you. I'll see to her ladyship now and will deal with you later."

Susie burst into tears, bobbed a curtsey, and fled. The housekeeper closed the chamber door, then let out a sigh.

"I take it you didn't know about his lordship's mother?"

Olivia shook her head. "Please don't blame Susie—I asked her to tell me. Did the previous Lady Devereaux really fall to her death?"

Mrs. Brougham sighed and nodded. "Poor lady—aye, she did. A miserable life she had, if truth be told."

"A-and was my husband there?"

The housekeeper tilted her head to one side, and shame pricked at Olivia's heart as she caught the understanding in the older woman's eyes.

"Surely you don't suspect the master of..."

Her cheeks flaming, Olivia shook her head.

"It was twenty years ago, Lady Devereaux," Mrs. Brougham said. "Master Charles was a boy at the time."

"Forgive me, I—"

"And if there's a boy in the world who loved his mother more, I've yet to witness it. He loved his mother very much, and her death..." Mrs. Brougham paused, her voice cracking. "It's not for me to tell. Doubtless the master will tell you in his own time, when he's ready, and when you're..."

Olivia swallowed her shame.

When you're deserving.

That was what Mrs. Brougham was going to say. When Olivia had shown herself worthy in her husband's eyes, and perhaps in the housekeeper's eyes also.

The older women placed a light hand on Olivia's shoulder. "Forgive me, dear, I see I've been too harsh," she said. "It's just...I've known Master Charles since he was in leading strings, and he wouldn't hurt a flea. He adored his mother, and she him. She died saving his life and he hasn't spoken a word since."

Olivia let out a low cry. "Oh, poor man! How he must have suffered."

"It pains me to think you'd listen to tales about him. Even more so if you give such tales any credence."

"I don't take any notice of gossip, Mrs. Brougham," Olivia

said. "I've been the subject of it enough to know that it serves only one purpose, which has nothing to do with the truth, and everything to do with furthering the entertainment of the spiteful."

The housekeeper smiled. "The master was always a good-natured boy," she said, "and a good-natured boy will turn into a good-natured man. He must think a lot of you to marry you and bring you home to us. I despaired of his ever taking a wife, but I'm that glad he has. He doesn't make friends easily, but there's none more loyal to those that deserve it. You'll see."

Her smile resumed and she patted Olivia's arm.

"Well!" she said brightly. "We'd best get you ready. I'm sure he'll be visiting you later, and you want to look your best for him. Not that you don't already. You're a pretty thing—I can see why he's so taken with you." She clasped her hands together. "Oh, I can't wait to hear the sound of laughter and children once more! This old house has been silent and empty for too long."

Shaking with embarrassment, Olivia rose, and Mrs. Brougham's hand flew to her mouth.

"Bless me, I admonish young Susie enough for rattling on, and here's me doing the same! What must you think of us?"

"I think you're all very kind," Olivia said. "And, if you have no objection, might I ask a favor?"

The housekeeper raised her eyebrows. "A favor? From me?"

"I-I could ask my husband's valet, but it might not be appropriate, and I don't want to disappoint anyone by acting improperly."

Mrs. Brougham frowned. "My dear child, what *are* you asking?"

"I-I couldn't help noticing that you understood what my husband was saying with his hands," Olivia said. "He's shown me some gestures"—she moved her hands—"this is 'no,' for example, but I have so much more to learn. I-I know so little of being the mistress of a house, but I do want to be a good mistress, and more than that"—she hesitated, aware of the heat in her cheeks—"a good wife."

Mrs. Brougham's expression softened and she took Olivia's hand. "My dear child, of course I'll teach you." She lifted her hand to Olivia's cheek and brushed away a tear. "Hush now—there's no need to distress yourself. Marriage can be an ordeal for any young woman—a new home away from her loved ones, new responsibilities, not to mention a husband to please. It'll take time, but I'm sure you'll settle here and be happy."

She patted Olivia's cheek in a motherly gesture. "I'll leave you to your rest, your ladyship. Shall I send someone to tend to you in the morning? Breakfast is at eight."

"Yes, please, send Susie at seven thirty if you would."

"Susie?"

"I-I'd like to try her out as my maid, if you've no objection."

The housekeeper smiled. "None at all, dear. You're the mistress and have no need of approval from me."

"Do I not?"

"No, dear. If you're good enough for Master Charles, then you're good enough for me. I suspect you're more than good enough for him."

She dipped into a curtsey, plucked the cup from the dressing table, then exited the chamber.

Olivia climbed into the bed and rolled onto her side, facing the doorway. Voices and footsteps echoed in the distance as the servants tended to their duties. At length, a heavier set of footsteps approached, and her skin tightened in recognition. They drew near, seeming to slow as they approached her chamber, and she caught sight of a shadow beneath the doorframe. Her body warmed with anticipation and shame as she recalled the events of the night before. But this time, she was prepared for him—for whatever he meant to do to consummate their union.

She curled her fingers around the bedsheet and held her breath. But, after a pause, the shadow moved and the footsteps resumed their path, diminishing until they faded into the distance.

She ought to have been relieved, but for the second night in a row, she lay back while the tears spilled onto her cheeks.

CHAPTER TWENTY-ONE

"A RE YOU WELL, sir?"

Charles spooned sugar into his teacup and stirred it. He lifted it to his lips, his hands trembling. Hot tea splashed onto the tablecloth and he lowered the cup with a clatter.

It had all been so real.

If he closed his eyes now, he'd see the same image that invaded his dreams last night—his mother's vivid blue eyes, wide with shock, staring into his own as the spark of life drained from them. He could almost taste the thick, metallic tang of blood that had choked the air, almost feel its sticky warmth as it seeped into his clothes and marked the floorboards with an eternal stain of death...

"Sir!"

He jerked his head up to see John staring at him.

"*Four* sugars, sir? Do you not want to keep your teeth?"

The valet chuckled then cut into his bacon. The knife scraped on the plate and Charles winced.

"At least Mrs. Groves can cook bacon," John said, chewing on a slice. "That pie last night! If you wanted to lose your teeth, you should have had some. Or you could use it as a doorstop if you prefer."

Charles pushed his plate aside and his fork clattered onto the floor. John's laughter died.

"What's the matter, sir?"

Charles lifted his trembling hands. *I'm not obliged to tell you everything.*

John tilted his head to one side. "You've had the dream again, haven't you? I should have known, considering how you behaved toward your wife, poor lady."

I've done nothing to her.

John snorted. "You gave her a fright when you grabbed her at the top of the stairs, then marched off as if the very touch of her disgusted you. She could be forgiven for believing that you want nothing to do with her. But she's hardly likely to suffer your mother's fate."

Why not?

"Because you're not your father."

Charles sipped his tea, wrinkling his nose at the sickly-sweet taste. Why was it that sugar was supposed to calm a person's nerves yet the taste of it made a man want to retch?

"You shouldn't have married her if you were going to shut her away and ignore her," John said. "Women don't like to be ignored."

I shouldn't have come here.

"What, to breakfast?"

Charles shook his head. *To this cursed house.*

"It's just a house," John said. "It's what you make of it that counts. Mrs. Brougham was right in that the house needs happiness and laughter. But the responsibility for that—and your little wife—lies with you."

I don't pay you to cast judgment.

The valet shrugged and took another mouthful of bacon. Charles waited for a response, another remark about his inadequacies as a master and husband, but none came. They continued to eat as the longcase clock in the hall outside struck eight times.

At length, Charles gestured with his hands.

My wife fears me.

"Is that why you ignore her?" John said. "Why you refused to dine with her last night? Perhaps you find her as distasteful as that pie?"

Of course not. Don't be a fool.

"Then do something about it," John said, his voice rising. "You made a vow to her brother, and Whitcombe isn't a man to be denied. With your estate still in need of funds, you cannot forgo that additional ten thousand. You must consummate the marriage. Surely you can't find her *that* repulsive? If I were you, I'd..."

John froze, then muttered a curse.

The skin on the back of Charles's neck tightened as he caught the faint scent of rose.

No...

Gripping the edge of the table, he rose and turned to see his wife standing in the doorway.

John leaped to his feet, as if a hot poker had been inserted into his arse. "L-Lady Devereaux, good morning."

She parted her lips as if to respond, then closed them again, the color draining from her face.

"Will you join us for breakfast?" John said. He approached the place setting opposite Charles and pulled the chair back. For a heartbeat she stared at it. Then she shook her head and retreated, her footsteps fading into the distance.

"You should go after her," John said.

And frighten her even more? Charles signed. *I have things to do.*

"Your steward can wait."

Not when today's the only day that suits us both. I must visit the tenants' properties while the weather holds.

"I suppose that's as good an excuse as any."

Charles let out a huff. Why did John always find a way to slip under his skin? Perhaps because he was one of the few people who could look into his soul. Did John realize that Charles was as fearful as his wife? Not fearful *of* her, of course, but of furthering her distress. She seemed such a fragile little thing, with no knowledge of the world and none of the hardness that glittered from the eyes of more sophisticated women.

But with each step he took, each gesture of his hand, he only succeeded in widening the gap that existed between them.

He was a coward for avoiding supper last night, and a fool for resisting the urge to visit her chamber. But the last thing he wanted to witness was the terror in her eyes of their wedding night.

Very well. Tell her I'll join her for supper tonight.

John grinned, revealing even white teeth—and a morsel of bacon stuck between them. "Very good. I'll tell her maid."

She has a maid?

"She appointed Susie as her personal maid last night."

Charles raised his eyebrows. Who the bloody hell was Susie?

"The one barely out of the nursery."

Oh, *her*. She'd scuttled away in wide-eyed terror when Charles encountered her in the hallway yesterday afternoon. She feared him almost as much as his wife.

Devil's breeches, what had he done to deserve their fear? No man could call himself a man if he terrorized the timid. It made him no different to those who had tormented him at school, no different to the man who sired him, who tormented his mother to death.

"I'll ask Mrs. Groves to prepare something other than pie for supper," John said. "You wouldn't want your wife to choke on her food while you're wooing her."

I want you to join us.

John stared at Charles's hands, then barked with laughter. "Are you in need of a chaperone to lessen your fear?"

No. To lessen hers.

John's laughter died and he nodded. "Very well."

They continued eating in silence, and Charles focused his attention on the sounds outside—the distant clatter of pans in the kitchen below, the chatter of servants. But the one sound he yearned for—his wife's soft footsteps—was absent.

A footman appeared to inform him that Mr. Carlton was

waiting in his study. Charles drained his tea, gestured for John to follow, and exited the breakfast room. Today he'd discover exactly how much of the ten thousand Whitcombe had given him would need to be spent.

And how badly he'd need the other ten thousand he had yet to earn.

CHAPTER TWENTY-TWO

*H*E DOESN'T WANT *you.*
You disgust him…

Olivia stumbled on the path as she turned her foot on a stone.

A jolt of pain shot through her ankle, and she lifted her head upward and screamed at the sky through the treetops.

"Leave me be!"

But no matter how hard she strove to banish the voices from her mind, they followed her everywhere. Even in this remote part of the estate they plagued her with their taunts, sharpening into the brittle tones of the debutantes who'd triumphed over her as she limped through her Season from one disastrous party to another.

Her husband had made no attempt to conceal his lack of regard for her, but it was another level of torment to hear his disdain declared so starkly by his valet.

Surely you can't find her that repulsive…

How he must loathe her if he couldn't bring himself to touch her, not even for ten thousand pounds.

As for Montague…

Her brother—the one man she believed actually cared for her—thought so little of her that he had to bribe her husband to bed her.

After the initial shock of hearing the valet so casually refer to the transaction as if she were a piece of rotten meat that not even a ravenous dog would dare take a bite of, Olivia had summoned sufficient courage, aided by a little brandy she'd appropriated from a nearby parlor, to return to the breakfast room to confront her husband. But he'd gone. According to the footman, Devereaux had ridden out with his steward and was not expected to return before supper.

An afternoon touring the gardens had only served to increase her despair. They were in a worse state than the house—overgrown, choked with weeds and the rosebushes in desperate need of attention, their leaves dotted with brown specks. As to her companions—Jacob was gallant enough, but his deep-set eyes only served to remind her of the man who'd declared his disgust of her. And Nicola—though more congenial than at their first meeting, showering Olivia with gratitude for employing her younger sister—could do nothing to lessen Olivia's melancholy. For Nicola clung to Jacob, her eyes filled with devotion and desire as he steered her about the gardens. And Jacob, though not returning Nicola's devotion, at least didn't look on her with distaste.

After she'd had her fill of their company, Olivia sought solitude elsewhere, unable any longer to conquer the sour taste of envy that clung to her soul at the sight of a couple who, while perhaps not in love, at least took pleasure in each other's company.

And the only refuge to be had was in the forest, away from the house, hidden deep among the trees.

Her foot caught another stone and pain exploded in her ankle as she crashed to the ground, reaching out to break her fall. For a moment, she lay still, biting her lip to stem the sobs, waiting for the pain to subside. What a pathetic creature she was, shedding tears at the slightest provocation!

No wonder he despises me.

When the pain had lessened to a dull, throbbing ache, Olivia struggled to her feet, wincing at the soreness in her palms, then limped toward a tree.

Heavens! That hurt.

She stiffened as she heard a rustle from behind and leaned against the tree. Then she heard a high-pitched squeal that was quickly silenced.

A mouse, most likely, meeting its end at the talons of a predator. A fox, perhaps? When she'd crossed the open land leading toward the forest, she'd spotted a russet-brown, bushy-tailed creature darting toward the tree line.

She glanced back, but there was no sign of a creature. Nor could she see the main house, concealed by the trees and the brow of the land, which sloped downward.

It would be a long trek back, but she had no wish to return just yet. For the first time since she arrived at Penham Park, she was free of its inhabitants, at least for a while, her only companions the rooks circling overhead, and the occasional cow lowing in the distance.

At least they *won't judge me for my birth or think me repulsive.*

Or have so little regard for her that they felt the need to pay another a fortune to bed her.

"Oh, brother, *why?*"

The forest muffled her cry, and she continued along the path, each step taking her further away from torment. The scent of pine filled the air, and she drew in a lungful, willing her mind to calm. Pain flared in her ankle again and she paused and drew her shawl about her shoulders, listening to the song of the wind through the trees.

But there was no wind. Closing her eyes, she focused on the sound. It was deeper, more musical, varying in tone, and it came from ahead, not above. The rush of water, perhaps? Jacob had said something about a nearby river earlier that afternoon, though he'd warned her not to look for it on her own.

Yet another man who considered her incapable, unworthy.

Olivia glanced at her palms where the skin was grazed and smeared with dirt, then she flexed her fingers, flinching at the soreness. If she could get to the water, she could at least wash the dirt off.

Jacob be damned. Devereaux be damned.

She glanced about, her heart beating in anticipation even though she'd spoken in her mind. But no response came. Emboldened, she tilted her head up once more and raised her voice, venting her frustration at the husband who did not want her.

"Devil take him!"

A twig snapped from behind, and Olivia stifled a scream.

It's just a fox, you simpleton.

Footsteps approached, and her gut twisted in fear.

Ignoring the pain in her ankle, she continued toward the sound of the water. She'd be safe there. Most animals disliked the water. Her brother's pointer refused to get his feet wet, much to Montague's frustration.

She heard another footstep, this time closer. Gripped by panic, she started to run. She cried out as pain shot through her ankle, and stumbled forward, almost losing her footing. The footsteps gathered in pace, the very earth beneath her feet seeming to vibrate, and she broke into a sprint.

Then a large hand caught her arm. She screamed, but the hand yanked her back and slammed her against a hard object. She struggled to break free, but an arm snaked around her waist.

"Let me go!" she cried, but her assailant made no move. She tore at the arms holding her, but they remained firm, neither tightening nor loosening their grip. They merely waited in silent patience, as if her captor knew she would tire eventually.

And he—or it—was right. Gasping for breath, an ache forming in her chest, Olivia's struggles weakened and, sobbing, she grew limp.

"Shh…"

The warm breath of a whisper caressed her neck, and she lifted her gaze and froze.

It was her husband.

Jaw bulging as if he gritted his teeth, he regarded her through hooded eyes. His brow was furrowed into the frown he permanently wore, but rather than anger in his eyes, she saw fear.

Then she blinked, a film of moisture covering her eyes. What a fool she was! As if *he'd* be afraid, while chasing her down like a hunted animal!

She resumed her struggles, but he remained firm, his expression unchanging, body unyielding. Then, slowly, he turned and nodded to the path. She blinked once more, then looked ahead.

Her heart plummeted at what she saw.

Not more than three feet ahead, the path disappeared. The ground fell away in a sheer drop to a mass of dark water that boiled and swirled some fifty feet below, forming spray that danced over jagged rocks.

Olivia curled her fingers into her husband's sleeve, clinging to his solid form. He stepped backward, slowly, until they were clear of the edge. Only then did he release her.

He gestured with his hands, and she shook her head, unable to temper the tremors in her body.

"I-I'm sorry, I don't understand you."

He pointed to the cliff edge, then repeated the gesture.

"I don't understand!" she cried. "Why won't you speak to me? Or is the notion of such a thing even more repulsive than the notion of being married to me?"

He flinched and shook his head. Then he gestured more slowly, pressed his hand to his heart, and pointed to the cliff edge once more.

"Are you saying I was a fool for placing myself in danger?"

He shook his head again and held his hands to his heart.

"Or...or that you feared I might fall?"

He nodded, then drew a finger along his throat.

"You feared I might die?" Olivia glanced toward the cliff edge, then the understanding that had sparked in her consciousness the moment she saw the river at the bottom of a sheer fifty-foot drop pushed to the forefront of her mind.

Had he not caught her, she would have fallen to her death.

She convulsed with nausea. A huge hand caught her sleeve, but this time she did not struggle as he drew her to him, holding her against his chest, his heartbeat pulsing faintly against her ear. A sob escaped her lips, but he remained still, the warmth from his big body seeping into her.

As her sobs subsided, he released her, then offered his hand. For a heartbeat, she hesitated, glancing up at him. But his eyes held no anger, nor judgment, only a plea. He gestured to the path leading back, and, understanding his meaning, she nodded.

The corner of his mouth quirked into a smile, but the smile morphed into a grimace as she stepped forward and stumbled against him with a moan of pain. He lifted his eyebrows in inquiry.

"My ankle's a little sore," she said.

His frown deepened, then, in a swift, smooth motion, he scooped her into his arms as if she weighed no more than a mouse.

"No, please! I can walk."

He arched an eyebrow and tilted his head to one side in the manner of a parent that refused to be deceived by a wayward child. Then he nodded toward her hands and dropped his gaze to his shoulders.

"Y-you want me to put my arms around your neck?"

His mouth quirked upward a little and he nodded.

"You're not going to put me down, are you?"

He shook his head.

She circled his neck with her arms, and a jolt of need rippled through her as she touched his skin. Then she winced at the soreness in her palms, and he frowned.

"I-I grazed my hands when I fell."

He dipped his head until his chin came into contact with her arm, closed his eyes, and inhaled. Then, tightening his hold, he opened them again, a determined expression in his eyes, and set off, following the path toward the edge of the forest.

Though Olivia had felt she'd been in the forest for hours, the return journey seemed to take mere moments. Her husband never broke his stride once, moving swiftly through the forest and the meadows, not slowing when the ground sloped upward more steeply. As they approached the house, Olivia caught sight of her maid running toward them, followed by the housekeeper.

"Oh, thank the Almighty!" Mrs. Brougham cried. "Lady Devereaux, I was so worried. We've been looking all over..." Then she let out a cry. "Oh my, *look* at the state of your gown! What's happened?"

Devereaux set her down, then made a series of gestures.

The housekeeper nodded. "Very good, sir. Come, Susie, stop dawdling and give me a hand."

Devereaux carried Olivia into the house, his boots clacking on the marble floor. He strode toward the morning room and kicked at the door, which swung back and slammed into the wall. Then he crossed the floor and laid her on the sofa.

"Really, there's no need..." she began, sitting up, but then he took her shoulder and gently, but firmly, pushed her back. He slipped a cushion under her feet, his touch featherlight despite the size of his hands.

Then he drew up a chair and sat. He placed his elbows on his knees and leaned forward, fixing his gaze on her.

"Husband, I—"

"Shh..." He placed a finger on her lips, and she held her breath as he traced the outline of her mouth with his fingertip. His eyes, which she had thought a dark, unforgiving color, were, at close quarters, the color of rich chocolate, with small accents of gold that seemed to glow in the candlelight.

Her skin tightened with want as he caressed her jaw, and her breath hitched as he placed his fingertip under her chin and tilted her head upward to bring her lips closer to his.

She parted them in anticipation, pushing aside the disappointment of their wedding day, when he'd refused to kiss her. He moved a fraction closer, and her heart soared with hope.

Then the door burst open, and he withdrew. He leaped to his

feet as Mrs. Broughman entered with a tray laden with bandages and bottles, followed by Susie carrying a brandy decanter—the same decanter that Olivia had taken an illicit sip from earlier that afternoon.

"Susie and I can take care of the mistress now, if you're wanting to get on, sir," Mrs. Brougham said. "Men are neither use nor decoration when it comes to tending to the sick."

Anger flared in his eyes, and he made a gesture.

"Very well, have it your own way," the housekeeper said, an undertone of mirth in her voice. "Far be it for me to interrupt when you're atoning for your neglect of your wife." She gestured to a jar on the tray. "Don't be putting that on her foot, now. It's for her hands. Though I wouldn't be surprised if you tried to feed it to her."

Olivia held her breath. Such incivility in a servant would surely warrant dismissal. But her husband merely rolled his eyes, then made another gesture. Mrs. Brougham raised her eyebrows in mock horror.

"The same goes to you, Master Charles. You're not too old for the strap, you know." Then she gave a smile of indulgence. "Now don't be drinking all the brandy. It's for Lady Devereaux, though you may pour yourself one as a reward when you've done your duty."

Behind her, Susie stood, eyes widened in fear as she glanced from the housekeeper to their master.

"Come along, girl, there's no need to be standing here gawking," Mrs. Brougham said. Then she lowered her voice to a whisper. "Your mistress is in good hands, though I hesitate to say that in front of the master in case it goes to his head."

"Yes, Mrs. Brougham." Susie bobbed a curtsey then exited the room, and the housekeeper followed, leaving Olivia with her husband.

CHAPTER TWENTY-THREE

A S SOON AS the door closed, Olivia's demeanor changed, and the fear returned to her eyes.

And I'm responsible for that fear, Charles thought.

Devil's breeches, he might have lost her today! Perhaps he'd overreacted seeing her at the top of the staircase last night, but today… Today, she had been running toward her death. Running away from him.

It was blind luck that had compelled him to search in the forest. Perhaps it was because it was where he'd sought sanctuary from his father's loathing and the taunts of others. Trees and animals did not judge a man—they simply *lived*. They never troubled him for being flawed, for being unfit to bear the name Devereaux, unfit to live.

And unfit to marry.

Though they were as different as two people could be, Charles and his little wife were also the same in that they were both misfits, unable to conform to the rules of the world.

Perhaps, in the ashes of the world's disapproval, they could forge their own world and make their own rules. Together.

Because, despite his attempts to keep her at a distance, she was never far from his thoughts. While he'd toured the estate, listening to his steward's tales of woe regarding the state of the farms, their depleted livestock, and the worsening finances, he couldn't banish from his mind the image of his wife's stricken expression. When he'd entered the dining room for supper, ready to make amends, his disappointment when she hadn't joined him turned into debilitating fear when that young maid tearfully told him that her mistress was nowhere to be found.

Then, when he'd spotted her in the forest, moving toward the ravine, oblivious of the danger…

Only then did the understanding hit him like a battering ram.

He couldn't live without her.

"M-my lord?"

What sweet relief it had been to hold her in his arms—her delicate body, so sweet and softly rounded, her lips parted in offering of a kiss…

Curse Mrs. bloody Broughman for interrupting! He was now left with a cockstand he could do nothing with.

"Husband!"

He glanced up to see his wife staring at him.

"Are you well?"

He almost laughed at the absurdity. Here she was, injured having narrowly escaped death, asking after *his* health!

Hurt flickered in her eyes. "Do I amuse you?" she said.

No, you intrigue me.

She stared at his hand movements, then shook her head. He rose and poured a brandy.

"Will I ever understand you?"

Her voice was almost inaudible, and when he turned to face her, her cheeks colored. He offered her the brandy glass, and his heart fluttered as her fingers brushed against his. Then he picked up Mrs. Brougham's tray, placed it at the foot of the sofa, and kneeled beside it. The tray contained a bowl of water, wisps of steam rising from the surface, strips of linen, small pieces of cloth, and a squat jar of deep-blue glass, stoppered with a cork.

He motioned to Olivia's hands, and she set the glass aside and held them out. The skin at the heel of her palm glowed red, jagged and broken in places and embedded with specks of dirt.

With his free hand he plucked a cloth from the tray, dipped it into the water, and squeezed it until droplets splashed into the bowl. Then he lifted his gaze to hers.

Forgive me, for I fear it will hurt.

She blinked, slowly, as if she understood, then lowered her gaze to her hand and nodded. An insignificant gesture, but it was an expression of trust for him to treasure.

He pressed the cloth against her palm and, though she stiffened, she showed no sign of pain. Emboldened, he continued, wiping her palm until all traces of dirt had gone, before repeating the process with her other hand. Then he placed her hands on her lap, palms upward. Tiny red droplets swelled on her skin, and he dabbed them with the cloth until the bleeding stopped.

He picked up the jar Mrs. Brougham had said was for her hands. Foolish old woman! Did she think he didn't know? How many times had she administered that salve to him when, as a boy, he'd sustained scrapes and cuts—some from falling out of trees, others administered at the hands of bullies...

He closed his eyes to suppress the memory of his father's beatings—the burn of the lash on his back, the screams he'd uttered, pleas for mercy, the last words he'd ever spoken as his mother had tried to defend him...

"Charles!"

His wife's voice returned him to the present, her wide-eyed expression heavy with concern.

Sweet Lord, she'd spoken his name! Not *my lord*, or *sir*, or *husband*. And his body responded, his manhood twitching in eagerness.

"I'm sorry, I didn't mean to..." She hesitated. "You've never said how you expect me to address you."

Devil's breeches, does she think herself no better than a servant?

He smiled and nodded.

Her eyes widened, as if in surprise. "A-are you trying to tell me that you have no objection to my calling you by your given name?"

He smiled again.

"D-do you like me calling you Charles?"

He nodded, and she rewarded him with a smile of her own.

Sweet heaven, she was a glorious thing when she smiled like that! What might it be like to kiss those lips? Of course, they were his, by right, to claim, but he had no right to take advantage of her. She already thought him a savage beast.

He uncorked the jar, releasing the woody aroma of herbs, then dipped a fingertip into the contents—the smooth, sticky salve—running it along the surface, leaving an indent. A globule of creamy-white ointment glistened on his fingertip, and he inhaled, reliving the comfort he'd once taken from its soft scent, so many years ago—in another lifetime.

Olivia closed her eyes, her nostrils flaring, then opened them.

"Lavender," she said, "and, if I'm not mistaken, chamomile and calendula. Are they from the gardens here?"

He nodded. Most likely it was the same jar Mrs. Brougham had used to treat him with as a boy.

"I saw lavender in the gardens today," Olivia continued. "Not the others, but there might be some beneath the weeds. Mrs. Brougham says there's only one gardener here, but a garden of this size would need more. We could make inquiries in the village. O-of course, it's not for me to direct you on how to spend your money, particularly when…"

Her voice trailed away and the color rose in her cheeks.

Particularly when the dowry was still ten thousand short.

"Forgive me, I—"

"Shh," he interrupted. Cradling her palm in one hand, he applied the salve, caressing her as delicately as if she were a brittle autumn leaf, running his fingertip slickly over the broken skin. Then he applied salve to the other hand and wiped his hands on a cloth.

"I-I ought to speak to Mrs. Groves about supper," she said, leaning forward in an attempt to rise. "It must be ruined now."

He placed a hand on her arm and shook his head, motioning for her to lie back, then gestured to her foot.

"Oh," she said, her mouth forming a perfect, round "O." He touched the hem of her gown and her color deepened. Slowly, he drew back the folds of her gown to reveal her feet, then eased her shoes off.

It was easy to tell which ankle she'd injured. Even through her stockings he could see that the left foot was more swollen than the right. A thread of one stocking had snagged, forming a runner that followed a line along her calf, disappearing beneath her skirts.

Charles took a strip of linen from the tray, then lifted his wife's feet, sat on the sofa, and placed them on his lap. Her breath caught as he touched her ankle. Then he lifted his gaze to hers and awaited permission. Her eyes clouded with confusion, then her blush deepened and she dipped her head, the coy gesture sending a pulse of heat through him. She nodded, an almost imperceptible gesture, but his hungry soul relished the consent it signified.

Holding his breath, Charles hooked his finger under the hem of her skirts and drew it along her leg, his fingertip following the line of the runner until he reached the top of her stocking, tied with a ribbon the color of honey that matched her eyes. He fumbled at the knot until the ribbon came loose, then he undid it and slipped the ribbon into his jacket pocket.

He paused and glanced up, to see her watching him, body tense, lips parted, her chest rising and falling with each breath. For several heartbeats they stared at each other, then she lowered her gaze to the top of her stocking and nodded. He hooked his fingertip around the stocking, then peeled it off her leg, his fingertips brushing against the soft pink flesh of her thigh. He gathered the stocking in his hand and began to lift it to his lips. Then, shame fluttering in his stomach, he dropped it on his lap and inspected her ankle.

The bones seemed sound, but a bruise was already darkening on the swollen flesh. He placed his hand over her ankle, caressing the skin with the pad of his thumb. Olivia caught her breath, but when he met her gaze, she smiled in response. On impulse, he rotated his hand, his gaze still fixed on her, and continued to caress her skin with his knuckles. Her eyes darkened, then she flicked out her tongue, moist and pink, and ran it across her bottom lip, leaving a sheen, emphasizing its sweet plumpness.

His cock strained in his breeches, hardening with each heartbeat. She shifted her feet, and her toes brushed against his rigid member. A low groan reverberated in his throat.

Sweet Lord, did she know what she was doing to him?

No. Her wide-eyed innocence was no act. He saw no slyness, no feigned desire designed to make him part with a coin. Instead, he saw gratitude, open and frank, with a frisson of pleasure.

Perhaps that was what whores spoke of when they talked of a woman's pleasure—not merely release, or physical gratification, but something to relish.

Might he also experience pleasure rather than merely a base release?

He lifted her foot and wound the strip of linen around her ankle, binding it firmly and securing the bandage with a knot. Then he lowered her skirts, placed his hand on her bandaged foot, and smiled.

"Thank you…Charles."

Her softly whispered words threatened to breach his defenses. How could he have ever thought she was anything but a true innocent, as pure and honest as he was tainted? She was an angel, and he was unworthy of her.

He moved to withdraw, but she caught his hand.

"*Please,*" she said, "don't leave me again. I-I must say something before I lose courage."

He raised his eyebrows, and her throat bobbed as she swallowed. Then she reached for her brandy glass and took a sip.

"M-my brother said that you could annul our marriage if you—if we—did not…"

She hesitated and closed her eyes. Then she opened them again and drained her glass, drawing in a sharp breath as she shuddered with a cough.

Did she fear him so much that she had to fortify herself with liquor?

"D-do you wish for an annulment?" she said, her voice wavering. "Am I so distasteful that you won't touch me—not even for ten thousand pounds?"

Shaking his head, he caressed her hand, then lifted it to his lips.

"Then, Charles, may I make a request?"

He nodded and kissed her hand.

"W-would you visit my chamber tonight? I didn't know what to expect before, but I'm ready now."

Sweet Lord Almighty! What had a beast such as him done to deserve such a sweet creature, offering herself even though she still feared him?

"Please, Charles," she said, moisture shining in her eyes.

He released her hands and gestured.

Yes.

Her eyes creased with a smile. "I remember what that means," she said. "Thank you."

He rose and crossed the floor to the bellpull and rang it. Shortly after, Mrs. Brougham appeared.

Bring my wife's supper in here so I may tend to her.

The housekeeper nodded, approval shining in her eyes, then patted his arm. "Maybe I don't need to take the strap to you after all, Master Charles."

Not the most appropriate response from a subordinate, but Mrs. Brougham's approval was something he'd craved since boyhood—perhaps because it was hard won, handed out only when he deserved it.

He glanced back toward his wife, settled on the sofa, a soft smile on his lips.

Perhaps, in time, he'd also come to deserve his wife.

CHAPTER TWENTY-FOUR

WHILE OLIVA SAT at her dressing table, Susie fussing over her hair, a soft knock came on the door. The maid opened it, then let out a squeak.

Olivia's husband stood in the doorway, dressed only in his breeches.

"Oh! L-Lord Devereaux, I-I didn't expect…"

"It's all right, Susie," Olivia said. "You may go."

"But…"

"I'll be all right," Olivia said, meeting her husband's gaze.

Susie approached the door and cringed, dwarfed by Charles's huge frame. Then she bobbed a curtsey and teetered sideways. He caught her elbow and she whimpered, but he smiled and nodded.

"Th-thank you, my lord."

She curtseyed again, then fled, closing the door behind her.

He sighed and glanced at the door, fingering his signet ring.

"She's young," Olivia said. "Anyone would be wary of a man such as yourself, let alone a maid hardly out of the nursery."

He tilted his head to one side and frowned.

"I-I mean a titled man," she said. "I was terrified of Montague when I first met him, and you're so much…so…" She gestured toward him.

So much bigger.

He approached her, his footsteps hesitant, then gestured with his hands.

"Wait," she said. "I've just the thing you need."

She plucked a piece of paper and pencil from the dressing table and held them up.

"I had Mrs. Brougham place these around the house—at least while I'm still learning your hand gestures."

Astonishment flicked across his expression, then a spark of pleasure flared in his eyes as he reached for the paper.

"I had better learn quickly," she said. "I wouldn't want to use all your paper, given how expensive it is, but I suppose after tonight…"

She broke off, cringing with shame, but when she looked up, she saw only kindness in Charles's eyes.

He stooped over the table and scribbled on the paper.

Thank you.

He glanced toward the bed, and Olivia's heart gave a flutter of anticipation. Trembling, she approached the bed.

He continued to write, then held up the paper. It trembled in his hands, as if caught in a breeze. But there was no breeze. He was as nervous as she.

She took the paper and read the words.

I will be as gentle as I can.

"I know," she whispered. "I-I trust you."

Doubt darkened his eyes. Did he think so little of himself that he was incapable of earning her trust? He had already earned it, tending to her with such kindness, not chiding her for her recklessness. Did he require another gesture of trust?

I have nothing to give him.

Except myself.

Swallowing her embarrassment, Olivia gripped the hem of her nightgown, then pulled it over her head, discarding it on the floor.

The cool air tightened her bare skin, and her husband stepped forward, a low growl rumbling in his chest.

Had she been too forward? Eleanor said that Montague liked

it when she removed her garments for him. Perhaps Charles had different tastes.

Aware of his gaze on her, Olivia climbed into the bed. Then he unbuttoned his breeches. Heat prickled on her skin as he stepped out of them, and that part of him that she feared, but also yearned to see once more, sprang free, jutting proudly from the nest of thick, dark curls at the top of his thighs.

He picked up the solitary candle and raised his eyebrows in inquiry.

Darkness would lessen her shame at being so exposed to him. But what if he preferred the light? Eleanor said that some men liked to look at a woman's body, and that she relished being looked at by Montague. But the sensations swirling throughout Olivia's body and mind—the heat from Charles's gaze and the shame as her wantonness—threatened to overcome her.

Then he blew sharply and extinguished the candle. A puff of smoke dissipated in the air, and a tiny orange glow at the tip of the wick reflected in his eyes before it disappeared.

Olivia exhaled, then her breath hitched as the bed shifted under his weight. He slipped under the bedsheet, and she suppressed a cry as their bodies touched. The raw, masculine scent of him filled the air and she inhaled, savoring his woody aroma. He cupped her face and coaxed her head around to face him, and she caught the faint glow of his eyes in the darkness.

He grew still. Did he not wish to continue? Had his valet spoken the truth and he found her repulsive? But then he brushed his mouth against hers. His lips were warm and soft, with the faint taste of spice. He let out a sigh, his warm breath caressing her skin.

Then she understood. He was waiting for her consent.

"Yes," she whispered. "I-I want this."

Gently, he rolled her onto her back, then climbed on top of her until they were chest to chest. A fizz of need rippled over her skin as he shifted position, and she focused on the delicious, unfathomable sensation until it centered on her breasts, where her nipples had hardened to painful points against his chest.

Sweet heaven, what was happening? Her skin burned as if it were on fire and a wicked heat bloomed between her thighs. She shifted her legs, and shame engulfed her as they grew slick with moisture.

Then she felt his length, as hard as steel, against her thigh. He placed a hand on her leg then teased her thighs open. But this time, she was ready. Conquering her embarrassment, she parted her legs for him, and he settled on top of her, as if he fitted there, the tip of him prodding against her center.

He grew still once more. She reached up and grasped his arms. His muscles, hard and toned, bulged with effort as he held his body up to prevent his weight from crushing her.

"Don't stop. Please…Charles."

As she whispered his name, he let out a deep sigh and sank inside her. He paused for a heartbeat, then thrust forward, and she bit her lip at the sharp nip of pain. He withdrew, slowly, then stilled once more, but she circled her arms around his neck, willing him to continue. With a low groan, he thrust inside her again. The pain lessened to a dull ache as he continued to move in and out, his breathing growing deeper and harsher. Then, with a sharp exhalation, he plunged into her, shuddering, and a rush of warmth flooded into her body. He clung to her, shaking, while his breathing subsided, then he withdrew.

Despite the soreness between her thighs, a sense of loss filled Olivia as looked up at him. Her eyes having grown accustomed to the dark, she saw his gaze fixed on her, brow furrowed with concern.

"I-is that… I mean—have we…?"

He nodded and sat up. Then he placed his hand against her cheek.

"Thank you," she whispered.

He shook his head, took her hand, and kissed it, brushing his lips over her knuckles. Then he climbed off the bed, pulled on his breeches, and padded over to the door. He opened it, paused for a moment to glance back at her, then slipped outside, closing it behind him.

The deed was done.

Eleanor had said that a woman's first time could be painful, but with a man who loved her, it could also be immensely pleasurable. Yet though Olivia had caught a faint glimpse of distant pleasure from her body's reaction, in the end, she had only felt pain.

Had *he* taken pleasure from it? Other than a few sharp exhalations, he'd given no sign.

Oh, Eleanor—if only I had you here to guide me!

Olivia rolled onto her side, swallowing her shame at the stickiness between her thighs. Sharp cramps jabbed at her stomach, and she curled her knees up, willing them to subside, then waited for sleep to come while the echo of her husband's footsteps faded.

CHAPTER TWENTY-FIVE

CHARLES HAD EXPECTED his wife to remain in her chamber the next day, but as he entered the breakfast room, his valet in tow, she was sitting at the end of the table, the morning sun forming a halo around her hair. She rose as he entered, but he gestured for her to sit.

Blushing, she turned her wide-eyed gaze toward John.

Charles raised his hands. *Leave us.*

John glanced at the pile of devilled kidneys on the side table, longing in his eyes, then nodded and approached the door.

Sometimes—just sometimes—the valet possessed enough insight to be sensible of the feelings of others. It was a well-known fact that new brides bled like sows on the wedding night and were delicate the following morning. And Charles was hardly a small man—both in stature and, according to the whores he'd taken over the years, in girth.

"Mr. Richards, there's no need—" Olivia began, but the valet interrupted.

"There's every need, Lady Devereaux," he said. "I'll take my breakfast in the kitchen."

She nodded, then reached for her teacup, which rattled against the saucer as her hand shook. She resumed her attention on the plate in front of her, though she merely pushed her food from one side to the other, then back again.

Charles approached the side table, his gaze wandering to the sheets of paper stacked beside the dishes, a pencil placed at the side, and helped himself to eggs and a spoonful of kidneys. Then, dismissing the attending footman with a wave of his hand, he resumed his seat and began to devour his food, forcing himself not to glance in his wife's direction.

At length, she spoke.

"May I ask you something?"

He nodded.

"Last night… D-does it always hurt?"

Only for the woman, and only the first time.

She stared at his hand gestures, then glanced at the pile of paper.

Shit—how could he bring himself to write *that* down?

He contented himself with shaking his head.

"A-and the blood," she said, a tremor in her voice. "Eleanor said…" She shook her head. "It matters not. I-is that why you cut yourself…that night at the inn? So, the maid tending to the sheets…"

Devil's breeches, he wasn't prepared for the sort of conversation that should take place between a bride and her mother.

But Olivia had no mother, only a sister-in-law who'd failed in her duty in preparing her for the marriage bed.

"Why *did* you do it?" she said. "I-I mean…cut yourself that night?"

A wife whom her husband neglects on the wedding night is a source of ridicule. I would not have everyone at the inn gossiping about you.

She watched his hands, then gestured to the paper. "Please, I don't understand you."

He plucked a sheaf from the side table and scribbled on it.

So as not to shame you.

She read the words, then returned the paper and picked up her fork, once more pushing a kidney about the plate.

"A-am I now with child?"

Bloody hell, had the duchess not told her *anything*? Such matters were not suitable for the breakfast table, even between women.

Wrinkling his nose, he picked up the pencil, wrote on the paper, and thrust it at her.

I hope to God you are not.

She stared at the paper, then crumpled it in her hand.

Perhaps he'd been too harsh, but surely she didn't want to bring a child into the world. Not *here*. He had endured nothing but misery in this godforsaken house. It was enough of a sin to have this innocent creature endure a life here, let alone a child.

"What do you mean?"

He glanced up to see her watching him, her eyes shining with intensity.

"Do not all men wish for a child—an heir?"

Charles shook his head.

Foolish girl! Didn't she realize by now that he was not like other men?

"Your father must have wanted an heir—and sons love their fathers, do they not? My father..." Her cheeks reddened further. "I mean, Montague's father—played his wife false, but Montague still speaks of him with fondness. And my nephew Horatio adores his father. Would you not what that for—*Oh!*"

She let out a cry as he slammed his fist on the table, causing the crockery to rattle. Moisture beaded in her eyes, and she picked up her teacup once more, her hand shaking more violently.

Fuck. The last thing he wanted was to frighten her.

Forgive me. I have no wish to speak of my father.

She stared as he moved his hands, then shook her head. But rather than ask him to write the words she continued to sip her tea, as if she no longer cared.

Or as if she knew that whatever he tried to say would distress her further.

Curse it! This was why he wasn't suited to married life. He knew not what to say to her, even armed with pen and paper.

Silence stretched around the room, save for the clock ticking on the mantelshelf. Then Charles heard hoofbeats and the crunch of wheels on gravel. Olivia stiffened and turned toward the window.

There was a knock before John entered.

"The carriage is ready when you require it, sir."

Bugger. So soon? I can't leave her now.

John glanced at Charles's hands. "Sir, you told me this morning that you needed to visit London, and I thought…"

You thought it opportune to visit my banker now I've earned the additional ten thousand? Charles smacked his fist into his palm. *You think I can fuck my wife then rush to London while the bed's still warm to claim the reward?*

"N-no, sir, I just thought, what with the new carriage and all the expenses agreed with Mr. Carlton yesterday, that…"

Charles banged his fist on the table again, and his wife's fork clattered to the floor.

"I should excuse myself," she said. "I doubt this is a conversation you wish me to partake in."

She stood, then paused as Charles raised his hands.

Tell her I'm going to London.

John rolled his eyes. "Lady Devereaux, your husband wishes to convey his apologies, but he's required in London for the next few days."

"How many days?"

John glanced at Charles. "A fortnight, perhaps. No longer than a month."

"For what purpose, if it's not unseemly of me to ask?"

The slight edge to her voice was cause for celebration, as was the firm set to her jaw. Charles's little wife had some spirit, after all.

Do not tell her.

John, the treacherous bastard, ignored the request.

"The cost of refurbishing the estate buildings is considerably more than anticipated, and…"

"And my husband wishes to claim the ten thousand from my brother that he earned last night?"

She stared at Charles unwaveringly, then dipped into a curtsey.

"I'll excuse myself so that you can go about your business unencumbered."

She approached the door, but Charles stepped in her path.

Don't go. I can delay my journey. I've no wish to leave you if you need me.

He glared at John, who repeated the message. Olivia continued to stare at him, her lips trembling as John spoke the words. Then, after drawing in a deep breath, she shook her head.

"Don't let me prevent you from undertaking your business, my lord," she said. "My need for you to remain is nothing compared to your need to go."

She bestowed a smile on John—the fortunate blackguard—then exited the breakfast room.

"You ought to go after her, sir, while I finish packing your trunk."

Charles shook his head. *It would only make matters worse. Instruct Mrs. Brougham to take care of her.*

"And Jacob?"

If you must.

"Mr. Carlton says he's a capable young man and, after all, Jacob is your heir." John gave a grin. "Though given the events of last night, I ought to refer to him as your heir *presumptive*."

Fuck off.

John chuckled at Charles's crude gesture, then exited the breakfast room.

Less than an hour later, Charles stepped out of the main doors. The servants stood to attention, forming a line that led toward the waiting carriage bearing the Devereaux crest on the side. At the end of the line of servants stood—

His heart gave a little flutter.

At the end of the line stood his wife.

She was the better person. Had anyone distressed him, he'd have not wished to show them respect. As a child, he recalled hiding in the attic rather than wishing his mother a safe journey after she'd admonished him over some transgression. Had he known at the time that within a month she'd be cold in her grave…

If only he could have relived all the moments he'd shown childish unkindness toward his mother, and behaved differently.

So many regrets—and they cut as deep as his regret over how he'd behaved toward his wife, the sweet young woman he'd vowed to honor and protect.

The servants bowed and curtseyed as he passed them, and he paused to nod and smile at each one, including the young maid who tended to his wife. When he reached his half-brother, he stopped and gestured to John.

Tell him to take care of everything, including her.

Jacob's eyes widened. "Who are you—and what have you done with Charles Devereaux?"

So, his brother understood him. Charles frowned, and Jacob stepped back, raising his hands as if in surrender. Then Charles approached Olivia.

"I hope you have a safe journey, my lord—"

She broke off as he took her hand and shook his head.

"Charles," she said, her voice almost inaudible. He smiled encouragement, and her lips curved in response. "I shall do my best not to disappoint…"

He placed a finger on her lips, and his blood warmed as her soft breath caressed his skin.

You could never disappoint me.

Though he neither spoke nor gestured, hope flickered in her eyes, as if she understood. He placed his fingertips beneath her chin and tilted it up, relishing the sight of those sweet, plump lips. Swallowing his embarrassment, aware that several pairs of eyes watched, he brushed his lips against hers.

Her eyes flared with joy, and, for a heartbeat, she gave him a glimpse of what it might be like to live in harmony and happiness, to exorcise the ghosts of his mother and father. But when he glanced back at the dark, forbidding building that cast a shadow across the land, his hope diminished.

He released his wife's hand, then climbed into the carriage, motioning for John to follow. The sharp odor of fresh paint thickened the air, reminding him of the expense of the carriage and the necessity of his visit to London.

Then they set off, and he leaned out of the window. The servants were beginning to disperse, but Olivia remained still, watching as the carriage rolled along the drive. Before the carriage turned a corner, she raised her hand. He mirrored the gesture, placing his hand on the window, fixing his gaze on her until she disappeared out of sight.

CHAPTER TWENTY-SIX

O LIVIA WAITED UNTIL the carriage had gone before she lifted her fingers to her lips.

"Do you need anything, Lady Devereaux?"

Jacob stood before her, hands in pockets.

"Perhaps you might call me sister, given that we're related." She smiled. "If I recall, I asked you to do so when you showed me around the gardens."

"Of course I will…sister."

She cast her gaze about the building.

"It's a large house," Jacob said, "especially when you're alone."

And I am alone.

Olivia glanced at the drive in the direction of the carriage.

"I can ask Nicola to accompany you today," Jacob said. "I'm over at Mill Farm with Mr. Carlton to oversee the repairs to the roof. I'll send her over to the great house once she's finished her chores at home."

Olivia nodded. "She can stay for tea if she wishes. Is the farm in disrepair?"

"It's only the roof that needs mending. Mr. Faulkes has been taking good care of the house otherwise. Well, I'd best be off if I want to impress Mr. Carlton."

He nodded and walked off, whistling, disappearing around the side of the building. Olivia glanced at the servants who were dispersing, then approached the cook.

"Mrs. Groves, might I ask a favor?"

"Are you wanting to discuss the menu for supper, Lady Devereaux?"

"No, but I wondered…might I be permitted to join you in the kitchen? I have a fancy for shortbread, and I'd like to bake some today—then, perhaps, for my husband when he returns home."

"Bless you, your ladyship, you've no need to ask permission, certainly not from me. And, begging your pardon, I expect you'll need a bit of company now his lordship's away, and we can't have you rattling around in that big house all on your own."

"Nicola is visiting later."

The cook wrinkled her nose. "There's better company to be had hereabouts, I'm sure."

"Jacob thinks highly of her," Olivia said.

"Not for the right reasons. A bit too free with her favors, that one. She's the sort who'll do anything to snare a man if she thinks it worth her while. She took little notice of Jacob when he were growing up, until she realized he was heir to this place."

"Didn't she know he was my husband's brother?"

"She knew, all right. Taunted him for being"—Mrs. Groves lowered her voice and glanced over her shoulder—"*born on the wrong side of the blanket.*" She shook her head. "Poor lad. The old earl separated him from his mother and refused to let him live upstairs. Treated him worse than a servant, he did. Jacob could have turned out very wild, but Mr. Carlton took him under his wing. He's a fine enough lad, for all that he's a natural child, but then…"

The cook hesitated, blushing. "Forgive me, Lady Devereaux, I didn't mean—"

"You didn't mean me?" Olivia said.

Did the whole household know of her birth?

"Of course not, your ladyship. And we all treat Jacob as one of the family."

"Except he spends his time downstairs rather than in the house."

"It's how he prefers it. He can't be bothered with the life of a gentleman, much to Nicola Faulkes's displeasure. That little miss was all over him when she found out he's the heir. Of course, he'll not be heir for long."

She flicked her gaze to Olivia's belly, then gave a gap-toothed smile.

"We're all right pleased you're here, your ladyship. I hope I didn't give no offense when I referred to…" She made a random gesture.

Olivia shook her head. "I've heard worse, Mrs. Groves."

Mrs. Groves took her hand and patted it. "Well, you'll not hear it from anyone's lips here, lass. Master Charles would have them strung up by the toes."

"I doubt that."

"He said as much—or that man of his said it for him. Young Jim made mention of it, and the master overheard and had him dismissed. Don't you recall the lad who served supper the night you arrived?"

Olivia shook her head.

"He's found a position at Alderley Hall in the next village, so there's no harm done, but he's lucky Master Charles didn't take a crop to him."

"Mrs. Groves," a deep voice said, "I trust you're not engaging in gossip with her ladyship?"

The butler stood in the driveway, his eyebrows kitted together in a frown.

"Beg pardon, Mr. Reynolds, I was…was just…"

"Mrs. Groves was discussing the method she uses for making shortbread," Olivia said. "I offered to make some for tea."

The butler bowed. "Very good, your ladyship. Now, if you'll excuse me, we're a footman short and I'm interviewing prospective candidates. I trust I'll not be obliged to advertise for a new cook as well."

Mrs. Groves bowed her head. "No, Mr. Reynolds."

The butler nodded then returned to the house, muttering to

himself. "Pity. We might be presented with a pie that doesn't break our teeth."

The cook gave no sign that she'd heard. Not that Reynolds had spoken a falsehood. Maybe Mrs. Groves might permit Olivia to bake a pie also.

The butler turned and winked at Olivia, and she suppressed a giggle. Perhaps, in time, she'd come to feel at home here, even if she could never hope to be as happy in marriage as her sister-in-law.

⟫⟪

"I MUST SAY, that's the tastiest shortbread I've had here. Did you make it, Olivia? For I doubt Mrs. Groves did."

Olivia smiled at her companion. Nicola—or Miss Faulkes, as Mrs. Broughman insisted Olivia call her—had completely shed the initial hostility Olivia had seen on her first arrival at Penham Park. She'd been a little quiet during the tour of the gardens, deferring to Jacob, but today, now Olivia was alone in her company, she seemed to blossom.

"Nicola!" Susie said as she poured the tea. "You oughtn't refer to her ladyship by her given name. She's a *countess*."

"But we're friends," Nicola said, fixing her pale-blue gaze on Olivia. "We might even be sisters one day."

"Has Jacob made you an offer?" Olivia asked. Susie's hand shook as she handed her a cup. "Thank you, Susie."

"There! What did I tell you?" Nicola said. "Olivia's not like other ladies who wouldn't bother to thank the staff. She even baked the shortbread."

"I *know* that," Susie said. "Lady Devereaux let me try a piece."

"That's kind of her," Nicola said, reaching for her cup.

"I know. I'm so glad she took me on as her maid."

"I *am* in the room, Susie," Olivia said, laughing. She nodded to the biscuits. "Take another if you like."

"Can I?"

"Susie, don't be so forward," Nicola said, "and you must take yours in the kitchen."

"You're just the same as me, Nicky."

"I'm Lady Devereaux's friend," Nicola said. "There's a difference, as I'm sure Mrs. Brougham would point out, even if Olivia's too kind to say anything. And if Jacob and I…" She sipped her tea and shrugged. "Jacob is the earl's brother."

"Jacob eats in the kitchen with the rest of us," Susie said.

"Well, he *shouldn't*."

"He's welcome to dine in the main house if he wishes," Olivia said. "He's to inherit, after all."

Nicola narrowed her eyes, then reached for a slice of short-bread. Susie bobbed a curtsey then exited the parlor.

"Do forgive my sister. She's young and has yet to learn deco-rum. I hope she's giving satisfaction otherwise?"

"She's delightful, Miss Faulkes."

"Nicola, please, Olivia."

Olivia nodded, swallowing her discomfort. Friendships forged in the country developed at a quicker pace compared to London Society, where formal introductions were required before one could even speak to another, and given names were only used after months of intimacy. Nicola would, in all likelihood, be the closest Olivia might come to having a friend hereabouts. Her upbringing couldn't have been so different to Olivia's—raised on a tenanted property on a grand estate. And if she married Jacob, she might come to live in the main house.

If Jacob asked her.

"Will Jacob join us for tea?" Olivia asked.

"I told him to," Nicola said, biting the corner off a piece of shortbread. "But he's busy with that Mr. Carlton."

"Isn't that a good thing?" Olivia said. "They're seeing to the repairs to your father's farmhouse."

"I don't see why Jacob has to do it. He is the heir—at least, until you…"

She gestured to Olivia's stomach, and Olivia averted her gaze.

"Forgive me if I offended you," Nicola said.

Olivia shook her head. "It matters not."

Nicola rose to take the seat next to Olivia on the sofa. Olivia bit her lip as a warm hand took hers, the skin smooth compared to her calloused hands.

She glanced about the parlor. By right of birth, neither she nor Nicola belonged here.

"You're distressed. I can tell," Nicola said. "Jacob said you seemed upset this morning when the earl left. Are you"—she lowered her voice—"with child?"

Recalling her husband's words, Olivia sighed. "I hope not."

A flicker of emotion gleamed in Nicola's eyes that Olivia couldn't fathom. Surprise, perhaps?

"Don't you *want* a child?"

"My husband…" Olivia hesitated, then shook her head. Friend or not, such matters were not for the ears of others. "It's nothing."

Nicola leaned forward and embraced her. "My dear friend, I won't tell anyone. Not even Jacob, even though there should be no secrets between sweethearts or a man and his wife."

She tilted her head to one side, and Olivia shivered at the intensity in her eyes.

"You're sensible in not wanting a child," Nicola said. "Women die in confinement. And your husband is so…"

"So what?"

Olivia stared at her friend, who leaned closer.

"So *big*," Nicola said. "Imagine the size of his child! The old earl was just as big. They say the late Lady Devereaux almost died giving birth. She bled for weeks."

Olivia shifted her thighs at the memory of the pain when her husband had taken her last night—the soreness that still pulsed between her thighs, and the tight cramps that had beset her body shortly after.

"Nicola, I'd rather not speak of—"

"And there's Lucy."

"Lucy?"

"Pa's second wife."

Olivia nodded. "Susie mentioned her."

"Did she tell you how Lucy died?"

"No."

"She died in childbirth. I was there."

"Sweet Lord!" Olivia cried. "How horrible. Does Jacob—"

"No!" Nicola said, and Olivia winced at the sharpness in her voice. "Forgive me, I'm not supposed to say anything. Pa has never recovered, and he gets angry if I speak of it. You mustn't say a word to anyone, not even to Jacob—*please.*"

Nicola wiped her eyes and sniffed, and Olivia took her hand. "Of course I'll say nothing. Your secret is safe with me."

"And yours with me."

"What secr—"

"About not wanting a child." Nicola glanced toward the door. "I can help," she whispered. "My grandmother can brew a potion to prevent a child. She does it for the women at the brothel in the next town and won't mind if I bring you some if you promise not to tell."

"I don't think—"

"I'm only thinking of you," Nicola said. "I wouldn't want you to suffer the same fate as poor Lucy. I loved her so much, and…" She wiped her eyes. "I know we've only been acquainted for a little while, but I see you as a friend. A sister." She let out a small sob.

"Very well," Olivia said, "but I'll not need it."

Nicola's eyes narrowed, the pale blue glistening like ice. "Has the earl not—"

She broke off as someone knocked on the door, then the housekeeper entered.

"Your ladyship, is now a convenient time to discuss the household accounts? I'm sure Miss Faulkes has plenty to be getting on with at Mill Farm."

Olivia rose, glancing at the mantel clock. "Yes, Mrs. Brougham. Forgive me, I hadn't realized how late it was. Nicola—would you mind?"

"Of course not, Olivia," Nicola said, rising.

Mrs. Brougham frowned, then rang the bell. Shortly after, a maid arrived.

"Ethel, please show Miss Faulkes out. The rear entrance, if you please."

The maid curtseyed, then ushered Nicola out. As soon as the door closed behind them, Mrs. Brougham gestured to a chair.

"May I sit, your ladyship?"

Olivia nodded.

"It's not my place, but I'd advise you to take care with that young woman. She displays a degree of overfamiliarity most unbecoming, given your difference in rank."

"Do you disapprove of my having a friend. Mrs. Brougham?" Olivia said.

"Of course not, my dear, but Miss Faulkes must understand the respect due to you as the countess. She's nothing but the daughter of a tenant who acts above her station."

"But I was once—"

Mrs. Brougham placed a hand on hers, but, rather than the stifling demands of friendship, Olivia sensed only maternal concern.

"I know of your origins, my dear," Mrs. Brougham said. "But you're a countess now and must recognize the difference in rank between yourself and those around you. I'm not saying that you cannot be friends with Miss Faulkes."

"What *are* you saying, Mrs. Brougham?"

"That you must take care in whom you place your trust. Do not be deceived by an overly friendly face. A new bride entering into a house of strangers can trust only one person."

Olivia cocked her head to one side. "Her housekeeper, I suppose?"

Mrs. Brougham smiled. "No—her husband. And until anyone

else has earned your trust, I'd advise you to be cautious. I understand the necessity of Master Charles's going to London, but he ought to have taken you with him."

"The necessity?" Olivia said. "You mean financial?"

The housekeeper had the grace to blush. "He was insistent on proceeding with the repairs to the buildings as soon as possible. I only pray that he doesn't drive the estate into bankruptcy. His father almost did, on three occasions, though for reasons of profligacy rather than generosity."

"Generosity?"

"It's not my place to speak of it, but Master Charles has insisted that he pay for the repairs himself. He's even ordered twenty head of cattle for the Baldwins' farm and won't take a penny from Mr. Baldwin. He's not like his father, for certain. I told him the garden needs work, not to mention this house, but he insisted on giving priority to the tenants." She eyed Olivia. "He's a good man, your ladyship."

"Why do you feel the need to tell me he's a good man?" Olivia asked.

"Because he'd never tell you himself. All his life he's been a disappointment to those whose good opinion he's sought."

"He has no need of my good opinion, Mrs. Brougham."

"Does he not?"

"He's a man. He's master here. He can do what he wishes."

"Had he followed his wishes, he'd never have returned here," Mrs. Brougham said. "He'd have found a way to settle the debts and remain on the Continent, handing over responsibility of the estate to Jacob, who would have inherited. But he chose not to. Instead, he's returned, to a home that gave him nothing but unhappy memories, and brought a wife." She gave an indulgent smile. "Though he may deny it, he's accepted the responsibility of the Devereaux name, and we're all mighty glad of it. I know he's a little…*difficult* at times, but he's just as daunted by the prospect of making a life here as you, though he doesn't show it."

She patted Olivia's hand. "Well! I'm sure you've better things to do than listen to my ramblings. Shall we discuss the household accounts? I could send for Ethel to bring you another pot of tea. You're looking a little pale."

Oliva nodded, another ripple of nausea flowing through her.

"Tea it is," the housekeeper said. "Forgive me for speaking out of turn, earlier—it was out of concern for you."

Despite Nicola's professions of friendship, Olivia found more to trust in Mrs. Brougham's more measured advice. The older women carried an air of Eleanor about her, and for that, at least, she deserved Olivia's trust.

"Thank you, Mrs. Brougham," Olivia said. "I'm glad you're here."

"And I you," came the reply. "As is Master Charles, even if he cannot say it."

She exited the parlor, and Olivia sank back into her seat and placed her hand over her belly.

What if she *was* with child?

Her husband didn't wish it, despite what Mrs. Brougham said. However, whatever she might say to Nicola, Olivia wanted a child more than anything—someone to love without condition and to love her in return.

But could she weather her husband's wrath—or worse, his disappointment—if she had a child?

Chapter Twenty-Seven

"This is a somewhat unusual request, Lord Devereaux."

Charles looked up from the sheaf of papers emblazoned with the legend *Stockton & Stockton* and raised his eyebrows.

"Of course," the lawyer continued, "you employ me to follow your instructions rather than comment on your decisions."

Charles gestured to John. *Excellent. The fool understands what I pay him for.*

Stockton tilted his head until he was looking over the lenses of his circular-framed spectacles.

"Lord Devereaux says that he is determined in his decision," John said.

"Your wife is already adequately provided for, Lord Devereaux. Her brother settled a substantial annuity on her at Drummonds Bank. He negotiated a very generous interest rate."

That's her brother's business. This is mine. I've no wish for her to be dependent on anyone should she outlive me, not even her brother.

Charles nodded to John, who conveyed his words.

"She's a countess, Lord Devereaux," the lawyer said. "She'll want for nothing."

Charles raised his hands. *I want to be absolutely sure. My brother is my heir.*

"Heir presumptive," Stockton said after John translated. "Your wife might produce an heir herself. And you might outlive her."

In the event that neither occurs, I must ensure that she will not suffer even the slightest risk of destitution.

The solicitor's eyes widened after John responded.

"Very well, Lord Devereaux. I applaud your consideration. Few husbands are concerned for the welfare of their wives should they predecease them."

Charles raised his eyebrows, and the solicitor let out a soft chuckle.

"Most men of your rank believe they'll live forever. If you don't mind my speaking out of turn, you must have a high regard for your wife."

Charles frowned. *I don't pay you to give me your opinion.*

John let out a laugh.

"What did his lordship say?"

"Nothing he's not said to me, Mr. Stockton," John said. "He appreciates your opinion—an opinion that I share myself."

That's enough, John. Must I remind you what I pay you for?

John ignored Charles's gestures.

"Hmm." Stockton tapped his pencil on the desk, then leaned back. "Very well—I shall proceed as directed."

He scribbled on his notepad, then picked up a bell on his desk and rang it.

"I should have the formal papers drawn up regarding your will in a week or so, then it's a matter of having the document signed and witnessed. As to the transfer of the outstanding portion of your wife's dowry into your account, it might take rather longer depending on whether the Duke of Whitcombe is in Town, given that the documents will require his signature. I shan't impugn your honor by referring to the terms of the marriage contract upon which the remaining ten thousand depended. That is a matter between yourself and His Grace."

Or, more to the point, a matter between Charles and his wife.

"Have you seen His Grace in Town?" Stockton asked.

Charles shook his head.

"We're only recently arrived in London," John said, "and Lord Devereaux prefers not to attend social events."

"How long are you staying?"

"As long as necessary," John said.

But no longer, Charles signed.

How was it that after only a few days, he already found himself missing his wife? Did she miss him also? Or had she not forgiven him for his crassness?

In claiming her body, Charles had gained far more than mere cash. He closed his eyes, relishing the feel of her body, soft and pliant beneath him, and her tight warmth that promised sweet pleasure, rather than mere base satisfaction…

He glanced up to see the solicitor staring directly at him, understanding in his eyes, his lips lifted in a slight curve, as if…

…as if the man, *damn him,* knew that Charles was sporting a painful erection in his breeches.

Charles crossed his legs, and Stockton's smile broadened.

The door opened and the clerk entered.

"Ah, Billings," Stockton said, "would you have these documents drawn up, and bring a bottle of brandy." He glanced at Charles. "Unless you prefer port? But I have a rather fine Armagnac that I keep for my most important clients."

Bloody fool. I'll wager he says that to every client.

"Lord Devereaux says he would very much appreciate a brandy, Mr. Stockton," John said, smiling at Charles's gestures. "He also asked if you'd be kind enough to permit his valet to have a glass also."

"Very well. Three glasses, if you please, Billings."

Impudent bastard, Charles signed.

John signed back. *Me, or the lawyer?*

Both.

The solicitor watched their exchange, a smile of amusement on his lips. Shortly after, the clerk returned with three glasses half filled with a deep amber liquid. Charles gestured to his valet.

I wonder why he doesn't keep his brandy in his office.

Stockton let out a laugh. "Because I don't offer my best brandy to just any client. Do I, Billings?"

The clerk's expression clouded with confusion and the lawyer chuckled once more then dismissed the clerk.

"How did you know...?" John asked.

Stockton smiled. "Contrary to what you might think, a lawyer doesn't merely draft legal documents. The chief objective of a lawyer is to earn a client's trust. He must therefore understand his clients' wishes and desires, as well as their deepest needs."

What is my deepest need?

Stockton's smile broadened. "Justice."

Any lawyer can make that claim.

"I see from your expression that you doubt my conclusion?" Stockton said, taking a glass from the tray. He gestured to the remaining two glasses. "Please."

Charles picked up a glass and took a sip.

"Justice is something that every lawyer is expected to serve," Stockton said. "However, in my experience, most clients don't seek true justice. Instead, they seek to further their own ends and act in the spirit of what suits *them* best, even if it's detrimental to the wellbeing of others. Whereas you, Lord Devereaux..."

Charles paused, his glass at lips.

"Whereas you," the lawyer continued, "wish to act in accordance with the true spirit of justice. Justice for your tenants, which redresses years of neglect." He sipped his brandy. "Of course, I mean no disrespect to your father. And, of course, justice for your wife to redress the imbalance imposed on us by a society where one's advantages are as a result of birth and sex rather than merit."

Devil's breeches, had the man managed to crawl into Charles's soul?

"I'm sure that many of my clients would act in accordance with similar principles had they the means—or rather, had they access to a substantial dowry from the Duke of Whitcombe. But you have my good opinion, Lord Devereaux, whether you value it or not."

Stockton raised his glass. Charles did likewise and clinked his glass against the lawyer's, nodding to John to do likewise. Then the three men drained their brandies.

"I shan't keep you longer than necessary if you're anxious to return to your wife, Lord Devereaux. Billings can send a message as soon as the documents are ready."

"Lady Devereaux is not in Town," John said.

"A pity," Stockton replied. "In which case, I'll do everything I can to ensure the documents are prepared as quickly as possible so that you may return to her. It's never wise to leave a bride alone for long. In the meantime, I trust you'll enjoy your stay in Town."

Did the lawyer's voice carry a note of judgment?

Perhaps Charles should have brought Olivia with him. But she disliked Society even more than he. And his lodgings were hardly suitable for a woman. For one thing, there was only one bedchamber.

Though that wouldn't necessarily be a bad thing.

He drew in a sharp breath to temper the surge in his groin. His body might be ready for her again, but hers…

Though he'd tried to be gentle with her, Charles hadn't missed the glimmer of fear in her eyes despite her pleading with him to take her, nor the sheen of pain that she'd tried her best to hide.

Their business concluded, Charles rose, and Stockton ushered him out of the office and escorted him to the door, where the bright sunshine of the London morning awaited him, reflecting off the bone-white façade of the buildings. He climbed into the waiting carriage and his valet followed.

"Where to?" John asked. "Savile Row, perhaps?" He gestured to Charles's jacket. "You could do with a new suit—the moths have got to that one."

Whose fault is that? Aren't you supposed to take care of my jackets?

"You've had that jacket for years, sir. I'll wager it's even older than your wife."

Charles let out a sigh and glanced out of the window at the passing buildings, which grew increasingly less ostentatious en route to Cheapside.

"Something must have unsettled you if you're not threatening to dismiss me for impudence," John said. "In fact, you've not made such a threat for two days. Since…"

Charles snapped his head around and glared at the valet.

Go on, John, I dare you.

John met his gaze and nodded in understanding. Charles's intimacy with his wife had unsettled him—not just because of the guilt he'd felt at taking her, but from the faint rush of pleasure that had swelled inside him as he claimed her body. But, unlike every previous encounter with a woman, their coupling hadn't been just a primal act of a male marking his female. It was something else. A union of bodies…perhaps even the beginning of a union of souls.

"If I'm permitted to express an opinion…" John began, and Charles gestured in return.

Since when have you felt the need to ask permission to force your opinion on me?

"Very well, I shall say it. I agree with Mr. Stockton. It was an unusual request to settle property on your wife should she outlive you without producing an heir. Few men in your position would enter into a negotiation with the trustees of his estate to split the assets should the contingency arise, even if those assets are granted as a life tenancy." John rattled out the words so quickly they stumbled over each other. Then he sat back. "There, I've said it. Of course, you don't owe me an explanation."

But you want one anyway. Charles let out a sigh. *My wife is in need of security. Her birth makes it so, and I want to ensure she has an indisputable right to it.*

"I'm sure she'll be relieved to hear that."

She is not to be told.

Charles leaned forward and fixed his gaze on John. Then the

valet leaned back, a flicker of fear in his eyes.

I am trusting you not to breathe one word of this to her. Betray that trust and I'll not only have you dismissed but will ensure that you never find employment elsewhere. Do you understand?

"I understand the consequences of betraying your trust, sir. But I don't understand why you won't tell her. If you're buying her gratitude, you'll only succeed if she knows of it."

I have no wish to buy her gratitude.

"Then what, sir?"

Charles hesitated, then moved his hands. *I wish to earn her trust.*

And her love.

More than anything, he wanted her to come to him willingly—not out of a sense of duty, or a wish to fulfil the terms of the marriage contract to satisfy her brother's sensibilities...but because she wanted him as much as he wanted her.

Charles reached inside his pocket and fingered the item he kept there—the ribbon he'd appropriated from his wife the day he removed her torn stocking.

They continued the journey in silence, the carriage rocking gently, punctuated by the occasional jerk as a wheels hit a rut, which grew more frequent the further they rode from Mayfair. Charles closed his eyes, but he could not dispel the image of his wife's tear-stained face, nor the memory of the small grunt of pain she'd tried so hard to disguise as he'd taken her.

Weren't women supposed to enjoy the act? The whores he'd visited might have uttered false cries of pleasure to secure an extra coin, but most men boasted enough about their prowess, about how it was measured not only by the number of women they'd bedded but by how frequently those women came to pleasure. Twice a night was, if the sordid tales were to be believed, sufficient to secure a man's place on the roll of fame at White's. If the same rumors were to be given any credence, the record was twelve times a night, held by the Duke of Foxton, the most prolific rake in London.

It was no wonder why Charles preferred to avoid Society when in Town. Men were nothing more than spotty adolescents who compared the size, and reach, of their cocks in the privies at Eton. And he was long done with pissing contests.

But what if he *could* give pleasure to his wife—to see her mouth open, not in a cry of pain, but a scream of ecstasy? Not, of course, to determine his own prowess, but for the simple joy of being the one to give her pleasure?

Perhaps he should have taken more notice of the tales his schoolfellows shared of the women they'd bedded—of how they made them writhe with pleasure until they were mad with want. But he could hardly petition the gentlemen of the *ton* to instruct him.

Then perhaps…

He glanced at John to see the valet staring at him, the corner of his mouth quirked in a smile.

His cheeks warming with shame, Charles gestured with his hands, his movements stilted. John's grin widened and he cocked his head to one side.

"You want to know if I'm well versed in pleasuring a woman?"

Hush! Charles gestured sharply, and John glanced at the window.

"The coachman can't hear." He grinned again. "Had he heard, he'd have fallen off his perch!"

Desist. It's no laughing matter.

John stared at Charles's hands. "Are you saying that you're in need of a few pointers in the art of bedding a woman?"

Charles nodded.

"I know my way around a woman, if that's what you're asking," John continued, "but I wouldn't call myself a proficient—at least not enough to teach another. I take it you wish to enhance your technique as much as possible, to please your wife?"

Fuck. Did the man have to be so blunt about it?

John grinned. "No need to reply. Of course, we both know

who's best placed to instruct a man on how to thoroughly pleasure a woman."

Do we?

"I can make discreet inquiries with the best tutor in London."

Surely you don't mean Foxton? Or—God forbid—Whitcombe?

John threw back his head and laughed. *Curse him!*

Charles smacked his fist against the carriage wall. Pain exploded in his knuckles and the carriage drew to a halt.

"Are you wanting to step out, Lord Devereaux?" the coachman called from outside.

Charles rubbed his hand—*fuck*, that hurt! Then he gestured to John, who leaned out of the window.

"Drive on!"

The carriage jerked into motion again.

"Forgive me, sir, I didn't mean to distress you. I have no intention of engaging a gentleman to teach you the skills required."

Who, then?

"What you need is a doxy. And I know just the woman."

CHAPTER TWENTY-EIGHT

"A PACKAGE HAS arrived for you, your ladyship."

Olivia set her teacup aside and glanced at the footman brandishing a silver tray. "For me?"

"Yes, ma'am. It arrived by messenger shortly after dawn."

"You mean someone rode through the night to bring it?"

Olivia's stomach tightened in apprehension. Had it come from Rosecombe? Was her brother unwell? Or Eleanor?

She reached for the package and read the inscription. But the hand was not her brother's, nor was it Eleanor's.

It was her husband's.

"It came from London, I believe," the footman said. "Mr. Reynolds said that Lord Devereaux has been in Town this past sennight. Perhaps it's from him?" His forehead creased into a frown. "I do hope there's nothing in there to give you cause for concern, ma'am. I can send for your maid if need be—or Mrs. Brougham."

Her heart racing, Olivia tore open the package. A note fell out, bearing her name, and carrying the faint aroma of masculine spices, together with a small package, tied with a thin white ribbon, on which was written the inscription *Mme Beaulieu, hosier.*

Hosier...

Olivia picked up the package and held it to her chest.

"You may go and take your breakfast now," she said. "I'll call if I need anything. Forgive me, I don't know your name."

"It's Colin, ma'am," the footman said. "Mr. Reynolds appointed me yesterday."

"Then you're newly arrived? Welcome to Penham Park, Colin," Olivia said, smiling. "I hope you'll be happy here. Tell Mrs. Groves I said to give you a good breakfast for your first day. I hope you like bacon."

A faint blush colored his cheeks, then he stammered his thanks, bowed, and exited the breakfast room.

Olivia waited for his footsteps to recede before she untied the ribbon and opened the package.

Cradled in a nest of tissue paper was a pair of silk stockings, together with a pair of brown garter ribbons. The stockings themselves had a fine weave, giving them a sheer appearance, like the surface of a pearl, and the tops were trimmed with delicate lacework. She ran her fingertips across the material, relishing the softness. Then, slowly, glancing toward the door, as if she were engaging in something very decadent, she lifted them up to the light. Sparkles shimmered across the fabric as if it contained tiny pieces of the sun.

They were the finest stockings she had ever seen.

Her hand trembling, she opened the note and read it.

Olivia,

I regret I am unable to return from London as soon as I would like and am likely to be required here for at least a month. Please accept this gift as a token of my desire to return home.

Yours,
Charles.

Not the most effusive of notes. Gallant suitors were supposed to shower the objects of their affection with professions of love and clever rhyming couplets.

But Olivia's husband was not a man to make gushing speeches—or any speech at all. A lengthy note filled with superlatives, a sonnet, or even a lavish gift of jewelry would have lacked sincerity. A husband who thought little of his wife would placate her with fine words and expensive gifts. Instead, Charles had written a short note, sincere in its brevity, and sent a gift that recalled the day he tended to her ankle with such gentleness that belied his brutish appearance and large, powerful hands.

After Olivia finished her breakfast, she rang the bell. The young footman appeared.

"Oh, Colin, I hope I didn't interrupt your breakfast."

"No, ma'am. I'm a fast eater. My ma always said that my brothers would starve if they didn't beat me to the table of a morning, and I'm partial to a bit of bacon. Mrs. Groves let me have five rashers! I'd have taken six, except Mr. Reynolds..."

"Except Mr. Reynolds what?" a stern voice said.

"Oh, lawks!" The footman winced, his face going as red as fire.

"What did I tell you about gossip, young man?" The butler stood in the doorway. "Lady Devereaux is not to be disrespected."

"It's all right, Mr. Reynolds," Olivia said. "I was just asking Colin whether he'd enjoyed his breakfast."

"Thank you, ma'am." The young footman bowed, then began clearing the table, stacking plates onto a tray.

"Which reminds me," the butler said, "I must ask Mrs. Groves to order another side of bacon from the village as I suspect our supply will diminish somewhat rapidly from today." His mouth curled into a smile, and he winked at Olivia. "No doubt Lady Devereaux summoned you to discuss the matter."

"Oh, beggin' your pardon, Mr. Reynolds, I didn't mean—"

"I believe Mr. Reynolds is teasing you, Colin," Olivia said. "But I was wondering if you could send for Mr. Carlton if he's free this morning. I'd like him to join me for tea."

The butler arched a dark brow. "It's not the done thing to take tea with the steward."

"But it is the done thing to discuss a matter concerning the estate expenditure with him, is it not?"

The butler's smile disappeared. "Very well, I shall send for him. I believe he's in the estate office and can attend to you directly. Do you wish him to bring the ledgers?"

"Would you recommend that he does?"

"Without knowing the purpose of your demands, I'm not in a position to say."

"Then he may bring them," Olivia said, rising.

What had caused the disapproval in his eyes? He'd almost acted as if he liked her earlier. When they'd taken tea yesterday, Nicola described the butler as "a pompous cockroach who thinks himself better than most," but until today, he'd given Olivia no reason to believe he looked down on her.

Perhaps the estate finances were not a woman's province—at least, not for a woman of questionable birth.

Would she ever be able to fit in here—prove herself worthy to be Countess Devereaux?

THOUGH STILL AS threadbare and shabby as the day she'd first entered it, at least the morning room had lost the stench of damp. A fire burned brightly, casting a soft orange glow about the room, giving it a warm, welcoming appearance—in contrast to the dull gray of the landscape outside that was overshadowed by a thick black cloud.

Olivia sighed, her breath misting on the windowpane. Then she traced the outline of a flower on the glass, peering through the marks toward the gardens, where a solitary man poked at the weeds. He was but a lone soldier attempting to hold back the tide. With each weed he pulled from the ground, doubtless another ten sprouted elsewhere.

There was a knock and she startled, then wiped the window with her sleeve and turned to see the butler enter with a smartly dressed man carrying a large leather-bound book, jet-black hair graying at the temples.

"Lady Devereaux, we have yet to be introduced. I am…"

"Mr. Carlton, the steward, yes," she said. "I appreciate your attending me at such short notice." She motioned to the butler. "Thank you, Mr. Reynolds, you may leave us."

"Very good, your ladyship." The butler exchanged a glance with the steward, then withdrew, closing the door.

"Please." Olivia gestured to a chair and the steward sat, clutching the book to his chest, as if he feared she might appropriate it. "First, let me I assure you that I've no wish to meddle in the affairs of the estate, or any decisions that my husband has made."

He seemed to relax.

"I have a number of arrangements I wish you to make," she continued, "but before I instruct you, I would ask for your discretion."

"You have it, Lady Devereaux."

"I take it you're aware that I have an annuity in my name?"

He colored and nodded.

"I wish to capitalize a portion of that annuity and would like you to act as my agent."

"B-but your husband…"

"My husband is not here, Mr. Carlton, and I do not want him to know of the arrangement until I deem it appropriate."

"Forgive me, Lady Devereaux, but I cannot act against the interests of his lordship."

He glanced toward the door, and Olivia tempered the anger simmering in her heart.

"I take it you've been talking to Reynolds, who no doubt has told you that as a woman and a *natural child* I have no right to make any requests of you and must restrict myself to matters concerning the household, such as how much bacon Mrs. Groves is permitted to order?"

Carlton's eyes widened, and the ledger slipped from his grasp.

"F-forgive me, Lady Devereaux, I knew nothing of your…"

He gestured toward her, a blush spreading across his cheeks and even staining the tips of his ears pink.

"I'm surprised to hear that," she said, bitterly. "I'd have thought the gossip would have spread halfway across the county by now. If not the circumstance of my birth, what did Reynolds tell you?"

"To comply with your requests, your ladyship, and treat you with respect."

"Oh, I-I thought…"

"You thought that because of your sex and birth I would not consider your wishes?"

"Isn't that what you're saying?"

He smiled and shook his head. "Of course not. I've often considered women to be the more capable sex—Mrs. Brougham, for example…" He paused, a smile on his lips.

"But?" Olivia prompted him.

"But I cannot act contrary to the best interests of Lord Devereaux. Which includes keeping secrets from him."

"You think I wish to act against my husband's interests?" Olivia said. "Would you not at least hear what I have to say? After all, it's my annuity. My brother settled it upon me when I married Lord Devereaux."

"The estate has little in the way of capital, Lady Devereaux."

"I am aware of that, Mr. Carlton. My husband has used the available capital for the benefit of the tenants. But tell me…has he spent any of it to his own personal benefit?"

The steward retrieved the ledger from the floor and placed it on his lap. "Lord Devereaux is not the type of man to indulge in frivolities for the sake of his own pleasure."

"Which is why I wish to indulge in them on his behalf."

"I beg pardon?"

"I would like to do something about the gardens—have them remodeled into something a little more…"

She glanced out of the window, where the gardener was still battling the weeds.

"Something more natural and welcoming. Easier on the eye and easier on that poor gardener. My brother knows of an excellent man—Mr. Baxter. Have you heard of him?"

Carlton nodded. "Mr. Lawrence Baxter? He has something of a reputation for originality when it comes to garden design. It was he who remodeled the gardens at Dartworth Park last year, but he's expensive. Four hundred, I heard his fee was, and the Dartworth gardens are not so extensive as the gardens here. The Devereaux estate simply does not have that kind of ready capital."

"But *I* do. The value of my annuity is ten thousand. And Mrs. Brougham tells me that my husband was fond of the gardens when he was a boy, though he disliked the house itself."

"I don't know…"

"Mr. Carlton, if my husband can spend his fortune for the benefit of the tenants, may I not spend mine for the benefit of my husband?"

"Yes, but why not inform him?"

"Because I don't want him concerning himself with the arrangements," Olivia said. "I would like to manage it myself, to show him that I can be useful, and therefore I want it to be ready when he returns from London."

"That's impossible, your ladyship. Lord Devereaux might return any day."

"My husband wrote to say he was expecting to be in Town for a month. Surely that would be sufficient time to at least make a start on the gardens?"

"He wrote to you?"

"He sent me a gift," Olivia said, and she blushed as she recalled the stockings. After breakfast, she'd hidden them in her bedchamber at the bottom of a drawer, to be taken out when Charles returned. Perhaps he might want to watch as she put them on, or…

…he might like to take them off.

"I daresay Mr. Baxter might be persuaded," Carlton said, "particularly if he's acquainted with your brother."

"Then I'll write to my brother and ask him to persuade the man. In the meantime, if you could arrange for the release of funds on my behalf, I'd be most grateful."

"Very good, your ladyship," the steward said. "I can make arrangements to release a sum of, say, five hundred? That should be more than sufficient."

"One thousand, if you please. Or, to be precise, one thousand and twenty five."

"I hardly think—"

"I wish to make a second purchase."

"Which is?"

"A horse."

"A *horse?*" Carlton shook his head. "A mare for your ladyship shouldn't cost more than fifty—a hundred at most. And I'm sure Lord Devereaux would be more than happy to arrange the purchase himself on his return."

"The horse is not for me," Olivia said. "I'm not much of a horsewoman, I'm afraid. It's for my husband. A very specific horse."

"For five hundred and twenty-five pounds?"

Olivia nodded. "That is five hundred guineas, is it not? If my brother's willing to sell, of course. I shall write to him directly."

"But…" Carlton hesitated, then understanding gleamed in his eyes and, for the first time that morning, he smiled. "I take it you don't wish me to inform Lord Devereaux until the purchase is completed?"

Olivia nodded.

"May I ask why?"

An onset of shyness threatened to overcome her, and she glanced toward the window, aware of the steward's eyes on her. Outside, the gardener had moved, though he continued to make slow progress, winning, perhaps, the battle against the weeds, but not the war.

"I want to be there when he first sees his gift," she said, her heart swelling. "I want to see him smile."

CHAPTER TWENTY-NINE

"Y OU'RE PROVING TO be an adept pupil, my lord."

Anne Brown parted her thighs once more and slipped her hand between them, pausing at the thatch of blonde curls.

"In theory, at least," she added, pursing her lips. "Of course, I've nothing against the theory of pleasure, but it is far more beneficial to engage in the practice of it."

Charles scribbled in his notebook and held it up.

Her gaze flicked over the words he'd written, then she let out a sharp huff. "I *am* discreet, your lordship, and assuming your man is equally so, your wife need never know whether you touch me or not. I have shown you everything I know about how to satisfy a woman."

Doubtless she had, having brought herself to pleasure in front of him in all manner of ways—some at her own hand, some with the use of marble artefacts, and others with the assistance of a fellow doxy.

Charles's cock had swelled with anticipation on several occasions, but there was only one woman capable of easing his torment. Much to the doxy's disappointment, he only wanted to practice the art of pleasure on his wife.

Olivia…

What might it be like to have her spread before him, offering her sweet body to be feasted upon. His mouth watered at the thought of tasting her pretty pink nipples, but he'd brushed the doxy aside when she offered her own. She might have elicited his release provided he imagined it was Olivia writhing in pleasure beneath him. But he couldn't bring himself to touch another woman. Better to seek an unfulfilling release at his own hand, which he'd done each time he'd returned to his lodgings, his wife's name circling in his mind.

At least John had been considerate enough to refrain from commenting on his master's stained bedsheets.

The doxy let her dressing gown slip to the floor, exposing her breasts, then she slipped her finger into her mouth and released it, glistening and moist. She caressed her breasts, then circled a nipple, before she pinched it and let out a sigh, her back arching.

"You see, my lord, how much pleasure this gives me?"

You are merely performing an act.

She glanced at Charles's hand gestures, then gave a knowing smile. Doubtless she understood what he'd conveyed. A good whore was adept at understanding the needs of men she serviced and reading his body and his mind—crawling under his skin as she crawled over his naked flesh, to delve into his deepest, darkest yearnings.

And Anne—or Angelina Bellissima, as she sometimes called herself—was the best whore in Town.

"Ah," she said, an undertone of slyness in her voice. "You doubt my sincerity."

She curved her lips into a smile and parted her thighs wider, and he caught his breath at the sight—her female flesh, glistening and ready.

"There!" she said. "Witness the evidence of my desire. A woman's body will always betray her. It is how you'll be able to tell whether your wife takes pleasure from the act. Do you recall our first lesson?"

He nodded, then gestured to his ears.

"That's it, my lord. You listen to her voice, the hitch of her breath. And then?"

He hesitated, then pointed to his nose.

"Excellent! Yes, you breathe in her scent. As I said, a *very* adept pupil." She cocked her head to one side. "Can you smell my desire now?"

He shook his head. The air in the doxy's chamber was thick with her cologne—an expensive Parisian scent, no doubt, but cloying nonetheless. He preferred delicate floral scents, such as rose and lavender…

The scent of his wife.

"And, of course, you can tell with your eyes," Anne continued. "Her skin will flush a beautiful pink, and her nipples…"

She flicked her nipple and smiled as it swelled.

"They will harden in readiness for your lips. Then…"

She widened her thighs, and her smile broadened as Charles's cheeks warmed.

"Do you take pleasure from looking at me, my lord?"

He remained still.

"There's no shame in it," she said. "All men who visit me take pleasure from the sight of a female form, whether they care for their wives or not. It's a natural male instinct, though your heart and loyalty may prevent you from acting upon it. Imagine, then, the pleasure you'll take from looking at your wife, spread before you, all willing and ready?"

He closed his eyes and drew in a sharp breath, willing his cock not to spend in his breeches. *Sweet Lord Almighty*—to imagine Olivia in such a pose, engaging in such debauchery!

Anne chuckled, and Charles opened his eyes.

"The woman takes equal pleasure from being looked at."

He raised his eyebrows.

"Oh yes, my lord," she said. "I said, during our second lesson, that what a man takes pleasure in is, more often than not, enjoyable for the woman also. I'll wager my body that your wife will take as much delight in the act as you. Not all men are as considerate as yourself."

Her expression darkened for a heartbeat, then the smile resumed.

"You can see *my* body's reaction today, my lord. I take great pleasure from being looked at intimately by a man."

Closing her eyes, she slipped her hand between her thighs, her chest rising and falling as she inhaled. She opened them again, and he caught a flash of shyness in her expression.

Then her smile slipped. She withdrew her hand and pulled her dressing gown around her body, securing it with a sash.

"I think your final lesson has come to an end."

She blinked, and Charles caught a sheen of moisture in her eyes.

Is something the matter?

She stared at his hands, then shook her head. "Forgive me, I don't understand you."

Yes, you do.

Charles fished in his pocket, drew out a sovereign, and placed it in the delicate porcelain dish together with the rest of the coins.

"Very well," she said. "A woman in my profession must abide by many rules. Not just to maintain the safety of her body, but she needs to temper her own desires such that she is not in thrall to them. A good whore ensures that her client is not only fully satisfied, but that he leaves an encounter already eager for the next. But when the whore herself is desirous of the next appointment with a client—not for coin, but for more personal reasons— then the time has come to part with the client."

Surely she wasn't saying that she'd fallen in love with him? He hadn't even touched her.

Charles held up his hands, showing three fingers on each.

She smiled and nodded. "Yes, Lord Devereaux, I'm aware that our arrangement was six lessons, and that we part company after today." She let out a sigh. "Have no fear, I'm not in danger of falling in love. But even the hardest-hearted whore must admit that there's something irresistible in a man who's in love with his wife."

Charles frowned.

Love?

A brute such as him wasn't built for love. He was the antithesis of men such as Whitcombe, whose ready wit supplied him with an endless stream of flowery declarations toward his wife.

The doxy gave a soft smile, something akin to affection in her eyes.

"You think yourself unworthy? Incapable, even?" She shook her head. "I'm visited by many men who'll fall over themselves to assure me how violently they love their wives, who continue voicing that love as they rut me from behind. But you, Lord Devereaux—you may be incapable of telling your wife that you love her, but by your deeds, the way you're so eager to learn how to pleasure her, yet torment yourself with the guilt of visiting another to teach you…"

She shook her head and wiped her eyes.

"By what greater means can a man demonstrate how sincerely he loves his wife—even if he has yet to admit it to himself?"

Charles approached her, tempering the urge to ease the pain in her eyes. Then she glanced at the clock on the mantelshelf.

"Mercy me, is that the time? My next client's due any moment. I believe you're acquainted with the Duke of Foxton?"

Charles grimaced. Did she seek to taunt him? Foxton was renowned for being the most successful rake in England—if success were measured by the number of women he'd bedded.

Anne let out a laugh. "Skilled in the art of pleasure he may be, Lord Devereaux, but I'm in no danger of finding Foxton irresistible, for he is a man with no heart."

Charles gestured to his chest and raised his eyebrows.

She smiled. "Yes, Lord Devereaux, you *do* have a heart. But you're astute enough to save it for the few souls deserving of it."

She approached the fireplace and yanked the bellpull. Shortly after, a young woman in a bright-pink gown appeared.

"Rosie darling, Lord Devereux is ready to leave. Would you find his man and show them out?"

The young woman nodded. "He was in with Jenny, Mrs. Brown, but I believe I heard them finishing a few minutes ago."

Anne let out a soft laugh. "Jenny's one of my best. I taught her everything I know. The two of you should compare notes."

She rose and offered her hand. Charles took it, and her slim fingers curled around his wrist.

"Good luck, your lordship," she said. "And remember, if you're ever uncertain as to whether your wife is taking pleasure, all you need do is ask her. As you learn how to give her pleasure, let her guide you by telling you where and how she likes to be touched. If you're fortunate, you may find her wanting to reciprocate and give you pleasure in return."

He nodded, then exited the chamber, returning to the corridor bedecked in deep-scarlet furnishings with gold trim, with wood-paneled doors behind which he could hear a symphony of grunts, cries, and professions of love. The young doxy led him to the main doors, where John stood waiting, a satisfied smile on his lips. The waiting footman opened the doors and Charles exited the building, his valet in tow. He turned to bid his farewell, but the door had already closed—a dark-painted door bearing a polished brass knocker and a nameplate with the legend: *Mrs. Brown's seminary for young ladies.*

"Well, sir, I don't know about yourself," John said, "but that was a very pleasurable way to spend an afternoon."

Charles allowed himself a smile and they set off. Before they'd taken half a dozen paces, Charles froze. Approaching from the opposite direction was a familiar figure.

Dressed in a white muslin gown and a burgundy redingote with matching bonnet, she exuded understated elegance. Their eyes met and she flicked her emerald gaze to the building from which he'd just come, then set her mouth into a hard line.

Surely she, like most women, had no idea of the true activities behind the door of Number 55 Green Street?

"Duchess Whitcombe!" John said, a little too brightly. "What a pleasure to see you."

She arched an eyebrow then regarded Charles with that unsettling expression of hers. "You must be careful," she said, turning her attention toward the building. "An excess of pleasure is not always advisable. I trust my sister-in-law is well? I see she has not accompanied you in your visit to"—she glanced at the brass plate, her expression hardening—"Mrs. Brown's seminary for young ladies."

Devil's bollocks—the duchess was an astute woman and would, most likely, sniff out a guilty man at fifty paces.

Tell her it's not what it looks like, Charles signed.

Say that *to a woman, sir, and she'll know you've been up to no good.*

"Lord Devereaux was just asking if we might accompany you anywhere?" John said.

"Thank you, but no," she replied. "I'm on my way to take tea with Duchess Sawbridge. Perhaps you know her, or at least you might know the duke. Disreputable rake—or he was until he married dear Jemima. I find it such a wonderful transformation when a rake is reformed by marriage. Of course, not *all* rakes are capable of redemption."

She lifted her lips into a smile, but her eyes darkened until they were almost black.

"Well, I shan't keep you from your…*business,*" she said. "Do give my regards to Olivia. Tell her I shall be writing to her. I'm afraid I've been remiss in my correspondence, and I promised not to let her down. I can't abide anyone who cannot keep their promises, can you?"

She dipped her head, then continued along the pavement.

Call her back, Charles signed.

"And say what?" John whispered. "If you try to justify your visit, you'll only confirm your guilt."

I'm not guilty! Charles signed, smacking his fist into his palm. *I care not what* she *thinks of me, but I have no wish to see my wife upset if the duchess sees fit to gossip.*

"Duchess Whitcombe is the last person to engage in gossip," John said. "You're concerning yourself over nothing. She's never liked you much—does it matter if she likes you even less?"

I care not whether she, or every soul in London, loathes me. I do, however, care whether the duchess distresses my wife by making unfounded accusations.

"Lady Devereaux won't believe them. Besides—you sent her a gift."

Fool! Charles smacked his fist into his palm once more. *You think a gift is enough to atone for the distress I've caused her? I want to make her happy. I care nothing for myself, only her.*

John stared at him, then placed a hand on his arm.

"Then that's all that matters, sir."

They continued in silence until they reached Charles's lodgings. John ushered him into the parlor, then returned with a brandy glass, which he placed in Charles's hand.

And, by heaven, was he in need of it!

But it wasn't the fear that the duchess knew whom he'd been visiting. It was the realization, brought about by Anne Brown's observations, and Charles's own admission regarding his desire, above all other things, that Olivia not suffer any distress.

Which meant only one thing.

He was in love with his wife.

CHAPTER THIRTY

OLIVIA GLANCED UP as someone knocked on the parlor door. "Come in!"

It opened and Colin entered. "Miss Faulkes for you, your ladyship. I believe you're expecting her?"

He stepped aside to reveal Nicola, holding a package.

"Thank you, Colin," Olivia said. "May we have some tea later? At four o'clock? I believe there's some shortbread left."

"Yes, ma'am. Mrs. Groves made a new batch yesterday and Mr. Reynolds hasn't eaten it all yet—though come four o'clock, it might have all gone."

He winked, then bowed again and exited the parlor.

"You oughtn't to let him speak so freely with you, Olivia," Nicola said, embracing her. "You're the mistress. He's just a *servant*."

"I'd rather the staff were happy here," Olivia said. "In any case, I suspect my upbringing was similar to his."

"But you're a *countess*, with a duke for a brother." Nicola sat, then held out the package. "I visited the post office on my walk here and took the liberty of picking up this parcel for you."

"Thank you," Olivia said, taking the package. "Oh! It's from Eleanor—her hand is so distinctive. There's always something so exciting about receiving post."

"I can't say I've thought about it, seeing as I've never received any letters. But I don't have a duke for a brother."

"Montague never writes to me," Olivia said with a laugh. "He dislikes letters, both writing and receiving them. Eleanor says that's because men only receive letters of business containing demands for the settlement of an account, or instructions to undertake some tedious task."

She began to unwrap the package then hesitated.

"Would you mind awfully if I read Eleanor's letter now? I've not heard from her for some time."

"Of course not," Nicola said, smiling. She rose, then crossed the floor to the window and looked out. "Mr. Baxter's making progress on the garden, I see. It must have cost Lord Devereaux an awful lot." She glanced toward Olivia. "Of course, it's not my place to speak of it. I see Jacob's helping him again today—which explains why he's not been at Pa's farm this week."

"I couldn't have made the arrangements without Jacob's help."

"Well, he is Lord Devereaux's heir."

Olivia glanced at her friend, who was staring out of the window, her eyes filled with longing.

"Shall we join him later, Nicola? I can show you the gardens and introduce you to Mr. Baxter. His wife, Lady Arabella, is a friend of my sister's."

Nicola let out a sigh, her breath misting the window. "It must be so beneficial to have a duchess for a sister."

"I don't love Eleanor because she's a duchess," Olivia said. "I love her because she's kind and intelligent—and would do anything to make me happy."

"Then you're fortunate to be loved."

"Your sister loves you."

"Susie's just a child," Nicola said, folding her arms. "Don't let me keep you from your letter."

Olivia nodded, then opened the parcel. Inside, she found a miniature watercolor landscape depicting Rosecombe, a letter, and a small, square box. She tore open the letter and read it.

Dearest Olivia.

Forgive me for not writing sooner, but I have been much occupied in Town. I trust you'll forgive me when you know the reason. I have been in Town on the most important business, namely the framing of the enclosed. I thought it might do for your parlor, to remind you of those who love and miss you every day. Though you are mistress of Penham, you will always have a home at Rosecombe. You must also forgive my indulgence in paying another visit to Rundell and Bridge, but what sort of sister would I be if I did not give you a pair of earrings to match your necklace?

I return to Rosecombe today. I confess I miss Montague when I'm parted from him. He was too busy overseeing the estate to visit London with me, and I confess to having been a little apprehensive about visiting London on my own. But I had no need for concern, as I find I have plenty of friends here. Dear Jemima has been in Town since the summer as her confinement draws near, and I took tea with Lady Portia and her husband yesterday. Mr. Reid asks me to convey his sister's best wishes and that she hopes to see you soon. Perhaps you and Lord Devereaux might come to Rosecombe for a visit over Christmas. Horatio is quite bereft without his beloved aunt. I fear he prefers his aunt to his mother, particularly when I am required to admonish him for teasing little Clarissa, who also misses her aunt. I miss you dreadfully, of course, and though Montague makes no mention of it, I know that he is anxious to see you again and to know that you are well, and happy.

And now I must conclude, if I'm to catch the post. I will only add that I happened to see Lord Devereaux in Town last week. He looked in good spirits, though I confess to being disappointed that you were not with him. Perhaps when he's secured his own townhouse he might be persuaded to bring you. Do persuade him, darling, if you can.

Yours,
Eleanor

Olivia folded the letter, held it to her breast for a moment, then set it aside. She picked up the box and ran her fingertips over the inscription, then lifted the lid. Nestled on a bed of dark-blue velvet was a pair of earrings, fashioned in gold, each bearing a single pearl suspended on a thin gold chain.

She lifted her hand to her throat, then sighed. Her throat was bare. She'd mislaid Eleanor's necklace last week, much to her distress—poor Susie had been heartbroken on discovering it missing.

"Oh, how pretty!"

Olivia glanced up to see Nicola standing before her, her gaze fixed on the earrings.

"A gift from my sister," Olivia said. "She's been in London. It's to match the necklace I lost."

"Can't she buy you another necklace? She's rich enough."

"I can buy another myself," Olivia said. "But it wouldn't be the same. That necklace was gifted with love, and I have an obligation to find it. I'm sure it will turn up eventually. I daresay I dropped it somewhere. Now—how about a turn in the garden, and we can ask Jacob to take tea with us."

She rose and caught her breath as nausea rippled through her. The world shifted out of focus for a moment, and she reached for the back of the chair to steady herself.

"Are you well?" Nicola said, drawing near.

"I stood a little quickly, that's all."

Nicola's eyes narrowed. "Susie said you fainted last week in the garden."

"I merely tripped on a loose stone on the path. It was nothing of any consequence, and Jacob was there to catch me."

"You were with *Jacob*?"

Olivia frowned at the sharpness in her friend's tone. "Mr. Baxter was there also," she said. "I was assisting him in the garden when I lost my footing."

"You were gardening?" Nicola shook her head. "But you're a *lady*. When I become..." She hesitated, then shook her head. "If I were in your position, I wouldn't be undertaking menial work."

Olivia laughed. "I wouldn't describe gardening as menial work, certainly not in front of Mr. Baxter." She held out her arm. "Come, let me introduce you."

Olivia's husband might be the largest man she had ever seen, but Baxter was of a similar build and height. With a tall frame and muscles toned from years of toil, he was a formidable sight. No doubt most women would enjoy the sight of him digging in the garden, shirtless, his muscles rippling with each movement. But Olivia could only regard him as he compared to her husband.

He paused in digging and straightened, stretching out his arms. Then he turned and raised his hand in greeting.

"Lady Devereaux! A pleasure to see you, as usual."

"And you, Mr. Baxter," Olivia said. "I trust you're not working too hard."

"Ah, that's where I'm fortunate, ma'am, given that I see my occupation as more enjoyment than work. This particular assignment has been more enjoyable than most."

"Mr. Baxter, I fear you're attempting flattery."

"My Bella would say the same, Lady Devereaux. Most of my clients demand a formal style, where every hedge is clipped into obedience to suit their tastes. My better clients prefer a naturalistic style, where the garden reflects the world around us. But they all pale in comparison to one such as yourself."

Olivia winced. Surely he wasn't referring to her birth?

"One such as myself?" she said.

"Someone with your vision, Lady Devereaux. Your idea for designing a garden that appeals to all the senses, not just aesthetics, is something I've long wished to put into being."

"All the senses?" Nicola said. "What do you mean?"

"The garden's going to appeal to every sense," Olivia said. "Even sound. Mr. Baxter has had some special items made that produce music in the wind. They're used in the Far East. Eleanor told me about them—her father brought some back from one of his business journeys. What are they called again?"

"Wind chimes," Baxter said, smiling. He settled his gaze on Nicola and raised an eyebrow.

"Oh, forgive me," Olivia said. "Mr. Baxter, this is Miss Faulkes. Nicola, this is Mr. Baxter, a man who performs miracles in the garden with wind chimes."

"The miracle was your imagination, Lady Devereaux," Baxter said. "I merely put it into being."

"Together with your wife," Olivia said. "I trust Bella will receive her share of the credit." She turned to Nicola. "Lady Arabella sketched all the designs for the garden."

"*Lady* Arabella?" Nicola said. "Then how come you're only *Mr.* Baxter?"

"My Bella's a duke's daughter," Baxter said, "though you wouldn't know it, seeing as she lacks the airs that most ladies have—and thank the Almighty for that, is all I have to say."

"Oh," Nicola said. "She's like Olivia."

Olivia flinched at her friend's reference to her birth. Would she never be free from the stain?

Baxter's eyes narrowed. "My wife is Lady Arabella and not Lady Baxter, because I have no title. But I fail to see why that should be something worth noting. Too many of us consider the possession of a title or the circumstances of one's birth to be the only factor that defines a person's worth. But I assure you, Miss Faulkes, birth only defines a person's position in society. It does not define their character."

Nicola's expression hardened and Olivia caught a flash of malevolence in her eyes. Then, in a heartbeat, it disappeared and she smiled.

"Jacob!" she cried. "I've not seen you for days. I was beginning to wonder whether you'd forsaken me."

Jacob approached them, shovel in hand. "That's the last of the sweet cherries in now, Mr. Baxter. I must say, they don't look like much."

"They never do when first planted," Baxter said. "But come the spring you'll see the blossom and understand why I chose them. It may take a year or two before it yields any fruit—or at least enough for one of Lady Devereaux's pies." He winked at Olivia. "My Bella tells me you're a miracle worker yourself in the kitchen. She says your shortbread is the finest she's ever tasted."

"Then I must give you some to take home when you're finished here," Olivia said. "Perhaps you'd take a piece now? We're having tea at four."

"No—best I get on while we still have the light. The nights are drawing in right quickly now winter's on its way. I want to get those herbs in before I finish today."

"What about you, Jacob?" Nicola said, an undertone of desperation in her voice. "Will you join us for tea?"

"I'd better help Mr. Baxter."

Olivia's heart ached at the hurt in Nicola's eyes. "Surely a little tea wouldn't hurt?" she said. "You've been working hard all day, and Nicola hasn't seen you for days. You've been neglecting her."

"Oh, very well." Jacob offered his arm, and Nicola slid her hand around it in a possessive grip. Baxter watched, his eyes narrowing.

"You must join us now, Mr. Baxter," Olivia said. "Just for a little while. In return, I'll help you plant the herbs after tea."

"Well, I'm not one to refuse an offer of shortbread and assistance in the herb garden." He offered his arm and Olivia took it, then they returned inside.

AFTER TEA, OLIVIA worked in the herb garden under Baxter's direction, relishing the feel of the earth beneath her fingers and the burst of woody aromas as she placed each herb plant in the ground. No wonder Charles had relished his time in the herb garden with his mother. Perhaps he might be disposed to smile again when he saw it on his return from London.

As darkness fell, she returned to the house to find Nicola waiting in the parlor, reclined on the sofa. She rose as Olivia entered, then gestured to Olivia's hands.

"Mr. Baxter has been working you too hard—look how soiled your hands are! I said you should have used those gloves, though I also said you shouldn't have been gardening.

Olivia stared at her fingernails. "A little dirt won't cause any harm. Besides, I'll wash it off before supper. Are you staying for supper? I've been trying out a new pie recipe with Mrs. Groves— for when my husband returns."

"If you wish it, my dear friend. I wish Jacob would join us. He seems to have been avoiding me lately. I don't know why he prefers to eat with the staff downstairs."

"I suppose he's grown used to it," Olivia said. "I have no objection if you wish to join him."

"He should be joining me in the dining room. After all, he *is* a Devereaux."

Nicola's voice sliced through the air, sharpening the pain that had settled behind Olivia's eyes during tea. Olivia rose and held her breath as her stomach rippled with nausea.

"I should dress for dinner," she said. "Susie will be waiting in my chamber."

"Shall I help you?" Nicola said.

"N-no, I'll be fine. Susie's turned out very capable."

"Susie's still a child. I'm your *friend.*"

"Very well," Olivia said, unable to summon the strength to resist, and she exited the parlor, Nicola at her side.

They passed Colin at the foot of the stairs, peering into the body of the longcase clock in the corner.

"Has Mr. Reynolds entrusted you with winding up the clocks, Colin?" Olivia said.

"Yes, your ladyship. He showed me how to do it last night and said I must not to pull the weights too high. But I'm afraid of causing damage."

"I'm sure that if Mr. Reynolds has entrusted you to wind the clock unsupervised, you'll perform the task properly, Colin," Olivia said, smiling at the young man. "You need to have a little more confidence in your abilities."

"Yes, ma'am, thank you, ma'am."

He reached back inside the clock and Olivia climbed the stairs, smiling at the familiar sound of the weights moving on their chains, followed by the deep ticking as Colin set the pendulum moving once more. Was there a sound more soothing than the ticking of a timepiece that had been lovingly crafted over two centuries before? Clocks seemed to take on a life of their own—living, breathing organisms that brought vitality into a building, turning it into a home.

And now, the clock had a distant cousin residing in the garden—a carved stone sundial nestling among the rosebushes that had taken four men to carry across the gardens.

Oh, I do hope Charles likes it!

She closed her eyes, willing herself to recall the expression in her husband's eyes when he'd smiled at her. Then she took another step up and her foot turned. Pain shot through her ankle, and she slipped sideways.

"Lady Devereaux!" a shrill voice screamed, and Olivia glanced up to see her maid's ashen face at the top of the stairs. "No!"

She lost her footing and fell on her side, the impact forcing the breath from her lungs. She reached for the banister, but failed to gain purchase, and slipped downward, bumping on each step. As she gathered speed, she let out a cry, flinging her hands out toward Nicola, but her friend stood, frozen halfway up the stairs, her mouth a wide "O."

Then a body arrested her fall and a pair of arms wrapped around her waist.

"I've got you, ma'am."

Olivia clung to the arms, shaking, as she was set upright. She placed her weight on her left foot and cried out, and the footman tightened his grip.

"Careful, ma'am—beggin' your pardon for touching you."

"N-no need to apologize, Colin. I dread to think what might have happened were you not there to catch me."

"Sweet heaven, Olivia!" Nicola cried, descending the stairs. "Are you all right?"

More footsteps approached and Mrs. Brougham appeared.

"Colin, what the devil are you doing? Mr. Reynolds told you to—*Oh!*" she cried as she caught sight of Olivia in the footman's arms. "What in the name of the Almighty has happened?"

"Lady Devereaux fell down the stairs, Mrs. Brougham," Colin said.

"Sweet Lord! And in the very same spot where…" Her voice trailed off as the color drained from her face. "We'd best get the doctor, your ladyship. Come along—we'll take you to your chamber. Susie, fetch your mistress some sweet tea and a brandy. Colin, help me with Lady Devereaux, then go and find Mr. Reynolds and ask him to send for Dr. Cheam."

"There's no need for a doctor," Nicola said. "It's just Olivia's ankle, and I can bind it—"

"And that's enough from *you*," Mrs. Brougham interrupted. "You're in no position to say what's best for her ladyship—not while Lord Devereaux is not at home."

"But I'm her friend."

"And I'm her housekeeper acting on Lord Devereaux's instructions," Mrs. Brougham said crisply. "He gave me strict instructions to take care of her ladyship. Or would you like to speak to him yourself when he returns to explain why you had no wish for her to see a doctor after taking a fall in the same place that killed his mother?"

Olivia's stomach twisted with horror as she glanced at the staircase and the solid marble floor at the bottom. Had Colin not been there…

She let out a low groan, and the housekeeper drew her into an embrace, her manner reminiscent of Charles's fierce determination to tend to her when she'd fallen in the forest.

"Can you walk?"

Olivia nodded, and between them, Mrs. Brougham and Colin helped her up the stairs and into her chamber. Ignoring her protests, they placed her on the bed.

"Ah, Susie—there you are."

The young maid stood in the doorway holding a brandy glass. "Mrs. Groves says supper will be ready in a minute, Mrs. Brougham. She'll send Ethel up with a tray."

"Very good," the housekeeper said. "Now, tend to your mistress." She turned to Nicola, who also stood in the doorway. "And you can be off now," she said. "Jacob's in the kitchen. Go and tell him to walk you home. If he argues, tell him I said so."

"But…"

"Must I ask twice? Lord Devereaux will hear if it if I do."

Nicola scowled and fidgeted with her hands, and Olivia caught sight of something small and shiny in her fist. Then she blinked and it was gone.

"I'll come and visit tomorrow," she said.

Before Olivia could reply, Mrs. Brougham shooed Nicola out.

"I know it's not my place to say, but there are more appropriate folk hereabouts whom you could choose as your friend, Lady Devereaux. That young miss has been giving herself airs ever since she set her sights on Jacob."

Susie blushed scarlet as she continued to tend to Olivia, turning back the bedsheet and plumping the pillows. Then she let out a sob.

"Now, none of that, Susie," Mrs. Brougham said. "Your sister can take care of herself."

"I-it's not that, Susie said, her lip wobbling. "It's—Oh, I'm so sorry, your ladyship!"

"It wasn't your fault," Olivia said. "And Colin was there. My ankle's a little sore, that's all."

"I-I'll bandage it, ma'am."

"I'd wait until Dr. Cheam's been," Mrs. Brougham said. "He'll want to examine it. You look after your mistress until he arrives. Now—where's Ethel with the tea?"

Olivia sank back onto the pillows, willing the pain in her ankle to subside. She caught her breath as another ripple of nausea washed over her.

"Here, ma'am, the brandy will make you feel better."

Olivia took a sip. "Thank you, Susie. I don't know what I'd do without you to take care of me."

The maid burst into tears.

"Don't be distressing your mistress," Mrs. Brougham said. "Come along with me. Lady Devereaux needs peace and quiet after her accident. Ethel can take care of her until the doctor arrives."

Susie's sobs only increased, and Olivia couldn't help exhaling in relief as the housekeeper ushered her out, closing the door behind them. Her head throbbing, she closed her eyes and awaited the arrival of the doctor.

AFTER DR. CHEAM examined her, Olivia drew the bedsheets around herself to hide her embarrassment. Though given that he'd poked and prodded every inch of her, there was no longer any need for modesty.

The doctor dipped his hands into the washbowl then dried them on a cloth, and Olivia's stomach tightened at the seriousness in his soft gray eyes.

"Is there anything the matter?" she said. "The pain in my ankle has subsided. Surely it's not broken?"

"No, Lady Devereaux. It's merely a bad sprain, exacerbated by your walking on it unbound before the original sprain was completely healed."

"Then what's wrong?"

"You're with child."

"I-I'm *what?*"

He peered at her over the top of his glasses. "Perhaps you now appreciate the seriousness of the situation. A fall down a staircase is dangerous enough for any woman, let alone one in your condition. I take it you didn't know?"

Hope flared in her heart and was almost immediately tempered by fear as she recalled the stark words that her husband had written.

I hope to God you are not.

"Dr. Cheam, are you obliged to tell anyone about my condition?"

"What happens between a doctor and his patient is nobody else's concern. Only when lives are in danger am I permitted to break my oath of confidentiality."

"A-and…my husband?"

His expression softened. "No, my dear, not even your husband has a right to know—though, of course, he'll discover the truth eventually. But I'll leave you to tell him in your own time."

"Thank you."

Olivia blinked and a tear slid down her cheek. Dr. Cheam produced a handkerchief and handed it to her.

"F-forgive me," she said. "I should be happy. Most husbands want an heir, don't they?"

He smiled. "It's a failing among my sex—the instinctive need for a son. I myself have four daughters, but I don't love them any less for not being boys. And my eldest is proving to be a better helpmate than a son could ever be—she's studying to be a doctor, and I intend for her to take over my practice."

"Then she's most fortunate," Olivia said, her mind drifting to poor Euphramia Lucas, who, despite being more capable than her father Dr. Lucas, was rarely given the chance to use her skills. "I have an acquaintance, a doctor's daughter, who is not given such consideration."

"I daresay she'd refute your claim to her good fortune when she's required to rise before dawn to tend to a long confinement."

Confinement…

Olivia swallowed the ripple of fear, and the doctor placed a hand on her arm.

"A confinement is nothing to fear," he said. "Not as it once was. And every activity carries a certain degree of risk, does it not? Even walking up the stairs. Now—I have a tonic I'll leave with you to alleviate your sickness. And I'd recommend eating little and often throughout the day to stave off the bouts of dizziness."

"Thank you, doctor."

"There's no need. I'm paid well to care for you."

"You are?"

"Lord Devereaux sent instructions as soon as he returned here married, to care for you should you need of anything. He pays a regular stipend—an overly generous one, if you ask me, but he was very insistent. Did you not know?"

Oliva shook her head.

"I-I didn't think he had the means. I…" She hesitated, her cheeks warming with shame. "Forgive me. I should not speak of such things."

He snapped his bag shut and rose. "In my experience, few husbands—even those of means—make such an arrangement for their wives."

He bowed, then exited the chamber.

Was he trying to tell her that her husband had made the arrangement because he cared for her? But even if that were true, what would he think when he discovered that she was with child, after he'd expressed so bluntly that he had no wish to be a father?

Olivia placed a hand over her belly.

"Hello," she whispered. "I'm sorry I placed you in danger today, but I'll be careful in future."

She closed her eyes, trying to form the image in her mind—cradling her child in her arms, handing him to his father, who smiled down at him with love…

But she could not.

"*I'll* love you," she said. "Perhaps you might love me."

She closed her eyes, unwilling to voice the words.

Even if nobody else does.

CHAPTER THIRTY-ONE

TWO MORE DAYS and I can be reunited with her.

About bloody time.

London had never held any pleasure for Charles, and right now he utterly was sick of the place. Sick of the buildings crammed against each other, sick of the bright colors and sharp voices of Society's finest all trying to outdo each other in ostentation, sick of the endless noise, even at night in a place that never seemed to take rest, and most of all…

Most of all, he was heartily sick of being separated from his wife.

But soon he could hold her in his arms again—not to mention indulge in giving her a taste of pleasure.

"Well! You're looking a little less like a thundercloud today, sir."

Fuck off, John.

The valet grinned. Charles drew in a lungful of air and glanced at his surroundings. At least Hyde Park gave him some respite from all the brickwork, though there was no relief from the people who, with their gaudy silks and bright waistcoats, visited the park to be seen rather than enjoy the little haven of greenery that made a passable attempt at resembling the countryside.

At least he could be thankful for having a limited acquaintance, which meant that few people stopped him to engage in inane conversation about the inclement weather that London had been suffering now winter was upon them, or the latest gossip about the prince regent's mistresses. In fact, the only soul Charles recognized—the Duke of Foxton—was too occupied with the painted ladies adorning each perfectly tailored arm to give him more than a cursory nod.

A volley of childish squeals filled the air, followed by a cacophony of quacks, splashing water, and a nursemaid's high-pitched admonishments. A young girl raced away from the edge of the Serpentine, toward a tree, yelling with laughter. Charles caught sight of a second child, a boy of five or six, swinging from a branch of the tree, then the boy released his hold and fell to the ground, landing in a heap beside a rhododendron. A lady dressed in bright-blue silk let out a cry and approached the child. Charles winced, in anticipation of the child receiving a beating, but instead, the lady scooped the boy into her arms, and they filled the air with their laughter.

"For shame!" a female voice huffed as a couple passed by. "But I suppose it's not unexpected, given her tomboyish nature. Earl Thorpe is to be pitied for marrying that misfit."

"He doesn't look all that pitiful, my dear," the woman's companion said in the muted voice of the henpecked husband.

A tall man approached the lady and joined in the laughter, then he picked up the girl and placed her on his shoulders. Charles found himself smiling at the little family—father, mother, son, and daughter—indulging in the simple, natural pleasure of a little tomfoolery. He knew Thorpe by sight, having seen him at Oxford, though they'd never moved in the same circles. He'd seemed a stuffy fellow, overly fastidious about decorum.

But marriage to a misfit must have transformed Thorpe— lucky bastard, able to appreciate, and be part of, the happiness of a child who was given free rein to express joy in merely being alive.

Perhaps that was what Mrs. Brougham meant when she'd said Charles was a different man to his father—that he had the chance to bring light and happiness to Penham…

Now that Charles had married his own little misfit.

He thrust his hands into his pockets and followed the path toward the park gates. Not long now and he'd be on his way back to her.

"I say! Devereaux!"

He glanced along the street to see his banker striding toward him.

"I *thought* it was you. What are you doing in London still? Now the papers have been signed, I assumed you'd be anxious to return to the country."

"Lord Devereaux leaves tomorrow, Mr. Coutts," John said. "He's just taking the air today."

"Quite right, given that this has been the only fine day all week." Coutts gestured along the road. "Care to join me? My club's not far. I was going that way for a brandy with Mr. Drummond."

Charles shook his head.

"I'll stand your drinks if that's your concern. I can afford to be generous."

Since when has a banker exhibited generosity?

John let out a snort, and the banker stared at Charles's hands.

"I take it you harbor a degree of cynicism when it comes to recognizing the generosity of men in my profession," he said, "but a banker can afford to be generous toward a client who has just deposited ten thousand in his account. Your man would, of course, also be welcome as my guest. The other members are hardly likely to object, given that my bank's issued loans to most of them, including the chair of the membership committee."

Charles raised his eyebrows and glanced at John.

"Come, come, Devereaux," Coutts said. "Your man is eager for you to accept on his behalf. Stranger things have happened at White's. Did you know that Viscount de Blanchard brought a doxy into the clubroom in a gentleman's garb claiming that she was his nephew? Most members would have called out a gentleman for having the audacity to bring a woman through the front door of White's. But I'm not an advocate of dueling, and I came to the conclusion that the poor woman deserved a little reward for having to endure De Blanchard's company."

"Does de Blanchard bank with you, Mr. Coutts?" John asked.

The banker shook his head. "While it's my business to make a profit from issuing loans, and the greater the risk of repayment, the higher the premium"—he glanced at Charles—"I'm an astute enough businessman to understand that some risks are simply not worth taking when the probability of repayment is slightly less than the probability of Sir Heath Moss joining a monastery. Forgive me, I trust neither gentleman is a friend of yours."

Quite the opposite.

John conveyed Charles's response, and Coutts chuckled. "That settles it. You must join me for a brandy to wish you a safe journey back to your wife."

White's was only a short walk from the entrance to Hyde Park, as was Foxton's London residence. Unsurprisingly, Foxton himself was settled in a corner of the clubroom, glass in hand, surrounded by sycophantic young men eager to ingratiate themselves with a duke. Doubtless he was rarely required to pay for a round of drinks in the clubroom.

The duke glanced up as Charles entered, raised his glass in salute, then resumed his conversation. Coutts led Charles and John to a quiet corner away from the rest of the members.

"My *very superior* usual please, Samuel," he said to an approaching footman, "and the same for my two friends."

The footman raised his eyebrows, gave a conspiratorial wink, then bowed and slipped away.

"I have a special bottle of Hennessy set aside here," Mr. Coutts said. "Very Superior Old Pale—some newfangled style. The name's something of an affectation, but it's smoother on the palate, so in that respect it lives up to its overly grand description. It was produced at the request of the regent himself, though I daresay he'd have me incarcerated in the Tower if he knew I'd got my hands on a bottle. I trust it will make your entering White's with me worth your while."

Not if it's like all other brandy in that it tastes like horse's piss.

John quirked his mouth into a smile and the banker laughed.

"I may not understand your gestures, Devereaux, but I take it your cynicism is coming to the fore again? If the brandy's not to your taste, I'm sure your man will drink yours for you."

The footman returned with three glasses on a salver. He bowed with reverence, as if he carried the regent's jewels, then watched as the three men took up their glasses and took sips.

The liquid burst with flavor on Charles's tongue, giving none of the harshness of strong liquor. He closed his eyes to savor the taste, then swallowed, letting it slip down his throat, radiating warmth through his body.

Devil's breeches, that was good.

Coutts raised his glass in salute, then leaned back in his chair as the three men fell into a companionable silence—preferable to the inane chatter of Society any day, and certainly preferable to whatever conversation Foxton was indulging in with his friends.

"Well, well, well!" a voice said. "You're the last man I expected to see *here*."

Charles glanced up to see Sir Heath Moss.

If ever a man epitomized the theory that beauty on the outside was matched with a black heart within, it was the man standing before him.

"Don't trouble yourself to get up," Sir Heath said. "I've no intention of joining you. I'm not a man to fraternize with *tradesmen*."

Coutts curled his lips in a smile. "Is that because you're in debt to most of them?" he said. "I flatter myself in not being among your numerous creditors. Mr. Drummond is to be pitied—you bank with him, I believe?"

"I say, old chap," Sir Heath said, his eyes glittering with spite. "Commerce is hardly an appropriate subject for a gentlemen's clubroom. But one can hardly expect you to engage in appropriate conversation, given the company you're keeping. Perhaps the club secretary should hear of this. He's a personal friend of mine."

"And a client of mine," Coutts said, sounding bored. "Which reminds me, the coupon on his bond is due for payment."

Sir Heath's expression hardened, then he glanced at John. "I suppose fraternizing with tradesmen is the lesser sin compared to fraternizing with those whose place is below stairs."

Coutts's knuckles whitened as he tightened his grip on his brandy glass. "My late wife was of humble origins."

"I meant no offense," Sir Heath said. "At least you had the discernment to refrain from marrying a girl stained by illegitimacy. Every man has his level, but I fear had you married someone's *natural daughter*, your bank would not have enjoyed the level of success is has to date. Which reminds me…"

He turned to Charles and gave him a broad smile, revealing large, white, even teeth—teeth that Charles itched to loosen with his fist.

"How is that wife of yours, Devereaux?" Sir Heath nodded to Coutts. "I happened across Lady Devereaux—Miss Whitcombe, as she was then—in an extraordinary position with Devereaux on a balcony. It was nearing the end of the Season, when unattached young women succumb to their desperation, so perhaps that accounts for it. Ingenuity in a woman is to be applauded when she devises stratagems to snare a marriage partner, and a woman of questionable birth has an even greater need for…"

His voice trailed away as Charles leaped to his feet and grasped Sir Heath's throat, turning his body such that his actions were not visible to the other occupants in the clubroom.

Sir Heath opened his mouth, but nothing came out save a strained gasp.

Speak ill of my wife again, and I'll ensure you never speak again.

As if he could read Charles's mind, the arrogance in Sir Heath's eyes disappeared, replaced by the raw, base terror of the bully being bested by his victim.

"Y-your wife…" he began, and Charles tightened his grip,

pressing his thumb against the other man's throat.

Go on, you blackguard, I dare you to say it. I only need tighten my grip a little more to end your life.

Sir Heath let out a low moan and Charles lowered his gaze to the man's breeches, where a dark stain was spreading across the fabric, moving down one leg.

Clearly Sir Heath's valet dressed his master to the left.

"C-Coutts, aren't you going to…" Sir Heath croaked, but the banker merely took another sip of his brandy and turned his attention to Charles's valet.

"Mr. Richards, I trust the brandy is to your taste," he said, "even if the company's a little lacking. There's little I can do about the former, of course, but much can be done to deal with the latter."

"I believe Lord Devereaux has the matter in hand," John said, with a smile. "You need have no concern regarding the brandy, which is particularly fine."

"I'll have my clerk send you a bottle, seeing as you display such discernment. Of course"—Coutts glanced at Sir Heath, whose face was turning a shade of puce—"some fellows have such little understanding of true discernment that I fear they'll never be satisfied with their lot—neither will they understand the difference between good and evil, nor have the good grace to apologize for their transgressions."

Sir Heath glanced toward Coutts then back at Charles.

"I-I apologize…" he sputtered.

Charles released him, and Sir Heath grasped his throat, drawing breath.

What for?

Sir Heath glanced at Charles's hands.

"Lord Devereaux wishes to understand the nature of the transgression you're apologizing for," John said.

"A reasonable question to ask," Coutts added. "When a man breaches the rules of decency and kindness at least a hundred times each day, he must make certain to clarify which transgression he's seeking absolution for. Sir Heath, if you wish to apologize for *all* your faults, I fear you'll be here all day."

"I-I apologize for insulting Lady Devereaux," Sir Heath said, gritting his teeth as if the words pained him.

"Unreservedly?" Coutts said.

Sir Heath nodded, massaging the base of his throat. "Bloody hell, Devereaux, that hurt," he said, his voice carrying a note of petulance.

"Go whine about it to your friends," Coutts said. "Better still, your banker. He must be a very sympathetic character, given the size of your loans with him." He raised his hand. "I say, Drummond! Care to join us? Sir Heath and I were just discussing you."

The fear in Sir Heath's eyes intensified—the fear of a man who valued his cashflow more than his life.

A neatly dressed man with a thick head of black hair peppered with gray approached.

"Coutts!" he said. "And Sir Heath Moss. A pleasure as always."

"Drummond," Sir Heath muttered, then he slipped away, ignoring the raucous greetings from Foxton and his set, and scuttled toward the exit.

"Something I said?" Drummond asked, settling into a button-backed chair.

"No, something he did," Coutts said, with a grin. "In his breeches."

"That explains the odor," Drummond said. He nodded to Charles. "Lord Devereaux, a pleasure. I didn't know you were in London, or I'd have arranged a meeting."

What for? I don't bank with you.

"To discuss your wife's arrangements," Drummond said after John conveyed Charles's question. "The sale of her annuity—at least, part of it. Forgive me, I thought it was undertaken at your direction, seeing as your steward—Mr. Carlton, isn't it?—issued the instructions. I can arrange a meeting tomorrow to discuss the particulars, though the sale was finalized almost a month ago."

Almost a month? Which meant that she must have made the arrangement shortly after he'd left for London.

For how much?

The banker raised his eyebrows in inquiry, and Charles placed his hands together then drew them apart slowly.

"You're inquiring as to the amount? One thousand, if I recall."

One thousand? *Devil's breeches,* what was she thinking?

"I say, Drummond, ought you to be discussing this here?" Coutts said. "After all, a client's confidentiality is—"

"There are no secrets between a man and his wife," Drummond said. "If I recall, Mr. Carlton said in his letter that Lord Devereaux approved the withdrawal. Lady Devereaux is unlikely to be capable of concealing the matter from her husband—after all, the release of such a substantial sum is bound to attract a man's attention, unless his wife is…"

Charles leaned forward. *Unless my wife is what? Purchasing trinkets for a lover?*

Drummond shook his head. "Forgive me, I don't understand you."

Charles gestured to John. *Tell him.*

John frowned and signed back, *I'm not asking such a question. Would you have me insult your wife in the manner of Sir Heath?*

I want to know what she's done, Charles signed.

Then ask her rather than listen to gossip. She may have a valid reason.

For spending a thousand pounds under false pretenses? Charles shook his head. *A wife's extravagance can only mean one thing when it is undertaken without her husband's knowledge behind my back. My father…*

John pushed Charles's hands away. "Your wife is not your father, sir."

"Ahem."

Bugger. John had spoken aloud.

Coutts cleared his throat. "Perhaps you should discuss the

matter your valet in private. Better still, your wife." He glanced at Drummond. "My friend here oughtn't have broken his client's confidence. I'm sure there's nothing untoward taking place. The Whitcombe family have banked with Coutts for generations—since our establishment, in fact—and we pride ourselves on discretion."

Discretion—*ugh*. Charles's father had used that word to justify his numerous affairs. Provided nobody knew of his infidelity, it mattered not whether it drove the Penham estate into near bankruptcy, or Charles's own mother into such despair that she sought comfort in the arms of other men.

Is that what my Olivia has been driven to, on account of my own neglect?

But whatever his actions had been, there was no justification for deception.

Perhaps it was Fate's way of repaying him for the sins his father had committed against his mother—a cruel twist of fate where the female sex redressed the balance against the male.

Coutts patted the seat of the chair next to him. "Come, Devereaux, sit, and I'll stand you another brandy."

But Charles didn't need brandy. He needed to know what his wife had been up to in his absence. And in two days he'd have the answer.

Whether he liked it or not.

CHAPTER THIRTY-TWO

*H*E'S HOME!

Olivia stood, flanked by the housekeeper and the steward, at the end of the line of servants, awaiting her husband's arrival.

As soon as she'd heard the sound of hooves in the distance, her heart lifted. Then the carriage emerged through the trees like the sun breaking through a cloud after a long winter.

Had he been counting the days until he could see her again?

And…might she see him smile?

She placed a hand over her belly. Would he be pleased, or angry, when he discovered that she was expecting his child?

Her eyes misted with tears once more and she wiped them away. What was happening to her? Lately she'd suffered bouts of melancholy that had gripped her for no reason. She'd been taking Dr. Cheam's tonic, which had reduced the nausea, though this morning she'd expelled her breakfast. But she assumed that was due to the anticipation of her husband's return, for a little voice whispered in her mind that a part of her still feared him.

"Lady Devereaux?" A warm hand took hers. "Are you well?"

"I-I'm just a little apprehensive, Mrs. Brougham."

The housekeeper patted her hand. "That's understandable, ma'am. But he'll be pleased to be home. He never liked London that much, and he'll be delighted with what you've done."

"Will he?" Olivia said, her confidence waning. "It's his home, and I have no right…"

"You have *every* right, my dear, and if he doesn't appreciate the efforts you've made, then I'll bend him over my knee and give him the strap."

Olivia smiled at the thought of the housekeeper wrestling her huge master to the ground.

"Mr. Carlton can hold him down while I administer the punishment," the housekeeper said. "What say you, Mr. Carlton?"

The steward nodded. "Anything you say, Mrs. Brougham. It doesn't pay to disagree with you."

Olivia suppressed a smile as the steward gave the housekeeper a look of devotion.

"There!" Mrs. Brougham said. "You've a little color on your cheeks now, ma'am. I feared you were going to swoon earlier. I don't suppose you're…"

Her voice trailed away as the carriage drew to a halt. A footman climbed down from the back and opened the door. Olivia's heart fluttered as a huge hand appeared on the window frame. Then the world before her blurred and she caught her breath and tilted sideways.

A strong arm caught her waist.

"I've got you, Lady Devereaux," Carlton said. "I *said* you've been working too hard."

"Sweet tea, that's what you need," Mrs. Brougham said. "I'll have Ethel take a pot to the morning room before luncheon."

Olivia nodded her thanks, her heart rate increasing as she caught sight of her husband. He swung his legs out of the carriage, then climbed out, unfolding his huge frame with some stiffness. His valet followed, leaping out of the carriage, before he stopped to brush his hands along his master's wrinkled sleeves.

Charles shooed him away, frowning, then turned toward the house, his eyes darkening as he fixed his gaze on her.

She motioned a greeting.

Welcome home.

He tilted his head to one side, studying her hands, but made no attempt to respond, then lowered his gaze to her waist. Carlton released her and stepped back.

"H-have I done it wrong, Mrs. Brougham?" Olivia asked.

"No, my dear—you were perfectly clear in your hand signs."

"Then why isn't he…"

Her husband's frown deepened, then he moved his hands.

"I-I don't understand," Olivia said. "He's doing it too quickly. Charles, what are you trying to say?"

He stopped, hands in midair, turned to his valet, and gestured again. John let out a huff and responded, his movements more measured and precise. Olivia recognized some of the gestures that Mrs. Brougham had been teaching her, two words…

Wife, and *deceive*.

"Are you accusing me of deceit, Charles?"

He gestured toward the steward.

"Lord Devereaux, I can assure you that your wife and I have not—"

Charles slapped his fist into his palm, and cold fingers clawed at Olivia's stomach. "Exactly what sort of deception do you think I've been engaged in, husband?"

Charles gestured again, and Mrs. Brougham let out a huff.

"Foolish boy!"

"What did he say?" Olivia said. "John—won't you tell me?"

John opened his mouth to reply, and the housekeeper stepped forward.

"*Pas devant les domestiques*, Mr. Richards," she said.

"Which means what?" Olivia asked.

Mrs. Brougham clapped her hands. "Return to your duties, all of you," she said. "Ethel, take some tea to the morning room. Colin, have luncheon ready in the dining room in fifteen minutes."

The servants dispersed, whispering among themselves.

"Enough of *that*!" the butler said. "Anyone caught gossiping, I'll dismiss them immediately without a reference."

The servants replied with a chorus of "Yes, Mr. Reynolds."

"Lord Devereaux," Carlton said, "it's not what you think."

Charles's gaze darkened further. He made a series of gestures, then nodded to his valet.

"Lord Devereaux wishes to know what you believe he thinks has been happening, and…" John hesitated, and Charles glared at him. "He wishes to know why you…"

Charles gestured again, and Olivia recognized, once again, the sign for *wife*. Then he nudged John, almost knocking him off balance.

The valet let out a huff. "Lord Devereaux wishes to know what you and his wife have been up to, spending large sums of money, having led the bank to believe that the expenditure had his approval."

Olivia's apprehension turned to indignation.

"Lord Devereaux, your wife and I—" Carlton began, but Olivia interrupted.

"It's my money to spend as I see fit, husband, or do you think me incapable of managing my money due to my sex?"

Charles's eyes widened, then he shook his head.

"Not my sex, then," she said. "Perhaps it's my birth that gives you cause for concern? Perhaps you believe I'm not entitled to my own money, given that I'm a bastard."

He slammed his fist into his palm, then gesticulated with sharp, angry movements. Olivia's stomach heaved and she clapped her hand over her mouth. But her attempts to stem the swell of nausea were in vain. Her body convulsed and she darted to the side of the house.

"Lady Devereaux, come back!" John called. "Lord Devereaux wants you to—"

"I care not what he wants!" she cried. "I want him to leave me alone! I want you *all* to leave me alone!"

She darted around the side of the building into a secluded part of the garden, then bent over and retched. She lost her balance and stumbled into the dirt, convulsing with nausea until her body ached. But her stomach was empty—there was nothing left to expel. At length, the nausea subsided, but a sharp pain throbbed behind her temples, and she groaned in pain.

Footsteps approached and she cringed, willing whoever it was to pass by. But they stopped.

"Leave me be," she whimpered.

"Why would I do that, my dear?" Mrs. Brougham said.

"I-I can't be seen like this. What will he think of me that he doesn't already think?"

The housekeeper let out a huff. "He ought to be more concerned about what we all think of *him*."

Olivia struggled to her feet, then burst into tears as she spotted a smear of mud on her skirts.

"Oh, Lady Devereaux! It's only a little dirt. That'll wash out, no trouble."

"I-it's not that," Olivia said. "I-I can't stop crying. Even when I think I'm happy, I find myself crying over nothing…when the pastry for that pie split yesterday, when I spilled my tea… And back then, I wanted to cry so badly, though it would make him angrier than he already is. What's the matter with me?"

Mrs. Brougham placed her arm around Olivia's shoulders. "Sweet girl, did your mother never tell you?"

"M-my mother died giving birth to me. I was brought up by the schoolmistress. She taught me to read and write."

"But not about marriage?"

Olivia shook her head. "Sh-she said I'd never find a husband because of my birth, so I'd have to work hard to support myself. Am I always to be blamed for how I came into the world?" She caught her breath to suppress a sob. "M-my brother took me in, tried to turn me into a lady, but I wish he hadn't. It would have been better if I'd not been born."

"Hush, my dear, you don't mean that," Mrs. Brougham said, drawing Olivia into her arms. "You're just a little overwhelmed, that's all. Some sweet tea and a rest will set you right."

"B-but it's happening all the time."

The housekeeper stroked Olivia's cheek. "The late mistress

was just the same, you know. It was how she could tell."

"Tell what?"

"That she was with child."

Olivia drew in a sharp breath.

Mrs. Brougham nodded. "How long have you known, child? Since you took your tumble down the stairs, I'll warrant—when Dr. Cheam was called?"

"You mustn't tell anyone."

"Surely Susie knows. It's almost a month since Dr. Cheam's visit."

"I've not told her."

"She's been tending to your bedsheets. But then, she's very young. Perhaps she's not realized. But someone will notice—and soon. You wouldn't want one of the chamber maids to know before Lord Devereaux, surely?"

"I-I'd rather Charles didn't know."

"He'll find out eventually."

"He won't be pleased," Olivia said, cringing at the memory of Charles's written words. "H-he told me he didn't want a child."

"Does he think a child springs from a woman uninvited?" Mrs. Brougham let out a huff. "Men! They play as much a part in begetting a child as women—more so, for they're always pestering a woman to engage in intimacy."

Oh, heaven!

Olivia clamped her mouth shut as another tide of nausea rippled through her.

"Oh, forgive me, I've shocked you," Mrs. Brougham said. "But you mustn't set any store by what Lord Devereaux tells you."

"He wrote it down."

"Foolish boy! But I've lived long enough in this world to know that men are all talk. They'll assert an opinion or make a promise merely to put an end to a conversation, with no intention of holding the opinion or keeping the promise."

"All men?"

"Without exception. They're the most insufferable creatures."

"Wh-what about Mr. Brougham?"

"He doesn't exist, Lady Devereaux. I'm neither married nor widowed. My address as Mrs. Brougham is merely a title afforded to housekeepers."

"Why didn't I know that?" Olivia said, shaking her head. "I'll never learn it all—or be a proper lady."

She let out another sob, and the housekeeper squeezed her hand.

"That's enough of that, my dear," she said. "You're mistress of Penham and deserve the respect that comes with the title. You've done admirably in the short time you've been here. In a matter of weeks, you've learned how to run a house, managed the works to the garden, learned several hand signs, and even taught Mrs. Groves to bake a passable pie! Not to mention the gift you've purchased for his lordship. In my ledger, that makes you far greater than any fine lady that Lord Devereaux might have brought here instead. Now, why don't you come back inside with me, and we'll see about that tea?"

Olivia shook her head. "I'd rather remain outside for a while."

"But..."

"Am I not the mistress of Penham?"

Mrs. Brougham smiled. "That you are, and I'm glad of it. Very well, come inside when you're ready and I'll have a pot of tea waiting for you. That is, if I've not poured it over the numbskull of a husband of yours."

She winked, then gave Olivia a motherly kiss on her forehead before she returned to the house.

⌘

CHAPTER THIRTY-THREE

"**B**LOODY HELL, SIR!" John cried as Olivia disappeared around the side of the house. "I told you not to come to conclusions about Lady Devereaux."

Charles raised his hands to admonish his valet, then lowered them again. John was, after all, in the right. But the sight of Olivia, with Carlton's hands all over her, was enough to boil his blood, and it was all he could do to restrain himself from smashing his fist into his steward's nose.

He approached Carlton, but Mrs. Brougham stepped in front of the steward, her eyes glittering with anger.

"Haven't you done enough harm for one day, Lord Devereaux?"

I ought to have you dismissed for insubordination.

She glared at his hand gestures. "Dismiss me and be damned," she said. "Do you honestly think Mr. Carlton has been behaving inappropriately toward your wife?"

"Mrs. Brougham," Carlton began, I hardly think—"

"And you can be quiet, Gerald."

Gerald?

Carlton flinched and nodded in acquiescence.

John let out a chuckle.

I fail to see what's so bloody amusing.

"Then you're doubly blind, sir," the valet said. "I think we may be assured that Mr. Carlton has no designs on your wife. For one thing, he values his position as your steward too highly, and for another, he values his balls."

Does he think I'll cut them off?

"Whatever punishment you dole out will be nothing compared to Mrs. Brougham's."

Charles frowned and turned his attention to the housekeeper, who was giving Carlton a look of frustration combined with not a little affection.

You mean my housekeeper and steward are...?

Charles made a random gesture, unwilling to articulate his suspicion.

"Isn't it obvious?" John said. "Even the biggest simpleton would have noticed the way he gazes at her like a lovesick puppy. But an even bigger simpleton would harbor suspicions about your wife."

In truth, I had no suspicions about her.

"Then why display such anger? Couldn't you see how eager she was to greet you?"

Charles had to admit that his wife's expression had carried a sheen of joy. But surely that couldn't have been due to his returning?

I'm not angry at her. He let out a sigh before continuing. *I'm angry because she continues to speak of her birth as if she believes it makes her worthless.*

He turned to Carlton.

I'm angry because she felt she had to deceive me with your assistance.

The steward shook his head. "I don't understand..."

"But I do," Mrs. Brougham said. "Perhaps, your lordship, you should ask your wife what she's been occupying herself with during your absence before you cast judgment."

Charles glanced in the direction Olivia had fled. He took a step forward, and the housekeeper caught his sleeve.

"No, sir. Let me. I'll not have her any more upset." She gestured to the coachman. "Well? Don't just sit there! Bring in his lordship's trunks."

Mumbling assent, the coachman climbed down and unloaded the trunks.

"Perhaps you'd like to take your luncheon," Mrs. Brougham said. "It should be all ready in the dining room. I'll see if Lady Devereaux wishes to join you. Mr. Richards, would you be so kind as to accompany Lord Devereaux while I see to her ladyship?"

"Of course." John caught Charles's wrist. "There's no good in your going after her, sir. Leave it to Mrs. Brougham. In any case, when you wish to earn the trust of a nervous filly, you don't rush out into the field and tether her right away. You wait for her to come to you."

Charles followed his valet inside, pausing to glance at the foot of the stairs, then he entered the dining room, where two footmen milled about, placing dishes of food on the table. In the center of the table was an enormous pie, the pastry golden brown and glistening in the sunlight. The top was decorated with motifs that had been fashioned into the shapes of vines and roses, curling around the body of the pie. The detail was exquisite, right down to the markings on the leaves and the thorns adorning the rose stems.

It was a thing of such beauty that he didn't know whether to cut a slice and eat it, or have it placed in a display cabinet.

"Have we a new cook, Colin?" John said, settling into his seat.

The younger of the two footmen glanced up, blushing as he caught Charles's eye, and shook his head.

"You may speak," John said, grinning. "The benefit of Lord Devereaux not speaking is that he won't shout at you. Has Lady Devereaux hired a new cook in his lordship's absence?"

The boy stepped back, his color deepening.

Not even the finest cook in the world would cost one thousand pounds.

"Now, now, sir, it's not the time to be churlish," John said. "Colin, who baked this pie? Lord Devereaux won't bite you, I promise. Only the pie."

"I-it was Lady Devereaux."

Charles rose, and the boy stepped back, fear glistening in his eyes.

"Sh-she was up late into the night making it, your lordship. All week she's been showing Mrs. Groves how to get the pastry just right so it's not hard on the teeth. I-it's pork and apple, sir. Pork from Mr. Faulkes's farm. Proper tasty."

How the devil would he know?

Ignoring Charles, John nodded to the boy. "Have you tried some?"

"Oh yes! When Lady Devereaux first made one, she shared it among all of us. She wanted to try it out to get it just right for when his lordship returned home."

"Thank you, Colin," John said. "You may leave us now."

The young footman exited the dining room, and Charles approached the door.

"Colin's done nothing wrong, sir. There's no need to go after him."

I know that, Charles signed. *I'm the one in the wrong.*

"Where are you going, then?"

To apologize to my wife. I've no right to eat a pie she made for me while she's unhappy elsewhere, especially when I'm the cause of her unhappiness.

He waited for a caustic response from his valet, but none came.

As he emerged from the dining room, a housemaid scuttled past, increasing the pace as she caught sight of him. He climbed the stairs and made his way to his wife's bedchamber. His heart sank as he heard sobbing from within, and he paused, his hand on the doorknob, swallowing his shame at eavesdropping on his wife's misery. Then he heard a voice.

"Don't be such a fool, Susie. You know as well as I that it's the only thing to be done."

"No! I cannot be party to this!"

"The bitch and her pup cannot be allowed to live. If you say anything, I'll tell everyone what you've done."

"B-but you made me do it even though I didn't want to!"

"Ungrateful brat, after everything I've done for you! I—Shh!"

The voice broke off, then footsteps approached, and the door opened to reveal a young woman. Behind her, standing at the fireplace, was his wife's maid. But there was no sign of Olivia.

"Oh!" The woman dipped into a curtsey. "Begging your pardon, Lord Deveraux. Are you looking for her ladyship?"

She was the one who'd been fawning over Jacob. Pretty enough, but behind the smile, a look of greed shone in her eyes.

What are you doing in my wife's chamber?

The woman glanced at his hands and shook her head. "I-I don't..."

"Nicola is my sister, your lordship," the maid said. "Sh-she's a friend of Lady Devereaux's and has visited several times." She wiped her eyes and sniffed.

Why are you distressed? What were you speaking of?

"Forgive me, your lordship, I don't understand."

He pointed to his right eye then ran his fingertip down his cheek. Then he gestured to both women.

"I-I'm merely upset b-because—"

"Because one of our pa's collies needs to be put down," Nicola interrupted. "She's broken a leg and can no longer run. Isn't that right, Susie?"

She glared at the maid, whose lip wobbled. Then she pulled her into an embrace. But Susie's distress only seemed to increase.

"My poor sister's a little weak-minded, your lordship. She becomes attached to anything and everything, and was quite taken with the dog. But you'll recover, won't you, Susie?"

The maid nodded, though her eyes were still clouded with distress—and something akin to fear.

"Were you looking for Olivia?"

Charles frowned. Who was this woman, to refer to his wife with such familiarity? Clearly he'd been away too long, and Mrs.

Brougham had been overly lax, if strangers treated his wife's chamber as if it were their own.

"Nicola, I think you ought to leave," Susie said. "Th-thank you for comin' to see me, but perhaps you should return downstairs. Or you could seek out Jacob, as it's him you came to see."

"He's nowhere to be found. I think he's avoiding me. I saw him looking at Mrs. Temple's youngest—Lily, or whatever the little slut's name is."

How dare they gossip before him like milkmaids! Charles clapped his hands and they stopped. Two pairs of eyes regarded him—one set filled with fear and misery, the other thoughtful and calculating.

Susie nudged her sister, who dipped into a curtsey. "Forgive me, Lord Devereaux, I ought to go and find Jacob. He'll be wondering where I am."

Charles frowned at her, and she curtseyed again then slipped out of the chamber.

"I-I think Lady Devereaux may still be outside, your lordship, if you're lookin' for her," the maid said. "Mr. Reynolds said I was to wait for her here, sayin' she might be in need of me. She was unwell this morning, you see, and I was concerned that..."

She paused as he raised his hand. Then he exited the chamber.

After he closed the door, the sobbing resumed. He leaned against the wall, waiting for it to subside, but it only increased. Surely the girl, no matter how sensitive her nerves might be, wouldn't be in such a state of hysterics over a sheepdog? But women were an enigma—it was the only adage his father uttered that he agreed with.

Father usually followed that particular maxim by saying it was not a man's responsibility to delve into the murky waters of a woman's mind, for there lay the path to becoming a henpecked husband. But Charles found himself wanting to understand his wife—not to delve into her mind, but to make amends. And he wanted to see her smile.

Was he turning into a henpecked husband? Or was he merely falling in love? Most men of Society, profligates such as Foxton, saw love as a weakness, or they considered it to be merely a surrender to one's physical needs—an act to commit for a moment's satisfaction before moving on to the next woman.

But Charles's mother had always said that love had little to do with attraction or desire, and everything to do with striving to make the world a better place for another, even if it were to the detriment of one's own happiness. It was the love a mother had for her child, a wife for her husband…

Much good it had done her. Though Mother had loved others, there was no one to love her other than a small child with little understanding of the world. And Charles had been too young when she died to understand the meaning of love, to see that, despite a marriage in which she'd suffered abuse and neglect, she had striven to make Charles happy. She'd given him every comfort—a warm pair of loving arms, someone to soothe him to sleep at night during thunderstorms…

Until she had been ripped away from him, her life taken from her at the foot of this very staircase.

And it had been his fault.

He closed his eyes, striving to see her beautiful smile, but all he could see was the memory of the day his life had changed…the terror in her eyes while Father beat him, her grim determination as she wrapped her arms around him, and finally…

…her wide-open stare as the spark of life left her while she clung to the boy she'd sacrificed her life to save. But he was a worthless soul incapable of love, whom the Almighty, in his cruelty, chose to save in exchange for the kindest, most loving woman who had ever lived.

Mama!

The last word he had ever uttered echoed in his mind, as sharp and clear as if the child he'd once been was there before him. Then the sightless eyes shimmered and changed color, becoming a clear, warm honey…

The sightless eyes of his wife.

He let out a groan, bent forward, and opened his eyes, rubbing them to dispel the image. What the devil was happening to him?

He blinked and caught sight of something small and shiny at the base of the longcase clock. He crouched down and retrieved it. A marble. Glancing underneath the clock, he caught sight of another that had rolled further back, too far to reach.

His wife's chamber door opened, and the young maid emerged. She gave a low cry as she caught sight of him.

"Oh, your lordship, what's happened?"

He held out the marble.

She stared at it, her eyes widening, then burst into tears again.

"Forgive me—it wasn't my fault. *Please!*"

Rising to his feet, Charles brushed the dust from his breeches then waved her away. Would that the Almighty could save him from overly hysterical maids! Mrs. Brougham ought to send the girl packing, or at least keep her away from Olivia.

Olivia…

What the bloody hell was he doing, wallowing in self-pity?

He pocketed the marble then went outside in search of his wife.

Where was she? Had she been foolish enough to venture into the forest again?

He crossed the driveway, his boots crunching on the gravel, then heard male voices coming from the gardens. He set off in the direction of the voices, turned a corner, then froze.

The garden had been transformed. The path that had previously stretched ahead in a straight line now curved from side to side, leading the observer's eye toward the midpoint where a large armillary sphere stood atop a stone pillar. A box hedge, newly planted, formed a series of arcs, dividing the garden into sections. At the far end of the path, a tall, broad-shouldered man with an unruly mop of brown hair stood, leaning on a shovel, talking to Carlton. He threw back his head and laughed, his breath misting in the winter air. Charles approached them, and the laughter stopped. The man smoothed down the front of his breeches and extended his hand.

"Lawrence Baxter, at your service, Lord Devereaux."

"Soon to be *Sir* Lawrence Baxter, if the rumors are true," the steward added. "And very well deserved if it happens. The gardens he's designed are among the best in the kingdom."

"Mr. Carlton, you're too kind," the man said, his voice rich and deep.

Charles cocked his head to one side and regarded the gardener. His body, toned and athletic, was in a relaxed pose, his shirt unbuttoned at the throat, sleeves rolled up to reveal muscular arms. Clear hazel eyes stared back at him in a face with strong features and a broad, honest smile.

"Have you heard of Mr. Baxter?" Carlton said. "His wife, Lady Arabella, is a friend of Lady Devereaux's...well, a friend of her sister's."

"Delighted to meet you at last, Lord Devereaux," Baxter said. "You're fortunate in your choice of wife. Her ladyship has a most extraordinary imagination, and it's been a privilege to bring her ideas to life."

What the bloody hell was the man rattling on about? Charles raised his eyebrows and glanced at his steward, who cleared his throat with some degree of trepidation.

"Ahem—I fear Lord Devereaux has been unaware of her ladyship's activities while he's been in London."

"Oh, lorks!" the gardener said. "Have I spoiled her ladyship's surprise? My Bella would have my ballocks if she knew. Chews them up something proper when I've done wrong. Mind you, she thinks up the most delicious penances and can be very forgiving when I..." He hesitated, his cheeks coloring. "Never mind that—I trust you'll forgive the words of a man who's been parted from his wife for too long. But you'll know how that feels, won't you, Lord Devereaux?"

Yes. Charles knew exactly how it felt, though doubtless Baxter wouldn't make an arse of himself when he reunited with his wife.

"Shall I show you around?" the gardener said. "There's just the hedging to finish, then we're done. Lady Devereaux was most anxious for it to be ready for your arrival."

He gestured about the garden. "We've divided the area into sections, each focusing on a sense—touch, taste, and so forth. This one"—he indicated the first section—"is for the eyes, for when one is in need of color to uplift the spirits. Lady Devereaux calls it the Rainbow Garden. I'm afraid it doesn't look like much just now, but come the spring, these shrubs will fill it with myriad colors. My Bella has designed the color scheme, and the seeds I've given your men to cultivate will yield flowering plants to fill the gaps."

My men? Charles raised his eyebrows.

"Lady Devereaux has hired two gardeners," Carlton said.

Charles stared at the steward. How could the estate afford the expense?

"Paid for out of her annuity," Carlton continued, "the remaining portion of it, at least. The garden's too much for one man, particularly old Mr. Jenks, but he has two sons who've been assisting Mr. Baxter. Lady Devereaux gave them permanent positions as under-gardeners to their father. They're good workers."

"*I'll* say they are," Baxter said. "Put my own employees to shame. They'll see you right, and I'll come over in the spring to make sure they're tending to things properly. Gardening's an art, you know. It's not just digging up weeds and clipping hedges. Shall we?"

He led the way through an iron-framed archway toward another section of the garden.

"I've planted some climbers that will soon cover this archway," he said. "They're fast growing, so in a year or two they'll form a tunnel. They flower twice a year—beautiful blooms. I've chosen a mixture of varieties to ensure you'll have flowers all through spring and summer. They're among my Bella's favorite, and we have them in our own garden."

As they continued, Charles caught the faint sound of music—deep, woody notes, as if nymphs chatted to each other, set against a backdrop of delicate chimes. At first he wondered if they were a figment of his imagination, but the music grew louder as they entered the next section.

"This is Lady Devereaux's particular favorite," Baxter said. "She calls it the music garden, which needs no explanation."

Hanging in a corner was a set of tubular structures fashioned from a light, irregular-shaped wood. As a breeze swept across the garden, they danced and swayed, emitting deep tones that formed a harmonious chord.

Then the gardener led Charles through the remaining sections, each one designed to enhance the senses, until they came to the final area, the walled garden accessed via an iron gate. As Charles stepped through the gate, he caught his breath at the memory…his beloved mama, tending to the herbs while he helped as best as he could, her plucking a sprig of thyme then crushing it in her slim fingers, her beautiful smile bathing his soul in light as he inhaled the rich aroma…

The garden before him had been restored to the little haven of love he recalled from boyhood. The paving slabs had been scrubbed clean such that they shone in the sunlight. Around the perimeter, the borders were filled with a large variety of herbs. To a casual observer, they appeared to have been placed at random, but each plant contrasted in color with its neighbor to give a rippling effect, as if light were dancing across the ground.

How was it that there could be so many shades of green?

A seat had been placed near one corner, fashioned from a single block of wood that looked as if it had sprouted from the ground. And beside the seat, set in the corner, was a statue, fashioned from white marble into the shape of an angel. Her head tilted downward, she gazed at the ground, a serene smile on her lips.

Charles's heart gave a jolt as he stared at the angel's face. Then he blinked and shook his head. It was just the memory that had rendered him a little senseless, but he could have sworn the statue bore a resemblance to his mother.

"The statue was Lady Devereaux's idea," Baxter said. "She planted most of the herbs herself."

Charles raised his eyebrows.

"Aye, she did," Carlton said. "There was no stopping her, sir. She was most insistent. She may be a quiet little thing, but when she's set her mind on something, well… Who am I to refuse a determined woman? Planned this all herself, she did."

And paid for it, most likely, having sold a substantial portion of her annuity.

Bloody hell.

Never had Charles felt so ashamed. Even though he'd feared only for a heartbeat that she was spending her money on frivolities, that heartbeat was enough to confirm that he was the very worst of blackguards, and she the most unfortunate of women to have been saddled with him for a husband.

Where is she?

Baxter frowned, and Charles gestured about the garden.

"Ah." Carlton nodded. "I've no idea where Lady Devereaux is. Perhaps she's returned to the house?"

"She was with me earlier," Baxter said. "She looked a little unwell, but insisted on staying outside. I believe she may be somewhere near the stables—to see to your other gift."

What other gift?

"Oh lorks, I've done it again, haven't I? I take it you've no knowledge of—"

"Perhaps Lord Devereaux should go and see for himself, Mr. Baxter," Carlton interrupted. "We can discuss the settlement of your account now the garden's almost finished."

The gardener nodded, and the two men slipped through a gap in the hedge, leaving Charles in the herb garden, a garden that was almost an exact replica of the one he'd recalled from his childhood—the one thing that had brought light to his mother's life in the months leading to her demise.

Bloody hell, what the devil am I going to say to her? I've been a complete and utter arse.

Thrusting his hands in his jacket pockets, Charles made his way to the stables in search of his wife.

As he approached, he caught sight of the brown faces of the three of the coach horses in the nearest building. The fourth stood patiently in the stable yard while a young boy groomed the animal's flank with a long, sweeping motion. The boy let out a squeak as he spotted Charles and dropped the brush.

"L-Lord Devereaux, beg pardon."

For what? For daring to taint his master with his presence? *Devil's breeches,* the boy looked positively terrified.

Am I such an ogre that small boys and maidservants flee from me in terror?

Yes, he was, for his wife had fled from him.

He forced a smile, and the stable boy returned it.

"Come to see your horse, your lordship? He's as fine a beast as I ever saw. He's in the building yonder."

My horse?

The boy pointed toward the stable block at the far end of the courtyard. Charles nodded in acknowledgment and approached the building. Then he paused as he heard voices.

"You must tell him, Olivia. He won't be as angry as you think."

"I-I can't, Jacob. At least not yet. Nicola said…"

"Nicola can go to the devil. She had no right to suggest such a thing. I trust you didn't—"

"No, I didn't! What do you take me for?"

"So you want—"

"Of course I do! But does my husband?"

"He's a damned fool if he doesn't."

"What about you, Jacob, your hopes and expectations?"

Charles rounded a corner to see his wife—and Jacob, who had her by the shoulders.

"Good God, woman," Jacob said, "you think I care for that? Are you such a simpleton that you believe—"

He broke off as Charles marched forward, grasped him by the lapels, and pulled him back.

"Brother, I-I... I mean—it's not what it looks like," Jacob stammered, but Charles rammed his fist into his brother's gut. Jacob bent over, coughing, and Charles advanced on him again. Jacob raised his hands. "Stop, please!"

Charles slammed his fist into his palm and gestured in quick, angry movements.

How dare you put your hands on my wife!

"I-I wasn't... We weren't..." Jacob shook his head. "Surely you don't think your wife would..."

Of course not. I trust her completely. But you...

"I-I don't understand..." Jacob coughed, and Charles grasped him by the lapels.

"Charles!" Olivia cried.

Charles turned to her, his heart aching at the distress in her eyes. He took her hands and drew her close, stroking her hair. Then he released her and gestured slowly.

Did he hurt you?

She frowned, watching his hands. "We were only talking. Surely you don't think I would..."

No. I know you are incapable of wrongdoing. My only concern is whether you've come to harm at my brother's hands.

Her eyes shone with tears. "I-I'm sorry. I'm learning—Mrs. Brougham has been teaching me—but you're moving your hands too quickly."

"I think my brother is saying that you're the last woman who'd break faith with anyone," Jacob said. "At least, I bloody well hope so." He drew in a sharp breath and winced. "Fuck—you've a bastard of a left hook, brother."

"Then why..." Olivia began.

Jacob let out a laugh that turned into another cough. "Why did he punch me to the ground? Because, like all men in love, he wishes to protect you from those he believes are placing you in danger."

Olivia turned her gaze to Charles. Her eyes, at first, showed only confusion. Then, as the two of them continued to stare at each other, he caught a flicker of hope in them.

"Is that what you said, Charles?"

He glanced at his brother. *Damn it*—must he have an audience when revealing his heart?

At length, he raised his hands and moved them in a slow, deliberate gesture.

Yes.

"Jacob's your brother," she said, "and as such, I see him as my brother also—like Montague, but perhaps with a greater inclination to smile. Besides, he's in love with Nicola, are you not, Jacob?"

Jacob's jaw bulged as if he were gritting his teeth.

"He's been helping me tend to…" She turned toward the far stall. "W-would you like to see?"

She offered her hand. For a moment, Charles stared at it. How could she offer her hand, and her trust, to someone so unworthy? But it was not a gift to be denied. Gladly he took it, his blood warming with desire as she entwined her little fingers with his and ran her fingertips over his signet ring.

She led him into the building, and he inhaled deeply, relishing the soft, warm scent of hay and horse. As his eyes adjusted to the light, he caught sight of the silhouette of a horse, ears pricked up as if in recognition.

Sweet heaven…

Surely his eyes deceived him!

He approached the stall, blinking to dispel the image, but it solidified the closer he moved to the horse that stood patiently, waiting to be reunited with his master.

Destriero.

My *Destriero.*

His wife approached the horse, and Charles shook his head. Destriero, wary of strangers, had a wild streak. But she merely smiled.

"It's all right, Charles. Destriero and I have been getting acquainted, haven't we, darling boy?" She reached up, then placed her hand on Destriero's nose. The animal nodded his head up and down, and she giggled. "Are you wanting an apple? You're in luck, for I've procured one from the pantry. Best not to tell Mrs. Groves, though, or she'll give me *such* a scolding." She stroked the horse's nose. "We're friends already, aren't we, my sweetheart? But I suspect I'm not your *best* friend. That position lies with another, does it not?"

She turned her clear honey gaze to Charles, and his heart almost broke at the expression in her eyes, as if she were pleading for his approval.

He stepped forward, and the horse nickered softly. Charles placed his hand on the animal's flank and leaned against it, relishing the soft warmth and familiar scent of the horse that had been the only living thing he truly loved.

Until now.

He closed his eyes, and the horse shifted position, leaning toward him.

Yes, my boy. You are home—brought to me by an angel.

"Shall I return to the house and give you some space—time to reunite with your horse?" Olivia said, stepping back. "Perhaps you'd like to take him for a ride."

She turned to leave, and Charles caught her sleeve, then gestured, slowly.

No. Stay.

She studied his hands, then rewarded him with a smile. "Very well. Let me first give Destriero a treat. I fear I've been spoiling him since he arrived. He's such a beautiful horse."

She made a soft crooning sound, and the horse whinnied in response while she retrieved an apple from her pocket and held it out, palm upward. She giggled as the horse's lips brushed over her hand while he plucked the apple and munched it.

Charles watched his wife, his heart almost melting at the pure joy in her eyes.

Jacob limped toward him, then pulled him close and whispered in his ear.

"I have never envied you as much as I do now, brother. Not for your title—I care nothing for that—but because you've found yourself that rare thing. A good woman—no, the *best* of women."

I know.

"Then bloody well *tell* her."

How?

"Very well then—*show* her." Jacob grinned, his eyes gleaming with mischief. "I wouldn't recommend beating into a pulp every man who lays a hand on her. A woman rarely appreciates such a primitive act—outside the bedchamber, at least."

He winked, then held out his hand. Charles took it, then returned to the stall, where his wife was stroking Destriero's nose. He offered his arm, and with a smile she took it. Then he led her back toward the house.

CHAPTER THIRTY-FOUR

OLIVIA CLUNG TO her husband's arm, struggling to keep pace with him as he steered her through the gardens in long strides. She'd almost forgotten how huge he was. His frame had filled the stable, and she had been beset with fear as she saw the anger in his eyes, but that ire had been directed at Jacob. It was the anger of a male beast laying claim to his female and warding off a rival. Primal and raw, it should have disgusted her, but she couldn't help the secret thrill coursing through her veins when he drew her close and caressed her hair, his huge hands gentle, treating her with something akin to reverence.

When he'd caught sight of his horse, his anger had been replaced by pure joy. Olivia's heart had almost broken at the sheen of moisture in his eyes. He—a brooding, taciturn man large enough to fell a dozen opponents at once—had revealed a piece of his soul as he caressed his horse's flank.

Then, when she offered to leave him alone, he'd pleaded for her to stay, almost as if...

No.

A voice whispered in her mind not to yield to the hope that he might love her. She still feared his anger if he discovered her secret—that she carried a child he did not want.

Another wave of nausea caught her, and she stumbled sideways. But before she could fall, her husband swept her into his arms.

"Charles!" she protested. "Put me down. I can walk."

He shook his head. He was not a man to be denied, and, in truth, she had no wish to deny him anything. She wrapped her arms around his neck then placed her head on his shoulder, breathing in his woody scent.

He carried her to the house, refusing to set her down until they reached the dining room, where he nudged open the door with his foot and set her on the chair at one end of the table.

"Shall I ring for Colin to serve us?"

He shook his head.

Instead of taking his place at the opposite end of the table, he picked up his cutlery and set himself a place next to her. Then he gestured to the pie in the center of the table and raised his eyebrows.

"I-I baked it, yes."

Would he be angry that she'd displayed such unladylike behavior as working in the kitchen?

He moved his hands again, and she shook her head.

"Forgive me, I don't understand."

He reached for the stack of paper and pencil on the side table, then scratched out a few words and held it up.

I'm blessed to have such a talented wife.

"Y-you don't mind that I've been in the kitchen?"

He took her hand and brushed his lips against it, and she suppressed the shiver of need rippling over her skin.

Then he made another gesture, slowly, which she recognized. *Thank you.*

Her heart warmed at the softness in his eyes, which had turned a rich, warm chocolate.

"It was my pleasure."

He picked up a knife and cut into the pie. Olivia held her breath—she never knew whether a pie was a triumph or disaster until it was cut open. He made another cut, then lifted a wedge onto his plate.

Encased in crisp, light-brown pastry, the meat was a soft rose color mottled with different shades of pink and red. It formed three layers, separated by the pale-green slices of apple. Between the meat and pastry, a thick jelly glistened in the afternoon light.

Thank heaven! The meat was cooked through and the jelly set. Charles picked up the wedge and took a bite. He frowned in concentration, and his jaw moved up and down, then his throat bobbed as he swallowed.

"Is it not to your liking?" she said.

He blinked, and a sheen of moisture glistened in his eyes, then he drew back his chair and stood.

"Charles?"

Olivia's stomach flipped at the dark intensity in his eyes.

"I-I know I should have sought your permission before instructing Mr. Carlton to assist me with the garden, and the purchase of your h—"

She broke off as he placed a finger on her lips.

Slowly and awkwardly, he lowered himself to his knees. He took her hands and dipped his head, his chest rising and falling as he drew in a deep breath, followed by a long sigh that rippled over her skirts. He closed his eyes and touched his forehead to her knees, as if in prayer, and grew still.

Not daring to speak, Olivia held her breath and waited. Then, at length, he looked up. Her heart almost cleaved in two at the expression in his eyes. He lifted a hand and cupped her cheek, caressing her skin with his fingertips. Then he blinked and a tear splashed onto his cheek. He opened his mouth, and her heart gave a jolt.

Would he speak—say her name?

Then he closed it again and shook his head. He lifted his hands and gestured, but his hands were shaking, and she could only make out a few words.

"Forgive me, Charles, I-I cannot understand you."

He nodded, then reached for the paper and scribbled on it.

Never ask for my forgiveness.

"But..."

"Shh…" He squeezed her hand, then continued writing.

It is I, not you, who requires forgiveness. I am proud to have you as my wife. The pie. The garden. My beloved Destriero. I am most fortunate.

Her heart soared as she read the words, but her joy was tempered by the absence of a declaration of love. Would it have hurt him to have spoken the words? His horse he referred to as *beloved*. But he'd known the horse longer than he'd known her. Doubtless he'd chosen the horse as his companion himself, whereas she…

He'd had no choice in marrying her. Their union had been one of necessity, on Montague's insistence, to prevent a scandal. Perhaps the best she could hope for was that he'd not regret that choice.

Then she lowered her gaze to her belly.

His regret would come soon enough.

She withdrew her hands, and a flicker of hurt crossed his expression. Then he resumed his seat beside her and cut her a slice of pie. But she could only eat a few bites. After he'd cleared his plate, he leaned toward her, his eyes narrowed with concern.

"I-I'm not very hungry," she said. "I think I might retire early."

As she rose, he caught her sleeve, unexpected shyness in his eyes. He paused, staring at her for a moment, as if contemplating something. Then, trembling, he scribbled on the paper once more.

May I visit your bed?

She stared at the words. After a pause, he started to scrunch up the paper, but she took his hand.

"Yes," she whispered. "Please."

Joy shimmered in his eyes, and he gestured once more, but she shook her head.

He let out a sigh, then scribbled on the paper again.

Go. Now. I'll join you as soon as I can.

He dipped his head and brushed his lips against hers. Pleasure tightened within her, and she parted her lips in invitation—but he withdrew, his cheeks turning pink, as if he were a callow youth wooing a young girl for the first time, fearful of rejection.

She placed a hand on his arm. "I shall await you with eagerness, Charles."

He closed his eyes, and his nostrils flared as she spoke his name. Then he shifted on his feet, his brow creasing as if in discomfort. She retreated to the door and glanced over her shoulder to see him seated at the table once more, scribbling on the paper, his hands shaking. Then she ascended the stairs, issuing instructions to a passing footman that she was not to be disturbed until morning, and made her way to her chamber.

BY THE TIME she heard her husband's footsteps, Olivia had lit the fire, changed into her nightgown, and climbed into bed.

A little pulse throbbed in her center as she glanced out of the window. There was something that felt so decadent, so *wicked*, about a marital visit in the afternoon. Eleanor had spoken of how a little wickedness enhanced the pleasure of a coupling—how Montague spent many hours loving her in all manner of positions and locations, including outdoors, where the risk of being observed added a piquancy to the occasion.

Would she ever know that pleasure herself? When Charles took her for the first time, her heart had ached at how gently he held her. But she couldn't forget the sting of pain or the absence of pleasure, save for the far-off promise of ecstasy that never came—like the end of a rainbow that she used to chase over the fields as a child but could never reach, no matter how fast she ran.

A soft knock came on the door, and she called out, her throat dry with anticipation. Her husband entered, fully clothed, clutching a folded note in his hands. He set the note aside then shed his jacket and shirt, fumbling at his necktie before it came loose.

Silence thickened the air, save for his breathing, and Olvia's nerves overcame her with the need to fill it with something—*anything.*

"D-did you enjoy your trip to London?"

The corner of his lip curved in a smile, and he nodded, then began to unbutton his breeches.

"Perhaps, if it's not too much to ask, you might take me with you next time? Eleanor said in her letter that she was disappointed to see you when—"

He lost his balance and stumbled against a chair, knocking it over. Olivia pulled back the bedsheet to climb out, but he raised his hand, shaking his head. She met his gaze and her stomach fluttered at the guilt in his eyes.

"Charles? What's the matter? Is it something to do with Eleanor?"

He gestured, slowly, with his hands.

I'm sorry.

"Sorry?" Olivia swallowed her apprehension. "Wh-what for? Is Eleanor unwell?"

He shook his head, then gestured again.

"I don't understand…"

He reached for the paper on her dressing table, wrote on it, and held it up.

I visited a doxy in London, but I did not touch her. I've not touched another woman since I married you. I swear on my mother's grave.

She read the words, suppressing the ache in her heart.

"And—Eleanor?"

He frowned.

"Did Eleanor see you there?"

He nodded.

"She didn't mention it in her letter." Olivia curled her fingers around the bedsheets. "Why did you visit a…a doxy?"

He gestured, slowly.

"Teach?" she said, concentrating on his hands. "And… I don't know what that means. Is it…happiness? Whose happiness?"

He gestured toward Olivia, and she caught her breath.

"The doxy was teaching you to make me happy?"

He lifted his hand and moved it from side to side as if to say she was almost, but not quite, correct.

"Oh my!" She let out a small cry as a nugget of desire pulsed in her center. "She was teasing you how to give me…*pleasure*?"

His eyes flared with eagerness, and he nodded. Then he unfolded the note and handed it to her. Trembling, she read the words as he touched his signet ring and rotated it.

I wish to give you pleasure but you must help me, for I've never tried to pleasure a woman before. You must therefore tell me when something I do is pleasurable so that I might continue. If you wish me to do anything that you feel you might enjoy, you must tell me what it is. We shall learn the art of pleasure together. Therefore, I ask that you place your trust in me, as I should have placed my trust in you from the moment we met.

Olivia's heart fluttered at the expression in his eyes—one of a young boy embarking on a new task, eager to please someone he respected.

And loved.

She folded the note, kissed it, then set it aside. Slowly she drew back the bedsheets. His eyes darkened with desire as he ran his gaze over her body, lingering on the neckline of her nightgown before moving along her skirts. When his gaze reached the hem of her nightgown and her stockinged feet, his nostrils flared.

"As you see, husband, I'm wearing your gift."

She grasped her skirts and pulled them up to her thighs until the tops of her stockings came into view, secured with the honey-colored garter ribbons.

He let out a low growl, the call of a beast ready to claim his mate. Primal, decadent, *scandalous…*

And she *loved* it.

He ran his hand over the bulge at the front of his breeches and closed his eyes, inhaling sharply. Then he continued to unbutton them and stepped out to stand before her completely unclothed.

Olivia's body tightened with apprehension as, once more, she let her gaze fall to the part of him that stood, proud and eager, waiting to claim her.

I ask you to place your trust in me.

She caught a shimmer of uncertainty in his eyes, a plea for her approval, and her consent.

She caressed the edge of her stockings, then caught the end of the garter ribbon between her fingers.

"Sh-shall I remove my stockings, husband?" she said. "Or, perhaps you'd prefer to—*Oh!*"

His breathing ragged, he reached forward and grasped the ribbon. Then he hesitated, his body vibrating as if he were fighting to maintain control. She shifted her thighs apart, swallowing her shame at the dampness in her center.

"It would please me very much if you removed them."

Slowly, he tugged at the ribbon until it worked loose. He dipped his head, and she suppressed a cry as his warm lips brushed against the skin of her thigh. Then he hooked a finger under the top of her stocking and peeled it off. Her whole body seemed to hum with pleasure as the soft silk slid down her thigh, her husband's fingertips brushing against her skin.

By the time he'd removed the other stocking, her body felt like it was on fire. Heat coursed through her veins, and the faint pulse in her center had thickened to a throbbing ache. Then he parted her thighs and looked at her body—at the secret place where she ached for him.

She ought to be ashamed at such wantonness, at revealing herself so intimately to another. But the raw need burning in his eyes made her feel beautiful…and *desired*.

He reached for her nightgown, which was—wickedly—bunched around her waist, then lifted his eyebrows and met her gaze.

"Do you wish me to remove it?" she whispered.

He continued to stare, in silence.

"I-I believe I would take pleasure from removing my nightgown."

The corner of his mouth quirked upward, and she pulled her nightgown off and tossed it aside.

His eyes flared with hunger and the tip of his tongue flicked out as he dropped his gaze to her breasts. Then he reached forward and took a breast in his huge hand, holding it with reverence as if it were a precious treasure. Gently he squeezed and caressed, and Olivia's heart ached to see the almost boyish delight in his eyes.

"Do you take pleasure from looking at my breasts, husband?"

He blinked.

"And…from touching them?"

Slowly, he nodded, and flicked his tongue out again.

"W-would you like to taste them?"

He caught his breath, as if in wonder, but remained still.

"Husband, did you not ask me to tell you when I might find an act pleasurable? You must do the same. We're embarking on a journey together, are we not, in search of pleasure?"

He blinked again and his eyes shone with moisture. Then he placed his free hand over his heart and nodded.

"Then please," she said, lying back, fighting her shame at her wantonness. "Taste my breasts."

The bed shifted as he climbed over her and covered her body with his. His arm muscles bulged with effort as he hovered above her so as not to crush her beneath his weight. Then he lowered his head and his hair brushed over the skin of her breasts. She caught her breath at the tickling sensation that drove a bolt of pleasure to her center.

Then he placed a soft kiss on her breast. She drew in a sharp breath, and he paused.

"Please continue."

Such a polite request for such a decadent act! His lips curved against her skin in a smile, then he peppered her breast with tiny kisses, flicking his tongue out at intervals. His kisses grew more insistent as he brushed his lips over her skin. Her nipple ached with need, and she arched her back in offering, unable to voice her plea. Then he took her breast in his mouth and flicked his tongue over her nipple.

"Oh yes," she breathed.

She inhaled and exhaled, focusing on the wave of pleasure building in her center. Then he clamped his lips over her nipple and sucked hard. Her body jerked as a bolt of pleasure tore through her.

He lifted his head, concern in his eyes, and she cried out in frustration.

"Don't stop—please!"

He lowered his head again, covering her skin with nibbling kisses, then he gave her other breast the same loving attention before sitting back to admire his handiwork.

How could something so wicked give rise to such pleasure? Was this what drove women to madness and ruination?

Olivia swallowed her shame as she saw herself, spread before him, thighs parted, breasts heavy and needy, nipples hard and distended, offering her body to the beast before her.

And beast he was. That part of him, the essence of the beast that made him a man, beckoned to her from the curls between his thighs—thick and erect, with a bead of moisture glistening at the top, to match the moisture between her thighs.

"May I…touch you? I think it would give me pleasure. Would it please you?"

She sat up and reached for him, and he let out a low groan.

"Forgive me, I didn't mean…" She retreated, but he grasped her wrist and shook his head. He released her, and she curled her fingers around his length. The faint echo of a pulse vibrated beneath her fingers and a slow smile curved his lips as he closed his eyes. She began to caress him, relishing the soft, silken skin encasing the hardness within, and he tipped his head backward.

"Am I giving you pleasure, husband?"

He exhaled sharply, then nodded while she continued to caress him, moving her fingers along his length. She ran her thumb over the tip, and his member jerked in her hand. He let out a groan, as if in pain. But the expression on his face, lips parted, mouth curved in a gentle smile, was one of pure bliss.

"Shall I continue?"

He opened his eyes and shook his head. Then he took her hand and kissed it, brushing his lips over her knuckles. Holding it in both hands, he pressed it against his chest and sighed. His heartbeat pulsed thickly against her palm. Dare she hope that his heart beat for her?

He pushed her back again, moved to climb on top of her, then hesitated.

She curled her fingers around his arms.

"Please, Charles," she whispered. "I want your body on top of mine. I want to feel you. I trust you not to hurt me."

He blinked again, and a tear splashed onto her chest. Then he lowered his lips to hers.

At first, the kiss was gentle, as if he feared he might harm her. Then, as his body relaxed over hers, the kiss grew more insistent. He flicked his tongue against the seam of her lips, and she parted them to welcome him. With a low growl, he slipped his tongue in and caressed the inside of her mouth in soft, sweeping gestures. He tasted of warmth and spice, and she curled her tongue around his to draw him in deeper.

Then she felt his manhood shifting against her thighs, moving slickly against her heated skin. The tip of him prodded against her center, and she caught her breath at the ripple of pleasure. He broke their kiss and raised his eyebrows, asking, once more, for consent.

Gladly, my love…

There was no need for words. As if he'd read her mind, his eyes widened in delight, and he eased himself into her. This time there was no pain, only a delicious friction where he filled her, pausing to let her body stretch around him before he slid in deeper until their hips met and he clung to her, his breathing labored.

"No pain," she whispered. "Only pleasure."

Slowly he withdrew, and she jerked at a little pulse of pleasure. Then he slid into her again and she lifted her hips to meet him, chasing both the friction and the pleasure.

"Again," she said, her breathing growing ragged.

He withdrew and plunged in again.

"Harder… Faster…"

A look of wonder flared in his eyes as she begged him to continue, willing the pleasure that was just out of reach to come to the fore. His breath came out in short, sharp puffs and he increased the pace while she met each thrust, causing a wave of pleasure that receded each time he withdrew then surged forward, each time stronger than the last. The swell rose above her and she closed her eyes, surrendering to the pure sensation as her rational mind began to dissolve.

He plunged his tongue into her mouth, mirroring the union of their bodies, and devoured her as he thrust into her body, slamming his hips against hers. The surge morphed into an explosion that shattered her soul, and she cried out his name as waves of ecstasy tore through her body.

"Charles! Sweet heaven… Oh… *Charles!*"

He exhaled sharply, shuddering, and a wave of heat filled her body. Then he fell forward, his weight bearing down on her, but she relished it. In a wicked little corner of her mind, she drew pleasure from the notion of being a female claimed by the beast who pinned her down while he took his—and her—pleasure.

As his breathing steadied, he enveloped her in his arms and rolled onto his side, still inside her. A flare of heat ignited in her center, and he smiled, thrusting once more inside her while she sighed with pleasure.

A delicious languor overcame her, and she relaxed in his arms while his heartbeat slowed to a deep, steady pulse. Then he exhaled, slowly, his breath fanning her heated skin until, at length, he fell asleep, cradling her in his arms.

Finally, Olivia understood what Eleanor had said about the delights to be found in the marriage bed, and how much she hoped that Olivia would take just as much pleasure from her marriage.

And Olivia's pleasure would be complete, save for two things.

The secret she carried in her belly and the fact that though she had screamed his name, declaring her pleasure and her love, she would never hear her husband speak hers.

CHAPTER THIRTY-FIVE

COULD THERE BE a more fortunate man in the world?

As his wife drifted about the breakfast room, Charles paused, his teacup at his lips, to let his gaze wander over her delectable form—the slender neck he'd peppered last night with kisses, the curve of her throat, the delicious breasts with their rosy nipples that seemed to get fuller as each day passed, and...

Desire heated his groin at the sight of her rounded hips, discernible through the fabric of her skirts when the sunlight shone at that particular angle.

She really ought to position herself in front of the window more often at that time of day.

Perhaps she'd be willing to engage in a bout of loving on the breakfast table, spread before him like a feast for him to devour while she screamed his name...

The teacup slipped in his grasp, and he drew in a sharp breath as hot liquid splashed onto his hand.

Devil's breeches! He'd have to be more careful to suppress such notions, especially now Jacob was taking his meals with them in the main house.

The footman rushed over, and Charles waved him away, his cheeks warming with embarrassment. It was the same young man—Colin, his wife said his name was—who'd almost caught them outside when, after a morning of anticipation in which they'd circled each other for almost an hour with lingering looks, almost-kisses, and a game of hide-and-seek, Charles found Olivia waiting in the garden wearing nothing but her chemise. Unable to contain the inferno of need, he'd torn the garment apart and taken her swiftly among the bushes, coming to shattering pleasure the moment he'd entered her while her body rippled and clenched around his cock as she sobbed with ecstasy.

What a fool he was to have believed that a coupling was a mere physical release to meet a man's baser needs! Over the past weeks, since his wife had first taken pleasure from his newly acquired skills, she had encouraged him to hone those skills in almost every room in the house. And who was he to object?

Finally, he understood what all the fuss was about—why some men were driven mad with desire over a woman, driving themselves to ruination to meet a doxy's increasing demands for coins and trinkets just to have a taste of her again. But rather than a grasping doxy, he had a willing wife who not only permitted him to indulge in her body, but actively relished the experience herself.

But it wasn't merely the needs of his body that she satisfied. Each time he buried himself inside her warm, welcoming heat, her eyes flared with desire and deepened in color to reveal her soul…

Save for a tiny part of her that she kept from him. He'd not noticed at first, but as they continued to explore each other's needs and desires, celebrating each other's bodies, a shadow occasionally clouded her expression, and she turned from him as if she could not give herself fully.

As if she did not yet completely trust him.

She approached the side table, eyeing the dishes, then spooned some eggs onto her plate and returned to her seat.

"Lady Devereaux, may I serve you some kidneys?" Colin said. "Mrs. Groves ordered them in special for you. It would be a shame for them to go to waste, though Master Jacob is fond of them also."

She shook her head and pushed her plate to one side.

"Some tea, perhaps?"

She nodded, then lifted her gaze to Charles and smiled. But the smile didn't quite reach her eyes, which still carried a flicker of pain.

Are you well?

She stared at Charles's hand gestures, then nodded.

"Perfectly so, Charles, but I-I find I'm not hungry. I'm a little tired."

And well she might be, given how little sleep they'd had last night. He'd brought her to pleasure three times, then woken her just before dawn to slip inside her once more while she writhed beneath him. Then he'd fallen asleep in her arms before rising the moment he heard his valet wandering about. Olivia had looked at peace when he left her in her bed. But now, she looked strained, lines creasing her forehead and a pale hue to her cheeks.

Will you join me for a ride today?

She frowned.

"Something about riding?" she said. "You're going riding?"

He gestured to her.

"You want *me* to come?" she said. "I-I've arranged to take a walk with Nicola today."

That harridan! Pretty enough, always trotting after Jacob with her tongue hanging out. But there was a look of cunning about her that made Charles uneasy.

Perhaps you should remain inside if you're feeling tired.

He gestured, slowly and deliberately this time, and she smiled.

"I think a walk will do me good," she said. "Dr. Cheam is an advocate for fresh air and exercise, and this is the only day that suits both myself and Nicola. Perhaps Jacob might accompany you? He's a better rider than I."

Charles suppressed a snort, and his wife's smile slipped.

"You disapprove of my friend."

The tone of her voice made it clear that it wasn't a question.

"Or do you disapprove of your brother—the fact that he now

dines with us? He's your heir, is he not?"

I don't disapprove of him.

She frowned as she watched his hands. "So, it's Nicola you disapprove of. Why? Is it because she's in love with Jacob? Do you not want your brother to marry beneath him—as you did?"

Her eyes glistened with moisture.

Surely she didn't still harbor fears that he resented *her* birth?

Do not speak so foolishly.

Her lip wobbled and a tear splashed onto her cheek. Charles rose from his seat then approached her and took her hand. Her fingers were cold, and she trembled. Was she sickening for something?

He caressed her fingers then brushed his lips against her hand.

"I…" She hesitated and caught her breath, as if she were about to faint. "I miss Eleanor," she said. "I-I didn't realize how much I would. Eleanor says little, but I took much comfort from her quiet presence. Nicola isn't Eleanor, but she's pleasant enough and I want to be kind to her. Her mother died, you see, not long ago. You must understand how painful that is."

He kissed her knuckles again.

"She was her stepmother really, but Nicola told me how devastated she was when she died in childbirth. I fear that…"

She broke off and leaned forward, trembling more violently, and Charles caught a flash of fear in her eyes.

Shall I invite your sister to stay?

"I—I don't understand."

He gestured to the sheaf of papers on the side table. The footman brought it over together with a pencil, and Charles scribbled on the top of the page. A visit from Olivia's sister-in-law might cure her melancholy, whatever the cause of it was. And it would have the added benefit of reminding her that there were better female companions to be had than an ambitious young miss with a little too much envy in her eyes.

Olivia read the words, then shook her head and another tear spilled onto her cheeks.

"I-I cannot invite her yet. I've lost her necklace—the one she gave me as a wedding gift—and she'll think me awfully foolish."

That was unlikely, given how much the duchess loved Olivia.

"She was kind enough to send me a pair of earrings to match it," Olivia continued, "so she'll expect me to wear them. I-I cannot..." She shook her head. "She might think I care little for her if I've been careless with her necklace."

He set the pencil down and gestured with his hands.

Of course not. She and I...

Love.

Charles paused. How was it that he had no hand gesture for love? Had his life been so devoid of love that he'd seen no need for it, that he'd never stopped to think that he might love another person enough to want to tell them?

"She and you...what?"

He picked up the pencil, his hand shaking. To make such a declaration, not as an ephemeral utterance, but written down such that it could never be unsaid...

I...

Charles jumped as the door opened and his hand jerked to one side, leaving a thick pencil line across the paper.

Jacob stood in the doorway, his mouth curled into a grin.

"Late again, aren't I?" he said, mischief twinkling in his eyes. "I forget the need for punctuality when eating in the house. But you must forgive me, brother, for I was just exercising caution."

"Caution?" Olivia said.

"A husband and his wife must never be interrupted, just in case," Jacob said with a wink.

A little color returned to Olivia's cheeks, and she lowered her gaze.

"Forgive me for embarrassing you, sister," Jacob said, "but I see nothing to disapprove of in a healthy marriage, eh, brother?"

He winked at Charles this time, then approached the side table.

"Devilled kidneys!" He spooned some onto his plate, then sat at the table and began to eat.

"Have you seen Nicola this morning?" Olivia asked. "She's meeting me here at eight for our walk today."

Jacob shook his head. "She's not my keeper." He swallowed a mouthful of tea and muttered something else that sounded remarkably like *thank fuck.*

"Jacob, Nicola is my friend," Olivia said.

Jacob set his cup aside. "Forgive me, I didn't mean to insult her. I just need a little respite."

"From Nicola? I thought you wanted to marry her."

He let out a snort. "Told you that, did she? Then you're a fool to believe her." Charles frowned at his brother, and Jacob let out a sigh. "Forgive me, Olivia. I'm a little bad-tempered this morning."

"Is Nicola here? Is that why you're in an ill temper?"

"She's in the kitchen, yes. I told her to remain there after she…"

"After she what?" Olivia said.

"After she demanded that I propose to her. She says that now I'm recognized as my brother's heir I must take a wife to continue the line."

Olivia drew in a sharp breath and held her hand to her mouth.

Charles smacked his fist into his palm. *How dare you distress my wife!*

Jacob shrugged. "I'm only repeating what Nicola said. But I don't want to marry her. She's always known that, despite what she might have said to Olivia."

"And—I take it you don't want her as your wife because she's not a lady," Olivia said.

Jacob gave a mirthless laugh. "You think I care for *that*? No—I want to marry a woman I love, and until I find her, I'll not be asking anyone."

"Are you so naïve as to think that men and women marry for love?" Olivia said, her voice tightening. "I—Oh, sweet Lord!"

She let out another cry and clamped her hand over her mouth. Then she leaped to her feet and ran out of the room.

Charles rose to follow, but Jacob placed a hand on his arm.

"Leave her be, brother. Let her calm down—women can be harridans when they've distressed themselves. I'll reckon there's a reason why she's been temperamental of late."

Charles stared at his brother. *What reason?*

"You've not noticed how she's changed?" Jacob said. "Perhaps it's because I don't see her every day that the change is more apparent to me. They do say that you can withstand having your hand in boiling water if you've had it in from when the water's cold because you don't notice it getting hotter. And your little wife's fit to boil."

Is she unhappy with me?

Jacob laughed. "You're a fool if you think *that*, given how many times I've heard her screaming your name. Last night as I was retiring…the other day in the billiard room…and, if I'm not mistaken, yesterday in the garden. Only a wife truly in love with her husband would let him rut her from behind with her skirts around her waist while she's—"

Jacob broke off as Charles thumped his fist on the table.

"What?" He shrugged. "You're a fortunate man and, I suspect, soon to be even more fortunate."

Charles raised his eyebrows.

"You really are a simpleton, aren't you, brother? Is it not obvious? Poor Lucy was the same."

Who the fuck is that?

"Mr. Faulkes's late wife—Nicola's stepmother. When she fell pregnant, she was unwell almost all the time, sickening in the mornings. Nicola said it was enough to drive her insane—but then, Nicola detested Lucy."

Sweet heaven—Olivia was *pregnant?*

Charles caught his breath as a nugget of joy ignited in his heart.

She's expecting my child?

Jacob grinned. "I'd say so, though perhaps you should wait until she tells you herself."

No wonder she's distressed, given that Faulkes's wife died in childbirth.

"In childbirth?" Jacob said, frowning. "Who told you that?"

My wife.

Jacob shook his head. "Lucy Faulkes fell down the stairs and broke her neck."

Like Mother…

"Dr. Cheam delivered her child, but it was too late. The baby was stillborn."

Dear God Almighty!

Jacob took Charles's hand. "Forgive me, brother, I ought not to have mentioned it. Lucy Faulkes slipped on a stone, or a marble, or something, at the top of the stairs."

Then why had Olivia lied about it? Or had Nicola lied to Olivia?

"It was an accident," Jacob said. "You needn't fear for Olivia. But if you're concerned, you can always send for her family—she's always speaking fondly of her sister-in-law."

You care for her, don't you?

Jacob laughed more softly. "Only as a brother cares for his sister. *You're* the one who loves her."

He was right. And when Charles next saw his wife, he had every intention of finding a way to tell her exactly that.

I'm going for a ride. Would you care to come?

Jacob's smile broadened and a flicker of delight shone in his eyes.

"There's nothing I'd like more."

The two of them exited the breakfast room and Charles made his way upstairs in search of his riding gloves and his wife. The former were in his dressing room, but the latter was nowhere to be found. Then he heard laughter outside and peered through a window to see Olivia, arm in arm with her friend, a basket over her arm, moving along the path toward the forest. He might disapprove of Nicola, but if she lifted his wife's spirits, then he'd tolerate her for Olivia's sake.

He pressed his hand to his heart and stood watching while they wound their way along the path then disappeared into the forest.

Then he made for the stairs, pausing at the top to glance at the longcase clock. He blinked and the image formed in his mind, the memory of the marble he'd retrieved from beneath the clock some weeks before.

What had Jacob said?

A stone…or a marble.

CHAPTER THIRTY-SIX

THE PATH WAS covered in a layer of frost that glistened in the winter sun, forming tiny diamonds on the ground. Olivia's breath misted in the air in short, sharp puffs as she approached the forest, Nicola by her side. Before they reached the tree line, she paused and caught her breath.

"Are you well, Olivia?" Nicola said.

"I'm just a little dizzy."

"You're pregnant."

Nicola's expression hardened, and Olivia shivered. "How do you know?"

"I've suspected it for some time. Susie said something about your bedsheets, and—"

Olivia's head throbbed as Nicola's voice sharpened, and she raised her hand. "Nicola, I know we're friends, but I'd rather not discuss it."

"Of course." Nicola's smile returned and she offered her hand. "Are you afraid?"

"Yes." Another wave of nausea rippled through Olivia's stomach, and she took the proffered hand. Nicola curled her fingers around Olivia's wrist.

"Does Devereaux know?"

"I've not told him," Olivia said. "How can I, when he made it clear that he didn't want a child?"

"I can still help," Nicola said, glancing over her shoulder

toward the house. "Old Mrs. Gibbs is very discreet. She'll have something to end a pregnancy as well as prevent one."

"No!" Olivia withdrew her hand.

"You could save yourself the prospect of death," Nicola said. "Don't you recall what I said about Ma Lucy?"

"Please desist," Olivia said. "If you continue, I must return to the house."

Nicola let out a sigh. "Forgive me. I'm only thinking of you." She caught Olivia's hand and kissed it. "I wouldn't want to lose my friend. You've been so kind to Susie—kinder than any other lady would be in your position, especially considering she's not the best of maids."

"Susie's an excellent lady's maid."

"That's generous of you to say. Come—we'll speak no more of it." Nicola gestured to her basket. "Mrs. Groves has given me all manner of good things for our picnic, and I asked her to pack some of her lemonade as well, seeing as I know how fond you are of it." She linked her arm with Olivia's, and they entered the forest.

Almost at once, the air was filled with the sounds of the forest—the rush of the wind through the trees and the rustling of woodland creatures investigating the undergrowth. The faint hammering of a woodpecker echoed in the distance, followed by a squeal—some creature caught in the jaws of a predator. The sun penetrated further now that most of the trees had shed their leaves, illuminating the forest floor with patches of light. Olivia thrust her foot into a pile of leaves, kicking them up into the air. Nicola followed suit, then threw back her head and laughed.

"I love this forest!" she cried. "I'm so fortunate to have you as a friend. Do forgive my earlier words."

"They're forgotten," Olivia said.

"You're like a sister to me," Nicola said, "dearer to me than Susie. I hope, one day, I might be able to call you sister."

"But Jacob doesn't—"

"Jacob doesn't what?" Nicola said, a sharp edge to her voice.

"Has he asked you to marry him?"

Nicola's eyes glistened and Olivia's heart ached at their expression. How cruel Jacob's words had been at breakfast! Didn't he realize how much Nicola loved him?

"He *wants* to marry me, but he needs…"

"Encouragement?" Olivia suggested.

"Convincing," Nicola said. "I fear he thinks I'm not good enough for him. Did you see him at breakfast this morning?"

Olivia nodded.

"Did he say anything?"

Olivia averted her gaze. "I-it wouldn't be right for him to discuss his feelings for you in front of me. Not when he knows you're my friend."

"I suppose not," came the reply. "But I fear he thinks I'm too far beneath him, especially now he's spending more time in the house. He's Devereaux's heir. What would an earl want with a farmer's daughter like me?"

Olivia placed a hand over her belly. "He may not be the heir for much longer."

Nicola tilted her head to one side. For a heartbeat, Olivia's stomach cramped with fear at the expression in her eyes.

"Perhaps your child will be a girl. And, of course, not all women…" She shook her head. "I'm talking nonsense. Shall we stop to eat? I know a perfect spot where the ground is covered in wildflowers."

"Flowers at this time of year?"

Nicola frowned. "Yes. Come on."

She stepped up the pace, and Olivia followed. The rushing sound of the wind in the trees deepened, forming musical notes.

"Are we nearing the river?" Olivia asked. "We ought to be careful."

"It's quite safe," Nicola said. "I know this forest well."

Olivia followed, and the rushing water grew louder. Then the path veered to the right, and she found herself on the edge of the ravine. She caught her breath and stepped back, but Nicola moved toward the edge and leaned over.

"Careful!" Olivia said. "You might fall."

"Nonsense!" Nicola replied. "Come and see the flowers. They grow among the rocks, just below the edge."

Olivia approached the edge and peered over. Her vision blurred as she saw the water at the bottom of the ravine, boiling and swirling like a live animal eager for its prey. Nausea rippled over her, and she leaned back.

"I-I can't see any flowers."

"Look *closer*."

Nicola's voice hardened until it carried an edge of steel. Olivia turned to respond, and her gut cramped in horror. Her friend's face was twisted with hatred, her eyes glittering with spite, mouth set in a hard line.

"What are—" Olivia began, then broke off as Nicola gripped her by the arms.

"Miserable whore," she said, her voice a low snarl. "You think you can destroy my hopes? Jacob was going to marry me until you started flashing your cunny at him. How do I know the brat in your belly isn't his?"

"I don't love Jacob—I love Charles!"

Nicola let out a cold laugh. "Devereaux isn't the sort of man to love another. You've told me that many times—he doesn't even want your brat!"

"H-he cares…"

"Don't be a fool! All you've done since you came here is mewl and whine about how your husband doesn't love you because you're some peasant's bastard who trapped him into marriage. He'll thank me when you're gone, and so will Jacob."

Nicola tightened her grasp on Olivia's arms and pushed her backward. Olivia screamed as her footing began to slip, and she clawed at her assailant. But the ground crumbled beneath her feet, and her ankle turned on a stone.

Just like the day she'd fallen down the stairs when she'd lost her footing…

…when Nicola had stood, watching, an expression in her eyes that Olivia hadn't been able to identify until now.

Loathing.

Then Nicola bared her teeth and thrust forward, shoving Olivia back until she could no longer feel the ground beneath her feet, only air.

"Sweet Lord—no!"

Olivia reached out, arms flailing in desperation for something—anything—to hold on to. She clawed at Nicola's sleeve, but it was too late, and she toppled over the precipice, calling the name of the man she loved.

"Charles!"

Images flashed before her mind—her husband's dark gaze, the joy in his eyes as she placed his newborn son in his arms…

But what little hope she might have harbored was now gone forever.

Her husband was not there to save her. She was going to die.

CHAPTER THIRTY-SEVEN

"C HARLES!"

A voice cried out, raw with terror. Charles reached toward the voice, then it was cut short with the dull snap of bone. Thick red bled into the blackness as a blurred shape took form— the shape of a woman, her body broken and twisted, her sightless eyes, as black as coal, staring out at him, the flicker of life fading until there was nothing but the dark shroud of death.

But the eyes were not those of his mother. They were the eyes of his wife.

Olivia!

He opened his eyes and sat up, his heart pounding against his chest, sharp pain stabbing behind his eyes.

He blinked, and his vision cleared. He was no longer a child trapped beneath his mother's body. He was a man, sitting in a wingback chair in the morning room, clutching the arms, his fingers curled into claws, digging into the leather.

But the echo of Olivia's voice still called to him.

He shook his head to dispel the echo then surveyed his surroundings. Someone sat in the chair opposite, silhouetted against the orange glow of the fireplace. He blinked, then swallowed his disappointment as the shape snapped into focus.

It wasn't his wife.

Jacob leaned forward. "Anything the matter, brother?"

Charles gestured with his hands. *How long have I been asleep?*

Jacob glanced at the mantel clock, where the hour hand was approaching four.

"Two hours, maybe more," he said. "I didn't realize how loudly you snored. Perhaps you're making up for being always silent, eh?"

Is my wife back?

"Not that I know of."

Charles rose and crossed the floor to the window, staring out at the landscape bathed in the soft pink of the setting sun. Perhaps, if he stared long enough, Olivia would appear—after all, she'd called to him in his dreams. He thrust his hands into his pockets and waited, fingering the smooth surface of his signet ring. Silence filled the room, punctuated by the ticking of the mantel clock and the crackling of the fire.

Four o'clock.

She should have been back hours ago. Charles approached the bellpull, then, changing his mind, returned to the window.

"Pacing about won't bring her back sooner. It'll only wear out the carpet." Charles made a gesture, and Jacob laughed. "I take it you're thanking me for my advice. Or you're telling me to fuck off. Why not take some tea? Ethel brought some in while you were sleeping, along with some of your wife's shortbread."

I don't want tea. I want my wife. Something feels wrong.

"Say again?"

Charles let out a huff, then signed again, slowly.

Jacob stared at Charles's hands. "You think something's wrong? What sort of thing?"

I heard her cry out. In my sleep.

"That's just your conscience plaguing you."

Unease continued to stab at Charles and his gut knotted with apprehension.

Jacob tilted his head to one side. "You really are concerned, aren't you?" he said. "I'm sure she and Nicola have just lost sense of the time. You know how women rattle on. Doubtless your wife's told Nicola she's expecting your child. Women like to share confidences, and Nicola's sister is Olivia's maid, so she'll have seen your wife's bedsheets."

Bedsheets? *Devil's breeches*, it was enough of a trial for a man to know about such things, let alone discuss them.

"Susie's always been loose-tongued," Jacob continued. "But she's much kinder than Nicola. She'll have plenty of admirers when she's older, then your wife will be wanting a new maid. As a young lass, Susie was always prattling on about this or that. I remember one summer when I was helping Mr. Faulkes with the pigs, I…"

He paused as Charles raised his hand and signed, *Does Mr. Faulkes keep pigs?*

"Don't you listen to anything Mr. Carlton says? He's always extoling the virtues of Faulkes's pigs. It was his pork that graced your dining table. Recall the pie your wife baked?"

And sheep?

"Heavens no!" Jacob laughed. "Faulkes comes out in a rash when he goes near a sheep. Always has done. The wool, Mrs. Faulkes said—the late Mrs. Lucy Faulkes, that was, before she died, God rest her soul."

Lucy Faulkes—the pregnant woman who fell down the stairs and broke her neck…

He has a dog, yes? A collie?

"Mr. Faulkes has never had a dog," Jacob said. "Plenty of cats, mind you, given that the barn's overrun with mice."

Icy fingers tightened their grip around Charles's stomach as he recalled the overheard conversation.

The bitch and her pup cannot be allowed to live…

Charles signed to his brother. *Do you think Nicola is a good person?*

Jacob opened his mouth to reply, then paused.

Be truthful.

"Well…" Jacob hesitated. "To be honest, meaning no disrespect, Nicola was none too pleased when you returned after the old earl passed. She said that you'd have been better staying on the Continent. At the time I thought it was just because this house has always had the specter of death hanging over it. But she then seemed overly keen on pushing me forward as your heir."

It's what you want, isn't it?

"Fuck no!" Jacob laughed. "What—to have to deal with all the comings and goings of lawyers, bankers, not to mention placating the staff and the tenants who think I'm some puffed-up nothing merely because I have the title? I'd rather do a proper day's work anytime, which is why I could never offer for Nicola. She doesn't want me as I am. I'd stake my arse on her only wanting to be the next Countess Devereaux. Ha! Put her nose right out of joint when you turned up with that lovely little bride of yours. Made her sick with envy. It was then that I realized Nicola wasn't the girl for me. I always wondered why she made such a show of befriending your wife when... *Holy cock*, brother, are you all right?"

Charles let out a groan as he shuddered, and he gestured to Jacob, his hands trembling.

"I don't understand what you're trying to say," Jacob said. "Sit down and let me get you a brandy."

Charles gestured more slowly. *My wife's maid. Send for her. And John.*

Jacob nodded and rang the bell. Shortly after, the young footman appeared and, after a brief exchange, scuttled off, then returned with the young maid.

She looked even younger than when Charles had last seen her, her eyes large and wide in her pale face.

"No..." she whispered, and she stepped back, trembling, and lifted her hand to her mouth. "Sweet Lord, no!"

"You've done nothing wrong, Susie," Jacob said. "My brother just wants a word with you."

Her expression glazed with fear, she glanced about, like an animal readying itself to flee.

Hold her.

"What?" Jacob said.

Devil's bollocks, why could nobody understand him?

Then the maid darted past the footman, but collided with John, who'd appeared in the doorway.

"Mind how you go, young Susie," he said, catching her wrist. "Hasn't Mrs. Brougham said that..." He glanced at Charles. "What the devil's happened, sir? You look as if someone's died."

The knot of fear in Charles's stomach turned to ice as he motioned with his hands.

My wife's missing. I think this girl knows where she is. Do not let her go.

John steered the maid into the room.

"Let go, you're hurting me!" Susie cried.

I'll do a damned sight more than that if my wife's in danger.

She stared at Charles's hands, then burst into tears.

"It wasn't me!"

"What wasn't you?" John said.

She glanced from John to Charles and back again. "I-I mean...wh-whatever it is you think I've done."

"What do you think we suspect you of having done, Susie?" Jacob said.

"*Please* don't hurt me!" the girl cried. "I-I didn't mean no harm!" She glanced toward John. "Mr. Richards, tell the master I've been with you all day seeing to the mending. You saw me, didn't you? I don't want to die!"

Charles approached her, and she burst into tears.

"Excellent work, brother, frightening a child," Jacob said.

"What, by merely looking at her?" John said. "You don't know your brother at all, if you think he'd stoop to hurting a girl."

"B-but she s-said he'd..." Susie began.

"*She?*" Jacob said. "You mean your mistress?"

"No, Lady Devereaux's never said a word against the master. It w-was my sister."

"Nicola?" Jacob said. "What did she say?"

The maid shook her head, her trembling becoming more violent.

Charles moved his hands. *Fetch the child a brandy before she faints.*

"Bring a brandy for Susie, would you, Colin?" John said.

The footman nodded and disappeared.

Let her sit, John. Then ask her where my wife is.

The valet steered the maid to a chair.

"I can't sit in the master's presence!" she cried. "Nicola said—"

"Nicola has been saying a great deal too much, Susie," Jacob interrupted. He kneeled beside her and took her hand. "Why don't you tell us what *you* have to say?"

"I…I can't."

"At least tell us where your mistress is," John said. "That's all we want to know."

Colin reappeared with a half-filled brandy glass and Jacob held it to the girl's lips. She swallowed a mouthful, then spasmed into a fit of coughing.

"Now speak," Jacob said. "You're not in any trouble."

"B-but the *necklace*… Nicola said the master would beat me to death if he knew I took it, and that she'd tell him if I told on her, a-and—" She broke off, sobbing, and Jacob pressed the glass to her lips once more.

What does a necklace have to do with my wife's disappearance?

"Susie, Lord Devereaux only wants to know where his wife is," John said.

"I-I can't tell you…"

"Can't, or won't? Do you wish to be dismissed? Lord Devereaux cares nothing for a necklace, but he does care for his wife. Where is she?"

"N-Nicola said she was just playing a joke on the mistress, seeing as they were such good friends. Like sisters, she said."

"Oh, she *did*, did she?" Jacob scoffed.

"What joke, Susie?" John asked.

"Th-the marble," Susie said, before bursting into tears again.

"I'm sorry! I'm sure she never meant for the mistress to come to no harm."

What do you mean?

The maid stared at Charles's hands.

"He wants you to continue," John said. "What marble?"

"Th-the marble on the stairs. When the mistress fell, I wanted to tell her about the marble, but Nicola said she'd tell on me about the necklace, then she'd push me down the stairs so that I'd end up like Ma Lucy, or the old mistress. The master was away, and I wanted to tell him when he returned, but that was when Nicola said he'd..." Her breath caught and she dissolved into tears again.

Charles's gut twisted in horror.

The marble he'd spotted at the top of the stairs...

Sweet Lord—was that why Nicola had lied about her stepmother's death?

And my Olivia is outside somewhere, alone with her.

"Sweet fucking hell," Jacob cursed. "You foolish girl! Where are they now?"

"I..."

Charles grabbed Susie by the shoulders, and she let out a whimper.

"N-Nicola said she was going to take her to the forest, and..."

She trailed off, and icy fingers squeezed Charles's heart as he recalled the image of his wife tumbling over the edge of the ravine as she had almost done before.

But this time, he was not there to keep her safe. This time her only companion was the woman who had, most likely, brought about her stepmother's death, and who saw Olivia as an obstacle to her ambitions.

What if she intended to remove that obstacle?

He leaped to his feet, then sprinted out of the house toward the stables, where Destriero stood patiently in his stall. Charles motioned to the stable boy to saddle the horse, then mounted swiftly and set off toward the forest at a gallop.

Fear swelled in his mind—a thick, black wave of terror that threatened to burst. He spurred Destriero on, and as they plunged into the darkness of the forest, the wave crested and burst. He tilted his head upward and a roar came from his lips, pushed to the surface through ten years of silence and the terror that the thing he loved more than the mother he'd lost—more than his own life—was lost to him.

"Olivia!"

His voice reverberated through the forest as he tore ahead, the branches of the trees whipping across his face. Then he heard the rush of water, angry, boiling water, a great beast waiting to devour its prey, and he reined his horse in. With a scream, Destriero pulled up, just shy of the precipice.

His throat aching, Charles summoned every ounce of his strength, then roared out again.

"Olivia, my love... Olivia!"

His heart hammering, he leaned forward as the world before him blurred and he clung to the reins to steady himself, willing the pain in his head to subside, praying that she would be safe.

But he was met with silence, save for the angry voice of the river below, mocking him with its vicious vitality.

He dismounted and, shaking, approached the edge and looked over. Then an invisible knife sliced through his heart as he caught sight of a shape at the bottom of the ravine.

It was the body of a woman—broken and twisted, lying at the water's edge.

Olivia...

He dropped to his knees and dug his hands into the earth, curling the fingers into claws. Then he lifted his head and let out a roar, cursing the world where the cruel and envious thrived but the virtuous and kind were destroyed.

It was a world he no longer wished to live in—not without his beloved Olivia, the woman who, despite his being so undeserving, loved him without condition, without expectation.

He'd never been able to tell her how much he loved her. And

now, his chance had gone.

Charles...

Her softly whispered voice slipped into his mind. *Devil's breeches.* Was he being taunted by her ghost?

"Wh-who's there?"

He stiffened and looked up.

It was *her* voice.

He crawled toward the edge, his stomach knotting at the prospect of seeing her broken body once more. His last memory of her should be her smiling face, her beautiful eyes filled with love.

Then he peered over, his gaze drawn to the angry, swirling river below and the lifeless form at the water's edge. Conquering his fear, he leaned farther over, casting his gaze along the wall of the ravine. Then he almost cried out as he caught sight of a white face looking up at him from about six feet below.

Clinging to a sapling that protruded from the rocks was his wife.

Chapter Thirty-Eight

THE COLD HAD long since seeped into Olivia's bones until she could feel ice in her veins, fingers of frost curling around her insides.

Darkness, blessed darkness, called to her, promising respite from the cold and the pain in her hands. But each time she shifted toward oblivion, the fear gripped her once more and she tightened her hold on the branch—the only thing that stood between her and death.

But she couldn't hold on forever. Her strength was draining from her, a great weight pulling her downward, toward the lifeless form below.

Nicola's screams still circled in her mind—the roar of triumph and hatred, followed by the scream of terror as Nicola had toppled over the edge, before it had been abruptly silenced.

Olivia glanced up, her gaze falling once more on the fissure higher up on the wall—large enough to shelter in, close enough to taunt her with its nearness, but too far out of reach to risk relinquishing her hold on the sapling.

Henrietta Thorpe would have scaled the wall with little effort. Eleanor always said how skilled Henrietta was at climbing trees. But Olivia was not Henrietta. She lacked both the strength and courage to scale a wall where the smallest mistake could result in her sharing Nicola's fate.

If only she'd listened to her heart rather than her fears! But it was Nicola who'd placed those fears in her heart—seeds of doubt that had sprouted into dark shoots, choking her soul.

Oh, Charles, why couldn't I have trusted you?

A cacophony of caws filled the air, warring with the angry rush of the river below. Something had disturbed the roosting birds, which squawked and protested. Shivering, Olivia tightened her grip, her heartbeat thrumming in her ears. The light was fading now the sun had dipped below the horizon. Soon, the night hunters would emerge to claim the world and await her surrender to the inevitable.

The heartbeat intensified until the earth seemed to thrum with it, as if a herd of beasts pounded on the ground with heavy, hungry footsteps.

Then she heard a roar, primal and savage, and her insides knotted with terror. It was the roar of a beast, deep and dark…

…and she could swear that the beast roared her name.

She was about to be devoured. Never would she see him again, the man she had grown to love.

"Charles!"

The footsteps approached, and she whimpered in fear. Then they stopped. She caught her breath, then heard a cry, filled with anguish.

The cry of a man.

She tilted her head back, straining to see the top of the ridge.

"Wh-who's there?"

She heard a gasp and held her breath as a shape moved above her. Then a face appeared.

A face she knew and loved.

"Charles? Is that you?"

His eyes widened, then he blinked, slowly, and parted his lips as he reached toward her.

"O-Olivia."

Sweet heaven! Had he spoken? His voice, though strained as if he were in agony, was raw and deep, reverberating through her bones.

"Nicola pushed me," she said. "I-I caught hold of her, a-and she…" She caught her breath as her body spasmed with cold and he raised his hand.

"Shh…"

"I don't know how much longer I can hold on," she said. "I can hardly feel my hands. I—*No!*"

She broke off as he swung his legs over the edge.

"Charles, it's too dangerous! You'll fall."

But he ignored her pleas and climbed down, moving his big body slowly over the rocks. His foot dislodged a rock, and Olivia screamed as he slid toward her. The rock rattled past her, and she held her breath until she heard a splash far below. Charles was now almost within reach, clinging to the side of the ravine. Then, slowly, he extended an arm toward her.

She glanced toward the river below. It was barely visible, save for the occasional cold glint of reflected moonlight in the dark swirls as it continued to rage over the rocks, bubbling and roaring.

"I-I can't move," she said. "If I let go, I'll fall."

He shifted closer until his hand almost touched hers. Fear coiled around her body like a rope, paralyzing her.

Then her husband drew in a deep breath, his eyes gleaming in the darkness, and spoke in a soft whisper.

"Trust me."

Slowly she uncurled one hand from the branch. Her body weight shifted, and her foot slipped. She cried out, fighting to regain her foothold, but found nothing but air beneath her feet. But the hand that took hers held it in a firm, strong grip, his huge fingers curling around her wrist. Then he pulled her up until she was close enough to circle her free arm around his neck.

"Charles!" she sobbed, glancing toward the top of the cliff. "Y-you won't be able to climb back up—it's too steep. Why risk your life for *me?*"

His eyes darkened and she shivered at the flicker of anger in them. He glanced about and gestured toward the fissure, then, slowly, he climbed upward, moving one limb at a time, testing each hold before committing to the movement, while she clung to him. At length they reached the fissure, and he pushed her inside, where she fell back. No longer clinging on for her life, she surrendered to exhaustion. Her body began to tremble violently, and her teeth chattered with the cold.

"I-I'm sorry," she said. "I didn't mean to cause such trouble. I—"

"Shh…"

He placed a finger on her lips, before leaning forward and brushing his mouth against hers. Then he removed his jacket and placed it about her shoulders.

"Charles, it's too cold. You'll freeze. It's not worth…"

He raised his hand, the flash of anger returning to his eyes. Then he gestured, slowly and deliberately.

Do not speak so. You are worth everything.

"Charles…"

Her voice trailed away as he placed his hand on her cheek, and she leaned into his touch, relishing his warmth.

I would willingly give my life for you. I…

He hesitated, then placed his hand over his heart and gestured to her.

His forehead creased as if he were in pain, and he parted his lips, his body tense, then closed his eyes.

"Love," he whispered, his voice a low rasp. "I l-love—"

He broke off and drew in a sharp breath.

"—you."

He exhaled, trembling, then opened his mouth once more. The pain in his eyes intensified and she placed her fingertips over his lips.

"No, my love," she said. Then she took his hand and placed it over her heart. "You have no need to speak, Charles. I love you as you are."

He moved his hands.

And I you.

She shifted toward him, to settle in his arms, but he raised his hand. Then he gestured to her belly and raised his eyebrows.

"Oh, Charles, I…"

He placed his hand on her belly and caressed it. His eyes gleamed, and she caught a flash of reflected light as a tear spilled onto his cheeks.

"Child," he whispered.

"Yes," she said, placing her hand over his. The twin rubies of his ring and hers winked in the twilight. "I'm carrying your child."

He took her face in his hands, and his eyes, wet with tears, creased with a smile. Then he pulled her close, encircling her in his large, muscular arms.

"Charles, what are we going to do?" she said. "I-I cannot climb back up."

"Shh…" he whispered, rocking her to and fro.

"Does anyone know where we are?"

He nodded against her, then tightened his embrace. "W-we wait."

"Yes, my love," she whispered. "I'll wait forever as long as I have you by my side."

He then placed a kiss on the top of her head. Drawing comfort from his silent solidity, Olivia nestled into his embrace and drifted into a doze.

Images flashed before her mind's eye—a dull orange glow, a flickering flame, a length of rope coiled around her waist. Then a softly whispered voice soothed the ache in her bones before it was accompanied by other voices—Jacob's familiar timbre, the gentle scolding of Mrs. Brougham, and finally the firm, professional tones of Dr. Cheam. But the one constant was the warm hand that enveloped hers, holding her firm, promising never to leave. Then a bitter taste swamped the back of her tongue, and she slipped into oblivion.

When Olivia next opened her eyes, she was surrounded by sunlight. She tilted her head and blinked, her eyes watering in the light. She was in her bedchamber, her husband still clinging to her hand, his dark gaze fixed on her. As she tried to sit, he shook his head and gently pushed her back.

"Ah, the patient's awake."

She turned her head, wincing at the ache in her neck to see Dr. Cheam rising from a chair.

"You've had quite an adventure, Lady Devereaux," he said. "First you tumble down the stairs, then, as if that's not exciting enough, you see fit to throw yourself off a cliff. I rather wonder whether—"

He broke off as Charles rose to his feet, anger in his eyes.

"Of course, I'm just jesting." The doctor held up a phial. "I can give you a little more laudanum if you're still in pain, though I'm not an advocate of its use when a woman is with child."

"I'm in no pain, Dr. Cheam," Olivia said.

"Is there anything that you need?"

She glanced at the huge hand engulfing her own, then lifted it to her lips.

"No, Dr. Cheam," she said. "I have everything I need—and will ever need—right here."

CHAPTER THIRTY-NINE

Five months later.

DEVIL'S BREECHES, COULD his beloved wife be in any more pain? Why weren't they *doing* anything? Surely no creature could endure such suffering for so long?

Charles winced when Olivia dug her fingernails into his palm as she shook with another spasm. She threw her head back and let out a primal roar, her face contorted with agony. He gestured toward Mrs. Brougham, but she ignored him.

They all ignored him.

So many bloody women, together in a confined space! It was enough to make a man weak with fear. And he would have been, save for the one person who made him strong.

His wife—the woman he'd fight the whole world to protect from harm.

Yet here she was, lying before him, racked with agony—agony that he was solely responsible for.

Dear God, what will I do without her?

He let out a whimper as she turned her face toward him, her eyes glazed with pain.

The midwife's crisp tones cut through the air. "Lord save me from weak-bellied men! Why a man thinks he has the stomach for a birthing, I'll never understand."

"Mrs. Cheam, Lord Devereaux is—"

"He's a *man*, and as such, has no place here."

Olivia's spasm subsided, and she lay back while Susie placed a cloth over her forehead. Treacherous little creature—Charles would never have forgiven Olivia's maid for the role she played in her mistress's accident, but an impressionable child, swayed by an older sister she'd worshipped, was perhaps to be forgiven. Her crimes had been born of folly rather than evil—at least, that was what Olivia had said. And Susie had tended to her mistress since that day with penitence and devotion.

"That's enough, Susie. Don't crowd your mistress."

"Yes, Your Grace."

Duchess Whitcombe shooed the maid aside then took Olivia's free hand.

"Your moment has come, dearest," she said. "Listen to Mrs. Cheam and all will be well." She glanced at Charles. "Lord Devereaux, I really think it's best if you join my husband in the drawing room. Olivia doesn't want you distracting her, and I don't want you fainting."

He arched his eyebrows, and she let out a huff.

"You think you're different from other men? My Montague passed out when I gave birth to Horatio. He'd convinced himself that he had the constitution of an ox, but at the first sight of blood, he fainted like a baby bird falling out of the nest. Fell against the armchair, cracked his head open, and bled all over my finest carpet. I suspect he soiled his breeches also."

Olivia let out a giggle between gasps for air.

"You think I jest, dearest?" the duchess said. "Poor Susie here, I am sure, does not wish to mop up the floor, or wash her master's breeches, after such an event—especially considering the enormity of the luncheon he consumed today. Two helpings of meat pie, and—"

"Eleanor, stop!" Olivia laughed. "I want my husband here. *I'll* scrub his soiled breeches if the need arises."

Was this how women discussed their menfolk when left unfettered?

But the smile in his wife's eyes was reward enough. If it made her laugh, he'd gladly empty his bowels and his stomach all over the floor and make an utter arse of himself.

That was, after all, the definition of love.

Olivia let out another cry. Charles placed his free hand on her cheek, gently turning her face until their eyes met.

Focus on me, my love.

As if she heard his thoughts, she tilted her head in a slight nod while the women bustled about at the foot of the bed. Then, her eyes focused on his, she let another long, low wail that heightened in pitch, crescendoing together with the chattering of encouragement from the women, until…

Until he heard another cry—weak at first, then growing stronger, a high-pitched wail that tugged at his soul, winding itself around his heart like a coiling spring.

The cry of a child.

"Well done, Olivia!" the duchess said, her voice muffled.

"Congratulations, Lord Devereaux," Mrs. Brougham said. "You have a son."

The spring snapped and Charles let out a cry, convulsing with sobs. He took his wife's head in his hands and kissed her. She parted her lips, and he slipped his tongue inside, gently at first, but she thrust her tongue greedily into his mouth, deepening the kiss as if she were a woman starved. When she broke the kiss, her eyes were wet with tears.

The duchess reappeared and placed a bundle in Olivia's arms. Charles caught sight of a round, pink face, tiny and wrinkled, among a sea of cotton and lace. Then the child opened his eyes and regarded Charles with a thoughtful, searching gaze as blue as the deepest of oceans—and his heart was lost.

How was it possible to love another person as much as he loved his wife? And how was it possible for that love to only increase the more he gazed at his son? He placed his hand over his heart and opened his mouth, but his throat tightened, and his body froze.

"No, my love," Olivia said softly. "You have no need to speak. I love you as you are. And why would I want a man who tells me that he loves me? Too many men will speak of their love, but I prefer a man like you, Charles. You have no need to tell me that you love me, because you show it every day. What wife—or son—would want for anything else?"

She placed another kiss on the baby's forehead.

"Hello, young sir. Would you like to meet your father?"

She offered the bundle to Charles.

Ye gods, surely she wasn't going to trust him, with his huge hands and clumsy frame, with something so precious, so fragile?

"Oh Lord," the duchess said, a hint of amusement in her voice. "Susie, you may have to fetch the mop and bucket after all."

Bloody hell, were they *laughing* at him?

Olivia let out a giggle, then silenced it as he met her gaze. She leaned toward him and whispered in his ear.

"Forgive me, husband," she said, her breath tickling his neck, sending a fizz of need into his groin. "I will permit you to think of a fitting way by which I can atone. In this bed, perhaps, though we have yet to share our love in the kitchen garden."

Then he grinned at her and motioned with his hands.

And over my desk in the library.

"Ah yes, husband. There's nothing I like more than a good book."

Could any man be as fortunate as he? Out of an unfortunate incident, he'd managed to find the best woman in all England. A natural child, a misfit, the very last woman who ought to have suited him. And yet, as misfits together, they were two halves of the same soul. He was ready to defend her against the world, while his beloved Olivia had, as his housekeeper had foretold, brought light and laughter back into his home—and his life.

About the Author

Emily Royal grew up in Sussex, England, and has devoured romantic novels for as long as she can remember. A mathematician at heart, Emily has worked in financial services for over twenty years. She indulged in her love of writing after she moved to Scotland, where she lives with her husband, teenage daughters, and menagerie of rescue pets—including Twinkle, an attention-seeking boa constrictor.

She has a passion for both reading and writing romance with a weakness for Regency rakes, Highland heroes, and Medieval knights. *Persuasion* is one of her all-time favorite novels, which she reads several times each year, and she is fortunate enough to live within sight of a Medieval palace.

When not writing, Emily enjoys playing the piano, baking, and painting landscapes, particularly of the Highlands. One of her ambitions is to paint, as well as climb, every mountain in Scotland.

www.ingramcontent.com/pod-product-compliance
Lightning Source LLC
Chambersburg PA
CBHW070513310726

48976CB00002BA/424